T0000050

PRAISE FOR

THE LAST GRADUATE

"Naomi Novik's Scholomance series, about kids at a preposterously deadly magical school, stands out in a ridiculously crowded field. Its sheer viciousness, its grim humor, and its complicated interpersonal politics are an immediate draw."

—*Polygon*

"Truly one of the best fantasy series out there right now, and it's not close."

—*Culteress*

"This second book is as compulsive a read as the first."

—*BuzzFeed*

"[*The Last Graduate*] rips along like a force of nature. In the abstract, this is a story about relying on others—but in the concrete, it is about how to survive when the odds are against you. As she did with [*A Deadly Education*], Novik changes the game again with the very last line."

—*Locus*

"Sardonic students, gruesome monsters, growing friendships, and a touch of romance create a highly readable story. Some questions remain to be answered in the trilogy's last volume. The end of this installment ensures that book three can't come fast enough."

—*Library Journal* (starred review)

"The climatic graduation-day battle will bring cheers, tears, and gasps as the second of the Scholomance trilogy closes with a breathtaking cliff-hanger."

—*Booklist* (starred review)

"Teen hormones and a never-flagging capacity for world-building underpin another great story about how easy it can be to sink into crab bucket thinking—even when you and everyone you know has the power to levitate themselves."

—*AV Club*

BY NAOMI NOVIK

THE SCHOLOMANCE

A Deadly Education
The Last Graduate

Uprooted
Spinning Silver

TEMERAIRE

His Majesty's Dragon
Throne of Jade
Black Powder War
Empire of Ivory
Victory of Eagles
Tongues of Serpents
Crucible of Gold
Blood of Tyrants
League of Dragons

THE LAST GRADUATE

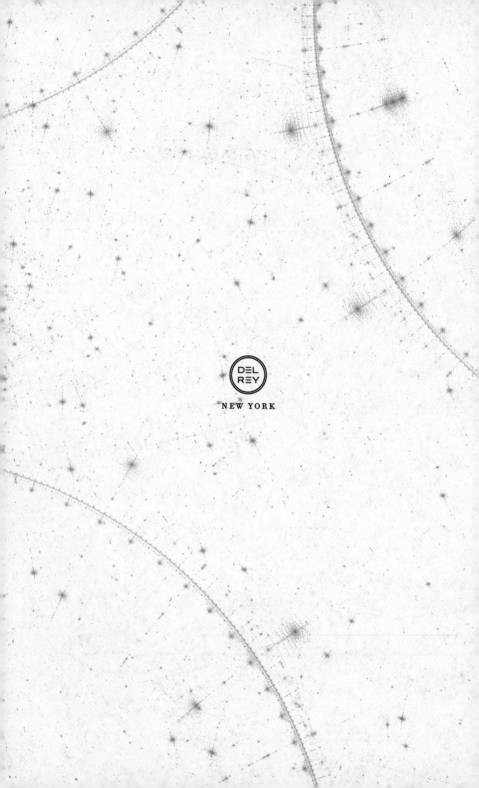

DEL
REY

NEW YORK

THE LAST
GRADUATE

A NOVEL

✦ *Lesson Two of The Scholomance* ✦

NAOMI NOVIK

The Last Graduate is a work of fiction. Names, characters, places, and incidents either are the product of the author's imagination or are used fictitiously. Any resemblance to actual persons, living or dead, events, or locales is entirely coincidental.

2022 Del Rey Trade Paperback Edition

Copyright © 2021 by Temeraire LLC
Illustrations copyright © 2020, 2021 by Penguin Random House LLC

All rights reserved.

Published in the United States by Del Rey, an imprint of Random House, a division of Penguin Random House LLC, New York.

DEL REY and the CIRCLE colophon are registered trademarks of Penguin Random House LLC.

Originally published in hardcover in the United States by Del Rey, an imprint of Random House, a division of Penguin Random House LLC, in 2021.

The illustration on pages viii–ix was originally published in *A Deadly Education* by Naomi Novik, published by Del Rey, an imprint of Penguin Random House LLC, in 2020. Copyright © 2020 by Penguin Random House LLC.

LIBRARY OF CONGRESS CATALOGING-IN-PUBLICATION DATA
Names: Novik, Naomi, author.
Title: The last graduate: a novel / Naomi Novik.
Description: New York: Del Rey, [2021] | Series: Lesson Two of The Scholomance
Identifiers: LCCN 2020055382 (print) | LCCN 2020055383 (ebook) |
ISBN 9780593128886 (trade paperback) | ISBN 9780593128862 (hardcover) |
ISBN 9780593357286 (International) | ISBN 9780593128879 (ebook)
Subjects: GSAFD: Fantasy fiction.
Classification: LCC PS3614.O93 L37 2021 (print) | LCC PS3614.O93 (ebook) |
DDC 813/.6—dc23
LC record available at https://lccn.loc.gov/2020055382
LC ebook record available at https://lccn.loc.gov/2020055383

Illustrations: Elwira Pawlikowska
Illustration design: David G. Stevenson
Illustration calligraphy: Van Hong and David G. Stevenson

Printed in the United States of America on acid-free paper

randomhousebooks.com

4 6 8 9 7 5

Book design by Simon M. Sullivan

ILLUSTRATIONS

Stabilize
with Polaxis
counter-resonators?

NOTE: Must be
3-step refined
or higher

Ⓧ Classrooms

Reading Room

Freshmen

Sophomores

Juniors

Seniors

Allow use of
empty classrooms
for work when
library seating
is filled?

Language
Laboratory

Workshop

Stockroom

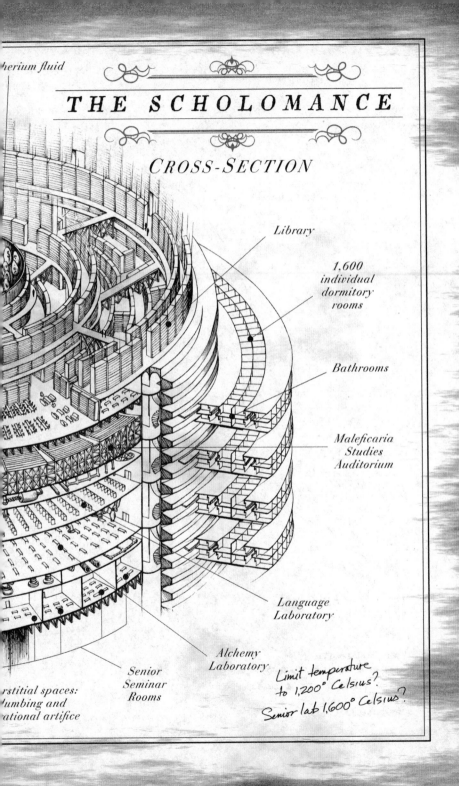

herium fluid

THE SCHOLOMANCE

CROSS-SECTION

Library

1,600 individual dormitory rooms

Bathrooms

Maleficaria Studies Auditorium

Language Laboratory

Alchemy Laboratory

Senior Seminar Rooms

rstitial spaces:
lumbing and
ational artifice

Limit temperature to 1,200° Celsius?
Senior lab 1,600° Celsius?

Note: Unavoidable point of vulnerability

SENIOR DORM

Seminar Classrooms

Furnace drainage

Secondary furnaces

Workshop

Primary furnaces

SENIOR DORMITORY ROOMS

Restock supply at end of term

POST-GRADUATION: RESTORE CONSOLIDATED ROOMS, REASSEMBLE INTO ORIGINAL CONFIGURATION AT FRESHMAN LEVEL

Seminar Cl

ROOMS

THE SCHOLOMANCE

FLOOR PLAN:
WORKSHOP LEVEL

~~50% physical education;~~
50% recreation

**REALLOCATE TO GRADUATION
TRAINING EXERCISE**

Gymnasium

SENIOR DORMITORY ROOMS

8983-9236 lms
weekly 3-year
maintenance cycle

NOTE: specialization in
botanical alchemy
will be required

Additional steel required
on senior level
to reinforce

- Ensure sufficient structural integrity to
complete rotation to graduation level

THE LAST GRADUATE

Chapter 1
VIPERSAC

KEEP FAR AWAY *from Orion Lake.*

Most of the religious or spiritual people I know—and to be fair, they're mostly the sort of people who land in a vaguely pagan commune in Wales, or else they're terrified wizard kids crammed into a school that's trying to kill them—regularly beseech a benevolent and loving all-wise deity to provide them with useful advice through the medium of miraculous signs and portents. Speaking as my mother's daughter, I can say with authority that they wouldn't like it if they got it. You don't *want* mysterious unexplained advice from someone you know has your best interests at heart and whose judgment is unerringly right and just and true. Either they'll tell you to do what you want to do anyway, in which case you didn't need their advice, or they'll tell you to do the opposite, in which case you'll have to choose between sullenly following their advice, like a little kid who has been forced to brush her teeth and go to bed at a reasonable hour, or ignoring it and grimly carrying on, all the while knowing that your course of action is guaranteed to lead you straight to pain and dismay.

If you're wondering which of those two options I picked, then you must not know me, as pain and dismay were obviously my destination. I didn't even need to think about it. Mum's note was infinitely well-meant, but it wasn't long: *My darling girl, I love you, have courage, and keep far away from Orion Lake.* I read the whole thing in a single glance and tore it up into pieces instantly, standing right there among the little freshmen milling about. I ate the scrap with Orion's name on it myself and handed the rest out at once.

"What's this?" Aadhya said. She was still giving me narrow-eyed indignation.

"It lifts the spirits," I said. "My mum put it in the paper."

"Yes, your *mum*, Gwen Higgins," Aadhya said, even more coolly. "Who you've mentioned so often to us all."

"Oh, just eat it," I said, as irritably as I could manage after having just downed my own piece. The irritation wasn't as hard to muster up as it might've been. I can't think of anything I've missed in here, including the sun, the wind, or a night's sleep in safety, nearly as much as I've missed Mum, so that's what the spell gave me: the feeling of being curled up on her bed with my head in her lap and her hand stroking gently over my hair, the smell of the herbs she works with, the faint croaking of frogs outside the open door, and the wet earth of a Welsh spring. It would've lifted my spirits enormously if only I hadn't been worrying deeply at the same time what she was trying to tell me about Orion.

The fun possibilities were endless. The *best* one was that he was doomed to die young and horribly, which given his penchant for heroics was reasonably predictable anyway. Unfortunately, falling in something or other with a doomed hero isn't the sort of thing Mum would warn me off. She's very much of the *gather ye rosebuds while ye may* school of thought.

Mum would only warn me off something *bad*, not something *painful*. So obviously Orion was the most brilliant maleficer ever, concealing his vile plans by saving the lives of everyone over and over just so he could, I don't know, kill them himself later on? Or maybe Mum was worried that he was so annoying that he'd drive *me* to become the most brilliant maleficer ever, which was probably more plausible, since that's supposedly my own doom anyway.

Of course, the most likely option was that Mum didn't know herself. She'd just had a bad feeling about Orion, for no reason she could've told me even if she'd written me a ten-page letter on both sides. A feeling so bad that she'd hitchhiked all the way to Cardiff to find the nearest incoming freshman, and she'd asked his parents to send me her one-gram note. I reached out and poked Aaron in his tiny skinny shoulder. "Hey, what did Mum give your parents for bringing the message?"

He turned round and said uncertainly, "I don't think she did? She said she didn't have anything to pay with, but she asked to talk to them in private, and then she gave it to me and my mam squeezed a bit of my toothpaste out to make room."

That might sound like nothing, but nobody wastes any of their inadequate four-year weight allowance on ordinary toothpaste; I brush with baking soda out of the alchemy lab supply cabinets myself. If Aaron had brought any at all, it was enchanted in some way: useful when you aren't going to see a dentist for the next four years. He could have traded that one squeeze of it to someone with a bad toothache for a week of extra dinners, easily. And his parents had taken that away from their own kid—Mum had *asked* his parents to take that away from their own kid—just to get me the warning. "Great," I said bitterly. "Here, have a bite." I gave him one of the pieces of the note, too. He probably needed it as much as ever in his life, after just being sucked into the Scholomance. It's better than the almost inevitable death waiting for wizard kids outside, but not by much.

The food line opened up just then, and the ensuing stampede interfered with my brooding, but Liu asked me quietly, "Everything okay?" as we lined up.

I just stared at her blankly. It wasn't mindreading or anything—she had an eye for small details, putting things together, and she indicated my pocket, where I'd put the last scrap of the note—the note whose actual contents I hadn't shared, even while I'd passed out pieces with an enchantment that should have precluded all brooding. My confusion was because—she'd asked. I wasn't used to anyone inquiring after me, or for that matter even noticing when I'm upset. Unless I'm sufficiently upset that I start conveying the impression that I'm about to set everyone around me on fire, which does in fact happen on a not infrequent basis.

I had to think about it to decide that I didn't, actually, want to talk about the note. I'd never had the option. And having it meant—that I was telling Liu the truth when I nodded to say *yes, everything's okay,* and smiled at her, the expression feeling a bit odd and stretchy round my mouth, unfamiliar. Liu smiled back, and then we were in the line, and we all focused on the job of filling our trays.

We'd lost our freshmen in the shuffle: they go last, obviously, and we now had the dubious privilege of going first. But nothing stops you taking extra for their benefit, if you can afford it, and at least for today we could. The walls of the school were still a bit warm from the end-of-term cleansing cycle. Any of the maleficaria that hadn't been crisped to fine ash were all just starting to creep out of the various dark corners they'd hidden in, and the food was as unlikely to be contaminated as it ever was. So Liu took extra milk cartons for her cousins, and I took seconds of pasta for Aaron, a bit grudgingly. Technically he wasn't owed anything for bringing the note, not by me; by Scholomance etiquette, that's all settled outside. But he hadn't got anything for it outside, after all.

It was odd being almost first out of the queue into the nearly empty cafeteria, with the enormously long tail of kids still snaking along the walls, tripled up, the sophomores poking the freshmen and pointing them at the ceiling tiles and the floor drains and the air vents on the walls, which they'd want to keep an eye on in the future. The last of the folded-up tables were scuttling back into the open space that had been left for the freshman rush, and unfolding back into place with squeals and thumps. My friend Nkoyo—could I think of her as a friend, too? I thought perhaps I could, but I hadn't been handed a formal engraved notice yet, so I'd be doubtful a while longer—had got out in front with her best mates; she was at a prime table, positioned in the ring that's exactly between the walls and the line, under only two ceiling tiles, with the nearest floor drain four tables away. She was standing up tall and waving us over, easy to spot: she was wearing a brand-new top and baggy trousers, each in a beautiful print of mixed wavy lines that I was fairly sure had enchantments woven in. This is the day of the year when everyone breaks out the one new outfit per year most of us brought in—my own extended wardrobe sadly got incinerated freshman year—and she had clearly been saving this one for senior year. Jowani was bringing over two big jugs of water while Cora did the perimeter wards.

It was odd, walking through the cafeteria over to join

them. Even if we hadn't been offered an actual invitation, there were loads of good tables still open, and all the bad ones. I've occasionally ended up with my pick of tables before, but that's always been a bad and risky move born of getting to the cafeteria too early, usually as an act of desperation when I'd had too many days of bad luck with my meals. Now it was just the ordinary course of things. Everyone else going to the tables around me was a junior, too, or rather a senior; I knew most of them by face if not by name. Our numbers had been whittled down to roughly a thousand at this point, from a start of sixteen hundred. Which sounds horrifying, except there're normally fewer than eight hundred kids left by the start of senior year. And normally, less than half of those make it out of graduation.

But our year had thrown a substantial wrench into the works, and he was sitting down at the table next to me. Nkoyo barely waited for me and Orion to take our seats before she burst out, "Did it work? Did you get the machinery fixed?"

"How many mals were down there?" Cora blurted over her at the same time, sliding into her own seat out of breath, still capping the small clay jug she'd used to drip a perimeter spell round the table.

They weren't being rude, by Scholomance standards of etiquette: they were entitled to ask us, since they'd got the table; that's more than a fair trade for first-hand information. Other seniors were busily occupying all the neighboring tables—giving us a solid perimeter of security—the better to listen in; the further ones were shamelessly leaning over and cupping their ears while friends watched their backs for them.

Everyone in the school already knew one very significant bit of information, namely that Orion and I had improbably made it back alive from our delightful excursion to the graduation hall this morning. But I'd spent the rest of the day holed up in my room, and Orion mostly avoided human beings unless they were being eaten by mals at the time, so anything else they'd heard had come to them filtered through the school gossip chain, and that's not a confidence-inspiring source of information when you're relying on it to stay alive.

I wasn't enthusiastic about reliving the recent experience, but I knew they had a right to what I could give them. And it was indisputably *me* who had it to give, because before the food line had opened, I'd already overheard one of the other New York seniors asking Orion a similar question, and he'd said, "I think it went okay? I didn't really see much. I just kept the mals off until they were done, and then we yanked back up." It wasn't even bravado; that was literally what he thought of the enterprise. Slaughtering a thousand mals in the middle of the graduation hall, just another day's work. I could almost have felt sorry for Jermaine, who'd worn the expression of a person trying to have an important conversation with a brick wall.

"A *lot*," I said to Cora, dryly. "The place was crammed, and they were all ravenous." She swallowed, biting her lip, but nodded. Then I told Nkoyo, "The senior artificers thought they'd got it, anyway. And it took them an hour and change, so I hope they weren't just faffing around."

She nodded, her whole face intent. It wasn't at all an academic question. If we really *had* fixed the equipment down in the graduation hall, then the same engines that run the cleansing up here twice a year, to burn out the mals infesting the corridors and classrooms, ran down there, too, and presumably wiped out a substantial number of the much larger and worse mals hanging round in the hall waiting for the graduation feast of seniors. Which meant that probably loads of the graduating class had made it. And much more to the point, that loads of *our* graduating class would have a better chance to make it.

"Do you think they really made it out okay? Clarita and the others?" Orion said, frowning into the churned mess of potatoes and peas and beef he was making out of what the cafeteria had called shepherd's pie but was thankfully just cottage pie. On a bad day it would turn out to be made of shepherd. Regardless of name, it was actually still hot enough to steam, not that Orion was appreciating its miraculous state.

"We'll find out at the end of term, when it's our turn through the mill," I said. If we *hadn't* got it working, of course, then instead the seniors in front of us had been dumped into a starving and worked-up horde of already-vicious maleficaria, and had probably been ripped apart en masse before ever getting to the doors. And our class would have just as good a time of it, in three hundred sixty-five days and counting. Which was a delightful thought, and I was telling myself as much as Orion when I added, "And since we can't find out sooner, there's absolutely no point brooding about it, so will you stop mangling your innocent dinner? It's putting me off mine."

He rolled his eyes at me and shoved a giant heaped spoonful into his mouth dramatically by way of response, but that gave his brain a chance to notice that he was an underfed teenage boy, and he began hoovering his plate clean with real attention.

"If it did work, how long do you think it will last?" one of Nkoyo's other friends asked, a girl from Lagos enclave who'd taken a seat one from the end of the table just to have access. Another good question I hadn't any answer to, since I wasn't an artificer myself. The only thing I'd known about the work

going on behind my back—in Chinese, which I didn't speak—
was the rate of words coming out of the artificers that had
sounded like profanity. Orion hadn't known that much: he'd
been out in front of us all, killing mals by the dozen.

Aadhya answered for me. "The times Manchester enclave
repaired the graduation hall machinery, the repairs held up
for at least two years, sometimes three. I'd bet on it working
this year at least, and maybe the one after."

"But not . . . more than that," Liu said softly, looking across
the room at her cousins, who were at their own table now,
along with Aaron and Pamyla, the girl who'd brought in Aadhya's letter, and a good, solid crowd of other freshmen kids
clustered around them: the kind of group that mostly only
enclave kids got. Which surprised me, until I realized they'd
picked up some glow-by-association from getting that close
to Orion, hero of the hour. And then it occurred to me, possibly even a bit of glow might have come from me, since to
all of the freshmen I was now a lofty senior who'd also been
on the run down to the hall, and not the creepy outcast of my
year.

And—I wasn't the creepy outcast by anyone's standards
anymore. I had a graduation alliance with Aadhya and Liu,
one of the first formed in our year. I'd been invited to sit at
one of the safest tables in the cafeteria, by someone who had
other choices. I had *friends*. Which felt even more unreal than
surviving long enough to become a senior, and I owed that, I
owed every last bit of it, to Orion Lake, and I didn't care, actually, what the price tag was going to be. There'd be one, no
question. Mum hadn't warned me for no reason. But I didn't
care. I'd pay it back, whatever it was.

As soon as I put it in those terms inside my head, I stopped
worrying over my note. I didn't even have to wish anymore
that Mum hadn't sent it. Mum had to send it, because she

loved me and she didn't know Orion from a cold welshcake; she couldn't help but warn me off if she knew I was on a bad road for his sake. And I could hold her love close to me and feel it, and still decide I was ready to pay. I put my fingers into my pocket to touch the last scrap I'd saved, the piece that said *courage,* and I ate it that night before I went to sleep, lying in my narrow bed on the lowest floor of the Scholomance, and I dreamed of being small again, running in a wide-open field of overgrown grass and tall purple-belled flowers around me, knowing Mum was nearby and watching me and glad that I was happy.

⚭

The lovely warm feeling lasted five seconds into the next morning, which is how long it took me to finish waking up. In most schools, you get holidays after term-end. Here, it's graduation in the morning, induction in the evening, you congratulate yourself and your surviving friends that you've all lived that long, and the next day it's the start of the new term. The Scholomance isn't really conducive to holiday-making, to be fair.

On the first day of term, we have to go to our new home-room and get our schedules lined up before breakfast. I was still feeling like moldy bread: it tends to slightly aggravate a half-healed gut wound when you get yourself bungeed around by yanker spells et cetera. I'd deliberately set an alarm to wake me five minutes before the end of morning curfew, because I was absolutely sure that wherever I was assigned for homeroom, it was going to take forever getting there. And sure enough, when the slip of paper with my assignment slid under my door at 5:59 A.M., it was for room 5013. I glared at it. Seniors hardly ever get any classroom assignments above the third floor, so you might think I should have been pleased, except it was only homeroom, and I was sure I'd never get a *real* class assigned that high. As far as I knew, there *weren't* any classrooms on that floor—fifth floor is the library. Probably I was being sent to some filing closet deep in the stacks with a handful of other luckless strangers.

I didn't even clean my teeth. I just swished my mouth out with water from my jug and started off on the slog while the first other seniors up were still shambling off to the loo. I didn't bother asking round to see if anyone else was going the same way: I was sure nobody I knew well enough to speak to would be. I just waved to Aadhya in passing as she came out of her room with her bathroom bag, and she nodded back in immediate understanding and gave me a thumbs-up for encouragement as she continued on to collect up Liu: we're all sadly familiar with the hazard of a long slog to a classroom, and our year now had the longest slogs of all.

There was no more *down* for us: yesterday, just as the seniors' res hall went rotating down to the graduation hall, ours had followed to take their place, at the lowest level of the school. I had to trot round to the stairway landing, then make my extremely cautious way through the workshop level—yes, it was the day after the cleansing, but it's never a good thing to be first onto a classroom floor in the morning—and then begin on the five steep double flights of stairs straight up.

They all felt at least twice as long as usual. Distances in the Scholomance are extremely flexible. They can be long, ago-nizingly long, or approaching the infinite, depending largely on how much you'd like them to be otherwise. It also didn't help that I was so early. I didn't even see another kid until I was panting my way up past the sophomore res hall, where the early risers had started trickling onto the stairs in small groups, mostly alchemy and artifice students hoping to nab better seats in the workshop and the labs. By the time I reached the freshman floor, the regular morning exodus was in full swing, but since they were all freshmen on their first day with no real idea where they were going, that didn't speed the stairs up at all.

The only saving grace of the whole painful trip was that I kept my storing crystal tightly clenched in my fist the whole time, concentrating on pushing mana into it. By the end of the final flight, where my gut was throbbing and my thighs were burning in counterpoint, every single deliberate step made a noticeable increase in the glow coming from between my fingers, and I had filled a good quarter of it by the time I came up into the completely empty reading room.

I badly needed to catch my breath, but as soon as I stopped moving, the five-minute warning bell rang from below. Stumbling around through the stacks looking for a classroom I had never even glimpsed before was a recipe for arriving late, not a good idea, so I grudgingly spent a bit of my hard-won mana on a finding spell. It cheerfully pointed me straight into a completely dark section of the stacks. I looked back without much hope at the stairs, but no one else was showing up to join me.

The reason for that became clear when I finally got to the classroom, which was behind a single dark wooden door almost invisible between two big cabinets full of ancient yellowing maps. I opened the door expecting to find something really horrible inside, and I did: eight freshmen, all of whom turned and stared at me like a herd of small and especially pitiful deer about to be mown down by a massive lorry. There wasn't so much as a sophomore among the lot. "You've got to be joking," I said with revulsion, and then I stalked to the front row and sat down in the best seat in the place, fourth from the near end. Which I could get without even a nudge, because they'd left the front row nearly wide open like they were still in primary school and worried about looking like teacher's pets. The only teachers in here are the maleficaria, and they don't have pets, they have lunch.

The desks were charming Edwardian originals, by which I mean ancient, too small for five-foot-ten me, and incredibly uncomfortable. They were made of wrought iron and would be hard to move in an emergency; the attached desk on mine, slightly too small to hold a sheet of normal-sized writing paper, had been very nicely polished and smooth roughly 120 years ago. It had since been scarified so thoroughly that kids had started writing on top of other kids' graffiti just to have room for their messages of despair. One had written LET ME OUT over and over in a neat red ink border all around the entire L-shaped surface, and another had done a highlighter pass over it in yellow.

There was only one other kid in the front row, and she'd taken what would have been the best seat, sixth from the far end—smarter to get a bit more distance from the door—except for the air vent in the floor just two seats behind it. Which was currently covered by a stupider kid's bookbag, so you couldn't know it was there unless you spotted that the other three air vents in the floor were laid out in a square pattern that needed a fourth one there. She watched me coming in as if she expected me to kick her out of her seat: age hath its prerogatives, and seniors are rarely shy about taking them. When I took the real best seat, she looked behind herself, realized her mistake, then hurriedly collected up her bag and moved down the row and said, "Is this seat taken?" gesturing to the one next to me, with a sort of anxious air.

"No," I said back to her irritably. I was annoyed because it made sense for me to let her sit next to me, since that only improved my odds by upping the nearby targets, and yet I didn't particularly want to. She was an enclave kid, no question. That was a shield holder of some kind on her wrist, the deceptively dull-looking ring on her finger was almost certainly a power-sharer, and she'd come in actively drilled on Scholomance strategy, such as how to identify the best seats in a room, even on the first day of class when you're too dazed to remember all the advice your parents gave you and instead just huddle with the other little kids like a zebra trying to hide in the herd. Also, the maths textbook in her bag was in Chinese, but she had good old Introductory Alchemy in English, and her notebooks were labeled in Thai script, meaning she was fluent enough to take magic coursework in not one but two foreign languages. Given the consequences of making even minor mistakes, that's a tall order for a fourteen year old. Likely she'd been in the most expensive language classes enclave wealth could buy from the age of two. She'd probably been planning to turn round in a moment and tell the other kids they were sitting in bad and dangerous seats, so they'd understand where they all stood in the pecking order: beneath her. I was only surprised she hadn't already made it clear.

Then one of the other kids behind us said tentatively, "Hello, El?" and I realized he was one of Liu's cousins. "It's Guo Yi Zheng," he added, which was helpful, as I'd gone out of induction day in perfect confidence that I wouldn't be seeing any of the freshmen I'd met ever again except by pure accident, and I hadn't tried to remember their names. There's not a lot of cross-year mingling in here. Our schedules make sure of that. Seniors spend almost all of our time on the lower levels, and freshmen get the safer classrooms higher up. If you're a freshman who regularly spends time hanging round the places where seniors are, you're asking to get eaten, and some maleficaria will grant your request.

But on the other hand, if you are somewhere with an upperclassman in range, you'd rather be closer to them than not. Zheng was already collecting up his bag and hustling over, which was just as well, because he'd been nearest the door until then. "May I sit with you?"

"Yeah, fine," I said. I didn't mind *him*. Liu being my ally didn't give her freshman cousin a claim on me, but he didn't need it to. She was my *friend*. "Watch out for air vents, even on the library level," I added. "And you were too close to the door."

"Oh. Yes, of course, I was just—" he said, looking over at the other kids, but I cut him off.

"I'm not your *mum*," I said, deliberately rude: you do freshmen no favors by letting them imagine there are heroes in here, Orion Lake notwithstanding. I couldn't be his savior; I had enough to do saving myself. "I don't need an excuse. I've just told you. Listen or don't." He shut it and sat down, a bit abashed.

Of course, he was right to stick close to the other kids: there's a reason zebras hang out in herds. But it isn't worth letting the other zebras put you in a really bad position. If you were unlucky, you learned that lesson when the lion ate you instead of them. If you were me, you learned it when you saw the lion eat someone else, one of the loser kids who wasn't quite as much a loser as you were, and who therefore had been allowed to sit on the end of the row, between the door and the kids who mattered.

And he had no business letting them put him on the end of the row, because he *was* one of the kids who mattered, or closer to it than anyone else here but the enclave girl. It's widely known that Liu's family are really close to founding an enclave of their own. They're already a big enough group that Liu got a box of hand-me-downs from an extended family member when she came in, and she'd given Zheng and his twin brother Min each a bag of stuff out of it, with the rest to come at the end of this year. They weren't enclavers, but they weren't losers either. But for the moment, he was still behaving as though he were an ordinary human being, instead of a student in the Scholomance.

A buzz of noise went up from the other kids. While we'd been talking, the draft schedules had just appeared on our desks, in the usual way: you look away for a second, and then they're there when you look back, as if they'd always been there. If you try to be cheeky and stare at your desk unblinkingly so the school can't slip it in, something bad is likely to happen to create an opportunity, like the lights going out, so other kids will shove you or put a hand over your eyes if they catch you at it. It's a lot more expensive, mana-wise, to let people see magic happening in a way they instinctively disbelieve, because that means you have to force it onto *them* as well as the universe. It's one of the reasons that people don't often do real magic round mundanes. It's loads harder, unless you dress it up as some sort of performance, or do it round people who aggressively work to believe in whatever magic you're doing, like Mum and her natural healing stuff with all her crunchy friends out in the woods.

And even though we're wizards, we still don't really *expect* things to appear out of thin air. We know it can be done, so it's not as hard to persuade us, but on the other hand, we've got more mana of our own to fight that persuasion with. It costs the school much less to just slip something onto the desk while we're looking away, as if someone had just put it there, than it does to let us watch it coming into existence.

Zheng was already trying to crane out around me to peek at the enclave girl's sheet; I sighed and said to him, "Go and sit next to her," grudgingly. I didn't like it, but my not liking it didn't change the reality that it was an obviously good idea for him to make up to her. He twitched a bit, probably more guilt: I expect his mum had lectured him on that subject as well. Then he did get up and went over to the Thai girl and introduced himself.

To be fair, she made him a polite wai, and invited him to sit down next to her with a gesture; usually you have to suck up a little more energetically to get in with an enclave kid. But I suppose he didn't have competition yet. After he sat down, a few other kids got up and moved into the seats behind them and they all started comparing schedules. The enclaver girl was already working on her own, with the speed that meant she knew exactly what she was going for, and she started showing the others hers and pointing out issues on theirs. I made a note to have a look at Zheng's after he was done, just in case she was a bit too helpful to her own benefit.

But first I had to take care of my *own* schedule, and one look told me I was in for it. I'd known going in that I'd have to take two seminars in my senior year: that's the price you pay for going incantations track and getting to minimize your time on the lower floors your first three years. But I'd been put into *four* of them—or five if you counted twice for the monstrous double course, meeting first thing every single day, that was simply titled Advanced Readings in Sanskrit, instruction in English. The note indicated that it would count as coursework for Sanskrit *and* Arabic, which made suspiciously little sense except for instance if we'd be studying medieval Islamic reproductions of Sanskrit manuscripts—such as the one I'd acquired in the library just two weeks before. That made for a really narrow field. I'd be lucky if there were three other kids in the bloody room with me. I glared at it sitting there like a lead bar across the top of my schedule sheet. I'd been counting on getting the standard Sanskrit seminar led in English, which should have meant being lumped into one of the larger seminar classrooms on the alchemy lab floor with the dozen or so artifice- and alchemy-track kids from India who were doing Sanskrit for their language requirement.

And I couldn't easily manufacture a conflict for it, since I didn't have so much as a single other senior in the room to compare schedules with. Usually at least one or two of the other outcast kids would grudgingly let me have a look, in exchange for getting to see mine, and that would give me at least one or two classes I could put in to try and force the school to shift the worst of my assignments around. You're allowed to specify up to three classes, and as long as you've met all your requirements, the Scholomance has to rework the rest of your schedule around them, but if you don't know what other classes there actually are or when they're scheduled, it's just a gambling game that you're sure to lose.

The Advanced Readings seminar would have been more than enough to make my schedule unusually lousy, but on top of that, I also had a really magnificent seminar on Development of Algebra and Applications to Invocation, which was going to count for languages, unspecified—a bad sign that I'd be getting loads of different primary sources to translate—as well as honors history and maths. I hadn't been assigned any other maths courses, so my odds of getting out of that one were very slim. Then there was the rotten seminar I'd actually been expecting to get, on Shared Proto-Indo-European Roots in Modern Spellcasting, which shouldn't have been my *easiest* class, and last but very much not least, The Myrddin Tradition, which was supposed to count for honors literature, Latin, modern French, modern Welsh, and Old and Middle English. And I knew right now that by the third week of class, I'd be getting nothing but straight-up Old French and Middle Welsh spells.

The rest of the slots were filled with shop—which I should have had a claim to be let out of entirely, since last term I'd done a magic mirror which still muttered gloomily at me every so often even though I had it hung up facing the wall—*and* I'd been put in honors alchemy, both meeting on mixed-up schedules: Mondays and Thursdays for the one, and Tuesdays and Fridays for the other. I'd be with different kids each day of the week, so I'd have it twice as hard as I already do finding anyone to do things like hold something I need to weld or watch my bag while I go and get supplies.

Up to that point, it was possibly the single worst senior schedule I'd ever heard of. Not even the kids aiming for class valedictorian were going to take *four* seminars. Except, as if the school was pretending to make up for all that, the entire afternoon on Wednesdays was literally unassigned to anything. It just said "Work," exactly like the work period we all get right after lunch, only it had an assigned room. Namely *this* one.

I stared at the box on my schedule sheet with deep and unrelenting suspicion, trying to make sense of it. An entire afternoon of free time, all the way up in the library itself, officially reserved so I wouldn't even have to protect my turf, with no reading, no quizzes, no assignments. That alone made this possibly the single best senior schedule I'd ever heard of. It was worth the trade-off. I'd been worrying about how I could possibly make up for all the mana I'd blown last term; with a triple-length work period once a week, I might be back on track before Field Day.

So there had to be a monstrous catch somewhere, only I couldn't begin to guess what it was. I got up and poked Zheng. "Keep an eye on my things," I told him. "I'm going to do a full check on the room. If any of you want to know how, watch," I added, and all their heads popped up to watch me go over the place. I started at the air vents and made sure all of them were screwed down tight, and made a sketch on a piece of scrap paper to show where they were in the room, in case something unusually clever decided to creep in and replace one of them at some point. I counted all the chairs and desks and looked under each one; I took out every single drawer in the cupboard along the back wall and opened all the cabinet doors and put a light inside the guts of it; I pulled it away from the wall and checked to make sure it and the wall were both solid. I shone a light along the entire perimeter of the floor to look for holes, I tapped over every wall as high as I could reach, I checked the doorframe to make sure the top and bottom were snug, and by the time I had finished, I was as sure as I could get that this was a perfectly ordinary classroom.

By which I mean, mals could get into it any number of ways: through the air vents, or under the door, or by gnawing through the walls. At least in this one, they couldn't get in by dropping down from the ceiling, because there was no ceiling. The Scholomance doesn't have a roof; you don't need one when you build your magic school jutting off from the world into a mystical void of non-literal space. The library walls just sort of keep going straight up until they're lost in the dark. In theory, they do eventually stop somewhere far up there. I'm not climbing up to prove it to myself. But anyway, the room wasn't infested to *start* with, and there weren't any obvious gaping vulnerabilities. So what could the school possibly mean, giving me the massive gift of an entire afternoon off in here?

I went back to my seat and stared at the schedule. Of course I understood that the afternoon off was the bait in the trap, but it was really *good* bait, and also a really good trap. I couldn't actually ensure a single good change in my schedule, since I didn't know when any other senior classes were being held. If I put down, say, that senior course in Sanskrit that I'd been expecting, to try and knock out that horrible Advanced Readings seminar, then even if the Scholomance actually did drop the seminar, it would have an excuse to shove me into an Arabic course on Wednesday afternoons. If I even tried to get something as minor as the matching shop class on Thursday afternoons, I'd undoubtedly be given alchemy lab on Wednesdays, and something else on Fridays. Anything I did would lose me the one really great thing about this schedule, with no guaranteed improvements.

"Let me see all of yours," I said to Zheng, without any real hope. One thing about being jammed in with freshmen, they all handed their sheets over meekly without even asking for a favor back, and I combed through the entire sheaf looking for any courses that I could take. But it was useless. I've never heard of freshmen being assigned to any class that a senior could possibly request, and they hadn't been. All of them had the standard Intro to Shop, Intro to Lab—enclave girl had wisely encouraged all of them to move those right before lunch Tuesday and Wednesday respectively, which are the best slots freshmen can get, since upperclassmen bagsie the afternoons—along with freshman-year Maleficaria Studies, wouldn't they have fun in there, and all the rest of their classes were literature and maths and history on the third and fourth floor. Except for one: outrageously, all of them also had the same Wednesday work session right up here with me, the lucky little snotnoses. None of them even appreciated how amazing it was.

I gave up and fatalistically signed my name at the bottom of my schedule without even trying to make any changes, then I went up to the big ancient secretary desk at the front of the room, cautiously lifted the roll-top—nothing there today, but just wait—and put my schedule inside. Most classrooms have a more formal place for submitting work, a slot that pretends to be shooting our papers through a network of pneumatic tubes to some central repository, but those broke early in the last century and were just patched up with transport spells, so really all you need to do is put your work out of sight in some common spot and it'll be taken up. I stared down at my sheet one last time, then took a deep breath and shut the roll-top again.

I was sure I'd find out just how big a mistake I'd made right after breakfast, when I headed down to my first seminar, but I was wrong about that. I found out not a quarter of an hour later, without ever leaving the room. I was bent with gritted teeth over a snarled mess of crochet, getting as much mana into my crystal as I could before breakfast, and already mentally strategizing what hideously boring calisthenics I could do in this room once I'd healed up a bit more—I hate exercise violently, so forcing myself to do it is wonderful for building mana. There wasn't much space, and never mind moving the desks. I'd probably have to do crunches lying across the top of two desks. But who cared: I'd be able to fill a crystal every two weeks, I thought.

Meanwhile the freshmen were all hanging about in the front of the classroom as if they didn't have a care in the world, chattering to one another. Just to improve things, all of them were speaking in Chinese, including the Indian boy, and the Russian boy and girl—I was fairly certain that was Russian they'd spoken to each other, but they'd dived into the general conversation without a hitch. They were undoubtedly all doing Chinese-track general classes—in here, your choices for things like maths and history are that or English.

I was doing my best to let the conversation just be background noise, but it wasn't working very well. One of the hazards of studying a ridiculous number of languages is that my brain has got the idea that if I don't understand something I'm hearing, it's because I'm not paying enough attention, and if I just listen hard enough I'll somehow be able to divine the meaning. I *should* have been safe from being hit with another new language for at least a quarter, since the Scholomance had started me on Arabic not three weeks ago, but sitting in a classroom for two hours every Wednesday with a pack of freshmen all speaking Chinese would undoubtedly mean I'd start getting spells in Chinese, too.

Unless they all helpfully got themselves killed before the month was out, which wasn't beyond the realm of possibility. Usually the first week of term is all right, and then just as the freshmen have been lulled into a state of false calm, the first mals creep out of their hidey-holes, not to mention the first wave of newly hatched ones from the ground floor start to find ways to squirm up here.

Of course, there's always the occasional overachiever. Like the baby vipersac that quietly worked its way up through the air vent just then. Probably it had stretched itself out skinny and long to get through the wards on the ventilation system, making itself look like a harmless little liquid dribble, and it snaked through the physical grating and coiled itself up on the floor behind one of the bookbags to form back into shape. It would have made some squelching noises in the process, but the freshmen were talking loudly enough to cover for it, and I wasn't paying very close attention myself, because for once in my life, I was the single worst target in the room by a thousand miles; no mal would pick me out of this crowd. I was already starting to think of the place as some kind of refuge.

Then one of the freshmen saw it and squealed in alarm. I didn't even bother to look what they were squealing at; I was out of the chair with my bookbag over my shoulder and halfway to the door—the boy had been looking towards the back of the room—before I even spotted the vipersac, hovering already fully inflated over the fourth row of seats like a magenta balloon that someone had Jackson Pollocked with spatters of blue. The blowdart tubes were starting to puff out. The other kids were all screaming and clutching at one another or ducking behind the big desk, a classic mistake: how long were they planning to stay back there? The vipersac wouldn't be going anywhere with a spread like this, and the instant they stuck their heads out for a peek, it would get them.

That was *their* problem, of course, and if they didn't find a solution for it on their own, they weren't going to make it out of homeroom on their first day of class, which probably meant they weren't going to last long anyway. It wasn't even the slightest bit my problem. My problem was that I'd been assigned four highly dangerous seminar classes, and I was already far behind on saving mana for graduation. I was going to need every last minute of my time in this room to build enough mana to make up for all that. I didn't have so much as a single crochet stitch's worth of energy to spare on a flock of random freshmen I didn't care about in the slightest.

Except for one. After I kicked the classroom door open, I did turn back to yell, "Zheng! Out, *now*," and he did a U-turn around from the big desk and ran towards me. The other kids might not all have understood me, but they were smart enough to follow him, and most of them were smart enough to abandon their bookbags while they were at it. Except for the enclave girl, of all people. She undoubtedly could have replaced every last thing she was carrying just by hitting up the older kids from her enclave, but she grabbed her bag before coming, so she was bringing up the very end of the pack when the vipersac got inflated enough that its three little eyestalks popped out and it started turning to track the last of the moving targets. As soon as it took her out, everyone else would get away. It was only a little bigger than a football; that newly hatched, it would probably stop to feed straightaway.

I was right at the doorway and about to go through and save my own neck, exactly as I should have done; exactly as I had done, any number of times before. It's rule one: the only thing you worry about, in the moments when something goes pear-shaped in here, is how to get yourself out of the way with skin intact. It's not even selfish. If you start trying to help other people, you get yourself killed and most likely foul whatever they're doing to save themselves while you're at it. If you've got allies or friends, you can help them *before-hand*. Share some mana, give them a spell, make them some bit of artifice, a potion they can use in a tight spot. But any-one who can't survive an attack on their own isn't going to survive. Everyone knows that, and the only person I've ever known to make an exception to the rule is Orion, who's a complete numpty, which I'm *not*.

Except I didn't go through the door. I stayed there next to it and let the entire pack of freshmen go galumphing through ahead of me instead. The vipersac went paler pink as it got ready to shoot Miss Enclave, and then it reoriented itself with a quick jerk towards the door as Orion, speaking of numpties, came bursting through it going the extremely wrong way. Two seconds later, he'd have been full of venom and most likely dead.

Except I was already casting.

The spell I used was a fairly obscure Old English curse. I'm possibly the only one in the world who has it. Early in my sophomore year, right after starting Old English, I stumbled over three seniors cornering a junior girl in the library stacks. Another loser girl, like me, except that boys never tried that sort of thing with me. Something about the aura of future monstrously dark sorceress must put them off. I put the three of them off the other girl just by turning up, even as a scrawny soph. They slunk away, the girl hurried off in the other direction, and I grabbed the first book off the shelf still seething with anger. So I didn't get the book I'd been reaching for; instead I came away with a small crumbling sheaf of home-made paper full of handwritten curses some charming beldame had come up with a thousand years ago or so. It opened up in my hands to this particular curse and I looked down and saw it before I slammed it shut and put it back on the shelf.

Most people have to study a spell at length to get it into their head. I do, too, if it's a *useful* spell. But if it's a spell to destroy cities or slaughter armies or torture people horribly— or, for instance, to shrivel up significant parts of a boy's anatomy into a single agonizingly painful lump—one glance and it's in there for good.

I'd never used it before, but it worked really effectively in this scenario. The vipersac instantly compressed down to the size of a good healthy acorn. It dropped straight out of the air, rattled on the grating for a moment, and then went down through it like a prize marble vanishing down a sewer drain. And there went my entire morning's mana with it.

Orion stopped in the doorway and watched it go, deflating himself. He'd been ready to launch some kind of fire blast, which would have taken out the vipersac—and also the three of us, along with any combustible contents of the classroom, since its internal gases were highly flammable. The enclave girl threw me and him a scared-rabbit look and darted out the door past him, even though there wasn't any reason to run anymore. He looked after her for a moment, then back at me. I took a single depressing look at my dimmed mana crystal—yes, completely dull again—and let it drop. "What are you even doing here?" I said irritably, shoving past him out into the stacks and heading towards the stairs.

"You didn't come to breakfast," he said, falling in with me.

That's how I learned that the bells weren't audible in the library classroom. Which at the moment meant I could either skip breakfast or turn up late to the first session of my lousiest seminar class, where I would very likely not have the least chance of getting anyone to fill me in on my first assignments.

I ground my jaw and started stomping down the stairs. "Are you okay?" Orion asked after a moment, even though I'd just saved *him*. He hadn't quite internalized the idea yet, I suppose.

"No," I said bitterly. "I'm a numpty."

Chapter 2
CUSHIONS

THAT ONLY GOT MORE CLEAR to me over the next few weeks. I'm *not* an enclave girl. Unlike Orion, I don't have a virtually limitless supply of mana to pull on for noble heroics. The exact opposite, because I'd just blown nearly half the mana stash I'd accumulated over the course of three years. For more than sufficient cause, since I used it to take out a maw-mouth, and if I never have to think about that experience again it'll be soon enough, but it doesn't matter how good my reasons were. What matters is I'd had a carefully planned timetable for building mana over my Scholomance career, and it was thoroughly wrecked.

My hopes of graduating would have been in equal shambles, except for that spellbook I'd found. The Golden Stone phase-changing spell is so valuable outside that Aadhya had been able to run an auction among last year's seniors that had netted me a heap of mana, and even a pair of lightly used trainers on top of it. She was planning to do another one among the kids in our year soon. With luck I would end up short *seven* crystals instead of *nineteen*. That was still a painful deficit to be making up, and I needed another thirty at graduation on top of it, at least.

That's what I'd planned to use my glorious free Wednesday afternoons for. Ha very ha. The baby vipersac turned out to be only the first of a series of maleficaria that all seemed irresistibly drawn to this specific library classroom. There were mals waiting to leap when we walked in the door. There were mals hiding in shadows that pounced while we were distracted. There were mals that came in through the vents halfway through class. There were mals inside the roll-top desk. There were mals waiting when we walked *out* the door. I could have avoided learning Chinese with absolutely no problem, just by not doing a thing. The entire pack of freshmen would have been gone before the second week of the term.

The writing was on the wall by the end of our first Wednesday session, in letters of dripping blood, literally: I'd just smeared a willanirga across the entire perimeter of the room, stomach sac and intestines and all. As we all headed to dinner in more-or-less bespattered condition, I swallowed my own irritation and told Sudarat—the enclave girl—that if she wanted more rescuing, she'd need to share some of her mana supply.

Her face went all red and blotchy, and she said, haltingly, "I don't—I'm not," and then she burst into tears and ran on ahead, and Zheng said, "You haven't heard about Bangkok."

"What haven't I heard about Bangkok?"

"It's gone," he said. "Something took out the enclave, just a few weeks before induction day."

I stared at him. The point of enclaves is they *don't* get taken out. "How? By what?"

He made a big arms-spread shrug.

"Have *you* all heard about Bangkok?" I demanded at dinner, wondering how I'd missed a piece of news that big, but actually I was ahead of the curve: Liu was the only one at the table who nodded, and she said, "I just heard in history."

"Heard what?" Aadhya wanted to know.

"Bangkok's gone," I said. "The enclave's been destroyed."

"What?" Chloe said, jerking so hard she slopped her orange juice all over her tray. She'd asked to eat with us—and nicely, not like she was doing us a favor gracing us with her presence—so I'd gritted my teeth and said yes. "That's got to be fake."

Liu shook her head. "A girl from Shanghai in our class confirmed it. Her parents told her little sister to tell her about it."

Chloe stared at us, still frozen with her glass midair. You couldn't blame her for being more than a bit freaked out. Enclaves don't just go popping off for no reason, so if an enclave had just been hit hard enough that it was taken out, it was a sign that some kind of enclave war was on the way, and New York was the prime candidate for being in the middle of it somehow, but after the third time in five minutes she asked for more of the details that neither Liu or I had, I finally said, "Rasmussen, we don't *know.* You're the one who can find out; your enclave's freshmen must know more about it by now."

She did actually say, "Watch my tray?" and then got up and went across the room to the table where the freshmen from the New York enclave were sitting. She didn't come back with much: not even that many of the freshmen had heard about it yet. The Bangkok kids weren't making any effort to spread the news, and Sudarat was literally the only freshman from the place who'd survived to be inducted. Everyone else in her year had gone down with the ship. Which alarmed all the enclavers even more. Even when enclaves are damaged badly enough to make them collapse, there's usually enough warning and time for the non-combatants to escape.

By the end of dinner, it became clear that *nobody* knew what had happened. We barely know anything in here to start with, since all our news about the real world comes in once a year via terrified fourteen-year-olds. But an enclave going down is big news, and not even the Shanghai kids had any details. Shanghai helped start Bangkok—they've been sponsoring new Asian enclaves these last thirty years, not incidentally while making increasingly pointed noises about the disproportionate number of Scholomance seats allocated to the US and Europe. If someone had taken out Bangkok as a first shot in coming at Shanghai, their freshmen would've come in with clear instructions to close ranks round the Bangkok kids.

On the other hand, if Bangkok had carelessly blown themselves to bits, which happens occasionally when an enclave gets a bit too ambitious in developing new magical weaponry without telling anyone, the Shanghai kids would've been given instructions to ditch the Bangkok kids entirely. Instead, they'd just gone—*cautious*. Meaning even their parents didn't have any better idea than the rest of us did, and if the Shanghai enclavers didn't know, nobody knew.

Well, except for whoever had *done* it. Which was its own source of complication, because if anyone were going to be orchestrating an indirect attack on Shanghai, the top candidate was New York. It was hard to imagine any other enclave in the world doing it without at least their tacit support. But if New York had secretly arranged anything as massive as taking out an entire enclave, they certainly wouldn't have told their freshmen a thing about it, which meant that not even the New York kids knew whether or not their enclave had been involved, but they—and the Shanghai kids—all knew that if it *had* been anything other than an accident, their parents were very likely at war outside *right now*. And we'd have absolutely no way of knowing one way or another for a year.

It wasn't a situation you'd call conducive to fellow-feeling among the enclavers. Personally, I didn't mind not knowing. I wasn't going to be joining an enclave myself. I'd made that decision last year—resentfully—and I wasn't going to be getting involved, if there *was* a war. Even if it was just some hideous maleficer going around taking out enclaves, it wasn't anything to me, except possibly my future competition, according to the unpleasant prophecy that would have made my life loads easier if it would just hurry up and come true.

What I *did* mind was that Sudarat couldn't help out with what was clearly about to be my *fifth* seminar, in freshman rescue. Their enclave's mana store had been fairly new and small to begin with, and now the Bangkok seniors had taken full control and were desperately trading on it to other enclavers to try and get themselves graduation alliances. They weren't even sharing with the juniors and sophomores. All of them had just become ordinary losers like the rest of us, scrabbling for allies and resources and survival. Their one big bargaining chip for alliance-building had been the chance of a spot in their fast-growing enclave, which they didn't have anymore, and they were operating under an aura of creepy uncertainty because no one knew what had happened. The other freshmen hadn't been avoiding Sudarat because they hadn't known she was from Bangkok; they'd been avoiding her because they *had*. She hadn't even been given a share of the gear that last year's seniors had left behind. That bag she'd brought in was all the resources she had.

I suppose I should've felt sorry for her, but I'd rather be sorry for someone who never had luck at all than for someone whose extreme luck ran out unexpectedly. Mum would tell me I could be sorry for both of them, to which I'd say *she* could be sorry for both of them, but I had a more limited supply of sympathy and had to ration it. Anyway, I'd already saved Sudarat's life twice before the second week of classes, despite my lack of sympathy, so she hadn't any right to complain.

And neither did I, since I was apparently determined to keep doing it.

Aadhya and Liu and I had made plans to take showers together that night. As we headed downstairs, I said to Liu bitterly, "Have you got any time after? I need to get down some basic phrases in Chinese." You might expect that to mean things like *where's the loo* and *good morning,* but in here, the first things you learn in any language are *get down* and *behind you* and *run.* Which I was going to need to stop the freshmen getting in the way of my saving them. Entirely at my own expense.

Liu bent her head and said softly, "I was going to ask you to help me." She reached into her school satchel and pulled up her clear plastic pencil bag to show me a pair of scissors inside: a left-handed pair with the remnants of ragged patches of green vinyl still clinging on stickily around the finger holes, one blade notched and the other a bit rusty. Promising signs: they were bad enough that they almost certainly weren't cursed or animated. She'd been asking round for someone who had a pair to loan for the last couple of weeks.

Her hair was down to below her waist, a glossy midnight black except at the very roots where it was coming in a color that anyone would also have called black, except by contrast to the slightly eerie darker shade of the long mass. Years and years of growing it out, and three of those years had been in here, having to negotiate terms and conditions for every shower we got. But I didn't ask *are you sure.* I knew she was, even if only on a purely practical note. Aadhya was going to use it to string the sirenspider lute that she was making for our graduation run, and anyway, she'd only been able to get away with growing her hair that long because she'd been using malia.

But then she'd had an unexpected and very thorough spirit cleanse, and she'd decided she wasn't going back down the obsidian brick road. So now she had to pay back three years of unreasonably good hair days all at once. We'd been taking it in turn each evening to help her comb out the truly horrific snarls that developed every day no matter how carefully she braided it.

After we were done in the showers, the three of us went back to Aadhya's room. She sharpened the scissors with her tools, then got the box she'd prepared for the hair. I started the cutting carefully, just taking off a bare centimeter from one very skinny lock of hair held as far from Liu's head as I could—you always want to start slow when it comes to an unfamiliar pair of scissors. Nothing terrible happened, and slowly I worked halfway up the strand, and then I took a deep breath and went in fast and cut, right at the visible demarcation line between the old hair and the new, and handed the one long section to Aadhya.

"You okay?" I said to Liu. I was making sure the scissors were all right, but I also wanted to give her an excuse to take a minute: I did expect it to be a wrench for her, even if she wouldn't start blubbing or anything.

"Yes, I'm fine," she said, but she was blinking, and by the time I'd taken off half the hair, she *was* blubbing, in a really quiet way, tears slipping away, and a fat one rolled off her cheek and splatted on her knee.

Aadhya threw me a worried look, then said, "I can definitely manage with this much, if you wanted to stop." Liu wouldn't even have looked bad: her hair was so thick I'd had to cut it in layers anyway, with the crap scissors, so I'd started from underneath. You never know when a pair of scissors might suddenly go unusable, and if she was walking round with the top of her head trimmed close and a long weird mullet of hair dangling behind, anyone she asked for a pair of scissors would charge her the earth in trade.

"*No*," Liu said, her voice quavery but also absolutely insistent. She was the quiet one of the three of us, usually—Aad could get plenty of heat going when she was annoyed, and if there's ever an Olympics of rage, I'll be odds-on favorite to take gold. But Liu was always so contained, so measured and thoughtful, and it was a surprise to hear her even that close to snapping.

Even to her; she paused and swallowed, but whatever she was feeling, it wasn't going back in the box. "I want it *off*," she said, with a sharp edge.

"Right," I said, and went at it faster, shingling every strand as close to her head as I dared. The glossy strands were trying to tangle round my fingers even as I chopped them off and handed them off to Aadhya.

And then it was done, and Liu put her hands up to touch her head, trembling a little. There was barely anything left, only an uneven fuzz. She closed her eyes and rubbed her hands over it back and forth like she was making sure it was all gone. She took a few deep watery breaths and then said, "I haven't cut it since I came in. Ma told me not to."

"Why?" Aadhya asked.

"It was . . ." Liu's throat worked. "She said, in here, it would tell people I was someone to watch out for." And it had worked, because you can't afford to have long hair unless you're a really rich and also careless enclaver—or unless you're on the maleficer track.

Aadhya silently went and dug a leftover half of a granola bar out of a small warded stash box on her desk. Liu tried to refuse it, but Aad said, "Oh my God, eat the freaking granola bar," and then Liu's face crumpled and she got up and put her arms out towards us. It took me a few moments longer than Aadhya—three years of near-total social ostracization leaves you badly equipped for this sort of thing—but they both kept a space open until I lurched in to join the hug, our arms around each other, and it was the miracle all over again, the miracle I still couldn't quite believe in: I wasn't alone anymore. They were saving me, and I was going to save them. It felt more like magic than magic. As though it could make everything all right. As if the whole world had become a different place.

But it hadn't. I was still in the Scholomance, and all the miracles in here come with price tags.

I'd only accepted my horrific schedule for the chance of building mana on those glorious Wednesday afternoons off. Since I'd been wrong about how wonderful my Wednesday work sessions would be, you might think I'd also been wrong about how terrible my four seminars were. And then *you'd* be wrong.

Not one of the Myrddin seminar, the Proto-Indo-European seminar, or the Algebra seminar had more than five students in it. All of them took place deep in the warren of seminar rooms that we call the labyrinth, because it's roughly as hard to get through as the classical version. The corridors like to squirm around and stretch a bit now and then. But even those paled in awful next to Advanced Readings in Sanskrit, which turned out to be an *independent study*.

I really *could* have used a dedicated hour a day of quiet time to work on Sanskrit. The spellbook I'd managed to get my hands on last term was a priceless copy of the long-lost Golden Stone sutras; the library had let it come in range in an effort to keep me from taking out that maw-mouth. I still slept with it under my pillow. I'd just barely managed to fight my way through twelve pages to the first of the major invocations, and it was already the single most useful spellbook I'd ever so much as glimpsed in my life.

But what I got instead was a dedicated hour a day, alone in a tiny room on the outer perimeter of the very first floor, squeezed in around the edge of the big workshop. To even get there, I had to go almost as far as you could possibly go into the labyrinth, open an unmarked windowless door, then walk down a long, narrow, completely unlit corridor that felt like it was anywhere from one to twelve meters depending on its mood that day.

Inside the room, the one large air vent at the top of the wall shared an air shaft with the workshop furnaces. It alternated between whooshing blasts of superheated exhaust air and a steady, whistling stream of ice-cold cooling air. The only desk in the room was another ancient chair-desk, the whole iron contraption bolted to the floor. Its back was to the grating. I would have sat on the floor, but there were two large drainage channels running across the whole room, coming from the workshop and going to a big trough along the full length of the back wall, and ominous stains around them suggested that they overflowed routinely. A row of taps were stuck in the wall overhanging the trough as well. They dripped constantly in a faint pinging symphony, no matter how much I tried to tighten them. Every once in a while, horrible gurgling noises came out of the pipes, and weird grinding sounds happened under the floor. The door to the room itself didn't lock, but *did* slide open or shut at unpredictable moments with an incredibly loud bang.

If that sounds to you like an absolutely magnificent setup for an ambush, well, a significant number of mals agreed. I got jumped twice in the first week of classes.

By the end of the third week of term, I actually had to dip into my mana stash instead of adding to it. That night I sat on my bed staring at the chest of crystals Mum sent in with me. Aadhya had done another auction, and now I had a grand total of seventeen of them glowing and full of mana. But all the rest sat there empty, and the ones I'd emptied taking out the maw-mouth were starting to go completely dull. If I didn't start reviving them soon, they'd become as useless for storing mana as the kind you buy in bulk online. But I couldn't find the time. I was building mana as hard as I possibly could and cutting every corner possible on my schoolwork, but I was still stuck on the very same crystal I'd been trying to fill back up since last term. That morning I'd been attacked in my seminar yet again, and I'd had to empty it completely.

I had gone back to doing sit-ups sooner than any doctor would've told me to, just because the struggle to do them with my aching gut actually made it easier to build mana. But I was pretty much healed up now, and I couldn't even rely on crochet anymore for real mana-building. I just didn't hate it as much when I was doing it at night hanging out with Aadhya and Liu. My friends; my allies. Who were relying on me to help me get them out the doors.

I closed up the box and put it away, and then I went out. It was still an hour to curfew, but already quiet: no one hangs out in the corridors senior year. Either they were up in the prime spots in the library, or taking the chance to go to bed early in the last week or so before the mals were expected to come back full-force. I went down to Aadhya's room and tapped on the door, and when she opened it I said, "Hey, can we go to Liu's?"

"Sure," she said, eyeing me, but she didn't push for details: Aadhya isn't a time-waster. She collected her bathroom stuff, so we could go brush teeth right after, and then together we went to Liu's room. She was down on our level, now.

Everyone gets a private room in here, so to squash in each year's delivery of freshmen, the rooms are arranged cellblock-style, stacked on top of one another with a narrow iron walkway outside the upper rooms. But at the end of term, as the res halls rotate down to their new levels, any empty rooms disappear and the space gets parceled out to the survivors. Often not in useful ways. I've had a delightfully creepy and useless double-height room since the start of sophomore year. Liu's had extended down in this last round, so we didn't have to climb up one of the squeaking spiral staircases to see her anymore.

She let us in and gave each of us our familiars-in-training to hold while we sat on her bed. I stroked the tiny mouse's white fur while she sat up in the palm of my hand nibbling a treat and looking around with bright and increasingly green eyes. I was still trying hard to name her Chandra, but the day I'd been thinking of names, Aadhya had said, "You should call her Precious," then laughed her head off while I whacked her with a pillow, and Precious was unfortunately sticking. Mum's never actually come out and apologized for saddling me with Galadriel, but I'm reasonably sure she knows she should be ashamed of herself. Anyway they kept forgetting Chandra and calling her Precious—all right, to be fair, *I* kept forgetting it myself—and pretty soon I was going to have to give up and accept it.

Assuming I was going to have her at all. I stared down at

her in my hand because it was better than looking at their faces, and I said, "I'm falling really behind on mana."

I had to tell them. They were counting on me to be able to pull my weight when it came time for graduation. If I wasn't going to be able to, they had the right to back out. They didn't owe anything to a bunch of freshmen they hadn't even met. Liu might have felt she owed me something for Zheng, but I could be saving just Zheng *without* laying out a week's worth of mana I didn't actually have saved up, and meanwhile she was breaking her back building mana for our team herself.

At this rate, I was going to be lucky if I had enough mana for maybe three medium-power spells, and I didn't even *have* any good medium-power spells. The only really useful spell I've got that doesn't need absolute heaps of mana is the phase-control spell I got out of Purochana's book, and it's not a great crisis option, since it's a good five minutes to prep the casting. I've *used* it in a crisis, but only when I had Orion thoroughly distracting the underlying cause for those five minutes, and he's going to be a bit busy come graduation killing monsters for everyone.

"Zheng told me about Wednesdays," Liu said quietly, and I looked up. She didn't look surprised; actually she looked kind of worried.

"This is your weirdo library session? What's going on?" Aadhya said, and Liu said, "It's her and eight freshmen, and they keep getting hit with major mals."

"In the *library*?" Aadhya said, and then she said, "Wait, this is on *top* of that horrible independent study and the three other seminars? Does the school have it in for you or something?"

We all fell silent. The question answered itself in the asking, really. My throat felt knotted up right around the tonsils, awful and choking. I hadn't even thought about it that way before, but it was obviously true. And that was worse, so much worse, than just being unlucky.

The Scholomance has been hurting for power almost as much as I have. It's not cheap to keep this place working. It's easy to forget from our perspective when we're suffering through this place and getting hit with mals on a regular basis, but they'd be coming at every last one of us in a continuous stream, and lots more of them, if it weren't for all those incredibly powerful wards on every single air vent and plumbing pipe, and all the highly improbable artifice that makes sure there are almost none of those openings in the first place, and despite that we're all breathing and drinking and bathing and eating, and all of that takes mana, mana, mana.

Sure, the story is, the enclaves put in some mana, and our parents all put in some mana if they can afford it, and we put in mana with our work, but we all know that's a story. The single biggest source of the school's mana is *us*. We're all trying to save mana for graduation; everyone's working on it all the time. The mana we grudgingly put into our schoolwork and our maintenance shifts is nothing compared with the amounts we put away for that rainiest of rainy days. And when the mals tear us apart, of course we grab for all that nice juicy power we've desperately been saving up, and they suck it out of us, only built up more by all our terror and final agony and struggles to live. The Scholomance gets the spillover, and then thanks to all those wards, it kills off a good healthy number of the mals, too, and it all ends up in the school's mana stores—where it goes to keep the rest of us luckier ones alive.

So when an enthusiastic hero—read, Orion—shows up and starts saving lives, and the mals start to starve, the school starts to starve, too. And at the same time, has more of us alive in here, breathing and drinking et cetera. It's all a pyramid scheme, and if there aren't enough of us on the bottom being eaten, there's not enough for the ones at the top.

That's *why* we had to go down and fix the cleansing mechanisms in the graduation hall: all those starving mals down there, waiting in the one place Orion wasn't, getting ready to tear the entire graduating class apart because they hadn't had enough to eat for the last three years. They were on the verge of breaking into the rest of the school because they were all so desperate that they started collectively pounding on the wards at the bottom of the stairwells.

And Orion—well, Orion's from the New York enclave, with a power-sharer on his wrist, and his affinity for combat somehow lets him suck power out of the mals he kills anyway. They don't even come after him, because he has a bottomless supply of mana and an almost equally infinite supply of fantastic combat spells.

But I don't. I'm the girl destined to make *up* for him, but who's obstinately kept refusing to become a maleficer and start killing kids by the double handful, and now I've gone the other way entirely. I stopped a maw-mouth heading for the freshman hall. I helped Orion keep the mals from breaking into the school. I was down there in the graduation hall with him, helping to hold up a shield so the senior artificers could fix the cleansing equipment. And now I'm even copycatting his stupid noble-hero routine one day a week.

Of course the school was going to come after me.

And if the Wednesday mals didn't work—it would try something else. And something else after that. The Scholomance isn't exactly a living thing, but it isn't exactly *not*, either. You can't put this much mana and this much thinking into a place without it starting to develop a mind of its own. And theoretically it's been built to protect us, so it won't just

start snacking on kids on its own—not to mention enroll-
ment would drop substantially when that began happening—
but of course it still wants enough mana to keep going; it's
meant to keep going. And I've put myself in the way, so the
school is coming after me, and that means anyone round me
is going to be in for it.

"The kids have got to start making mana for you," Aadhya
said.

"They're just freshmen," I said, dully. "All eight of them
together make less mana in an hour than I can build in ten
minutes."

"They could reset your dead crystals, though," Liu said.
"You said you don't need a lot of mana to wake those up, just
a steady stream. They could each carry one around."

Liu wasn't wrong, but that wasn't actually going to solve
the real problem. "I won't *need* the dead crystals. I'm not
going to have enough mana to fill my other empties, at this
rate."

"Then we can trade them," Aadhya said. "They're loads
better than most storage. Or you know, I could try building
them into the lute—"

"Do you want out?" I said, breaking in, harshly, because I
really couldn't handle sitting there while they worked through
all the options I'd spent the last three weeks clawing through,
trying to find a way out myself, until I'd realized there wasn't
going to be one for me. There was only the one for *them*.

Aadhya stopped talking. But Liu didn't even pause; she just
said, "No."

I swallowed hard. "I don't think you've thought—"

"*No,*" Liu said, strangely hard, and after a pause, she went
on more quietly, "I used to take Zheng and Min around all
day on a leading string when they were little. At school, if
one of the other boys was hurting something like a frog or a

stray kitten, they would stop it and bring the animal to me, even though they got teased for 'being girls' because of it." She looked down at Xiao Xing in her hands, stroking her thumb over his head. "No," she repeated, softly. "I don't want out."

I looked at Aadhya, my feelings in a confused knotted mess: I didn't know what I wanted her to say. My practical friend, whose mum had told her it was a good idea to be decent to losers, and so had been decent to *me*, all the years while everyone else treated me like a piece of used kitchen roll no one wanted to pick up even long enough to put in the bin. I'd liked her *because* she was practical, and hard-nosed: she'd always driven a solid hard bargain, the kind you could believe in, without ever cheating me, even though she'd more often than not been the only person who would have traded with me. She hadn't any reason to care about the freshmen in the library, and she had *choices*: she was one of the best practical artificers in our year, with a magical lute in the finishing stages that was going to be worth something *outside*, and not just among students. Any enclaver would've gladly snatched her up for a graduation alliance. That was the smart thing, the practical thing to do, and I almost wanted her to do it. She'd already taken half a dozen chances on me that anyone else would have called a bad bet. I didn't want her to drop me, but—I couldn't be the reason she didn't make it out.

But she only said, "Yeah, no," almost dismissively. "I'm not a ditcher. We just need to figure out a way to get you some more mana. Or better yet, get the school off your back. I don't get why the Scholomance is pulling this whole complicated stunt on you. You're not an enclaver, it's not like you were going to have tons of mana anyway, so why is it so into making you spend the little you've got?"

"Unless," Liu said, and then stopped. We looked over at her; her lips were pressed together, and she was staring at her hands in her lap, twisted up. "Unless it's about—pushing you. The school—"

"Likes maleficers," Aadhya finished for her.

Liu nodded a little without looking up. And she was absolutely right. That was surely why the Scholomance had given me that Wednesday session. It was trying to give me—an easier choice to make. The school wanted me to have to make the first selfish choice, to save my own mana, instead of saving a random freshman I didn't care about. Because then it would be easier for me to make the second selfish choice after that, and the one after that.

"Yeah," Aadhya agreed. "The school wants you to go maleficer. What could you do if you decided to start using malia?"

If you had me make a list of the top ten questions I go to great lengths to avoid asking myself, that one would have comprehensively covered items one through nine, and the only reason it wasn't doing for item ten as well was that *So how do you feel about Orion Lake* had quietly crept onto the bottom of it. But it's a long way down from the rest. "You don't want to know," I said, by which I meant *I don't want to know.*

Aadhya didn't even slow down. "Well, you'd have to get the malia somehow—" she was saying thoughtfully.

"That *wouldn't be a problem,*" I said through my teeth. She wasn't wrong to raise the question, since that's the top roadblock facing most would-be maleficers, and the solutions generally involve spending a lot of time on intimate encounters with entrails and screaming. But my own main concern is how to avoid *accidentally* sucking the life force out of everyone around me if I ever get taken by surprise and instinctively fire off something really gargantuan. For instance, I've got this great spell for razing an entire city to the ground, which will certainly come in handy if I ever turn into one of those people who write furious letters to the editor about the architecture of Cardiff, and I suppose it would do to wipe out any mals on the same floor as me. Along with all the other people on the same floor as me, but they'd probably be dead by then, since I'd have drained their mana to cast the spell.

That did finally stop her; she and Liu both eyed me a little dubiously. "Well, that wasn't creepy and ominous at all," Aadhya said after a moment. "Okay, I vote for you *not* turning maleficer."

Liu put up an emphatic hand to agree. I let a choked snort of laughter come out and put up my hand. "I vote no, too!"

"I'm even going to go out on a limb here and say that pretty much everyone else in the school will be right there with us," Aadhya said. "We could ask people to chip in for you."

I stared at her. "*Hey, everybody, it turns out El is some kind of mana-sucking vampire queen, we should all give her some mana so she doesn't drain us dry.*"

Aadhya scrunched up her mouth. "Hmm."

"We don't need to ask everyone to chip in for you," Liu said slowly. "We could just ask one person—if it's Chloe."

I hunched my shoulders forward and didn't say anything. That wasn't a terrible idea. It might even work. That was why I didn't like it. It had been almost a month since we'd gone down to the graduation hall, and I still remembered what it had been like with a New York power-sharer on my wrist, all that mana right in front of me like getting to plunge my head into a bottomless well and drink cold water in careless gulps.

I didn't trust how much I'd liked it. How easy it had been to get used to it.

"You think she'll say no?" Liu said, and I looked up: she was studying me.

"That's not . . ." I trailed off and then blew out a sigh. "She offered me a spot."

"In an alliance?" Aadhya said.

"In New York," I said, which only means one thing in here: an enclave spot, a *guaranteed* enclave spot. For most people, if you're lucky enough to get picked by an enclaver to join their alliance, it means their enclave will *look* at you, maybe give you a job. Usually four hundred kids graduate each year. Maybe forty enclave spots open up worldwide, and more than half of them will go to top adult wizards who've earned them with decades of work. A guarantee of one of those spots, fresh out of school, is a prize even if you weren't talking about the single most powerful enclave in the world. Aadhya and Liu were both gawking at me. "They're freaked out over Orion."

"After you've only been dating two months?" Liu said.

"We're not dating!"

Aadhya made a dramatic show of rolling her eyes heavenwards. "After you've been doing whatever you're doing that is not dating but totally looks like dating to everyone else, for only two months."

"Thanks ever so," I said, dryly. "As far as I can tell, they're shocked that he's talking to another human being at all."

"To be fair, you're the only person I've ever met who'd come up with the idea of being wildly rude and hostile to the guy who saved your life twenty times," Aadhya said.

I glared at her. "Thirteen times! And I've saved *his* life at least twice."

"Catch up already, girl," she said, unrepentantly.

It's not that I'd *rather* have had Aadhya and Liu ditch me to face the rest of my school career alone and desperate instead of asking Chloe Rasmussen for help, but I had definitely managed not to see asking her as an option. I wasn't actually sure what she'd say. I'd turned *down* her offer of a guaranteed place in New York, after all. I was still sullen about having to do it. I'd spent the better part of my life carefully planning out my campaign for an enclave spot. It had been a really comforting plan that ended in the fantasy of me having a nice happy long life in a safe and luxurious enclave with endless mana at my fingertips like all the other enclave kids, and by making sure the campaign was long and involved and never quite completed successfully, I'd neatly avoided having to think about how I didn't really want to be an enclaver at all.

Even Chloe—she's a decent sort, and better than that if I'm being fair. When the enclave kids started courting me last term—because of Orion—they all behaved as though they were doing me a generous favor by so much as talking to me. All it got them was my violent and unstrategic rudeness in their faces, so they stopped talking to me at all. But Chloe stuck it out. She's already asked to sit with us ten times this year, and she hasn't brought any tagalongs with her. I don't know that I'd have bent my neck the way she did, apologizing to me and even asking to be friends after I bit her head off. I'm not sorry for doing the biting, I had more than enough cause, but I still don't know that I'd have had the grace.

Oh, who am I lying to? My supply of grace wouldn't overflow an acorn cap.

But Chloe's still an enclaver. And not like Orion. All the New York kids have a power-sharer on their wrists that lets them exchange mana and pull from their shared storage, but

Orion's is one-way, going *in*. Because otherwise, he'll just pull as much mana as he needs to kill the nearest mal and save other kids. It's so much of an instinct for him that he can't actually stop himself. So the son of the future Domina of New York doesn't get access to the shared mana pool, although he sure gets to contribute, not to mention come running if any of them get into danger.

Chloe's one of the kids who gets the benefit of all that power he puts in. She doesn't need to budget her spells. She throws up a shield anytime she feels anxious. If a mal jumps her, maybe she has to keep her head and figure out what spell to use on it, but she doesn't have to worry that she can't afford to cast it. When she came in as a freshman, on top of bringing in a bag of the most useful magical items that wizardry can devise, she inherited a massive chest crammed full by more than a century's worth of other kids from New York, each of them bringing in a new set of useful items and making others in here—items they can afford to leave behind, because when they get out, they're going home to one of the richest enclaves in the world. And they *do* get out, because they're the worst targets in the room when we get dumped into the graduation hall, and there's lots of tasty losers available to be the cannon fodder.

I can't forget that whenever I'm with her. Or more honestly, I *do* forget it after a bit, and I don't want to. I find myself wishing she'd just gone on being awful, so I could go on being awful back. It feels unfair for her to get to have real friends, the kind of friends who don't care about how rich you are and how much mana you have, and also have all the mana and the money and the eager hovering sycophants on top of it. But whenever I really get into that mean sour squirrely thought, I immediately get the sensation of Mum looking at me with all this love and sympathy, and I feel like an earthworm. So hanging about with Chloe is a constant roller coaster from guarded to relaxed to resentful to earthworm and back again.

And now I had to ask her to let *me* in on the mana pool, because if I didn't, I'd be laying out Aadhya and Liu and all the freshmen in the library, and possibly everyone else in the school if I ever *do* screw up one fine morning when a rhysolite tries to dissolve my bones or a magma slug squirms up the furnace vent and launches itself at my head. I'd have even less excuse for being resentful of her than I've already got. I half wanted her to say no.

"Wait—do you mean you'll take the spot?" she said instead, sounding hopeful about it, as if I was meant to think that it was on perpetual offer, and I could claim myself a place in New York anytime I liked.

"No," I said, warily. I'd come to her room—I didn't want eavesdroppers for this conversation—and the whole place made me feel twitchy. She had one of the rooms above the bathrooms, where the opening to the void is overhead instead of out one wall. On the bright side, you never need to worry about falling out. On the downside, you've got an endless void over your head. She'd dealt with that by putting up a canopy of opaque cloth with just one spot open over the desk. Anything at all could have been hiding above it or in the folds.

She'd also kept all the standard-issue wooden furniture that I'd almost immediately replaced with thin wall-mounted shelves that didn't provide loads of dark corners. She even had two half-empty bookcases: her room had just gone double-width in the last reshuffle, which I could tell because she had a bright cheerful mural painted over the wall alongside the bed and was still working on continuing it onto the new space. It wasn't an ordinary painting, either; I could feel mana coming off it. She'd probably imbued the paint with protective spells in alchemy lab. Even so, I kept my back to the door and didn't come far into the room. She was snuggled in doing some reading on one of three luxuriously plush beanbag chairs amid a pile of other cushions, and I didn't trust a single one of them. My hands were itching to pull *her* up out of the heap before it suddenly swallowed her whole or something. "I'm just asking to borrow mana. I'm running out."

"Really?" she said dubiously, like that was an extraordinary thing to imagine. "Are you feeling okay?"

"It's not mana drain or a pipesucker," I said shortly. "I'm *using* it. I've got three seminars, a double independent study, and once a week I'm stuck with eight freshmen in a room and things try to eat them."

Chloe's eyes were all but popping before I'd finished. "Oh my God, are you nuts? A *double* independent study? Are you making a last-ditch run for valedictorian? Why would you even do that to yourself?"

"The *school's* doing it to me," I said, which she didn't want to believe was possible, so I spent the next ten minutes standing there with metaphorical cap in hand while she earnestly informed me that the fundamental intent of the Scholomance was the shelter and protection of wizard children, and the school couldn't act contrary to that intent, as if it didn't toss half of us to the wolves on a regular basis, and also that the school couldn't violate its standard procedures, which it also did on a regular basis, and after she had laid out those lines of argument, she finally wound up triumphantly at, "And why on earth would it be out to get *you*?"

I really didn't want to answer that question, and I was already sick of hearing her trot out the enclave party line. "Just forget I asked," I said, and turned to go; she was going to turn me down anyway.

"What? No, El, wait, that's not—" she said, and even scrambled up out of the heap to come after me. "Seriously, wait, I'm not saying no! I'm just—" and I gritted my teeth and turned round to tell her that if she wasn't saying no, she could get on with saying yes, or else stop wasting my time, except instead what I did was grab her arm and yank her sideways onto the bed with me as the cushions *did* have a go at swallowing her whole, and me along with her. Her own beanbag chair had split open along one seam to let out a gigantic slick greyish tongue that swiped across the floor towards us. It moved horribly fast, like a slug on a mission, and after we got out of the way, it kept going and swiped over the doorway, leaving every inch of the metal coated and glistening with some kind of thick gelatinous slime that I was confident we didn't want to touch.

I always keep my one decent knife on me; I already had it out and was slicing fast through all the canopy ties along the wall over the bed, so I could yank it down to envelop the slugtongue. That bought us a moment, but not a very long one, since the fabric almost immediately started to hiss and smoke: yes, the slime was bad. I didn't recognize this particular variety of mal, but it was the kind that's smart enough to play a very long game, waiting until it can take a victim without sparking suspicion. The dangerous kind. A glistening tip was already wriggling out through the first dissolving hole in the canopy, but Chloe had got past her own instinctive shriek and was grabbing a pot of paint from the rack at the foot of the bed; she threw the paint over it. A gargling noise of angry protest came from under the disintegrating canopy, and it rose to a higher pitch when she threw on another pot: red and yellow streaming together over the silky fabric, staining through and running off in rivulets, coating the thrashing tongue.

The mal pulled the tongue back in through the hole and back under the canopy, making a lot of ugly squishing and gurgling noises underneath that unfortunately sounded less like death throes than a mild attack of indigestion. "Come on, quick," Chloe said, grabbing another pot of paint and jerking her head towards the door, but halfway there, we ran out of time; there was a large gulping noise and the whole canopy, paint and all, was sucked into the slit of the beanbag chair with a slurp of tongue, and then the whole pile of bean-bags and cushions heaved itself up together and came at us in a humping rush.

There was no chance Chloe had been stupid enough to inherit that entire pile and never even move the pillows apart over the course of the past three-odd years, so that meant it was the kind of maleficaria that can animate wizard posses-sions, and it was also the kind of maleficaria that had a corpo-real flesh-digesting body of its own—each of which is a significant branching on everyone's favorite cladogram from Maleficaria Studies, meaning it was actually *two separate mals* that had formed some kind of wonderful symbiotic relation-ship. Trying to take out two mals at once when you don't know what either of them are isn't what you'd call easy. The only way to do it, at speed, was something grandiose—the kind of thing that would eat a heap of the mana I had left, and if I blew it all on Chloe and she *didn't* pay me back, I'd be saving her, choosing her, over everyone else who needed me.

Or I could just have—waited. Chloe had thrown the paint over the slime to neutralize it, and she was already sliding the door open. The cushion-monster was lumping straight towards her back: it would get her before she got ten steps onto the walkway. If I held back until it caught her, I'd be able to make it out the other way and get clear. She wasn't even looking to see if I was behind her. She hadn't looked back when we'd been in the stairwell, either, fighting together to try and keep the argonet from getting into the school. She'd taken off to save her own skin. Aadhya and Liu had stayed with me, but she'd abandoned us. And she'd just spent ten minutes telling me at length that I was making up reasons why I needed mana, which is to say reasons why she shouldn't feel bad about saying no to me.

"Get out of the way!" I said through my teeth, and pointed at the cushion beast. Chloe darted a look back that went wide when she saw the thing coming at her. She gave a terrific heave and shoved the door and flung herself out into the hall even as it slid open, where she collided bodily with Orion, who was already off-balance because he'd been holding on to the door handle from the other side. She took him down to the floor beneath her in a heap.

The spell I used was a really terrific higher-level working I'd just learned in my Myrddin class. It had taken me a solid week to plow through the antique Welsh manuscript—time enlivened by the many lavish illustrations of the way it had been used by a tidy-minded alchemist maleficer to flay the skin off hapless victims, neatly drain their blood, pop the organs into separate containers, and then the flesh into a desiccated heap, leaving behind the cleaned bones.

The incantation did a remarkable job of whipping off the outer layer of cushion covers and beanbag chair casings, sending them into a beautifully folded pile that might have come straight from a laundry. That step briefly exposed a glowing translucent sac full of tongue and undigested canopy and, gruesomely, a half-digested person. Thankfully the face was already unrecognizable, even before the sac shredded into a stack of inch-wide strips of some vellum-like material, and dumped the whole tongue out flopping onto the floor. The tongue proceeded to roll up into a very thin spongy mat, a huge puddle of viscous fluid squeezing out of it, which after a moment of alarming uncertainty and struggle finally separated into three different liquids: one ectoplasmic, one clear, and one sort of jelly-pinkish, which all leapt like graceful fountains into the emptied paint cans on the floor. The excess more or less reluctantly went down the drain in the middle of the room.

Orion was trying to fight his way back up, hampered because Chloe was frozen not halfway off him, staring open-mouthed at the elaborate dismemberment. To be fair to her, it was more of a show than I'm letting on. When I cast spells, there are usually copious side manifestations, generally designed to convey to anyone watching that they should probably be fleeing in terror or alternatively dropping to their knees and doing homage. The whole dismemberment happened in roughly the span of half a minute, and there was a lot of futile but violent thrashing involved, along with wailing disembodied shrieks and gusting flares of phosphorescence as the apparition bit went. After it was all over, everything was left neatly lined up in a row, exactly like the supply shop of an alchemist maleficer's dreams. The remnants of the last victim had *also* separated themselves tidily into cleaned bones, flesh, and scraps of skin, in line with the bits of mal. The skull was sitting atop the pile of bones with thin trails of smoke coming out of the sockets. And as the finishing touch, the spongy roll that had been the tongue wrapped itself into a square of the fallen canopy, and another strip of canopy tore away and tied a little bow around it before it rolled into the line.

I'd jumped on a chair to get clear of the various gushing

fluids, and the last wafting clouds of phosphorescent smoke were winding around me. My mana crystal was glowing with the power I'd had to pull, but I wasn't casting a shadow, which meant I was probably glowing myself. "Oh my God?" Chloe said, a little faintly, sort of like a question, frozen in place.

"Hey, can you get off?" Orion said, sounding a bit squashed.

Chapter 3
LESKITS

"J UST SO YOU KNOW, I was going to say yes anyway," Chloe said miserably, like she didn't think I'd ever believe her, as she handed me the power-sharer. "Really, El."

"I know you were," I said grimly, taking it, but her expression didn't change; probably my tone didn't sound very encouraging. So I added, "If you were going to say no, it wouldn't have jumped us," a little pointedly, because she should have figured that much out by then. A mal smart enough to have been quietly lurking in her floor pillows—floor pillows she'd probably inherited from a previous New York enclaver—for years and years, conserving its energy and slurping up anyone *other* than her who was unlucky enough to be left alone in her room—which is the kind of thing enclavers do, invite friends over for a study group after dinner with the understanding that one of *them* is going to arrive first and make sure the room is all right—hadn't just leapt at us because it suddenly lost all self-control. It had done it because Chloe was about to get on board with *me*, meaning that especially delicious me was about to become a much harder target.

Chloe frowned, but she's not dim, and she'd just had her face shoved in it very firmly, so once she got over the hump of her basic programming, she worked through the implications fast enough that the associated emotions traveled over her face in quick succession. It meant I hadn't been making everything up. The school really *was* out to get me, and the mals were, too; I really *was* as powerful as that implied—her eyes darted over to the still-standing array of grotesque ingredients as that hit—and anyone hanging round me was almost certainly asking to be in the line of fire.

When she got there, I said, "I have a bunch of storage crystals. I'll just fill them up and then give this back to you."

She didn't say anything for a moment; she was still looking at the ingredients on the floor, and then she said, slowly, "You're strict mana. Is that—*because*—" She didn't go on, but that was because she didn't have to. Like I said, she's not dim. Then she looked at me and raised her chin a bit and said in a high voice, like she was declaring it to the world and not just me, "Keep it. You might need more." I was already fighting down the violent urge to scowl at her like a monster of ingratitude when she added tentatively, "Would you—do Aadhya and Liu need them?"

Which made it a request to *join our alliance.*

I couldn't even just blurt out a flat unthinking no, because I couldn't give her an answer to that question without talking to Aadhya and Liu. That meant that I'd have too much time to recognize that the obvious and sensible and even *fair* answer was yes.

I didn't want to be allied with Chloe Rasmussen. I didn't want to be one of the lucky ones whose alliance gets scooped up with enormous condescension by some enclaver with mana and friends and a chestful of useful things to spare, which is of course the goal that most people are actively aiming for when they put together a team without an enclaver already in it. Even if that wasn't what Chloe meant or what we meant, that's what everyone would think it was. And after all, they'd be right; we'd get Chloe out, and Chloe's mana would get us out, and we'd be leaving other people behind who didn't stand a chance.

But she had a right to ask, when I was here asking for her help to start with, and she'd had the guts to ask, when instead she could just have got clear after paying me back for saving her from the attack that only happened because she'd been willing to help me in return for nothing at all. She was offering more than fair value, even if it wasn't fair that she had it to offer, and if I still wanted to say no to her despite all of that, Aadhya and Liu had the right to tell me I was being a colossal twat.

"I'll talk to them," I muttered ungraciously, and as you would expect, the end result was that three days later I had to add Chloe's name on the wall near the girls' bathroom, where we had written up our alliances. Liu also put her name on the Chinese translation next to me, the power-sharer on her wrist gleaming and shiny, and then we all went to breakfast together and I had to hear at least twenty bazillion people congratulating us, where by "us" I mean me, Aadhya, and Liu, for having scored Chloe. We hadn't got nearly as many congratulations when we'd written ourselves up near the end of last term, even though we'd been one of the first alliances to go on the wall.

To cap it off, Orion didn't congratulate me exactly, but he said, "I'm glad you and Chloe have become friends," in an alarmingly hopeful way that was very clearly only one unfortunate literature assignment away from turning into *come live with me and be my love,* optionally etched onto metal with little hearts around it.

"I've got to get to class," I said, and escaped to the comparative safety of my independent study down in the bowels of the school, where the worst thing that was going to leap at me with devouring attention was a flesh-eating monster.

In a month of school, I'd so far translated a grand total of four additional pages out of the Golden Stone sutras. They contained a single three-line spell in Vedic Sanskrit whose purpose I couldn't even guess at from the start. It had seven words I'd never seen before which all had multiple translation options. The rest of the four pages was a commentary in medieval Arabic explaining at length why it was just fine to use the Sanskrit spell even though it might seem haram because of the wine used in the casting process. The commentary mostly avoided anything useful like explaining what the spell did that was so great and how the alcohol was meant to be used. Except it didn't *completely* avoid anything useful, so I had to dig through the whole frothing thing for the handful of nuggets.

That morning I finally figured out which of the ninety-seven possible meanings went together, and reached the conclusion that the spell was for tapping into a distant source of water and purifying it—something of extremely great interest to people living in a desert and much less so to someone living in an enchanted school equipped with functional if antiquated plumbing. I was just glaring at my finished and useless three-line translation when the furnace vent rattled at my back and a whirling mass of fur and claws and teeth leapt out onto me, exactly as anticipated.

And then it promptly bounced off the shield that I didn't even have to cast, because Aadhya's shield holder on my chest had automatically pulled mana from the power-sharer to block the physical contact. Even as I whirled round, the leskit went skidding over the floor into the corner and twisted itself up on its twelve feet. It was odds-on which of us was more surprised, but it recovered quicker; it came at me again and stopped just short to give the shield an experimental swipe, striking a cloud of bright orangey sparks off it.

My normal strategy in a situation like this would have been to distract and run. But by then I could hear screams and more hissing coming from the ventilation: there was a pack of them in the workshop. Leskits don't usually hunt individually. Mine opened its toothy maw and emitted a loud *krrk krrk krrk* noise like an angry ostrich—I've never heard an angry ostrich but it's the noise I'd imagine coming from one—and there was some scrabbling in the vent and another one's head came poking out. It dropped down and the two of them discussed in *skrrks* for a moment and then charged me together, clawing, scraping more deep flaring gouges in the shield.

I stared at them from behind it, and then I slowly said, *"Exstirpem has pestes ex oculis, ex auribus, e facie mea funditus,"* which was a slight variation on an imperial Roman spell meant to eradicate a host of annoyances that are trying to get at you but are temporarily held back—such as, for instance, a mob of angry locals besieging your evil tower of wizardry and torture. I waved my arm in a broad sweeping-away-vermin gesture at the leskits, who promptly disintegrated, along I presume with all their pals inside the workshop, since the screaming I could hear filtering in through the vent died off into a vaguely confused silence.

For another moment I went on staring at what were now two little piles of ash on the floor, then for lack of anything else to do I slowly sat back down at my desk and went back to work. There wasn't any reason for me to go running out into the corridor, and still twenty minutes left before the bell. After a few minutes, the door—which had done its slamming routine again just a few minutes before the leskits made their appearance—slid back open in what I possibly imagined was a disappointed way. It didn't even bang all that loudly.

I spent the rest of the period making a clean copy of the original Sanskrit spell, along with a formal spell commentary of my own, including word-for-word translations of the spell into modern Sanskrit and English to help convey meaning, with several possible variations in connotation, an analysis of the Arabic commentary, and notes on the potential usage. It was the kind of stupid flashy work that you only do if you *are* trying for valedictorian, or eventual journal publication, which is a less violently competitive approach to getting post-graduation enclave interest.

I didn't need to do any of that. There wasn't an assignment I had to hand in, and I certainly didn't need to do the work to cast the spell. In fact, I could've done that as soon as I'd worked out the pronunciation. Except, of course, that if I ever took the risk of casting a spell without knowing for sure what it was meant to do, it would definitely turn out to be meant to do a lot of murder.

I did all of that silly make-work because I didn't want to start on a new section. More accurately, I didn't want to have the *time* to start on a new section. Obviously I didn't have any regrets about spending New York's mana on wiping out a pack of leskits, saving my own skin in the process, but I wasn't going to let myself feel *happy* about it. I wasn't going to be grateful, and I very much wasn't going to get used to it, only that was hopeless nonsense; I was already getting used to it. My shoulders wouldn't stay tense, and I kept forgetting to check the vent behind me, as if it wasn't the most important thing in the room.

And then at the bell, I went out into the corridor and the crowd of sophomore artificers came spilling out of the workshop, talking excitedly about what had happened to the leskits, and I overheard one of them saying, shrugging, "*Comment il les a eus comme ça? J'en ai aucune idée. Putain, j'étais sûr qu'il allait crever,*" and I went to my Myrddin seminar in a cloud of outrage as I realized Orion had been *in there*, and my leskit-clearing stunt had somehow saved his neck, so I *did* have to be happy I'd been able to do it, and also what had he even been doing down in the workshop with a bunch of sophomores?

"Were you lurking outside my classroom door or something?" I demanded at lunch, as we got in line.

"No!" he said, but he also didn't offer a remotely convincing explanation. "I just . . . I had a feeling" was what he served up, and hunched away from me looking so sour and grouchy that I almost wanted to let him off the hook, except my wanting that was so horribly wrong that I didn't let myself.

"A feeling like you needed to get your arse saved from a pack of leskits?" I said sweetly instead. "My count is up to four now, isn't it?"

"I didn't need to be saved! There were only eight of them, I could've taken them," he snapped at me, and he had the nerve to sound actually annoyed, which annoyed *me*.

"That's not what *I* heard about it," I said, "and if you don't like getting rescued in turn, you haven't got a leg to stand on, have you?"

I took my tray and stalked away across the cafeteria to the table Liu was holding. Orion slunk after me and sat down next to me with both of us still mad—you don't break up a table in here over anything as minor as a violent quarrel—and we both steamed away in silence for the entire meal. We cleared our trays and walked out of the cafeteria at what I thought was meant to be pointedly different times, since he seemed to be in a rush to get out ahead of me, so I slowed down, and when I came out, I spotted him talking to Magnus just outside the doors, and a moment later Magnus held out his hand and I realized Orion was asking him for *mana*.

"You bag of jumbled screws, you could've *said* you were running low," I said, after giving him a swat across the back of the head when I caught him down the corridor, just before the stairs. "Also, going after mals when you're low to try and make up for it is even more stupid than your usual line, which is saying something."

"What? No! I wasn't—" Orion started, and then he turned round and caught my hard glare and paused, and then looked awkward and said, "Oh," like he'd just noticed that was in fact exactly what he'd been doing.

"Yes, *oh*," I said. "You're *entitled* to a fair share of the New York mana! You've probably put in loads more than *your* fair share just this past week."

"I haven't," Orion said shortly. "I haven't been putting anything in at all."

"What?" I stared at him.

"I haven't taken out any mals this whole month," Orion said. "The only ones I've even seen are the ones I've seen *you* taking out."

If you can believe it, there was even still a faint accusatory tone in there, but I ignored it in favor of gawping at him. "Are you telling me you haven't saved anyone all term? Why haven't I been hearing howls of death and dismay all round the place?"

"There aren't any!" he said. "They're all lying low. I think we wiped out too many of them down in the graduation hall," as if the words *too many* had any business taking up room in that sentence, "and the ones left are still mostly in hiding. I've been asking people, but almost nobody's been seeing mals at all."

I can't actually coherently describe the level of indignation I experienced. It was one thing for the school to be out to get me, which I think all of us secretly feel is the case from the moment we arrive, and another for the school to be out to get *only* me, to the exclusion of literally everyone else, including even Orion, even though the school's hunger was really his fault in the first place. Although I suppose it *was* getting him by keeping mals away from him. "What do you have Wednesdays after work period?" I demanded, when I could get words out past the incoherent rage.

"My senior alchemy seminar," he said: four levels down from the library. So he couldn't come up and give me a hand even if he wanted to, as he apparently very much did.

"What are your first periods?"

"Chinese and maths." As far away from the workshop level as a senior class could get.

"I hate everything," I said passionately.

✕

"The rest of New York is going to say something if this keeps going," Chloe said unhappily, perched on Liu's bed cross-legged with her own mouse cupped in her hands. She'd named him Mistoffeles because he had a single black spot at his throat like a bow tie, which had started looking much more like a bow tie just in the week she'd been holding him. He was also already doing things for her: just yesterday he'd hopped out of her hands and run scampering off into the drain and then come back a few minutes later and offered her a little scrap of only slightly gnawed-on ambergris he'd somehow found down there.

It irritated me: I'd been working on Precious for more

than a month and a half now, giving her mana treats and try-ing to give her instructions, and she still wasn't doing much but accepting the treats as her due and sitting there on my hand graciously permitting me to pet her. "Shouldn't you at least be able to turn invisible or something by now?" I'd told her in a grumble under my breath before tipping her back into Liu's cage. She just ignored me. Even Aadhya had been able to take her mouse Pinky permanently back to her room by now, where she'd built him a massive and elaborate enclo-sure full of wheels and tunnels that kept getting expanded up the wall. "It just takes time sometimes," Liu told me, very tactfully, but even she was getting a faintly doubtful expres-sion as the weeks crept on.

Of course, I still wouldn't have given up a single minute of getting to cuddle Precious even if I could have had them all back a hundredfold in study time. She was so alive and real, her soft fur and her moving lungs and the tiny beat of her heart; she didn't belong to the Scholomance. She was a part of the world outside, the world I sometimes found myself thinking maybe only existed in the dreams I had of it once in a while. We'd been in the Scholomance for three years, one month, two weeks, and five days.

And in that last one month, two weeks, and five days, no-body but me or the me-adjacent had been attacked by a sin-gle mal, as far as we could double-check without making people suspicious. People hadn't realized yet only because some of the attacks had spilled over into the workshop, which was on the other side of my independent study room, and also it was still early enough in the year that everyone sepa-rately thought they were just getting lucky.

"But the other New York kids *are* going to notice the mana pool getting low," Chloe said. "Magnus was already asking me the other day if I'd been doing any major workings. I've got a right to share power with my allies, but not to let them take it all."

"We're all putting as much as we can back," Aadhya said. "And there're seven seniors from New York. You have to be putting in loads yourselves. How low is the pool going to get?"

"Well," Chloe said, in an odd, awkward way, darting a look at me, and then she said haltingly, "We don't really— I mean—"

"You don't build mana at all," I said flatly, from the corner, as I instantly realized what she wasn't saying. "None of you ever put any mana in the enclave pool, because Orion was putting in enough for all of you."

Chloe bit her lip and avoided our eyes; Aadhya and Liu were both staring at her, shocked. *Everyone's* got to build mana in here. Even enclave kids. Their big advantage is more time, better conditions, people watching their backs and doing homework for them and giving them little presents of mana and all the other things that the rest of us have to spend mana to get. They all have their own efficient mana stores and power-sharers. So by the time they get to senior year, they're all way ahead. But never having to build mana at *all*— never having to do sit-ups or struggle through making some horrible doily, because all of them were just coasting on Orion's back—

And he had to beg mana from *them* when he started to run out.

Chloe didn't raise her head, and there was color in her cheeks. Mistoffeles made a little anxious chirping noise in her hands. She probably hadn't even thought about it since freshman year. The way I already wasn't thinking about it, day-today. And I'd sniped at Orion for needing help, after killing monsters with the mana he'd built up over three years of risking his life.

✖

"So what?" Orion said, and sounded like he meant it.

I hadn't been near his room since last term; I was doing my best to avoid being alone with him at all these days. But I'd put Precious down and walked out of Liu's room and straight down the corridor to his, without saying another word to Chloe. Orion was there, busy failing to do his alchemy homework, judging by the total blankness of the lab worksheet on his desk. He let me in so nervously that I almost stopped being angry long enough to reconsider being there, but despite him and his mostly futile attempts at straightening up his piles of dirty laundry and books, anger won. It usually does, for me.

I might as well not have bothered, for all he cared when I did tell him. I stared at him, and he stared back. It wasn't even just him being happy to help the useless wankers out; he sounded like he didn't understand why I was bothering to mention this odd piece of irrelevant information.

"It's *your mana*," I said through my teeth. "It's *all* your mana. Do you get it, Lake? The whole parasitic lot of them have been clinging on your back for three years and change, never putting in a minute's worth of effort themselves—"

"I don't care!" he said. "There's always more. There's always *been* more," he added, and that *did* come with an emotion, only it was flat-out whinging.

"I'm sorry, are you *bored*?" I snarled at him. "Are you missing the good fun of saving people's lives six times a day, the regular dose of adoration?"

"I miss the *mana!*" he yelled at me.

"So take it back!" I said, and yanked the power-sharer off my wrist and shoved it at him. "Take *all* of it back! You want more mana, it's yours, it's all yours, they haven't a right to a single drop."

He stared down at the power-sharer, a half-hungry expression flitting over his face, then he shook his head hard with a jerk. "No!" he said, and shoved his hands in his hair, which hadn't grown back long enough yet to support the drama of the gesture, and muttered, "I don't know what to *do* with myself," plaintively.

"I know what to do with you," I said, by which I meant kicking him into next week where maybe he'd have got over himself, only he actually had the nerve to say, "Yeah?" in a challenging, pretending-to-be-suave double-entendre sort of way that lasted only long enough for him to hear it coming out of his own mouth, at which point he went red and embarrassed and then darted a look around the room with nobody but us in it and turned even more red, and I went out of the place like a shot and ran straight back to Liu's just to escape.

Where I came back in with all of them still sitting there and the power-sharer still in my hand. Chloe jerked her head up and looked at me anxiously. But as far as I was concerned, she could discuss it with Orion herself if she wanted to know what he thought about it. "So what now?" I said, holding it out to her instead. "You want out?"

"No!" Chloe said, and then Aadhya actually hauled a book out of her school bag, the thick kind we call larva-killers, and threw it at me with enough intent behind it that I had to jump aside or it would've nailed me in the bum.

"Stop it!" she said. "I think that's like the third time you've asked to be ditched. You're like one of those puffer fish, the second anyone touches you a little wrong you go all *bwoomp*," she illustrated with her hands, "trying to make them let go. We'll let you know, how's that?"

I put the power-sharer back on more or less sullenly—let's be honest, more—and sat back down on the floor with my arms wrapped round my knees. Liu said after a moment, "So the real problem isn't that you're using mana. The problem is that Orion's not putting any in."

"Yes, all we need to do is find a surefire way to lure him some mals," I muttered. "If only we had a bunch of tasty adolescent wizards all in the same place. Oh, wait."

"I've got more things to throw over here," Aadhya said, waving another deadly book—this one had some actual suspicious splotches on its cover—threateningly.

"Maybe we could build a honeypot, like they do for construction sites?" Chloe said.

"Like who does for what?" Aadhya said, and Chloe looked around like she expected me or Liu to be any less confused.

"A honeypot?" she said, more tentatively. "Is there another word for it? You know, when there's a major project for a circle of wizards, and they're going to be working for a long time, days, and you don't want mals to be coming for them? So you have to lure all the nearby mals out and clean them up, like the week before? New York used one for the Tri-State Gateway expansion a couple of years back."

It certainly *sounded* brilliant, but only in the sense that it was clearly too good to be true. "If you can lure them places, why wouldn't you do it all the time?" I said. "Just stick one of these honeypots in the middle of a trap, and no more mals around ever."

"You've still got to *do* something with them!" Chloe said. "What kind of trap is going to hold a thousand giant mals? We had to hire a team of three hundred guards just for the one week." That was starting to sound a bit more plausible, and worth considering, and then she added, "Anyway, you can't just keep a honeypot going all the time, it's too expensive to run."

We all stared at her. She stared back. "It's *too expensive*," I said pointedly. "For *New York*." I'd seen Orion toss fistfuls of mana-infused diamond dust into his homework assignment potions like it was all-purpose flour. He didn't even bother to sweep up the leavings from his lab bench afterwards.

Chloe bit her lip, but then Liu said, "But it can't be that hard to lure mals. They want to come for us anyway, you're just reinforcing their existing desire."

"Oh, hey," Aadhya said abruptly. "How *far away* did you lure mals from?"

"We covered all of Gramercy Park and one block out in each direction," Chloe said, which meant nothing to me, but Aadhya was nodding.

"Yeah, okay," she said. "Any artifice is going to be crazy expensive to run when you try to push the effect out over six city blocks. But we don't want to lure *all* the mals in the school." We very much didn't; in fact we all cringed instinctively just because she'd said it out loud. "We just want a few of them for Orion." She rummaged round in her bag and dug out a copy of the blueprints that she must have made at some point in her career: artificers often get assigned to do detailed studies of the school, since it helps reinforce the workings. "Here." She pointed to a spot on the first floor. "There's a major pipe junction here running through the workshop wall. If we build a honeypot and set it next to the nearest drain and run it from there, I bet we'll catch him plenty of mals even if we only cover a two-foot radius."

"Brilliant," I said. "So how does one of these honeypots work?"

We all looked at Chloe. "Um, there's a container—you

need to put in some kind of bait, and then the artifice blows the scent out . . ." She trailed off unspecifically and shrugged. "I'm sorry, I only know about it because my mom had to do the presentation for the requisition process."

"The requisition process," I said even more pointedly, because anything that New York bothered to make you *requisition* had to be insanely complicated on top of expensive.

But Aadhya was waving it away. "That's enough to go on. Liu's right, it can't be that hard. You just brew up some bait that smells like teenage wizard, and I'll see what I can come up with to disperse it."

Chloe was nodding. "How fast do you think you can do it?" she asked anxiously.

"No clue," Aadhya said, with a shrug.

"And in the meantime, all of New York has to start building mana," Liu said. "If Orion can't put in mana anymore, and none of you are, you're going to run out sooner or later anyway. You don't want to find out that the honeypot doesn't work in three months, just when it's time to start doing obstacle-course runs."

"But if I tell everyone that we have to start putting in mana because Orion can't anymore, the first thing Magnus will want to do is run an audit on our power-sharers to see how much everyone is using," Chloe said. "Then they'll know why it's going to be *sooner.*"

"I don't think he'll insist on an audit," Liu said, with a glance towards me. "Not if you tell them the right way."

"What's the right way?" I said warily.

❦

The right way was, Chloe whispered around to everyone in New York, that *Orion's girlfriend* was keeping him from hunting mals because I didn't want him getting hurt, and now I was getting suspicious about why the mana was suddenly running low.

The New York enclavers were all as eager for me to learn the truth about the source of their mana as Chloe had been, so they did start quietly contributing after all—which it turned out they could do by the bucketload without even getting anywhere close to their mana-building capacity. That of course didn't keep them from being grumpy about the work they *were* doing. I confess I enjoyed catching a glimpse of Magnus stalking into the boy's bathroom at the head of his entourage, soaked in sweat and red-faced from what I assume was a hearty session of building mana with annoying physical exercise.

But after a month of what I suppose they found unbearable suffering, they all began to interrogate each other in accusatory ways about mana use, and meanwhile the honeypot project ran into a serious snag. Aadhya had made up a special incense burner, a set of nested cylinders of different kinds of metal, with holes punched carefully in each one to control the path that smoke took through them. Chloe had mixed a dozen small batches of mana-infused incense and left them out around a drain in one of the alchemy labs during dinner. We came down afterwards—warily—and picked the one that showed the most signs of having been poked at with various appendages, including a snuffler's face, which had left a distressing imprint roughly like a lotus seedpod.

"Great, let's go," Orion said promptly; he would have grabbed the cylinder off the table and headed straight for the door, but Aadhya put out a hand against his chest and stopped him.

"How about we *don't* try it out for the first time next to a big junction going straight down to the graduation hall," she said. The rest of us all agreed heartily. The diameter of the school's plumbing is open to a determined interpretation, and if we were *deliberately* luring mals, our intent would actually be helping them squeeze themselves through.

Orion sat on a stool in visible impatience, tossing the burner from one hand to the other, while the rest of us discussed the best place for a trial run. We finally settled on the lab itself, on the grounds that the incense had been out here for a bit already, and we didn't want to carry it through the corridors to somewhere else, possibly accumulating a trailing horde in the process.

Aadhya put the incense into the burner, fussed with the positioning of the cylinders a bit longer, and finally said, "All right, let's give it a shot," handing it to Orion.

We all backed well off towards the door while he did the honors. He lit the small blob of incense—"Ow," he said, burning his fingers with the match, which he was more worried about than the possibly impending mals—and dropped it into the middle of the cylinders. Then he put the burner on the lab stool and set it right near the drain.

The first threads of smoke came out and visibly wafted over the drain before dispersing. Orion hovered over it eagerly, but nothing came out. We waited another few minutes. The smoke began to pick up, making a thin stream that circled the drain and went down into it. Still nothing.

There had been a couple of small agglos in the lab, stealing the floor leavings—we'd ignored them as they're quite handy when fully grown, and completely harmless otherwise—which had started slowly humping their way towards the drain to escape when we'd come into the room. While we were still waiting, they reached the drain and kept going, straight through the thickest smoke, showing no interest in it whatsoever.

Orion looked over at us. "Shouldn't it work on them? They're still mals."

"Yeah, I guess," Chloe said, a bit nasally. The burner was certainly doing something; even all the way back at the door, the air was taking on the same distinct aroma that regularly wafted out of the boys' loo.

Aadhya frowned and took a few cautious steps towards the burner. "Maybe we should," she started, and that was when Pinky stuck his head out of his carrying cup and gave a loud excited squeak. Aadhya had made each of us a bandolier-style strap with a cup attached, for the mice to ride around in during the day, since Liu wanted us to keep them with us more often. Before she could stop him, Pinky leapt directly out of the cup on her chest all the way down to the floor, raced over to the stool, scampered up the leg like a tiny streak of white lightning, and did a full-body flying lunge for the cylinder and knocked it onto the floor. While we were still yelping, Mistoffeles and Xiao Xing emerged from their cups and made their own mad dashes to join him.

They were certainly interested in the incense. Together they spent the next half hour rolling the cylinder around the lab in mad glee, sending it under cabinets and tables and squirming out of our grip every time we tried to grab it or them. It turns out that magical mice high on incense are really good at *not* being caught. There was a lot of swearing and yelling and banged elbows and barked shins before we finally managed to get the cylinder away from them and put the smoke out, at which point they collapsed in exhausted furry lumps with their paws curled and glazed expressions that somehow conveyed dreamy pleasure on their faces.

Chloe drew several thick lines through the incense recipe in her notebook, and Aadhya disgustedly dumped the set of cylinders into the scrap bin. When a first experiment goes that far awry from your expectations, it's usually not worth the risk to keep going. It means you're missing something quite important, and in this case, we had no idea what the something we were missing was. So if we tried again with just minor tweaks, we'd *expect* it to go wrong, and at that point, not only would it go wrong, it would almost certainly go wrong in a much more dramatic and possibly painful fashion.

The only positive outcome was my getting the first sign that Precious was actually becoming a familiar. She hadn't joined the frenzy; instead, as soon as Pinky went for the burner, she'd run up my shoulder and jumped onto a high shelf of the lab, where she tipped a large beaker over herself and sat there disapprovingly watching the other mice having fun with her tiny forepaws held over her nose. After we put out the incense, she climbed back into my bandolier cup and pulled the lid firmly on top of herself and made clear that she was coming home with me instead of going back to the group cage in Liu's room with the other stupefied mice.

So that was tidy, but the honeypot project was back to square one.

Meanwhile the New York enclaves weren't my only problem anymore. Everyone *else* was starting to look into the pattern of mal attacks, or lack thereof. We all spend a great deal of time thinking about mals and what they're going to do. Almost half our freshman and sophomore courses are devoted to the study of maleficaria, their classification, their behavior, and most important, how to kill them. When mals start behaving unexpectedly, that's bad. Even if the unexpected behavior is that they're not leaping out to kill you anymore. That usually just means they're *waiting* to leap out and kill you at a much more opportune moment.

The next Wednesday, at the end of our cheery library death seminar, Sudarat waited until the kid on my other side got up and then said softly to me as we packed up to leave, "A girl from Shanghai asked me if our class had been attacked again."

We were getting into striking range of midterms by then, and a grand total of twenty-three people had been killed so far the whole year. More than half of them had been freshmen blowing themselves up in shop or poisoning themselves in alchemy lab, which was barely like dying at all by our normal standards. The others—bar one—had all been cafeteria mistakes. Even that was radically below the usual rates, since almost everyone could afford to cast sniffer spells and brew antidotes, since *they* weren't getting jumped by maleficaria.

Death number twenty-three was the only upperclassman, a junior-year charmer named Prasong who'd been another former Bangkok enclaver. He had been very unhappy to discover he wasn't an enclaver anymore, and he'd made himself obnoxious enough in the years he'd been one that he found sympathy and friends in very short supply. As he couldn't see any other way to continue in the lifestyle to which he'd become accustomed—or to reliably continue living, for that matter—he made the decision to go maleficer. And obviously the best and safest way for him to get a big helping of malia stored up, enough to see him through graduation, would be draining it out of a group of unsuspecting wide-eyed freshmen.

If that sounds unimaginably evil to you, I should mention that it wasn't to us. Most years there are somewhere between four and eight kids who go for the maleficer track, and since most of them haven't planned it out carefully in advance and brought in a supply of small mammals, targeting younger students is their standard order of business. We're all warned about it quite prosaically in the freshman handbook, and told to be wary of older or more successful kids showing too much interest in our activities. I owed my own charming gut scar to one of them, the late unlamented Jack Westing, who'd also done for Orion's neighbor Luisa back in our sophomore year.

Sudarat was the only freshman that Prasong could talk to without arousing suspicions. He didn't even have to go out of his way—she was going as far out of hers as she could to maintain her connections to the older Bangkok ex-enclavers. Even if all that got her was a chance to sit with them in the cafeteria once in a while, or the last hand-me-downs they couldn't sell as seniors, that would still be better than nothing. So all Prasong needed to do was agree to let her fill an empty seat at his table for a single meal. She must have told him enough about her weird library seminar to convince him it was the perfect meal: eight freshmen in an isolated room with no witnesses around. I assume she didn't mention me.

A few days later, he snuck upstairs just before the end of lunch period and laid down a flaying hex circle on the floor under the desks.

It wasn't very good. You can't exactly look up malia-sucking hexes in the library; officially there aren't any malicious texts available in here. That's nonsense of course, I've stumbled across at least a hundred of them. But anyone who went *looking* for them would probably have harder luck getting one. Anyway, Prasong wasn't as ambitious as dear Jack. His hex was good enough to rip off a substantial patch of skin on his victims, opening us up so he could pull a tidy bit of malia out of us through our pain and horror, and I imagine that was all he wanted. Actually killing eight wizards at once, even freshmen, is no joke for a budding maleficer; the psychic damage would've left him visibly marked in the ominous sorts of ways that make your fellow students—particularly your nearest neighbors—gather up a sufficient group to put you down before you get any more bright ideas that might involve extracting mana from *them*.

Unfortunately for him, I noticed the hex before I even crossed the threshold. I assumed a construct mal had done it; some of the more advanced kinds can draw spell inscriptions, although usually not very well. That didn't rule out this example. I could've done better without half trying, and that's exactly what I did: I grabbed a piece of chalk off the nearest board, rewrote half the sigils to turn the spell back on the original inscriber—correcting the various mistakes and adding a few improvements while I was at it—and invoked it with contemptuous ease and barely an ounce of mana. I was even a little smug that the first attack of the afternoon had been so easy to deal with.

I only found out who had cast it at dinnertime, when people were gossiping energetically about how Prasong's skin just completely flew off him in the middle of the language lab and how he ran around in circles screaming wildly until he died of massive blood loss and shock.

I won't say I was sorry. I won't. I vomited after dinner, but it was probably something I'd eaten. Sudarat left the cafeteria looking moderately ghastly herself. She and all the kids in the library had known at once what had happened: I'd made a point—smug, smug, smug—of showing them the hex circle, what it was trying to do to us, and how I was cleverly turning it back on the creator. She'd been extra quiet in the couple of weeks since, which was saying something. This was the first peep she'd let out in my direction since.

"From Shanghai?" I said slowly.

Sudarat nodded, a small jerk of her head. "Some people from Bangkok heard," she said. "About the attacks we've had.

Some other people. When I told . . ." She trailed off, but I'd got the picture. When she'd told Prasong about the library attacks, other older Bangkok kids had been at the table, too. And now her former enclave mates were using her as the source of useful gossip to pass along, just to score a few points. Just like all of us loser kids do, because you can't know which of those points is going to be the one that gets you through the graduation hall gates.

"What did you tell them?" I said.

Her head was bent down towards her desk, the short blunt edge of her hair hiding her eyes, but I could see her lips and throat work when she swallowed. "I said, I didn't remember. Then I said no."

She was learning, the way every loser freshman learns. She'd understood that they weren't asking out of consideration for her: they were hunting for information that was valuable to them. She understood that they were sniffing around after me. But she hadn't learned the full lesson yet, because she'd done the wrong thing. What she should have done, obviously, was find out how much the information was worth, and sell it to them. Instead, she'd lied to protect me, to someone who had hope to offer her: hope of help, hope of a new home.

Thoughtful of her, although I'd have been happier if someone from Shanghai hadn't been suspicious enough to be asking her questions in the first place. That meant a raft of bad things. For one, the seniors in Shanghai enclave were actively trying to figure out what was going on with the mals—and they had nine students in our year alone, not to mention all their allies. For another, they already knew that our library session *had* been attacked by a mal at least once, which made us unusual this year. They were surely trying to put that information together with any other known mal attacks, which would be the handful that had spilled over into the workshop from my seminar room. As soon as someone found out that there was a single-person language seminar held next to the workshop that was getting attacked, and the single person happened to also be the only senior in the library room that was getting attacked, that wouldn't be a difficult blank to fill in.

I had no idea what would happen when the information all came out. The other New York kids might decide to cut Chloe and us off from the pipe. If Orion wasn't supplying them with fresh mana anyway, they didn't have a lot to lose from ditching his "girlfriend." And that could—would—be the least of it. If people worked out that the school was gunning for me in particular, they'd want to know *why,* and if they couldn't turn up a reason, someone would probably decide to poke me with a sharp stick to find out. If they didn't just decide that it was a good idea to give the school what it wanted.

So, my midterm study sessions were exceptionally cheery.

Except actually they *were.* The shine of studying with other people still hadn't dulled for me. We'd cleaned up Chloe's double-width room, and found new stuffing for the cushions—if you think we'd turn up our noses at reusing some perfectly good and comfortable cushions just because they'd previously been home to a pair of monsters and a half-digested fellow student, you haven't been paying attention—and we gathered there almost every evening, with a little basket in the middle where our mice could snooze between getting petted and even occasionally fed a treat by anyone invited to join us.

It was almost never just the four of us. Whatever subject we wanted to cover, it was a sure bet we could get in more people for the asking. I had plenty of help for Arabic: Ibrahim and a couple of his friends were happy to come by and give me advice as the price of admission. Nkoyo came almost every night, too, and she was doing that general Sanskrit seminar I'd expected to get. Thanks to their help, I was making some real headway on the Golden Stone sutras: just that week I'd actually got to the first of the major workings.

Except, ugh, that was a lie. It wasn't their help, not really. It was the time I had because I didn't have to desperately watch my own back every second of the day. It was the energy I had because I wasn't constantly scrabbling to build mana. And it *was* their help, too, only their help and the time and the energy all came from the same thing, and that was *Chloe's* help, Chloe's bountiful generosity, and I didn't like it. Except of course I did like it loads, I was just bitter and sullen about it, too.

But I couldn't manage being bitter and sullen on the day I turned the page and found myself looking at a gorgeously calligraphed heading that I didn't need to translate into Being the First Stone upon the Golden Road to understand what it was saying: *This one's really special,* with the Sanskrit incantation set in a finely bordered window on the page, every character flavored with gold leaf and paint in the main curves. Even at a first glance I could pick out bits of all the other spells I'd gone through so far: the phase-control spell, the water-summoning spell, another one I'd just finished working through that was for dividing earth from stone; they were woven together and invoked as part of the overall working.

I didn't just stop being sullen. I stopped worrying about mana, about what was going to happen when and if my cover was blown; I stopped working on my midterm assignments and ignored the rest of my classes entirely. For that whole week, in every waking minute that I wasn't actually stuck in session or killing mals, I was working on the sutra. Even during meals I had my head in a dictionary.

I knew it was stupid. My midterm assignment for the Myrddin seminar was a long involved piece of Old French poetry that was sure to contain at least three or four useful combat spells I could probably use during graduation. Meanwhile Purochana's great working was on the scale of architecture and probably needed an entire circle of wizards to cast anyway. The Golden Stone sutras were meant for building enclaves, not killing off mals: it would only do me any good if I lived long enough to get *out* of here.

But if I did—then I could offer it to groups like Liu's family, like the kibbutz that Ibrahim's friend Yaakov was from: established communities of wizards who wanted to set up their own safe, sheltered places. The Golden Stone sutras probably weren't the best way to build enclaves anymore, otherwise more of the spells would have survived into the modern day, the way the phase-control spell had, but it would be a sight better than having to mortgage your entire family to another enclave for three generations just to get access to the spells, much less for the resources you'd need to use. And Purochana's enclave spells probably weren't going to be as expensive as the modern spells, either. No one was building skyscraper enclaves back in ancient India: even if you'd imagined one, you couldn't exactly call your local builders and order some steel girders and concrete.

So my golden enclaves wouldn't be as grand as a top modern-day enclave, but who cared? It would still keep the mals from getting to your kids, and if you had that, if you had *safe*, at least you'd have a choice. A choice that someone could make without being Mum. You wouldn't have to suck up to enclave kids and bribe them. They'd still have advantages, they'd still have more hand-me-downs and more mana, some people would still court them, but it wouldn't be everyone, desperate to survive. They wouldn't get piles of free help just for dangling the slim hope of getting into their alliances and the even slimmer hope of getting into their enclaves.

I liked the idea; I loved the idea, actually. If *this* was how I'd bring destruction to the enclaves of the world, I was on board with my great-grandmother's prophecy after all. I'd take Purochana's spells and spread them all over the world, and I'd teach people how to cast them, and maybe they wouldn't *like* me, but they'd listen to me anyway, for this. They'd let me stay in the enclaves I helped them build, and I'd make it part of the price that they had to help others build them, too. Either they'd donate resources, or they'd make copies of the spells, or train teachers—

While I was busy putting the world to rights in my spare time, what I wasn't doing was any of my other schoolwork. I completely forgot the midterm assignment for my Proto-Indo-European seminar, and I would have been well on the way to outright failing if it hadn't been for Ibrahim; when I remembered it on the Monday night before the due date, with less than one hour to curfew, he brokered me an emergency trade with an enclaver from Dubai that he'd got friendly with. He and I had sat near the Dubai kids in the library for one evening last term. They all still gave me dirty looks if we passed in the corridors, and he'd made one good friend and four nodding acquaintances. Story of my life. But now I got to benefit, because when I yawped in alarm, that night in Chloe's room, Ibrahim said, "Hey, Jamaal's probably got a paper for that." It turned out that Jamaal was the youngest of five, and had inherited a priceless collection of hand-me-down papers and schoolwork for nearly every class he might possibly have taken, and more besides. I handed over a copy of the paper I'd written about the water-summoning spell and got back a nice, solid essay handed in for the PIE seminar of ten years ago.

I still had to rewrite the essay in my own handwriting, and while I was doing that, I got annoyed at some of the dumb things it said and ended up changing about half of it, staying up until all hours. I fell asleep on my desk and had to work on it the next day during my independent study. Afterwards I shuffled into the PIE seminar, full of unjustifiable resentment, and as I stuffed it into the submission slot still yawning, an eldritch vapor wisped out and went straight into my wide-open mouth.

Forget any preconceived notions you might have of gigantic Cthulhian monstrosities. Eldritch-category mals are actually relatively fragile. They hunt by driving people insane with enchanted gases that fill your senses with the impression of untold horrors, and while you thrash around screaming and begging everything to stop, the mal creeps out of its hiding place and tries to hook your brains out through your nose with its partially embodied limbs.

The problem with using this clever tactic on me was that there really isn't an untold horror that the human brain is capable of experiencing that's worse than being enveloped by a maw-mouth. So the vapor made me flash back to that particular experience, and I reacted just as I had at the time, which can be summed up as me yelling *die immediately you horrible monstrosity* with enormous and violent conviction. Only this wasn't a maw-mouth, it was just a drippy ectoplasmic cloud, and I slammed it with the full force of a major arcana murder spell like someone trying to light a match with a flamethrower.

My handiest killing spell doesn't kill things by destroying their bodies, it just goes straight to extinguishing life on a metaphysical level, so that's what spilled over. More or less, I informed the eldritch horror it had no business existing with so much aggression that I shoved it entirely out of reality, and I then went on from there to try and insist that a whole lot of the stuff around it should also stop this absurd pretense of continuing to exist.

This was especially awkward because a lot of the Scholomance *doesn't* exactly exist. It's made of real material, but the laws of physics get quite flexible in the void, so most of that material has been stretched thinner than it should be, the engineering doesn't meet the regs, and the number one thing keeping it up is that we're all believing in it as hard as we can stare. And that's what I took out: in one horrible moment, I made the four other kids in my seminar extremely aware that the only thing between them and howling nothingness was a tin can held together by happy thoughts and pixie dust. They all screamed and tried to get to safety, only they couldn't, since they were carrying the lack of belief along with them, and the seminar room and then the entire corridor started to come apart around them.

The only thing that stopped us taking out a massive swath of the school was that I hadn't stopped believing myself. Still half groggy with eldritch vision, I stumbled after them out of the room into a corridor which was starting to bend and warp like aluminium foil under the weight of the entire massive school above it, and in my confusion I thought it was just me being drugged, so I shut my eyes and told myself firmly that the corridor was not by any means wobbling and put out my hand to the wall with the expectation that the wall would be there and solid, and so it was again. I yelled after the other kids, "It's fine! It's just eldritch gas! Stop running!" and when they looked back and saw that the corridor was fine around me, they were able to persuade themselves I was right, and then they started believing in the school again.

A moment later, I realized that actually I'd been wrong, because as soon as the corridor stabilized, the Scholomance slammed the door of the room shut and sealed it away behind a permanent hazard wall, which are normally reserved for lab rooms on the second floor where there's been an alchemical accident so horrible the deadly effects won't resolve for a decade or more. As the hazard wall shot down from the ceiling beside me, almost taking off my thumb in the process, I startled and glanced over long enough to catch just half a glimpse of the excessively real wall of the seminar room beyond it, crumpled into accordion folds. That's how I worked out what I'd done.

I didn't really know any of the other kids in the seminar. They were all languages-track seniors like me, of course, and one of them, Ravi, was an enclaver from Jaipur, so the other three had sat round him, the better to offer him help on his papers and exams. None of them had ever spoken to me. I only knew Ravi's name because one of the others was a blond German girl named Liesel who had a violently annoying habit of cooing "Ravi, this is extremely excellent," every time he let her edit his papers. It made me want to hurl a dictionary at both their heads, and all the more so because I'd seen her submitting a paper once—that's how I knew *her* name— and that one peek had been enough to tell me she was probably going for valedictorian and at least ten times smarter than him, since he wasn't even smart enough to have figured out that she was the best in the class; he usually gave his papers to one of the other boys and wasted class time flirting with her and staring at her breasts.

Of course, brains aren't everything in all circumstances.

Ravi was able to convince himself everything was fine a lot quicker than anyone else; by the time I got over to them, he was recovered and saying with easy assurance, "We'll go to the library. We can't be marked down if the classroom's been shut. You're welcome to come," he added to me, in a tone of lordly generosity, and had the gall to gesture to the corridor, indicating that I was to take point position in exchange for the condescension. What made it even worse was that just a few weeks ago, without Chloe's power-sharer on my wrist, I'd have had to do it and be grateful for the lucky chance of company.

"If I'm taking point for a walk mid-period, I'll go by myself," I said, rude. "Especially since none of you thought of mentioning the eldritch shine." They'd all been in class before me. Since none of them had been attacked handing in their own assignments, they'd clearly spotted the signs—there's a sort of faint iridescent glitter to the air near an eldritch horror that I wouldn't have missed ordinarily—and pushed their own papers in from a distance. None of them had said a word as I'd stepped up to the slot myself.

"You've got to have your own lookout," one of the boys said to me, a little defiantly.

"That's right," I said. "And now you can have yours."

"What was that?" Liesel said suddenly. She'd been looking at the stabilized walls and the hazard door with a lot more suspicion than the rest of them, which she'd now translated into staring at me. "That spell which you used. Was that—La Main de la Mort?"

It had, in fact, been La Main de la Mort. She'd obviously done French at some point, assuming she hadn't grown up bilingual anyway, and it's not a hard spell to recognize; there're not that many three-word killing spells. The difficulty of casting it isn't learning the *words,* it's just got a really extreme amount of the *je ne sais quoi* that a lot of French spells have: you've got to be able to toss them off blithely, effortlessly. Since La Main de la Mort kills you instead of your target if you get it even the slightest bit wrong, very few people feel blithe about giving it a go, unless for instance they're inside a maw-mouth where death would be a reasonably good outcome. Also you've got to be able to channel a truly outrageous amount of mana without displaying the slightest effort, which is tricky for most people who aren't designed to be dark queens of sorcery et cetera.

"Look it up yourself if you want to know," I said, taking refuge in more rudeness, and walked away from them as fast as I could towards the stairs, but even Ravi was gawking at me.

At that point it wasn't exactly transmutation of matter to work out that I had something substantial and disturbing under the hood. When I came in at lunchtime, I saw Liesel stopping to talk to Magnus at the New York table, and he was waving a couple of his hangers-on over to open a spot for her to sit down next to him. "Well, I'm fucked," I told Aadhya and Liu, succinctly, as soon as I reached our table and sat down with them. And how right I was.

Chapter 4

MIDTERMS

MUM SPENT A LOT OF TIME in my formative years gently reminding me that people don't think about us nearly as much as we think they do, because they're all busy worrying what people are thinking about them. I thought that I'd listened to her, but it turned out I hadn't. Privately I'd believed, on some deep level, that everyone was in fact thinking about me all the time, evaluating me, et cetera, when really they hadn't been giving me much of a thought at all. I had the pleasure of uncovering this exciting truth about myself because all of a sudden, a substantial number of people *did* start thinking about me quite a lot, and the contrast was hard to miss.

In retrospect, everyone had quickly written off the weirdness of Orion Lake falling for the class loser. He was already weird by all our usual standards. Even Magnus and the other New York enclavers, offering me a guaranteed spot: they hadn't really thought *I* was anything unusual; they thought Orion was choosing to be odd in yet another way. And as for my surviving the graduation hall escapade, everyone had assumed that was Orion saving me. But Liesel spreading it around that I could sling La Main de la Mort while high on eldritch vapors was one straw too many for the collective camel. And once the other New York kids did actually spend a few moments thinking about me, of course it took them less than a day to realize where all their mana was going.

That night when I left the library to go down to bed, I glanced back and saw Magnus and three friends closing in on Chloe around a couch in the reading room, the dismay on her face clear to read even from between their backs. I thought about going back, but what was the use? Was I going to ask Chloe to lie to her enclave friends, the people she'd spend the rest of her life with, just so I could keep sucking down mana from them? Was I going to beg them to keep letting me cling on? Obviously not. Was I going to threaten them? Tempting but no. There wasn't anything else to say or do. So I just turned my back and went down, in the firm certainty that they'd insist on Chloe cutting me off first thing the next morning. Actually, that was my optimistic scenario. Really I expected Magnus to appear at my door leading a school-wide mob with not-necessarily-metaphorical pitchforks.

The thing is, I'm not actually unique in the history of wizard society; not even Orion is, really. We're both once-in-a-generation talents, but those happen, as you might have guessed, once in a generation. It is a bit of a coincidence that we're in school at the same time, and that we're both fairly extreme examples. But I'm reasonably sure that's because there's some violation of balance being redressed on our backs. Dad nobly walks into a maw-mouth for an eternity of pain to save me and Mum; she gives out too much healing for free; I end up with an affinity for violence and mass destruction. The year before that, twelve maleficers murdered the entire senior class, so a hero who would save hundreds of kids in school got conceived. The moral physics of the principle of balance: equal and opposite reactions totting up on both sides.

The point is, wizards like us do come along every so often: a single individual powerful enough to shift the balance of power among the enclaves depending on where they land. Roughly forty years ago, a hugely powerful artificer with an affinity for large-scale construction came through the school. Every major enclave made him offers. He turned them all down and went home to Shanghai, where his family's ancient former enclave had been occupied by a maw-mouth. He organized a circle of independent wizards to help him, personally spearheaded the effort to take out the maw-mouth, and as you might imagine was immediately acclaimed as the new Dominus, not three years out of school. It still looked like a bad deal for him: the enclave he rescued was ancient and had soaked up magic for centuries, but it was small and poky by modern standards, and at the time most of the really talented Chinese wizards headed straight to New York, to London, to the California enclaves. Even Guangzhou and Beijing had to recruit from the second string.

Well, after four decades of Li Shan Feng's rule, Shanghai's got six towers and a monorail *inside* the enclave, they just opened their seventh gateway, and lately they've been signaling that they're thinking of splitting off the Asian enclaves and building a new school themselves. And that's part of what makes Orion so important, so important that New York was willing to throw a priceless guaranteed enclave spot at some loser girl just because Orion liked her. Everyone knows there's a power struggle coming, and Orion's not just a top student inside the Scholomance; he's a game-changer on the outside. No one's going to go to outright war with an enclave that has an invincible fighter, and that's not even touching on the resource he represents if he can convert *mals* into *mana*. And he belongs really securely to New York: son of the very likely future Domina, no less, and I'm sure he's at least partly responsible for her being in that position. All the kids from Shanghai in here probably came in with instructions to keep a close eye on him, and gather as much information as they could. They haven't got any less anxious about him over the last three years, while he's been busy building a substantial fan club of all the kids he's saved.

What I hadn't realized, as I went down to bed, was that I was about to be promoted to game-changer status alongside him.

Chloe didn't try to lie to Magnus—she's a terrible liar anyway. She fell back on desperately arguing that they had to keep giving me mana *or else,* and went into a lot of detail about the grisly potential else, with a vivid description of my dismemberment of her cushion mals. A normal person would have been terrified to find out about nuclear bomb me waiting to go off. Magnus decided that he quite fancied bringing a tidy nuclear bomb home to his parents.

By breakfast the next morning, I'd gladly have faced any number of pitchforks instead of having to see his smug rubbish dump of a face smirking at the Shanghai kids across the cafeteria, like he'd done something clever or recruited me by hand, instead of having done his level best just last term to *kill* me. The Shanghai kids all looked grim and worried back, for that matter. By that afternoon, I knew for a fact that they were offering stuff to people for *details* about me, because they had another go at questioning Sudarat: one of them had actually offered her a power-sharer for the rest of the year, which was almost guaranteed to keep her alive that long. "Take it," I told her bitterly. "Someone ought to do well out of this."

I suppose I didn't have the right to complain: New York wasn't cutting me off after all, so I still had lovely torrents of mana coming. If anything, the other New York kids had all got *more* enthusiastic about building mana now that they knew where it was going. Because of course they expected to get a handsome return on investment, namely *me*, a massive gun tucked neatly in their enclave's back pocket, ready for use in case of emergencies. They were all delightedly hoping to give me exactly the post-Scholomance life I'd dreamed of for years. The bastards.

Two days later, Orion said to me, of all things, "Hey, after graduation, what do you think of taking a road trip?"

I stared at him. "What?"

"The guys were talking about our doing a group road trip," he said earnestly. "The enclave has this really great cus- tomized RV, they'd let us take it, we were thinking . . ." He trailed off, possibly alerted by my expression of total incredu- lity that there was something odd about this conversation. It wasn't just that he had actually out-loud attempted to make *concrete plans* set in the future that required making the as- sumption that we'd all survive to appear for these plans— horribly taboo among all but the richest enclavers, and even they have the tact to avoid the topic in mixed company—but he was trying to suggest that I voluntarily spend time with the rest of the New York enclavers.

I knew he hadn't come up with the idea on his own. Chloe had once told me with a perfectly straight face that Orion didn't want anything except to kill mals, which was absolute bollocks, but it was the kind of absolute bollocks that I'm certain everyone around him his entire life had so strongly encouraged that it had got lodged in his own head. And the power-sharer he wore only went one way, so he *had* to go round killing them if he wanted mana, which all of us do. They'd programmed him really thoroughly to spend all his time thinking about hunting. The only other thing I'd ever heard him actually express wanting was me, which I choose to believe meant anyone at all who'd treat him like a person instead of a mal-killing automaton.

That was the scale of things for which he could express desire: friendship, love, humanity. But he didn't care where in the cafeteria he sat, he didn't care what shirt he wore, he didn't care what classes he was in or what books he read. He did his work more or less dutifully, was polite, and preferred to avoid hero-worshippers while feeling guilty about it, and if I said, "Let's go stand on our heads on the cafeteria mezzanine stairs," he'd probably shrug and say, "If you want to." He certainly hadn't come up with the sudden desire to go on a road trip away from his enclave. He'd been *fed* the idea, and the idea was very clearly to get *me* into the New York crowd. Before they'd been worrying about someone else using me to get Orion; now they were trying to use Orion to get *me*.

"Lake," I said in measured tones, "why don't you tell Magnus actually you'd like to go backpacking in Europe with me instead. See what he thinks of that. We could do the Grand Tour! Start in Edinburgh, visit Manchester and London, go on to Paris, Lisbon, Barcelona, Pisa—" I was rattling off the names of every city with an enclave I could think of, and Orion got the point, scowled at me, and sloped off.

I felt pretty pleased with myself afterwards, until that evening when I went on a snack bar run with Aadhya, and Scott and Jermaine from New York passed us on the stairs and said a cheery, "Hey, El, how's it going? Hey, Aad," with a friendly wave.

She waved back and said, "Hey, guys," like a civilized human being, while I delivered the coldest possible, "Hi," in return. As soon as they were out of sight, she looked at me and said, "What *now*?"

I hadn't ranted about the charming road-trip scheme to her because I couldn't without breaking the horrible taboo myself, and being tactless into the bargain. Aadhya's family lived in New Jersey, and while she hadn't said outright that she'd have liked a New York enclave spot herself, it was what virtually every wizard for three hundred miles around the city aspired to, since they were all more or less working for the place anyway. "They'd like to make plans for my future," I said, shortly.

She sighed, but once we were back in her room and eating our makeshift parfaits—strawberry yogurt out of slightly aged tubes, topped with fruit-and-nut mix and whipped cream out of a can; we'd regretfully discarded the tin of vienna sausages, which had been not merely dented but slightly punctured, with a bit of greenish ooze round the edges of the hole—she said, "El, they're not that bad."

I knew she wasn't talking about the parfaits, which were fairly ambrosial by our standards. "They are, though," I said, revolted.

"I'm not saying they're sterling examples of grace and nobility," Aadhya said. "They're all kind of dickish, but they're the same kind of dickish that anyone is when you put them in an enclave. Magnus, okay, that boy is trying way too hard to be big man on campus. But Jermaine's a nice guy! Scott is a nice guy! Chloe is practically *too* nice. And you actually *like* Orion, who is kind of creepy—"

"He's not!"

"Excuse you, he totally is," Aadhya said. "Half the time he can't recognize me unless I'm *with you*. He pretends to when

I say hi to him in shop, but every time his brain goes into this panicky loop like *who is she oh no I'm supposed to know her oh no I'm failing at human.* And it's not just me, he does it to everyone. He could probably tell you every last mal he's killed in the entire time he's been at school, but us human beings all get filed under the generic category of future potential rescue. I don't know why he *can* see you, I think it's because you're some crazy super-maleficer in waiting. *Creepy.*"

I glared at her indignantly, but she just huffed and added, "And *you* have a hard time accepting that anyone has a right to exist if they *won't* jump three lab tables to save the life of a total stranger, so you guys are totally perfect for each other. But sorry to break it to you, you both still need to *eat* and *sleep* somewhere and, even worse, occasionally interact with other humans. Why are you setting every available bridge on fire?"

I put down my empty yogurt cup and pulled my knees up and wrapped my arms round them. "I'm going to start thinking Magnus put you up to this."

She rolled her eyes. "Oh, he tried. I told him that *I* wasn't a crazy person and I'd take a place in New York in a hot second if he offered it to me, but he wasn't going to get any closer to bagging you. My point is—look, El, what are you even going to *do?*"

Aadhya wasn't asking me to make plans; she just wanted to know what I was going to do with my life. She waited for me to offer *something*, and when I didn't she said, to drum it in, "I know what *I'm* doing. I don't freaking need Magnus to make me offers. I've sold seventeen pieces of spell-tuned jewelry out of the leftover bits of sirenspider shell and argonet tooth you gave me. They're not just junky senior stuff, they're really good, people are going to keep them. I'll get my own invites. I know what Liu's doing. She's going to do translations or raise familiars, and her family are going to have that enclave up in twenty years. Chloe's going to be getting her DaVinci on and putting frescoes up all over New York, and she doesn't even really need to do that. And I know that you're *not* going to an enclave. That's it. And not-enclaver is not a life."

She wasn't wrong, but I couldn't say anything. My beautiful shining fantasy of the life of an itinerant golden-enclave builder withered in my mouth completely before her recitation of excellent and sensible and thoroughly practicable ideas. I couldn't bring myself to describe it to Aadhya: I could just see her face going from doubtful to incredulous to horrified with worry, like listening to a friend earnestly telling you about their plans to climb a tall mountain, with dangerously insufficient preparation, and then going on to describe how, once they got to the top, they'd jump off and sprout wings and fly away to live in the clouds.

She sighed into my stretching silence. "I get you don't like to talk about your mom, but I've heard about her and I live on another continent. People talk about her like she's a saint. So in case it doesn't go without saying, you don't have to *be* your mom to be a decent human being. You don't have to live on a commune and be a hermit."

"I can't anyway, they won't have me," I said, a bit hollowly.

"Based on what you've said about the place, I'm going to go out on a limb and say they're justifiably afraid you're going to set them all on fire. It's *okay* for you to go live in New York with your weirdo boyfriend if you want to."

"It's *not*," I said. "Aad, it's not, because—they *don't* want *me*. They want someone who's going to cast death spells on their enemies. And if I gave them that, I wouldn't be *me* anymore, so I might as well *not* go live in a bag of dicks. And you think that, too," I added pointedly, "because otherwise you'd have told Magnus that you'd try and talk me into coming if he'd get you in the enclave."

"Yeah, because that would *work*."

"It might work to get *you* in," I said. "He'd promise you an interview for sure."

She gave a snort. "That's not actually a stupid idea. Except I don't want to talk you into *New York*, I'm just . . ." she trailed off. "El, it's not *just* Magnus," she said bluntly. "I've had a bunch of people asking me. Everyone knows about you now. And if you *don't* go to some enclave—they're going to wonder what you *are* planning to do."

And I didn't even need to lay my idiotic plans out before her to know without question that they'd believe in them even less than *she* would.

To further gladden my heart, our midterm grades were coming in that week. No matter how hard you've worked, there's always something to worry about. If you're going for valedictorian, anything less than perfect marks is a sentence of doom, and if you *do* get perfect marks, then you have to worry whether your courseload is heavy enough that your perfect marks will scale well against all the other kids going for valedictorian with *their* perfect marks. If you're not going for valedictorian, then you have to spend the bare minimum of time on your actual coursework in order to maximize whatever you are actually working on to get you through graduation—whether that's expanding your spell collection or creating tools or brewing potions, and of course building mana. If you get good marks, you wasted valuable time you should have spent on other things. But if your marks are *too* bad, you'll get hit with remedial work or worse.

If you're wondering how our marks get assigned when

there are no teachers to evaluate anything, I've heard a million explanations. Loads of people, mostly enclavers, say with great assurance that the work gets shunted out of the Scholomance and sent to independent wizards hired for the marking. I don't believe that for a second, because it would be expensive, and I've never met anyone who knows one of these wizards. Others claim the work gets graded through some sort of complicated equation based almost entirely on the amount of time you spend on it and your previous marks. If you want to really set off any valedictorian candidate, try telling them that it's partly randomized.

Personally, I'm inclined to think we're doing the marking ourselves, just because that's so efficient. After all, we mostly know what marks we deserve, and we certainly know the marks we want to get and what marks we're afraid of getting, and whenever we see bits of someone else's work we get an idea of what *they* ought to get. I'd bet that the school more or less goes by the sum of the parts, depending on how much will and mana each person has put behind their judgment. Which also handily explains the bloc of self-satisfied enclavers who annually fill up the class rankings only a little way down from the actual valedictorian candidates, despite not doing nearly as much work and not being nearly as clever as they think they are.

None of these possibilities told me what to expect in the way of marks for myself, since this year I was entirely alone in the one seminar to which I'd devoted massive amounts of time and energy and passion and mana, and apart from that I was in three other small-group seminars that I'd aggressively neglected.

You'd think that marks wouldn't matter very much senior year unless you were going for valedictorian, since we literally don't take classes for the second half of the year. After the class standings are announced at the end of the first semester, seniors are given the rest of the year off to prep for their graduation runs.

But that's in the nature of a grudging surrender. Graduation wasn't *designed* to be a slaughterhouse gauntlet of mals. The cleansing routine we fixed last term was intended to winnow them down to a reasonable level every year before the seniors got dumped in to make their escape back to the real world. After the machinery broke four times in the first decade, and the enclaves gave up on repairing it, seniors largely stopped going to class, because there's a point where training and practicing with the spells and equipment you've got is more important than getting new ones. When there're a thousand howling starved mals coming at you from all sides, you want your reactions worked thoroughly into your muscle memory.

So the powers that be running the school at the time— London had taken it over from Manchester by then, with substantial support from Edinburgh, Paris, and Munich; opinions from St. Petersburg, Vienna, and Lisbon taken under advisement; New York and Kyoto occasionally given a patronizing ear—decided that they'd accept the reality and turned it into a deadline. And up to that deadline, the school does its best to *make* marks matter. The penalties get especially vicious for our last semester. Finals are the worst of it, but even midterms are generally good for taking out at least a dozen seniors.

I was relatively safe for the Proto-Indo-European seminar because I'd cheated on that one essay, which always gets you good marks. The school's perfectly willing to let you leave dangerous gaps in your education. The only risk there was that I'd actually done some work on the thing beyond copying it out; I'd get marked down for that, although probably still not to failing level.

The translation I'd handed in for my final Myrddin seminar poetry assignment was a rotten half-baked job I'd run through in two hours, guessing wildly at the many words I didn't know. It hadn't left me with any spells I could even sound out, at least not if I didn't want to risk blowing the top of my own head off. I'd got top marks on the lovely deconstruction spell I'd used on Chloe's cushion-monster, though, which was likely to pull my grade there to safe levels.

Aadhya had helped me with the maths in my Algebra course, and I'd done a load of translations for her. Artificers don't get language classes in their senior year; instead they just get assigned a design project in one of their other languages. Design projects are a really special fun thing for artificers. You're given a set of requirements for some object, you write down the steps to build the thing, and then the Scholomance builds it *for* you. Exactly according to your instructions. Then you have to try the resulting object out and see what it does. Three guesses what happens if your instructions turn out to have been wrong or insufficiently detailed.

Having to do a design project in a second language makes it even more exciting. And in this case, Aadhya's languages are Bengali and Hindi, both of which she knows really well, except the school swerved and gave her the projects in Urdu instead, which happens sometimes if it's feeling particularly nasty. She didn't know the script well, and anyway subtle differences in meaning matter quite a lot in these circumstances. You'd really like to be confident that you're not building a blasting gun backwards, for instance.

You would also really like to build something that might be of some use at graduation, but her choices were a mana siphon, a shell-piercer, and a garden planter. A mana siphon is a flat-out maleficer tool and anyway the last thing anyone allied with me would ever need. A shell-piercer would've been a terrific weapon against constructs, except in the very last line of the specifications, the assignment said that the purpose of this particular one was to acquire usable miercel shells. Miercels are these self-reproducing construct mals that look rather like wasps the size of my thumb. Their shells are made of a mana-infused metal and *are* quite useful, but a shell-piercer of any combat-appropriate size would fracture them to tiny bits.

"You could probably sell that second one to an enclaver?" I said.

"Not until we're out," Aadhya said, making the face it deserved: she was right, nobody inside the school was going to buy a modestly good artificer tool. It wasn't like the phase-control spell from my sutras, where it was so useful and so expensive on the outside that it was worth someone trading a substantial advantage in here to get it for their family's future use. Also, there was the question of how the Scholomance would have her test it. I'm sure it would have been generous enough to provide an entire hive of live miercels to practice on.

The last option was a combination sunlamp and self-watering planter that could be stacked to make a vertical garden while using very little mana, for setting up a greenhouse in a tiny space with no natural light. It would have been very nice to have in a Scholomance room, so of course the specifications required the planter to be fifteen feet long, which meant it wouldn't fit in even a double-wide room. After I finished translating that bit, I realized to my dismay that the one place these planters would have worked perfectly was in those small Golden Stone enclaves I'd been so energetically dreaming of setting up. It was probably my fault Aadhya had got stuck with it: spend a lot of time with your allies, and sometimes their intent can start to influence your own work.

"Sorry," I said grimly when I handed it over for her to look at.

"Ugh, and it's going to take *forever* to meld these layers of chalcedony with the sand," she said in dismay. "And I'm still not done with the lute."

She'd been working on the lute in her every free minute since last term, but she badly needed more of them. Aadhya's got an affinity for exotic materials, especially ones taken from mals. As you might imagine, they have loads of power, but most artificers can't handle them; either they just don't work, or more likely the artifice goes wrong in some excitingly malicious way. Aadhya can almost always coax them along into her projects, but the lute was ten times more complicated than anything else she'd done. The sirenspider leg I'd given her had gone to make the body of the lute, and the argonet tooth had made the bridges and the frets, and she'd strung it with the hair Liu had cut off at the start of the year. And then she'd etched sigils of power over the whole thing and lined them with the enchanted gold leaf her family had sent her on induction day. Pulling the whole thing together would've been a challenge for a professional artificer with a full workbench of favorite tools, and we'd pinned a large number of our graduation hopes on it.

Senior year, you spend half your time staying alive, half your time on your lessons, and half your time working out a graduation strategy to get you through the hall. If you can't make that equation add up properly, you die. Most teams spend a lot of time identifying their best approach—are you going to rely on speed and deflection, dodging your way through the horde; are you going to build a massive forward shield and try to bowl yourselves straight to the doors; are you going to turn yourselves gnat-sized and try to hop from one team to another and let them carry you; et cetera.

Our alliance had a very obvious basic strategy: everyone else would keep the mals from interrupting my casting, and I would slaughter everything in a tidy path straight to the doors. Perfectly simple. Only it wasn't, because most spells can't slaughter *everything*. Even La Main de la Mort doesn't work on *everything;* it's useless on the entire category of psychic maleficaria, since those more or less don't actually exist to begin with. They can still kill you, though.

And not even a share in the New York mana pool was going to be enough to power more than one of my major workings. There were six other New York seniors who'd be in the graduation hall at the same time as Chloe, all wanting hefty quantities of mana for themselves and their own teams, and even if they didn't mean to cut me off beforehand, they were very definitely going to ration just how much mana I could take during the main event.

So all our planning took place at one remove: how could we get enough mana for me to *keep* slaughtering mals all the way to the gates. The two key pieces were Aadhya's sirenspider lute and Liu's family spell. Liu's grandmother had sneaked her a really powerful song-spell for mana amplification to bring in, even though she couldn't cast the spell alone—her affinity was for animals, and anyway it usually took two or three of her family's most powerful wizards to make it work. After a lot of careful Chinese coaching, I'd got the words down. Our strategy was, just before we sailed into the hall, Liu would play the melody on the sirenspider lute while I sang out the lyrics, and then she'd carry on playing even after I finished. With a magical instrument, the spell would keep going, and our whole team would have the benefit of amplified mana. So Liu would be in the middle of our team, sustaining the spell; Chloe and Aadhya would be on either side of her, covering her and me, and I'd take the lead.

That was the theory, at any rate. Unfortunately, the lute wasn't quite working according to plan. We'd made one experiment with it a few weeks back while still urgently trying to make a honeypot for Orion. Liu had written a Pied Piper spell for mals with the idea that we'd do a little parade through some section of the corridors one evening, me singing and her playing, and Orion whacking the mals one after another as they popped out at us.

I'll leave you to imagine how appealing I found the prospect of wandering around loudly calling, *Here, kitty, kitty.* I've spent my entire life trying *not* to lure mals. But we needed to try out the lute, and Orion didn't *quite* beg and plead for us to get him some mals to kill, but he clearly *wanted* to beg and plead, so after Aadhya finished the last bit of inlay, we agreed to give it a go.

We bolted our dinners and hurried to a spare seminar room down on the shop level, so everyone else would still be upstairs and not in range to see us doing anything this unbelievably stupid. Orion hovered around hopefully, and this time we tied all the mice securely into their bandolier cups as a precaution. That seemed to have been a good idea, because they all set up a frantic squeaking from inside as soon as Liu started tuning the lute and I hummed the line of melody.

In retrospect, the mice were just trying to warn us. Liu hit the first notes, I sang three words, and the mals came from everywhere. The *baby* mals. Agglo grubs came out of the drain and larval nightflyers started dropping from the ceiling and thin scraps that looked like flat handkerchiefs that were probably going to be digesters peeled off the walls and blobby mimics the size of a little toe and a thousand different unrecognizable flabby things all started coming out of every possible nook and cranny of the entire room and converging on us like a slow horrible creeping wave swelling out of every surface around us.

"It's working!" Orion said delightedly.

The rest of us, not being absolute madmen, all ran for the door at once, with mals crunching and squishing under our feet and more of them still coming, crawling out of tiny gaps between the metal panels and oozing from the corners and falling from the ceiling and pouring in a torrent out of the air vent and the drain. Orion barely made it out before we had the door slammed and were barricading it fervently against the solid mass of mals. Chloe rushed to seal up all the edges with an entire syringe of mana-barrier gel while Liu and I reversed the invocation and Aadhya unstrung the lute. We locked in place there staring at the door, ready to flee, until we were sure it had stopped bulging out any further, and then we all jumped up and down and shook ourselves wildly and pawed and batted at one another to get the larvae out of our hair and clothes and off our skin and onto the floor where we stomped and crushed them in a frenzy. We're used to flicking off larval mals—it's always satisfying to take them out that small when you have the chance—but there's a horrific difference between one tiny digester trying very hard to eat a single square millimeter of your skin and a *thousand* of them speckled all over your body and clothes and hair.

All the while Orion stood in the corridor behind us and said, exasperated and plaintive, "But you barely even tried!" and other insane and stupid things until we turned on him in unison and yelled at him to shut up forever and he had the gall to mutter something—under his breath, he wasn't suicidal—about girls.

I *was* grateful that we no longer needed to find a way to

provide Orion with mals, because after that experience, none of us wanted to keep trying. Except him. He even went so far as to talk to other human beings to try and get more information about honeypots himself. He spent a lunch period with half a dozen kids from the Seattle enclave and a desperate expression, and came up to our study corner in the library afterwards and said, "Hey, I've found out how you make honeypot bait," urgently. "The main ingredient is wizard blood. You just hold a blood drive and everyone donates . . ." He trailed off, I presume as he heard the words coming out of his own mouth and saw our faces, and then just stopped and sat down with a glum expression. That was the end of working on honeypots.

However, we did still urgently need the lute. And instead of getting to work on that, or at least something else useful, Aadhya had to very carefully design a garden planter, then I had to rewrite her design back into Urdu for her, also very carefully, and when the Scholomance delivered the finished product to be tested, the most useful thing she could do with it was plant some carrot tops from the cafeteria. It produced carrots roughly the size of a gnome's top hat. We fed them to our mice. Precious ate hers very daintily, sitting up and holding it in her forepaws and nibbling it from tip to end before carefully handing back the leafy top to be planted again.

At least the planter was reasonably sure to net Aadhya a decent mark. I was less sure to get decent marks in Development of Algebra: all the readings were in the original languages, and specifically in Chinese and Arabic, the ones that I'd just barely started. Aadhya could generally figure out for me what the actual equations being described were, so I could do the problem sets, but sitting the midterm essay exam—*compare and contrast Sharaf al Tusi's explanation of polynomial evaluation with that of Qin Jiushao, including exam-*

ples of usage—had been an experience worth forgetting as quickly as possible. The only part of those readings I had actually done were the names, which had been enough for me to look the authors up in the library, find out that Horner had reinvented the same process, and learn it in English instead. I'd felt so clever, too.

So I was holding my breath when I went to class that whole week. We don't know *exactly* when we're going to get our marks. Predictably, I got my safest one first: a B+, for the Proto-Indo-European seminar. Our class was now being held on the second floor, but in an even smaller room and sharing a wall with the alchemy supply room, so we were constantly hearing banging as people went in and out. Liesel glared at me through every class session with cold resentment, and mals would often attack the alchemy supply room thanks to my being on the other side, which made me as wildly popular as you'd think. Enough mals were creeping out of the woodwork at this point in the year that they'd finally started to come after people other than me once in a while, but I remained top item on the menu.

The rest of my marks trickled in grudgingly over the next couple of days: a B+ for the Myrddin seminar and a pass on my shop assignment—a sacrificial obsidian dagger, clearly intended for unpleasant purposes, which I'd chosen because it was the quickest of my options to knock off, so I could use the free time to finish the book chest for my sutras. I also netted a pass for my alchemy section, where I'd had to brew a vat of sludging acid that could etch through flesh and bone in three seconds.

The next Monday morning I finally got my algebra results, a D, and wiped my metaphorical brow, and then just had to wait for my last mark, on my independent study. I'd really wanted the bad news already, so the whole week after

midterms, I tried to bait it out: I kept my head down and focused on my desk the entire time, and then looked away for
a solid thirty seconds only right in the middle of class, so
there was only the one opening for it to drop, which usually
gets you the mark early on. But instead it didn't come until
the tail end of the week.

Except that day I was working on the last piece of the first
major working of the sutras, and I'd got so deep into it that I
forgot to pause mid-class. My bolted-down desk was a monstrous thing of wrought iron—I scraped my knees on the un-
derside every other week at least—and the only silver lining
of it was having the space to spread out. I always kept the
sutras right in front of me, wrapped up in a leather harness
Aadhya had made me: it went over the ends of each cover,
with soft wide ribbons that I kept tied down around all the
pages except the handful that I was working on that day. It
had a foot-long strap attached that buckled around my left
wrist, so at an instant's notice I could just leap up and the
book would stay with me even if I had to use both hands for
casting. I stood my dictionaries open on end above it, and I
used a three-inch memo pad for my notes, which I held in my
hands braced on the edge of the desk so it wouldn't touch the
sutra pages.

It's not that the book was so fragile; it was made out of
really lovely heavy paper and didn't look like it had aged more
than two months since the last bit of gilt had dried. But that
was clearly because it had snuck away from its original owner
roughly two months after the last bit of gilt had dried, and I
didn't want that to happen to *me,* so I cosseted it as much as
possible. It was worth having sore wrists at the end of each
class. Whenever I ran out of space on my tiny notepad—
often—I just tore off the filled sheet and stuck it into a folder

I kept on the side, and each night I rewrote them into a larger notebook in my bedroom.

That day I had filled about thirty tiny pages with tight handwritten notes. The bell was about to ring and I was still going when the whole folder did a sort of angry jerk and went flying sideways off my desk, scattering paper everywhere; I gave a yowl of protest and grabbed for it, too late, and then had to pack up in a hurry, expecting something to jump me at any moment. I only realized that it had been my mark being delivered when I finally had all my notes collected again. I opened the folder to stuff them back in, and the little slip of green paper was tucked in the pocket, with ADV. READINGS IN SANSK poking out above the top. I pulled it out and glared at the A+ with a footnote asterisk going to SPECIAL COMMENDATION at the bottom, which was just rubbing it in: *Look at all your misspent time.* I could practically hear the Scholomance sniggering at me from the ventilation system. But that was just pettiness, and overall I heaved a sigh of relief; it could've been loads worse.

It *was* loads worse for other people. At lunch that day, Cora came to our table with her face tight with pain and her arm wrapped up in her beautiful yellow head tie with the embroidered protection charm, blood soaking through it in spreading dark patches. "Failed shop," she said, her voice ragged. She had her tray held tight against her waist with her other arm, and the contents were pretty scanty. But she didn't ask for help. She probably couldn't afford it. She hadn't nailed down an alliance of her own yet.

She and Nkoyo and Jowani were friends, and they'd been great help for one another for tables and walking to class, but the same reason they'd been great for that was why they weren't a viable graduation team: all three of them were incantations-track, and doing all the same languages. And Nkoyo was going to get decent alliance offers. In fact, she probably had one already, since just that morning she'd carefully mentioned that she might sit with someone else tomorrow for breakfast. A lot of alliances happened after midterm marks cleared. But Jowani and Cora were going to be stuck until after the end of the semester, when the enclavers had got their alliances set and the leftovers sorted themselves out.

It's not that they were loads worse as students, even. As far as I knew, they were all three somewhere in the middle of the pack as far as classwork went. But Nkoyo was a star, and they weren't. She'd always been the one who made the friends and connections, and when you thought of the three of them, you always thought of her in the lead. They'd leaned on her social skills the whole time, and that had been good for them—right until now, when everyone thought *Nkoyo,* and not one of them.

Most years, that meant their odds were going to be somewhere in the 10 percent range. The rule is that 50 percent of the graduating class makes it out, but that doesn't mean it's even odds. The kids in enclaver alliances almost all get out, with maybe one or two members picked off each team— rarely the enclave kids themselves—and that's roughly 40 percent of the class. So the ones who die almost all come out of the 60 percent who don't have an enclave on their side. Of course, even that leaves you with better odds than you get on the outside of the Scholomance, which is why kids keep coming.

If the cleansing machinery down in the graduation hall really had got fixed, if it stayed fixed this year, they might make it out after all. But it wouldn't improve Cora's odds any to be going into the second half of the semester with a bad arm that she'd got because she'd screwed up and misjudged the amount of effort to put into her shop assignment. No enclaver was going to look at that arm and ask her to join their team. She sat down carefully, doing her best not to jostle the wound, but once she was down she still had to shut her eyes for a few long minutes, taking deep breaths before she tried to fumble at her milk one-handed and shaky.

Nkoyo silently reached over and got it and opened it. Cora took it and drank without looking at her. Nkoyo hadn't taken unfair advantage. She'd helped them make it this far; it wasn't on her if she couldn't take them the whole way, if they weren't good enough and she had to jettison them to make it herself, like boosters of rocket fuel falling away spent while the orbital module went flying on past gravity. There wasn't anything she could do to save them, and they'd made their own choices, getting here. But Cora still didn't look her in the face, and Nkoyo still didn't say anything to her, and all of us at the table pretended we weren't looking at Cora's blood-stained arm when of course we were.

I didn't know I was going to say anything until I did. "I can patch the arm if everyone at the table will help," I said, and everyone paused eating and stared at me, either sidelong or just straight-out gawking. I hadn't thought it through, just blurting it out, but the only thing to do in the face of the stares was push onward. "It's a circle working. No one has to put in any extra mana, it'll work if we all just hold the circle, but everyone already here has to do it."

That's actually a simplification of how the spell in question operates. The underlying principle is that you have to get a group of people to willingly put aside their selves and offer their time and energy to help perform a working for someone else's benefit that doesn't help any of them directly. And the trick is, once you ask a particular group, if anybody in the group refuses or can't make themselves do it, the spell fails. It's one of Mum's, if you couldn't tell already.

Nobody said anything for a moment. It's not even remotely how things work in here. You don't do anything for anyone without some kind of return, and the return's always got to be something solid, unless there's some more substantial connection in place: an alliance, dating, something. But that's why I knew the spell would work if everyone *did* agree. It means a lot more in here than outside to do something for nothing. Even Cora herself was just staring at me confused. We weren't even friends; she was willing to sit at a table with me *now*, when Chloe Rasmussen from New York was my ally and Orion Lake himself would be here as soon as he came off the line with his tray, but she'd barely tolerated my company all those years when Nkoyo used to let me tag along behind them on the way to language lab in the mornings. She was standoffish in general, and had always been a bit jealous of Nkoyo's company, but it was more than that: she was aces at spirit magic, her family had a really long tradition of it, and she had clearly thought—and probably still did—that I was carrying some kind of unpleasant baggage on mine.

Nkoyo didn't say anything. She was staring at her own tray without looking up, her lips curled in between her teeth, her hands curled on either side, waiting, waiting for someone else to speak. I really wished Orion had made it to the table already, and then Chloe said, "Okay," and held a hand out to Aadhya, who was sitting between us.

Aadhya was definitely in the sidelong-eye camp, less at the request than at me: I could all but hear her saying *okay, El, are you trying to develop a martyr thing of your own now or what*, but after one good hard look, she just sighed and said, "Yeah, sure," and took Chloe's hand and held her other out to me. I took it, and as soon as I did I felt the living line of the circle building. I turned and offered my other one to Nadia, Ibrahim's friend. She glanced over at Ibrahim but then after a moment took it, and he took hers and reached out to Yaakov across the table.

I'd been in circles with Mum a handful of times. She hadn't asked me very often, almost always only when it was magical harm, usually someone suffering from a spell a maleficer had put on them or a complication from some spell they'd cast themselves, or the attack of some maleficaria. Healing something like that is a lot easier if you have another wizard helping, even a kid, instead of just you and a bunch of enthusiastic mundanes who can't actually hold mana. But she didn't ask me a lot, because most wizards who came to her for help couldn't keep from getting uneasy round me. They were already vulnerable, so when they looked at me they were rabbits looking at a wolf—a half-starved wolf who sometimes snapped even at the hand that fed her because it also kept her on a leash. I never really wanted to help them. They were sick and weak and cursed and poisoned and desperate, but they were still part of the pack that hated me, that left me alone and scared and desperate myself. So Mum only asked me when she badly needed the power that came from me agreeing to help anyway, because otherwise she knew I'd say no sometimes. And I'd done it, grudgingly, partly to make Mum happy, partly to try and prove to myself I wasn't what they saw when they looked at me.

But I'd never cast a circle by myself before. The idea's straightforward enough: the mana everyone puts in flows through all of us in the circle, and because everyone shares the same purpose, it gets intensified. So you just let the mana keep circling around until it builds up high enough. But just because the idea is easy to describe doesn't mean it's easy to *do*.

In fact, I realized too late it was going to be even harder *because* everyone else around the table was a wizard. With Mum's spell, you can heal internal injuries with a circle of ordinary people because you don't need any more mana than you produce just by making the effort to stay in the circle, and you just need one wizard in the mix to "catch" the mana and hold it for long enough to pour it into the spell. With a bunch of almost adult wizards, we were building up a lot of mana really fast, and I could already feel everybody else sort of *tugging* on it. It wasn't even on purpose; if anyone had deliberately tried to grab the mana for themselves, the circle would've fallen apart. But all of us are actively thinking about *some* kind of magical work every minute of the day and most of the night; we've all got spells half worked out and artifice projects in progress and potions brewing in the lab and graduation graduation graduation in our heads, and here was all this mana to work with, and I was asking them to think about using it to save Cora's arm instead of their own necks.

It was hard for them and hard for me. I had to concentrate ferociously hard on the healing spell while the circle grew along the sides of the table and one by one everyone a little uncertainly added their hands. Jowani and Nkoyo closed it at the end, their hands clasped behind Cora's back, and when they did, the circle established and the full mana flow started. Everyone jumped or squeaked. I should've warned them, but I couldn't actually say anything at this point that wasn't the spell. Anyway, I didn't have any mental energy to spare. Everyone kept hold, the mana of that choice feeding along, being reinforced over and over by all of us intent on the same goal, one that wasn't *for* us, so there wasn't much of either hope or fear to cloud the intention. And the surprise didn't hurt, it helped, because everyone chose to stay in the circle anyway.

Well, it helped build mana. But I started to feel more or less like I'd volunteered to ride a particularly violent horse and it was doing its best to heave me off while I clung in desperation to the edge of the saddle. The mana was a building wave traveling around the circle, getting bigger as it went; I tried to cast the spell literally the first time it came by me, but it happened so fast that I missed, which meant the wave got even bigger the next time around and even more unruly: that much mana surging through everyone was extremely inspiring to everyone's imagination. When it came back a second time, I had to make a tremendous mental heave to drag it firmly out of the circle and into the spell.

At least the words weren't hard to remember. Mum doesn't like complex or detailed incantations. You don't need them when you go straight for the requirement of pure noble unselfishness. "Let Cora's arm be healed, let Cora's arm be whole, let Cora's arm be well," I said, feeling like I was gasping it out while treading in deep water, my head tipped back to keep my mouth above the surface, and the mana went roaring through me and out of me.

The spell blew the wrap off Cora's arm with the crisp snapping sound of someone shaking out a freshly laundered pillowcase. She made a squawking noise and grabbed at her elbow: just like that, her whole arm was smooth and unmarred as if nothing had happened to it at all. She opened and closed her hand a couple of times, and then she burst into tears and put her head down on the table with her arms huddled around it protectively, trying to hide from us all while she sobbed. The yellow tie, hanging from the crook of her elbow, fluttered one more time like a banner, even the bloodstains gone.

The rule is, when someone has a breakdown, you carefully don't pay any attention to them and just carry on the conversation until they get hold of themselves. But the circumstances were a bit unusual, and it's not as though there were an existing conversation to carry on. Yaakov said a prayer in Hebrew softly to himself, and bowed his head, but none of the rest of us were religious, so while he had a nice spiritual moment with himself, we all just carried on being awkward and glancing round at each other to avoid staring at Cora, which obviously we all wanted to do. Jowani, who was on her left, was losing the fight and letting his eyes slant down to peek.

"What did you do?" Orion demanded, and made me jump; he'd come up to the empty seat Aadhya had left for him, next to me, and he was staring at Cora exactly the way the rest of us were trying so hard not to. "What was that? You just—".

"We did a circle healing," I said, dismissively, which took some effort. "You'd better hurry up and eat, Lake, it's nearly to the warning bell. Have you got your alchemy seminar marks yet?"

He put his tray down and sat next to me almost like he was moving in slow motion, without taking his eyes off Cora. He hadn't shaved in a week, and he'd been looking unkempt even before that; his hair had grown back out to a length that required at least running your fingers through it to keep it in order—we have low standards—but he wasn't doing even that. His Thor t-shirt hadn't changed in four days and was more than usually aromatic, and there were lingering smudges of soot and glittery blue asphodelium powder on his cheek. I was resolutely not saying a word, because it was none of my affair and it was going to keep being none of my

affair until he became so stinky that I could justify complaining purely on the grounds of sharing a table, by which point
maybe someone else would beat me to it. Probably not: most
kids in here are more likely to bottle the scent and sell it as
Eau de Lake or something. I suspected that he'd been spending the last few weeks hunting those just-past-larval-stage
mals that had started creeping out of the plumbing.

I jabbed him in the side with an elbow, and he finally jolted
out of it enough to stare at me instead. "Food. Alchemy
marks. Well?"

He looked down at his tray: oh, how surprising, food!
Things to eat to keep you alive! That's about as much as you
can say for Scholomance cuisine. He started eating it fast
enough after he got over the massive surprise of rediscover-
ing its existence, and said out of the corner of his mouth,
"No, today I guess, or Friday," but he kept staring at Cora
until I poked him again for being a rude wanker and he realized it and jerked his eyes down to his plate.

"You've had to see a circle working sometime, living in
New York," I said.

"They don't feel like *that*," he said, and then had the nerve
to ask me, "Was there any malia in it?"

"That's meant to be funny, is it?" I said. "No, you aardvark,
it's one of my mum's healing circle spells. You don't get any
return at all."

That's not true, at least according to Mum: she insists that
you always gain more than you give when you give your
work freely, only you don't know when the return will come
and you can't think about it or anticipate it, and it won't take
the shape you expect, so in other words, the return is completely unprovable and useless. On the other hand, no ven-
ture capitalists are lining up to give me rides in their private
jets, so what do I know?

"Huh," Orion said, sounding vaguely dubious, like he wasn't sure he believed me.

"It's negative malia if it's anything," I said. Occasionally, a repentant maleficer comes to Mum for help, someone like Liu was on the way to being: not the gleefully monstrous ones but the ones who went partway down the road—usually to make it through puberty alive—and have now changed their minds and would like to go back. She won't do spirit cleansing for them or anything like that, but if they ask sincerely, she'll let them join her circle, and generally once they've spent as many years doing the circle work as they did being maleficers, they come right again, and she tells them to go and make a circle of their own somewhere.

"Maybe that's why it feels weird to you," Aadhya said to Orion. "Are you seeing an aura?"

"Nmgh," Orion said with half a pound of spaghetti dangling out of his mouth. He heaved the rest of it in and swallowed. "It's more like—for a minute, she had these really crisp edges. Like you do sometimes," he added to me, and then he blushed and stared down at his plate.

I glared at him, completely unflattered. "And why exactly did that make you think it was using *malia*?"

"Uh" was the feeble response. "It's—maybe it's just power?" he tried, kind of desperately.

"Do *mals* have these crisp edges?" I demanded.

"No?" Under my continuing glare, he wilted. "Some of them? Sometimes?"

I stewed over it while shoving in the rest of my own dinner. Apparently I looked like a maleficaria to him occasionally? Although Orion *didn't* see anything odd about human maleficers: he hadn't noticed our life-eating neighbor Jack was one until after that charmer had tried to leave my intestines piled on the floor of my room. And all right, there're so many wizards who use small bits of malia here and there, stolen from things like plants or bugs or filched from a piece of work that someone else left unattended, that Orion could plausibly have a hard time picking the hardcore maleficers out. Those of us who strictly use only mana that we've raised ourselves or that someone has given us freely are the minority. But still: apparently I'm visibly more of a monster than an evil wizard is. Hurrah.

And an even larger hurrah: Orion found that appealing. It sounded too much like Aadhya had been right about what Orion saw in me. I'm not some sort of pallid romantic who insists on being loved for my shining inner being. My inner being is exceptionally cranky and I often don't want her company myself, and anyway one of the main reasons I'd been avoiding Orion's room lately was the strong feeling that it would be for the best for all concerned if I didn't see him with his shirt off again anytime soon, so that would be pot and kettle. But I was unenthusiastic about the prospect of being found attractive *because* I seem like a terrifying creation of dark sorcery instead of *despite* it.

I stewed enough over it that I completely missed the implication of the rest of what Orion had said until I was slogging upstairs to my Wednesday library session. Just short of the top stair—where my entire gaggle of freshmen were waiting for me to lead them to whatever potential doom I was scheduled to save them from today—I halted, and realized that if Orion hadn't got his results from his senior seminar yet, it wasn't because he was going to get an A+, since he'd been falling down on everything badly enough to forget changing his t-shirt. He was going to *fail*.

And when you fail alchemy, you don't get attacked by mals. You just get to interact very intimately with your last brewing assignment, and being an invincible monster-killing machine does you absolutely no good against being doused in a vat of etching acid used to carve mystical runes into steel, which had been Orion's midterm assignment.

I stared up the last few stairs at the eight freshmen, who were all peering anxiously back at me, and then I said, "Right, field trip today," and turned round to lead them downstairs on a three-stairs-at-a-time rush barely short of sending them pell-mell the whole way to the bottom. I had to actually grab Zheng to stop him tumbling past the alchemy floor landing. Once I'd steadied him, I ran for it down the corridor with the pack of them behind me, as fast as their considerably shorter legs could carry them. I didn't know what room Orion was in, so I just shoved open every lab door I saw and yelled in, "Lake?" until someone yelled back, "He's in two ninety-three!" I turned and ran past the pack of freshmen still going the other way, all of them wheeling to follow me like a flock of confused geese. I passed the landing and went on the other way, threw open the door to 293, and without even breaking stride tackled Orion away from the lab bench, just as the bell for the start of class rang and all the complex brewing equipment at his station started to rattle and belch smoke.

The large copper vat foamed over so energetically that the whole lid got lifted off and clanged away onto the floor atop a massive and expanding column of violet foam that poured over the sides and then cascaded down from the surface of the table and over the floor, enormous black billows of smoke hissing up in its path. There was a lot of screaming and running from the rest of the students that only made things worse, other experiments going up as they were hastily abandoned. We fumbled up to our feet together, but we couldn't see a thing; I kept a death grip on Orion's wrist and would have walked us both the wrong way, only the freshmen all started yelling from the door, "El! El!" and Zheng and Jingxi and Sunita—I'd been trying really hard not to learn their names, but it wasn't going very well—even made a line into the room and cast light spells to give us a path.

We were still coughing horribly by the time we managed to make it out into the corridor, and I couldn't speak afterwards until Sudarat came round, giving us each a drink of water out of her charmed portable flask, but I could and did immediately smack Orion along the back of his unnecessarily thick skull and then waggled my hand with all five fingers spread out in his face, for emphasis. He gave me a halfhearted scowl and batted it away.

Chapter 5
QUATTRIA

"I SHOULD DO THIS in the lab," Orion said.

"You don't need the equipment in front of your face to copy out a clear recipe, Lake, and you needn't think you're being clever, either," I said, because what he really meant was, he should get to wander around the corridors and poke his beaky nose into every room on the alchemy floor until he found some poor unsuspecting half-grown nightcrawler or striga and got to slaughter them. "How you've got through three and a quarter years in here without learning when you have to pay attention to your work is beyond me."

He groaned deeply and put his head down on the desk, which was my old study carrel in the nook of the library. I'd taken great pleasure in using New York mana to clear out the still-waiting booby trap that Magnus had left for me last term; it was one of the first things I'd done when Chloe had given me the power-sharer. Hauling Orion up to the library and shoving him into a dark corner was my latest attempt to actually get him to do his remedial alchemy assignment, which was absolutely going to disintegrate him before the end of the month, along with several innocent bystanders and possibly *me* if he didn't actually buckle down to it. I'd started making him show me his progress every evening at dinner, and since there hadn't been any in the week and a half since the *last* time he'd nearly got me disintegrated, I'd dragged him out of bed at first bell this fine Saturday morning and marched him upstairs after breakfast.

Even in here, with no distractions, he spent at least ten minutes gazing woebegone at his lab instructions for every one minute he spent actually reading them. "What *is* wrong with you?" I asked, after another hour and several more heaved sighs. "You weren't a complete incompetent before. Are you getting senioritis or something?" That's a highly fatal condition in the Scholomance.

"I'm just *tired*," he said. "The mals keep hiding from me, there aren't enough of them, I'm low on mana all the time—no, I *don't* want it!" he added with a snap, when I reached for the power-sharer on my wrist again. "If I could find any mals to use mana on, I wouldn't need to suck it from the pool!"

"What you need to use mana on is *your alchemy assignment*, so stop being a numpty, *take some*, and get it done!" I said.

He ground his teeth and then said sulkily, "Fine, but just give me some, don't give me the sharer."

That made less than no sense, since you lose some mana in each transfer. Not loads or anything, but even a little bit was a pointless waste of someone else's deeply annoying work. "Is this some sort of kinky thing you've got going?" I said suspiciously.

"No! You know I can't have access to the pool."

"Right, because you've got lousy mana discipline and

you'll pull gobs when you're not paying attention," I said. I wasn't going to *coddle* him about it. "So what? Pay attention for five seconds."

His alchemy assignment had suddenly developed a powerful fascination, judging by how hard he was staring down at it. "It's not—it doesn't work that way."

"What, if you get access you'll suck the whole thing dry involuntarily?" I said, sarcastically, except he flushed red as though that was really on the table. "Are you speaking from some kind of experience here, or—"

"I got a power-sharer to practice with six months before induction, like everybody else," Orion said in totally flat tones. "I sucked the entire enclave's active reservoir dry in half an hour. Even my mom couldn't pull me off it." I gawked at him in disbelief. He didn't turn his head, just twitched his shoulders in a stiff, brief shrug. "She thinks it's got something to do with me being able to pull from mals. That it's the same kind of channel, and I can't tell the difference."

I was staring at him in fascination. "Why didn't you just— pop?" It sounded like filling a water balloon from a firehose. I've got what anyone would call a reasonable mana capacity, namely a hundred times the average, and even that couldn't be a noticeable fraction of the active mana reservoir of the entire New York enclave. He only shrugged impatiently, as if he'd never bothered to give it a thought.

"And what on earth did you use it all for? That much mana, you should still be coasting along for the next ten years even if you were doing major arcana every day."

"I didn't *want* to take the mana! I put it back! As soon as my dad made me the one-way sharer." He held up his wrist with his narrow band around it. He sounded a little frayed, and it occurred to me: of course those wankers at his enclave

THE LAST GRADUATE ✦ 129

had probably made him feel like a maleficer over it, or worse. One of the more common ways that enclaves get taken down is if one of their enemies gets a traitor on the inside to steal a batch of the enclave's mana pool and hand it over, and then the enemy enclave can destroy them using their own power. It's happened a handful of times, all of them a popular subject for wizard storytelling, at least among kids who don't live in enclaves. It might well be how Bangkok had been taken down, in fact.

"How long did it take your dad to make it?" I asked, and Orion's shoulders hunched.

"A week," he muttered. I imagine all the grown wizards in New York had really enjoyed a thirteen-year-old walking around with the mana to wreck their entire enclave in his belly, and had made sure he enjoyed that week just as much as they did.

I wanted to go throw rocks at them, and also possibly to put my arms round Orion and hug him, but obviously those were equally impossible, so instead I just gave him a bracing thump on the shoulder and said heartily, "Let's set you to rights, then."

I pulled a substantial helping of mana through the power-sharer. I'd only ever been taking mana out of the pool for crisis situations; it felt odd doing it deliberately, without anything threatening me. It wasn't like getting mana out of the crystals Mum gave me, the mana I stored myself; that mana had a different kind of feel to it, a bit rougher round the edges, like I could still feel the work and pain that I'd put into it. Or maybe it was just that when I did it, I was always thinking of the work and pain I'd have to go through to replace anything I took. It was easier and smoother to pull mana back out of the shared pool, the pool I didn't have to fill up all by myself, and I was already hopelessly used to it. Orion wasn't the only greedy one. I could've gladly drunk of it until I filled up every empty corner of myself.

But instead I took a carefully measured amount, the amount I usually put in on brewing an alchemy recipe myself, and I put my hand on his chest and nudged it at him. He gave a gasp and shut his eyes, covering my hand with his and pressing it there a moment, and I could feel his chest expanding and his heart beating thump and his skin warm through the thin worn fabric of his t-shirt—at least it was clean, I'd made him change it and shower this morning, but we'd climbed four flights of stairs and I could smell him a bit anyway, except it was a nice smell, and he opened his eyes and stared at me and kept his hand over mine, mana flowing between us, and I was almost certain *something* was going to happen and that I wasn't going to stop it happening, and while I was also almost certain that it was a bad idea, it felt like the sort of bad idea that's great fun at the time, and then Orion yanked his hand back squalling, "Ow!" His thumb was dripping blood. Precious had climbed out of her cup and down my arm without me even noticing and *bit* him.

I glared at her incredulously while Orion whimpered his way through digging out a plaster from his backpack and covering up the mark of her deeply planted incisors. She sat on the edge of the desk washing her face and whiskers with an air of enormous satisfaction. "I don't need a chaperone, much less one who's a *mouse*," I hissed at her under my breath. "Aren't you lot having babies when you're a month old?" She only twitched her nose at me dismissively.

Orion avoided looking at me at all the rest of the morning, which was quite a trick when we were sitting next to each other. Of course, I managed it myself, too. I wasn't at all tempted to do otherwise. Even in the moment, whatever we'd been about to do had seemed like a bad idea, and thankfully I wasn't in the moment anymore. I'd never been in a moment with anyone before and I didn't like it at all. What business did my brain have coming up with a patently stupid idea like kissing Orion Lake in the stacks instead of doing my classwork? It felt like nothing more than the symptoms of a mindworm infestation, per the description in the sophomore maleficaria textbook: mysterious and uncharacteristic foreign thoughts inserting themselves at unwanted and unpredictable times. If only I had a mindworm infestation. All I had was Orion sitting next to me in his too-small t-shirt from sophomore year that was the only clean one he had left this week and his arm about four inches away from mine.

I spent those three hours staring at my latest poem from Myrddin class, which strangely refused to translate itself. At this rate, soon I'd start failing my own classes. To add insult to injury, when the bell for lunch rang, Orion sat back in his chair and sighed and said, "There, I got it," and he'd finished the entire worksheet. He'd still have to actually brew the potion, but that wasn't a horrible burden: it was a reflex-boosting concoction that would make him even more of a terror to mals everywhere. It was an outrageously good remedial assignment. My remedial alchemy assignments are always poisons that kill instantly, kill gruesomely, or sometimes kill instantly *and* gruesomely.

"Good," I said sourly, packing up. "Do you need any more help with it, Lake, or do you think you can manage the measuring spoons after lunch without supervision?"

"I'll be fine," he said, with a glare, and then he remembered that something had almost happened and apparently he didn't think it had been such a bad idea as all that, because he stopped glaring and blurted, "Unless you want to come," which was horribly absurd: *Want to come help me with my reme-*

dial alchemy assignment down in the lab was possibly the worst date ever and he had absolutely no business inviting anyone to do it, and I had absolutely no business even thinking about saying yes.

And I'd also promised Aadhya to help her tune the lute this afternoon, so I couldn't say yes. Just as well. "Don't be ridiculous," I said coolly, as I snatched up my last two books. He went sheepish and curled in, and I swept away into the aisle back towards the reading room and the stairs, silently congratulating myself on having stomped on his aspirations, except as we started to clear our trays, Aadhya said to me, "Are we still on for tuning the lute now?" and Orion shot a narrow-eyed look across the table at me like *Oh so you would have said yes otherwise wouldn't you.* I avoided his eyes. He didn't need any more ideas than he already had, and neither did I. Instead I hurried off with Aadhya to an empty classroom to work on the lute, only the instant we got clear of other people she nudged me in the arm and raised her eyebrows and was all, "Wellllll?"

"What?" I said.

She gave me a shove. "Are you dating *now*?"

"No!"

"Oh, come on, seriously, look me in the face and tell me you didn't kiss at least once up there," Aadhya said.

"We didn't!" I said, in glad and perfect honesty, and at dinner I grudgingly gave Precious the three ripe red grapes out of the fruit cup I'd bagged that was otherwise only full of tired-looking honeydew and pale underripe pineapple chunks that stung in my mouth. "Don't take this as encouragement," I told her. She accepted them with smug graciousness and ate all three one after another and went to sleep in her cup with her tiny belly distended.

There're almost no holidays in the Scholomance. They'd be a pointless fiction, but that's not why we don't have them; we don't have them because we—and the school—can't afford them. We need to be *working*, all the time, just to keep the lights on. So there's only graduation and induction day, on the second of July, and the semesters are divided around the first of January, which is also when the senior class rankings get posted and the winter cleansing happens. But that leaves one extra day in the first semester, which the Americans decided was a terrible problem that obviously had to be addressed. So one day each fall, after the last of the remedial post-midterms work has been turned in—or not—we have Field Day.

It *is* a notable milestone in the year: it marks the start of the killing season. By then, all the mals that go into hibernation or reproductive phases after graduation have woken up and are finding ways back upstairs, or their adorable new babies have squirmed their own way up, and the competition among them gets more aggressive. Roughly one in seven freshmen die between Field Day and New Year's, as I'd loudly and repeatedly informed all of mine, whose names *had* all got into my head at this point despite my best efforts. It's never a good idea to get attached to freshmen, and doing it this early in the year was an invitation to misery, but after they'd saved me and Orion from blundering around almost choking ourselves to death, it had worn off enough of the cold-aloof-senior mystique I'd cultivated that they'd started *talking* to me. Even my most aggressive snappishness wasn't discouraging them sufficiently anymore.

I gather that the usual purpose of a Field Day is to build

school spirit by letting people run around doing sport in the fresh air and cheering each other on in their achievements. We don't have any fresh air or school spirit, so instead we all gather together down in the gymnasium and cheer each other on for having stayed alive long enough to experience another Field Day. Attendance is mandatory, and enforced by the cafeteria being closed all day, so the only place to get food is the buffet that gets laid on in the gym in an enormous bank of antique Automat-style cases that are trundled out for the occasion. I have no idea where they go the rest of the time. You can only unlock them by feeding in tokens, which you can only get by participating in the various delightful games like relay races and dodgeball. To add to the festive atmosphere, normally at least one or two kids get eaten on the way down to the gym, since there are enough mals out there who can remember dates and know there's going to be a buffet laid on for *them* along the stairs and corridors.

When the Scholomance first opened back in 1880, there were several really complex multilayered spells on the gym to give students the illusion of being outside in nature, complete with trees and open skies above that would go from day to night. It was the masterpiece of a crack team of artificers from Kyoto. Even at the time, Kyoto was powerful enough that Manchester couldn't afford to just blow them off completely when the school was being constructed, so instead Manchester fobbed them off with the gym. Kyoto took revenge by making it so spectacular that everyone who got to tour the place couldn't talk of anything else. There are several raving accounts framed up on the walls amid the blueprints, with antique photos that are supposedly of the gymnasium but look exactly like photos from a guidebook to the Japanese countryside.

No one's seen the illusions working in more than a hundred years. After Patience and Fortitude, our resident maw-mouths, first made themselves at home in the graduation hall, and all the maintenance started being done by students, the whole thing fell apart. The plants all died so long ago that there's not even dirt left, just the empty ironwork planters, and the color has faded out of the distant shifting murals of hills and mountains, so now they look like a landscape out of the afterlife. There's one week in springtime when a scatter-ing of bleached-white ghostly scraps come drifting down mysteriously—all that's left of the cherry blossom experi-ence. Occasionally stark bare trees sprout up, and there's a small pagoda that occasionally appears and vanishes again. I don't think anyone's ever been mad enough to go inside, but if they have, they've never come out again to report.

But the sunlamps still work, and at least there's wide-open room to run around and move, with an enormously high ceiling that lets you see mals dropping on you with plenty of warning. Most kids love the gym. I've avoided the place for virtually my entire Scholomance career. Mals come to the gym all the time; it's on the lowest floor, so it's the first stop for any of them who have managed to squirm past the wards from below. It's a bad place to be a solitary zebra. And if I ever tried to join anything as casual as a game of tag, within a few minutes everyone else in the group had mysteriously decided they were moving on to something else that involved picking teams, and I'd always be odd one out. I did try to go running on my own instead, but that made me just a bit of an appealing target, and the other kids would make things worse. They'd deliberately move their game or some piece of equipment they'd cobbled together so that I'd have to run through a narrow lane near the walls, or cross some convo-luted bit of greyish landscaping just right for mals to hide in. It wasn't simply out of pure dislike. Not that they didn't dislike me, but anything that got me would be something that didn't get them.

So I don't go to the gym. Instead I exercise alone in my room to build mana, and it's always good for a boost if I first dwell on *why* I've got to do it alone in my room, and being rejected and outcast. That's the kind of thing that makes you really not want to exercise and just lie on your bed and eat ice cream, except there's no ice cream to be had in the Scholomance, which makes you feel worse, and if you can force yourself to exercise anyway despite being miserable and not wanting to, voilà, extra mana.

But I've gone to every Field Day. I could never afford to miss a day of eating, much less one of the best days of eating we get each year. At least on Field Day, the activities are set and you just queue up to do each one, so I couldn't be left out comprehensively. And because of all that exercise I do alone in my room, I usually come out with a fair haul of tokens. And an even larger haul of resentment, since I'm clearly a good choice for teams and still never get picked.

Even this year, going into the gym I was ready, automatically, for Aadhya and Liu to ditch me. I don't mean I expected that to happen—it would've been a horrid surprise—but some part of my brain was planning for it anyway, working out the kind of strategy I've always needed to have for Field Day. First I'd go for the rope climb, because everyone avoids it early on, when there still might be some mals hiding in the ceiling panels or camouflaged against the dingy mottled grey that was once the sky. So the queue is short and you can get the tickets quick, and while you're up there, you take a look round and see which other activities have the short queues, because if you don't have allies watching your back, overall your best odds are to take a few risks up front and get enough tickets to spend the rest of the day eating and performing perfunctory cheers until people start to head back to their rooms.

So I was primed and ready to be abandoned and left on the sidelines. What I wasn't ready for was Magnus. Oh, I'd have reacted at speed if he'd tried to slip me some kind of contact poison or if he'd sent some minor gnawing construct to chew through a rope while I was on it. I was, however, completely unprepared for what he actually did.

A shoving match started while I was queued up with Aadhya and Liu and Chloe for the relay race, and a bunch of big senior boys went tumbling across the queue, cutting me and Chloe off. It turned into everyone shoving angrily, trying to keep their places or get better ones in the confusion, and we ended up pushed out of the queue and staring at Aadhya and Liu across a messy knot of people. We'd already been queuing for twenty minutes, and the line had grown a lot longer in that time. If Aadhya and Liu gave up the spot and came back to us, we'd all end up losing the time for a full activity or two. But everyone in the queue was keyed up, and no one was going to let us get back to our original places without a fight.

"Chloe!" Magnus yelled from the nearest queue, where he was about to go into the tug-of-war. "That's Jaclyn and Sung behind your allies, let them have your spots and come over here!" Aadhya was already waving a thumbs-up at us from over the sea of heads, and Chloe grabbed my hand and ran with me over to where Magnus and Jermaine had stiff-armed a couple of juniors in the queue behind them, who weren't brave enough to start arguing when they let us in.

I was so completely bewildered by Magnus going out of his way to be helpful that I had my hands on the big rope before I worked out that the whole thing had been a setup: his ally Sung had definitely been one of the kids in the shoving match, and I was sure a couple of the others had also been New York hangers-on. I craned over for a look at the other queue: Aadhya and Liu were still another five minutes back from the start of the relay races, which meant that when we had finished here, in order to hook back up with them, Chloe and I would have to waste that time just standing around like target mannequins. It would make much more obvious sense for them to stick with Jaclyn and Sung and for us to go on to something else—with *Magnus,* who apparently now *wanted my company.* Or rather wanted to cut me away from Aadhya and Liu, and make sure I was firmly embedded in the New York crowd.

"Tebow, if no one's ever told you, you're a soggy dish-cloth," I told Magnus when we got off the tug-of-war—our side had won; I'd yanked with a lot of vengeful fury involved. He stopped open-mouthed in the start of whatever hurrah-go-team speech he'd been about to deliver, so likely no one ever had, even though the resemblance was uncanny in my opinion: cold, useless, clings when all you want is to shake it off. "Sorry, Rasmussen, I'm not spending all day with this wanker," I told Chloe, and marched off towards the long line for the egg-and-spoon races. Those are always popular, de-spite being possibly the stupidest activity a human being could engage in, since even if a spoon turns out to be a mimic or an egg hatches something unpleasant halfway through the race, they usually can't be very terrible if they're only the size of a spoon.

Chloe joined me on the line a moment later, with a belea-guered expression that annoyed me by reminding me of the similar look Mum occasionally gets when she's been trying to make peace between me and the most recently irritated commune-dweller. At least Chloe didn't try to persuade me that I ought to try and see things from Magnus's side, and call forth his understanding by offering my own, et cetera. She was still trying to think of what she *did* want to say—I don't know why Americans won't just talk about the weather like reasonable people—when Mistoffeles suddenly put his head out of the little cup on her chest and emitted a few alarmed squeaks, at which point I noticed that eight kids from Shanghai enclave had casually been drifting off the lines on either side of ours and were now very-not-casually closing in around us. And one of them was already muttering away at an incantation for something unpleasant that he was about to throw in our faces.

Chloe darted a scared look over towards Aadhya and Liu—deep in the relay race and not even glancing our way—and then looked around for anyone else from New York, except Orion wasn't anywhere to be seen, I presume too busy hunting the mals in the stairways and corridors, and of course Magnus the Magnificent had flounced off with the rest of his pals to huddle on the other side of the gym and discuss what to do about my refusal to accept their wide-armed welcome.

"A *filthy* soggy dishcloth," I said, trying to vent enough of my fury to think through the situation. It wasn't the numbers: I can handle a thousand enemies as easily as seven, as long as by *handle* you mean "kill in a grisly fashion." I hadn't any idea what to do about them otherwise. I do have a top-notch spell to seize total control over the minds of a group of people, only there isn't a constraint on the size of the crowd: you have to cast it on a defined physical space isolated by things like walls, and then it grabs everyone in it. In this case, we were inside the gym that was holding literally every kid in the school. Also, the spell was quite vague on the aftereffects on the minds in question.

I could just have waited until the other kid threw his spell, and then caught it and thrown it back at him. It's hard to describe how that works, and in fact it doesn't work for most people; the first-year incantations textbook informed us firmly that you're much better off either doing a defensive spell or trying to get your own offensive spell out before the other wizard fires off theirs. But I'm brilliant at reflecting as long as the spell being thrown at me is malicious or destructive enough, and I had a strong presentiment that wasn't going to be a problem in this case.

And then I would have the pleasure of watching up-close while *his* skin flew off his body, or his intestines exploded out of his mouth or his brains dribbled out his ears or whatever horrible thing he meant to do to us, and it would just be the purest self-defense; no one would even criticize me for it. Not to my face, at any rate.

I would really have liked to be angry at them right then. I often haven't any difficulty in contemplating extreme violence and even murder when I'm angry, and I can get angry at an enclaver at the drop of a hat. But I couldn't be angry at them, not that way, not with that helpful burning righteous rage, because I'm really very good at knowing the right thing to do, the smart thing to do, and picking a fight to the death with a wizard who's capable of killing with a wave of her hand isn't it. If I was dangerous enough to warrant killing, the smart selfish enclaver thing for *them* to do was to keep the bloody hell away from me, as far as possible. They ought to have kept their heads down, got out safely as they were all sure to do, and then gone home to tell their parents about me. They were teenagers; they had every right to let me be the grown-ups' problem.

Instead here they were, all of them gambling with their safe, sheltered lives—they had to assume I'd take out at least *one* of them, and as far as I could tell, they didn't even have loser allies along with them to take that mortal blow. The boy in front getting ready to cast was an enclaver: his face was vaguely familiar from the language lab, round and spotty with a mustache he'd valiantly been trying to grow for the last two years. We'd never studied any of the same languages; I didn't know his name. But Liu might: her mum and dad had worked for the enclave a few times. Their parents might know each other.

And I did know the girl backing him up, Wang Yuyan, because everyone in languages track knew her: she was doing twelve languages, which no enclave kid needed to do. Either she was ambitious or she loved languages madly or maybe she was just a tremendous masochist, I had no idea. I didn't really know her, we'd never had a conversation or anything. But we'd been in the same Sanskrit section sophomore year, and one time I'd had a dictionary she needed—when you're trying to get the meaning of a more obscure word, you often need to chase it down through three or four dictionaries until you end up in a language you're fluent in—and she'd asked me to look the word up for her in a perfectly civil way, and offered to look one up for me in return.

That might not sound like much, but for comparison's sake, in freshman year an enclave kid from Sydney glanced down at the really good French–English dictionary I'd found that week in the library and said, "Let's have that, there's a good girl," not even asking. And because I told him exactly where he could hop off, at the end of class he had two of his minion-friends trip me going out of the room while another grabbed my entire bag and ran down the corridor shaking all my things out, yelling, "Free supplies!" while everyone laughed and grabbed.

I got up in the doorway with my lip bleeding and my forehead bruised. He was standing right there with two more of his pals to enjoy the show, all of them grinning, and then I turned and looked him in the face and thought in a red haze of all the things I could have done to him, so he stopped grinning and they fled the other way. Ever since, he's firmly ignored my existence. Ah, the advantages of being a monstrous dark sorceress in embryonic form.

But he wouldn't have stopped on his own. That's what enclavers are like, most of them. Like Magnus, who was the reason we were exposed and also the reason the Shanghai kids were putting themselves on the line to take me out. Because they could imagine what someone like that would do with the kind of power I had.

And probably, maybe, at least half of those enclaver kids closing in round us were like Magnus themselves, but Yuyan wasn't. I knew that much about her, and I also knew what she was casting, because I'd overheard people talking about this fantastic spell she'd got in her languages seminar that allowed you to get behind someone else's spell and *push*, meaning that whatever spotty mustache boy was about to throw at us, she'd double it. That meant that when I flung it back, she'd get hit with the reflection, too. And maybe she deserved it, but I didn't want to give it to her, to any of those kids getting ready to kill us for no reason other than being absolutely terrified of me and what I might do. It felt like making them *right* to have come after me.

But I even less wanted to let them kill me and Chloe, so I was just steeling my gut to go ahead and reflect the spell back anyway, when Chloe pulled a tiny plastic spray bottle filled with blue sparkling stuff from her pocket and spritzed it in the air all round us. On the other side of the glimmering, the whole room slowed down like everyone but the two of us was moving through mud—which meant of course she'd sped the two of us up; much easier.

"Do you have enough for us to run for it?" I asked her, but she shook her head, holding it up for me to see: the reservoir was the size of an underfed caterpillar, and there was barely any of the blue stuff left in the bottom.

"I just couldn't think of anything else to do that would be quick enough," she said. "I've got a blinding spray on me, but if I use it on those two incanters, Hu Zixuan in the back is going to hit us, and I'm almost sure that thing he has is a reviser. We've heard rumors about him working on one since he got here, and he'll have it powered up by the time they go down—"

She was pointing at a kid all the way in the back of the group on the other side. I hadn't paid much attention to him, because he was so shrimpy he looked like a sophomore at best; I'd assumed he was just helping to provide mana. But as soon as Chloe pointed him out, I realized it was the other way round: the five people fanned out in front of him were screening him and feeding mana *back* to him. Zixuan had a small pale-green rod almost completely hidden in his hand, which was connected by a thin gold wire to what had to be the rest of the artifact in his pocket: I could see slowed-down light gleaming along the line.

"Right," I said grimly. "Go ahead and blind the incanters. Is it permanent?"

"You really want me to explain how it works *now*?" Chloe said. "It's a migraine inducer, and maybe they'll keep having them for the rest of their lives, and they're about to *fry us*!"

"Yes, all right!" I said hastily. I *was* in fact perfectly all right with giving someone migraines in exchange for attempted murder. "Go after the boy with the mustache: Yuyan's just doing an amplification; if you get him, her casting won't do anything."

"But what about the reviser?" Chloe said.

"That I can handle," I said, and I really hoped I wasn't lying, but anyway we were out of time. Chloe threw me one last desperate look that also hoped I wasn't lying as she got out the blinding spray, and then the blue haze was settling down and my throat was hurting as if I'd been shrieking at the top of my lungs. The people on either side of us in the line were cringing away, so probably that's about what our conversation had sounded like. Chloe was already lunging with a last bit of unnatural quickness across the empty space towards mustache boy, whose eyes went wide in alarm but stayed resolute. He'd known he was going to pull the first attack, brave bastard, although he screamed and crumpled when the spray hit him in the face just the same.

I turned towards the other group just as they parted and Zixuan, owlish with his eyes magnified behind enormous farsighted lenses, brought the jade rod up to mouth level and sang a single clear line at it. I couldn't understand his request, as he was casting in Shanghainese, but I could take a reasonable guess: it was probably something on the order of *please alter the floor so it no longer encloses this girl.*

I'd only seen a reviser in illustrations before. They're used all the time, but only in major enclave projects. It's a generic device that allows artificers to create vastly more complicated and difficult pieces of artifice—something that no one person could keep in their heads—by starting with a completed piece and then making it more complex, little by little. The first ones were used to help build the Scholomance, in fact.

It was quite a clever approach to take against me. Dropping me out into the void beneath the gym would certainly remove me as a problem, and I couldn't stop it with any kind of shield or even throwing the spell back, because he wasn't actually aiming a spell at *me*; he was aiming it at the school itself. It was a small enough edit that he could get away with it, too. And I couldn't exactly destroy the piece of artifice he was using it on, at least not without dumping us *all* into the void.

Fortunately, I knew what to do in this situation, because I'd had to spend two months in my freshman year translating a charming cautionary tale in French all about a truly horrible maleficer who maintained herself in gory evil for about a decade at the expense of many wizard children in her vicinity. Her shielding was so good that she was effectively invincible in a fight, so she killed all the wizards who attempted to end her reign and mounted their heads on the parapet of her elaborate and well-warded tower. She finally got taken out by a young artificer she'd snatched: a boy with an affinity for stoneworking. He didn't try to attack her; instead he cast a working on the stone of her tower, and walled her up with all her six layers of shielding, so closely that she couldn't move, and left her entombed to suffocate.

The school then assigned me a long essay—in French—explaining what I would do in the same situation. It even flat-out failed my first half-arsed attempt in which I suggested running away and *not* killing any more children, so I had to spend a week in the library doing research for the makeup.

The answer I found was, when facing an artificer who's about to turn the environment against you, kill them first. But if that's not an option you like, your second best chance is to try and intercept the spell power, and then override their alteration with your own.

Chloe wasn't wrong to be worried about my doing that, however, because if two wizards start wrestling over the same piece of artifice—which in this case was the school itself—almost always the better artificer is the one who ends up in charge.

If Zixuan could *make* a reviser of his own—you can't bring

one in with you through induction, because they've got to be fed with a tiny thread of mana constantly or they burn out—he had to be an absolutely brilliant artificer. And I'm *not* good at artifice myself. Artifice is fundamentally about giving the universe a long and complicated story complete with attractive props in order to coax it to accommodate your wishes. I'm really more about shouting the universe into compliance with mine.

But there was some tidy coaxing right at hand that had already been done for me, more than a hundred years ago, by a whole pack of artificers far more skilled than any senior kid could be. So when the green wave of power came towards me, ready to revise the floor beneath my feet out of existence, I stepped into it and spread my arms to greet it and said, "Set this right instead, why don't you?" then just heaved it up at the gym ceiling, with a push of extra mana to help it along.

The power went boiling up from my arms into the mottled-grey ceiling. It ran cascading down over the domed surface with the wild frothing of a power washer, trickles of green dripping down and kids screaming and running everywhere around me trying to dodge the rain. I was only vaguely aware of them, deep in the breathless shock like standing under a waterfall, having to look straight up into the flow with my whole face desperately scrunched up, barely able to see or breathe or hear for the rushing fury of it. Zixuan and the other kids had put a *lot* of power behind his working: if I had stopped redirecting for a second, his original instructions would have been carried out, too.

I didn't notice when the screaming and running stopped around me; I was still in the middle of the torrent, and I had to stay there until the last reluctant trickling flowed through and I sank out of it gasping, to find Chloe standing there in front of me with her hands over her mouth, crying in just a shocking way—outright blubbing with her mouth turned down like a clown. I couldn't see Zixuan or any of the other Shanghai kids anymore, or anyone else I knew. Everyone had been scattered around the gym like giant hands had gathered them up in a sack and then shaken them out into the room again at random, except for the small area right around me.

Almost all of the kids were crying, the older kids especially, or huddled up on the floor like they wanted to be curled into a fetal position but they couldn't bear to put their heads down. All of us under the crisp blue of an autumn sky, dry leaves on the air and crunchy under us, sunlight dappling in a slant through the leaves of dark maple trees in a mix of brilliant crimson and yellow and green around the edges of the room that was suddenly a forest clearing, the faint gurgle of water running over stones somewhere not far away like a promise, large grey stones emerging like islands from a carpet of moss and leaves, while in the far misty distance a hill climbed a little way above the tree line, with the wooden balcony and roof of a pavilion just peeking out from more cascading colors.

I stood there stupid for a minute or two and then a bird called from somewhere and I started blubbing myself, too. It was horrible. It was almost the most horrible thing that had happened to me in here; it wasn't exactly as bad as the mawmouth, but it was hard to compare because it was horrible in such a completely different way. I have no idea what they were thinking when they'd made it, except of course I do. They wanted to make a room that would look charming on tours and impress other wizards, and make them all say how lovely it would be for the kids to have such a nice place to come to for exercise, how lovely to have this to make up for being trapped inside the school for four years without ever seeing the sun or feeling the wind or seeing a single green leaf, all the water you drink tasting faintly of sour metal, all the food the regurgitated slop of massive kettles filled with different vitamins and barely there enchantments to fool you into believing it's something else, knowing the whole time you're probably never coming out again, and it didn't make up for any of that at all.

People started running out of the gym in droves. The only ones who didn't were the stupid freshmen, who were all wandering around burbling out nonsense like, "Wow," and "Look, there's a nest!" and "It's so pretty!" and making everyone who'd been in here for more than five minutes during the safest year on record want to stab them with knives. I would have gone running out myself, only my legs were as mushy as if I'd just been born, and so I just sat down on one of the picturesque rocks sobbing until Orion was there grabbing me by the shoulders saying, "El! El, what *happened*, what's *wrong*?" I waved my hand frantically and he looked around with his face only confused, and then he said, "I don't get it, you fixed the gym? But why are you *crying* over that? I gave up hunting a quattria to come back here!" in a faintly accusatory voice.

It did help. I got a breath and told him flatly through my snot and tears, "Lake, I've just saved your life again."

"Oh for—I can take a quattria!" he snapped.

"You can't take *me*," I spat at him, and I heaved myself up onto my feet and stormed out on the energy of pure fury, which at least carried me out the doors and away from the grotesque lie of the grove.

I lurched away down the corridor, wiping my streaming nose on the hem of my t-shirt—*his* t-shirt actually, the New York one he'd given me, which I'd stupidly worn today, like a declaration; maybe that had been part of why the Shanghai kids had come at me. Because they were afraid of what I would help New York do to their enclave, their families, and why wouldn't they be afraid? I could do anything.

There were kids crying in huddles scattered around the corridors. I went into the labyrinth and all the way to my seminar classroom, where at least I could be alone except for any maleficaria that wanted to try to jump me, which I'd have really appreciated at that moment. I went down the narrow corridor into the room and shut the door and put my head down on the ugly massive desk, and through the vent a faint breath of autumn leaves came into the room, and I cried for another two hours without anything at all trying to kill me.

Chapter 6
SPELLED DYE & MORTAL FLAME

NOBODY BOTHERED ME the last few weeks of the semester, except by sort of sidling around me warily like I was a bomb that might go off unexpectedly. Faint wafts of fresh air scented with crisp leaves and early frost were now coming through the vents at occasional moments that emphasized how awful the air was all the rest of the time. My delightful classroom up in the library got them quite often. My freshmen all took deep breaths of it while I did my best not to vomit. I saw kids occasionally burst into tears in the cafeteria when one blew into their face. Every time, people would glance at me sideways, and then pretend really hard that they hadn't.

The Shanghai kids had all backed a mile off, and for that matter so had the New York kids. During the previous month, people had briefly started doing things like asking me to trade books or passing me a jar in lab or loaning me a hammer in the shop. I'd been irritated at the time, since I'd understood very well it was because they'd decided I was an important person worth courting. But now they didn't ask me for anything, and if I did say, "Can I have the psyllium husks," four kids would jump at the same time to shove whatever thing I needed at me, more often than not knocking it over and spilling it all over the floor, at which point they would collectively go into a frantic routine of apologies and babbling while cleaning it up.

I did try saying things like, "I won't *bite*," only I said it while seething, so the message that actually got conveyed was that biting would be mild by comparison with whatever I would do instead. And of course they believed me. I'd already done something horrible beyond imagining: I'd made the Scholomance *worse*. Top marks for inflicting mass trauma. It was even getting the freshmen, too: three of them had *died* in the gym during the last couple of weeks. I made clear to mine that none of them were to go near the place, but other, less-well-advised ones, kept making excuses to go down there to play fun games of keep-away-from-the-surprise-mal or get-eaten-in-the-doorway. The death toll would've been higher except Orion had begun patrolling the place on a routine basis to hunt for the mals that were using it as a hunting ground. I wasn't clear on whether it counted as him using the freshmen as bait if they were the ones staking themselves out.

We're all wary of one another in here as a general rule. Budding maleficers are at the top of everyone's list of potential threats, followed by enclavers, older kids, the better students, the more popular ones. Any other kid could become a mortal enemy without so much as a moment's notice if the right conditions—usually a mal planning to eat at least one of us—came along. But we knew how to be afraid of one another; what we might do to one another had sensible limits.

No one would ever in ten thousand years have imagined that if someone tried to kill me in the gym, I'd respond by rebuilding the gym fantasia and creating a fresh torment for everyone in the school, including myself. I certainly wouldn't have imagined it.

So now I wasn't just a dangerously powerful fellow student, to be flattered and watched and strategized over. I was an unpredictable and terrible force of nature that might do anything at all, and they were all shut up in here with me. Like I'd become part of the school myself.

As if to confirm it, the mals all suddenly stopped coming after me. I didn't know why. I spent a few weeks panicking until Aadhya worked it out. "Right, here's what's going on," she said, sketching it out on paper for us to understand, on a stick-figure diagram of the school's screw-top shape. "It takes mana to run all the wards. Early in the year, when there's not a lot of mals, the school does this neat trick: it *opens* a few of the wards, aimed right at you, and uses that mana to reinforce the *other* wards. The mals take the path of least resistance, and voilà, you're target number one. But by now there's too many of them and they're squeezing through on their own as usual."

"And no maleficaria are going to come at you if they have any other choice," Liu finished, as if that were obvious.

"Yeah, aces," I said. "Even the mals agree I'm poison. Ow! Get off me, you little—!" Precious had just bit my earlobe. I swatted at her but she scampered handily across my hunched shoulder blades and grabbed the rim of my *other* ear meaningfully, a fairly potent threat given the stabbing pain in my first one. "No treats for *you*," I told her coldly, after I took her off—carefully—and put her back into the carrying cup. But I did say, "Sorry," to Aad and Liu in a mutter. It really wasn't on for me to be whining about being *unpalatable*. I still remembered exactly how I'd felt about Orion telling *me* that mals never came after him.

Of course, even if the mals had gone, my hair trigger hadn't. I was still jumping at every noise and nearly obliterating the occasional solitary fool who came bumbling across my path at unexpected moments. They were always the kind of pathetic friendless loser no one else would warn off from going into the library corridor where I was lurking or taking a seat too close to me. Just like I'd been. I'd almost have appreciated the distraction of actually being attacked.

Orion would've appreciated it even more. He was still grumpy about having passed up a full-grown quattria to race to my rescue. It seemed to grow in size each time he complained about having missed it. No one had seen the thing since—or rather, no one who'd made it out of Field Day alive. There were four kids who'd gone missing during the mass exodus from the gym, so almost certainly the quattria had successfully scored itself four separate meals of sobbing kid in flight, one for each mouth, and had hidden away somewhere in the depths for the next four years to digest until it split up into four separate littler quattria.

I suppose I'd traded those four kids for the ones from Shanghai who'd actually attacked me. Was that better because I hadn't meant to do it? Or was I just being a stupid wanker who thought she was too good to look people in the face while I killed them?

I knew what Mum would say: it hadn't been me killing them, it had been a quattria—or better yet the alchemist who'd taken four innocent baby animals and squashed them together. Alchemists make quattria because if you starve them of solid food for a month or so, then feed each one of the mouths a different reactant, you get highly useful alchemical fusions out the other end, some of which you can't get any other way. But the quattria don't like being starved, as you might imagine, so they break out fairly often, and then they start eating other creatures with mana because that's the most efficient way to get enough mana to keep themselves going.

It's always convenient to be able to blame things on people who aren't in the room, but I wasn't sure it made me feel any better. Fine, some vicious alchemist had bashed together a quattria a century ago and it was his fault really, but he was long dead and the quattria had eaten four people just last week.

Meanwhile Orion was scrounging around in corners for scrawny and pathetic mals that even a freshman could have taken out. He did catch a nice fat polyphonic shrieker in one of the sophomore girls' bathrooms a couple weeks after Field Day; I understand there was a lot of non-maleficaria shrieking while he chased it through the communal showers during the evening rush, although no one really objected to him barging in on them, given the alternative had a lot more tentacles and smelled even worse than unwashed boy, which he wasn't anymore by the time that fight ended.

The week after that, a gelidite quietly grew itself over the doors to the big alchemy lab during work period, froze them completely shut, and then started creeping steadily onwards into the room. Happily for all concerned—namely the thirty-odd kids in the room—Orion was sulkily doing his—already-late—homework in one of the smaller labs at the time, and he instantly abandoned it to be of service. Normally you can only kill a gelidite by piercing its solid core with a specially enchanted fire arrow, but Orion just started whacking big chunks off it with a metal chair and incinerating those with fire blasts before they could merge back into the rest. Eventually he took off enough mass that he could jam the remaining chair leg down onto the core, and then he heated the leg until the metal melted and ran down all over the core.

"Well, Lake, it's not getting added to the recommended means of destruction in the textbook, is it?" I said coldly at dinner that day, when he displayed the metal globe that was all that was left of the gelidite, ostensibly because he wanted opinions on whether the thing was really dead or not. I wasn't fooled: he was just trying to excuse himself for having left a week's worth of lab work to dissolve on his own bench, when he could have spent thirty seconds to suspend the reaction *before* he'd charged heroically to the rescue.

What business of mine, you might say, and then I'd explain at length how I'd had to rescue him *yet again* just two days before. He'd got to his lesson and started straight in on an overdue batch of spelled dye without paying any attention to the fact that the four other members of his senior lab section had all skived off that day. Of course all the ventilation in his lab had quietly shut itself down, and he didn't notice, just went straight on blithely stirring up more toxic fumes for himself to inhale while increasingly vivid daydreams of pythagorans and polyvores filled his head.

The only reason I'd known in time to save his stupid useless life was because one of the *other* students noticed all of her other classmates were in the library working, and decided to score points with New York by scuttling over to Magnus to tell him that Orion was all alone in a lab section. She could have scuttled over to me directly: I was at the center table in the reading room at the time, with seven fat dictionaries spread out round me in a vengeful spirit. There were nine seats completely open at the best table in the reading room because Chloe and Nkoyo were the only ones there who dared sit with me. Magnus didn't even nerve himself up to come over; he sent one of his minions to get Chloe, told her, and let her come back and tell me.

By the time I got down to the lab, Orion was hallucinating so hard he thought I was a pythagoran myself and tried to throw an immobilizing spell at me. If it had landed, I suppose we'd have died hallucinating together; how romantic. I caught it and hurled it right back at his head, and he promptly toppled over with a crash, taking out three stools on the way down. At least that got him out of my way so I could get on with vaporizing his cauldron of increasingly toxic dye, along with a substantial chunk of his lab table. Overkill, but I was vexed. I didn't get any less vexed after dragging his lockjaw-rigid body out into the corridor. I vented my spleen by haranguing him for the next five minutes while he still couldn't move, but he was still high as a kite and only kept staring at me glassily until I finished and then he said in a soupy way, "El? Is that you?" Then the immobilization spell wore off and he sat up and vomited purple all over my feet.

So he had no business getting himself into avoidable trouble with his classwork, and he knew it, and he could just stuff his large frosted beach ball into the nearest bin. He squirmed away from my glare and looked an appeal over at Chloe, who'd been trained up to be nice to him all her life. "Well, I *think* it's probably dead, but you could try a scrying on the internals," she said cooperatively.

"Yes, you could, if only you weren't six weeks behind on your schoolwork," I said through clenched teeth.

"I'm not!" Orion said. "I'm only *four* weeks—" He stopped himself too late and glared at me while everyone at the table, including even Chloe, made the appropriate squawks of horror at him. I smirked back over folded arms. That evening he got told off by Magnus and Jermaine, by which I mean they cornered him in the boys' bathroom and earnestly talked to him about the need to catch up properly and how silly he was being to let his work get away from him for no reason when it could be so easily managed. I wasn't there to hear it, but I didn't need to be; they were enclavers.

I did see them going in after him, so I hurried to brush my own teeth and then waited in the corridor until Orion sloped out again, properly chastened; I fell in with him and said, "So, Lake, going to let your enclave pals shove your schoolwork off onto some poor sod desperate to get in with them?"

He threw me a look of outrage: having got him into trouble in the first place, couldn't I at least have the decency to let him just look away while Magnus made his work conveniently disappear? But as I clearly couldn't, he sighed and muttered, "No," reluctantly.

I nodded and asked very sweetly, "Going to keep shoving the *consequences* off onto *me*?"

The right answer to that question wasn't very hard to find, either, although he did scowl at me before handing it over. "*No.*"

"Good," I said, with satisfaction, and stopped by his bedroom door and pointedly waited for him to go and shut himself in with his overdue homework.

He looked at the door and then back at me. "El—if the cleansing runs down in the graduation hall again—"

"At New Year's, you mean?" I said. The end-of-semester cleansing isn't nearly as thorough as the graduation day cleansing. School maintenance had to be cut back a great deal in quantity and ambition once they had students doing it instead of teams of grown professional wizards coming in through the graduation hall. One of the places where they decided to cut back was the mid-year cleansing. Only about a quarter of the walls of mortal flame go, in order to save on wear and tear. That leaves plenty of survivable escape routes available, so the cleansing really only winnows back the more mindless mals.

Of course, where a lot of the smarter ones retreat to is the graduation hall. If the machinery did run down there, then we'd very likely end up with all the mals cut down back to the nonexistent levels from the start of the year.

"Yeah," Orion said, glumly. Poor him: the greatest hero in generations and no evil monsters for him to fight. Precious made a dismissive squeak from her cup, but lucky for him, he wasn't in range for biting. At least he wasn't trying to complain of it to anyone but me, the one other person who had a decent reason to dislike the idea. If the mals did get cut back that far, the school would probably be able to funnel all of the attacks right back at me again.

But I wasn't going to commiserate with him out loud. I *was* in range, and I'd been bitten twice that week already. "Much difference it'll make if you get yourself turned into goo beforehand because you couldn't be arsed to do a few worksheets," I said. "It's thirteen seconds more to New Year's, and then you won't need to do any more classwork ever, unless you completely flunk everything. Do you need another helping?"

"No, I'm okay," he said, although he had to drag his eyes away from the power-sharer when I waved my wrist at him. "I've got enough, I just—got used to it, I guess." He shrugged away the misery of his lot with one shoulder, but he was still staring at the floor, and after a moment he brought out the real problem: "It's not like there're loads of mals in New York. In the enclave, I mean," he added. "Not much gets through."

I couldn't help myself. I blurted out, "No one's chaining you down in New York."

That was a nice and sympathetic thing to say to a boy who

wanted his mum and dad and his own bed as much as I did. But I'd been overwhelmed by an instant éclat of idyllic vision: the two of us wandering the world together, welcomed everywhere by everyone, him clearing out infestations and then watching my back while I put up Golden Stone enclaves with the power from the mals he took out.

You could say I was just offering him a different future, and I had as much right to put that future on the table for him as he did asking me to come to New York, only I didn't feel as though I did. I'd *like* to have felt that way; I'd have argued myself breathless and blue if anyone else had tried to tell me I didn't. But there wasn't any convenient opponent around to be argued with, and on the inside of my own head, I didn't really believe I had any right to ask Orion Lake to walk away from a future of safety and ease in the most powerful enclave in the world, just to spend his life as an itinerant bodyguard at my heels.

And even if I could squash that particular squidgy feeling, my vision would still mean asking him to walk away from his family and everyone he knew. He wasn't saying he didn't want to *go home*, he was saying he didn't like the idea of spending the rest of his life having to go begging to Magnus Tebow every time he wanted a cup of mana. I wouldn't have liked asking Magnus Tebow for pocket lint. I felt like a selfish beast as soon as the words came out of my mouth.

"If you just set up shop, you'll get booked to come out and kill the worst mals the world over," I added, as if that was all I'd meant. "Orion Lake: Maleficaria Hunter for Hire, no mal too large, some too small."

He huffed a noise that aimed for laughter and stopped at a sigh. "Am I a jerk?" he asked abruptly. "Everyone always acts like—" He made a frustrated wave of his hand in the direction of the legions of his fan club. "But I know that's just . . ."

He was being about as articulate as, well, the average seventeen-year-old boy, but I understood him perfectly. He'd been trained to think he was only good if he ran around being a hero all the time. Naturally as soon as he dared think about what *he* might want, surely that made him a monster. But as someone who's been told she's a monster from almost all corners from quite early on, I know perfectly well the only sensible thing to do when self-doubt creeps into your own head is to repress it with great violence. "What do I look like, your confessor?" I said bracingly. "Go and do your homework so I don't have to cobble you back together out of spare parts, and have your existential crisis another time."

"Thanks, El, you're such a pal," he said, in tones of deep syrupy affection.

"I am, aren't I," I said, and left him to it. And then I went to my room and didn't do any of my own homework. Instead I spent the entire time reading the Golden Stone sutras and translating more bits of it and doodling stick pictures of tidy little enclaves in my notes. Precious scampered around the desk messing my pens about and cracking sunflower seeds out of her food bowl and occasionally coming to inspect my work. She didn't approve of the bit where I scribbled in a little stick figure with a sword killing mals; when I looked away, she slipped under my arm and deposited a dropping in exactly the right spot so I put my hand right down on it when I started writing again and squished it over my own artwork.

"It's not like he's any use in an enclave," I muttered while I poured half my jug out over my besmirched hand, scrubbing it clean over the room drain. "I expect he'd *rather* come round the world hunting mals with me."

But of course she was right; it was an unbelievably stupid thing to be thinking about. There were very good odds that at least one of the small handful of people in the world that I loved only had months left to live, and that one might well be me if I let myself get distracted. I'd lectured Orion about neglecting his work, but at least his hunting was to some reasonable immediate end: he actually got mana out of it, and every mal he killed in the corridors would be one less jumping at our heads at graduation time. But I wasn't going to be building any enclaves until *after* I got myself and everyone I cared about through the doors, so I could stop wasting my time on the idea right now.

Go on, ask me how much time I wasted on it before the end of the semester. Or don't; I don't really want to do the gruesome tally of the hours I poured down that drain. The school rubbed it in for me well enough on New Year's Day. The whole day was screwed on the wrong way from the very beginning: the night before I fell asleep still reading the sutras—I was starting to be able to get a vague general understanding of a new page just by sounding it out a few times—and when I woke up, they were still open on my bed. I made the mistake of looking at the page again and started sounding it out from the beginning. It felt as though it had become easier overnight; it was amazing. Half an hour and two paragraphs later, I noticed what I was doing, and had to run unwashed to catch up the last few stragglers and get into the very tail end of the senior queue for the cafeteria line. All I got for breakfast was a scanty bowl of the dried-out scrapings from the sides of the porridge vat.

"You could have bitten me *usefully* for once," I told Precious as I came out with my unpleasantly light tray. She ignored me to keep gnawing on the dry heel of the loaf I'd scrounged for her, and only squeaked a complaint when I jumped a mile because the food service door slammed shut behind me: I had literally been the last senior to get breakfast.

That wasn't nearly the end of it. Sudarat was queueing up along the wall with the other freshmen waiting for their turn to come, and as I passed her, she said to me, "Congratulations, El," like she meant it.

"What?" I said. She pointed at the class standings, which had been posted up in gold letters under our class year on the big placard on the wall. I hadn't bothered to look at them yet, since I didn't really care which one of the twenty snarling beasts who'd been fighting it down to the wire had actually made valedictorian, and I knew I wasn't anywhere near the top hundred myself.

Well, I was right about that bit; I wasn't near the top hundred. My name was listed well above everyone else—next to ALGERNON DANDRIDGE SINNET PRIZE FOR SPECIAL ACHIEVEMENT IN SANSKRIT INCANTATION. I didn't even know there *were* prizes to be awarded; I've never seen anyone get one before.

And before you ask, yes, there was an actual prize. I slunk over to the table with my allies, who could now all see in bright gilt letters just how much time I'd been frittering stupidly away, and when I put down my tray, it didn't lie flat. Obviously I said, "Look out, clinger on my tray," and jumped back from the table along with everyone else except Orion.

He promptly reached out a finger and zapped my entire tray with one of his stupid but highly effective lightning-bolt spells, charring the already inedible porridge into a solid cinder, and then he frowned and said, "No there isn't," and tipped the still-smoking tray up to reveal that what was making it lie askew was my award: a small round medal stamped out of some dull grey metal, hanging from a blue-and-green-striped ribbon with a top bar pin, apparently designed to be worn on a lapel along with my other military honors. It was only lightly singed.

"Oh, that's really cool, El, congrats," Chloe said, in all apparent seriousness. She wasn't even a freshman.

I dangled the thing out to Aadhya without dignifying that with a response. "Is it worth melting down?"

Aadhya picked it up with both hands and rubbed her thumbs over the front surface, murmuring a quick artificer's testing charm. The little relief carving—possibly meant to be Ganesh; the nose looked vaguely elephantine—glowed pink for a moment, and she shook her head, handing it back. "It's just pewter."

"Congratulations, Galadriel," Liesel said to me a little coldly—she had in fact bagged valedictorian—when she went by the table a few minutes later. But what she meant was *fuck you.* At least that was fair enough; if I'd spent all that time cooing at enclaver boys and doing their homework, I'd have wanted to stab anyone who'd got their name jumped up over mine for a single seminar. But I wasn't going to be sorry for her. She was walking away from breakfast with Magnus, and she'd scored her first points with him by carrying tales of me. I suppose she'd decided to make New York her target. I wouldn't have gone for it at the price of courting Magnus, but she obviously had a higher tolerance for soggy dishcloths than I did.

A *lot* higher, in fact. I came down from the cafeteria late, because Zheng ran over to me while Min held his place in the freshman queue, and told me that he and the other kids from the library seminar would try and get me something when their turn came. You rarely manage to get much more than you want as a freshman—the opposite, in fact—and that was even before the survival rate in the Scholomance rose to

Orion Lake levels. But across the eight of them, they were able to rustle up a bread roll and a carton of milk, so at least I wouldn't lose our whole free morning light-headed as well as irritated.

It was worth waiting for them, but by the time I finished, the first early warning chimes were going off delicately, *ding dong death by fire coming,* to remind anyone who'd missed it that the cleansing was about to get under way. I made a dash to the girls' to get my teeth brushed and my face washed, so I wouldn't be grotty for hours, and stopped short in the doorway aghast: Liesel was in there doing her makeup.

The use of cosmetic in here is roughly as high as it was in my first year of primary school. However low the odds that you make a mistake when mixing up your lipstick in the alchemy lab and melt half your face off, they're still too high for most people. If you're good enough to be sure you won't, you're good enough to get an alliance in a more reliable way. Dating doesn't guarantee you an alliance any more than friendship does. But nevertheless here Liesel was, putting shiny pink lip gloss on her valedictorian mouth and dabbing a bit of it as color onto her cheeks. She'd already taken her hair out of the tight short plaits she always wore and had shaken the blond waves over her shoulders. She'd put on a crisp white blouse, actually ironed, and she'd unbuttoned it just far enough to leave a decent bit of cleavage showing, with a gold pendant hung round her neck. She would have looked nice enough for a date outside; in here, by comparison with our usual state, she might as well have stepped off the cover of *Vogue* to dazzle ordinary mortals.

I have to confess, I reacted atrociously. "Not *Tebow*," I blurted, from the door.

Her shiny lips pressed into a thin line. "Lake seems quite

THE LAST GRADUATE ✦ 165

busy," she said, through her teeth, and I couldn't even say anything to that under the circumstances; she had every right to
be as angry with me as she was. Maybe she *wanted* to shag
Magnus, who was after all heading for six feet and would
himself have not looked out of place in—well, an Argos catalog, or at least a pound-shop flyer.

Yes, *maybe,* but my imagination has limits and that's beyond them. So I didn't even leave bad enough alone; I said,
"Look, it's no business of mine," which coming out of my
own mouth should have been a strong hint to me to stop
there, but instead I went on, "but you should know, they've
already offered me a guarantee."

In my defense, that piece of information probably did matter a great deal to her. Even if Magnus Tebow was her ideal
of manhood and charisma, she'd made bleeding valedictorian with three and a half years of brutal unrelenting work,
and she couldn't have wanted to throw that away on someone who couldn't even offer her a guaranteed spot in an enclave. New York had too many eager applicants, most of
them proven wizards who'd left school years ago and done
significant work; there wasn't any way they were letting their
kids give out more than one guaranteed place in a year to a
raw eighteen-year-old, and Chloe had made anxiously clear
at every opportunity I gave her that the spot was being *held*
for me. Even if I didn't ever take it up, that didn't mean that
Liesel would get invited after the fact.

Of course, it wouldn't have said much for her brains if she
wasn't smart enough to make sure that she was getting a
guaranteed spot *before* she unbuttoned her blouse the rest of
the way, so even if I was handing her useful information,
there was an implied insult going along with it. She took it
accordingly. "How nice for you," she said, even more furious,

closed her lip gloss with a snap, swept the handful of jars and things on the counter back into her washbag, and marched out of the loo without looking back.

"Well done," I told myself in the mirror around my toothbrush. I had to rush now, since the first warning bell was going, so I scrubbed my teeth as quick as I could before dashing back out into the corridor, where I skidded right off my heels and smashed my head backwards onto the floor. Liesel had poured out the rest of her hard-brewed lip gloss into a puddle just outside the door, enough of a sacrifice to cast a clever little *trip the next person who comes along* hex. I knew what had happened even while I was on the way down: the moment I'd stepped on the slick patch, I'd felt the malicious intent of the spell, only it was too late for me to do anything about it.

I did manage to twist a bit falling, which either helped or made things worse, I don't know. I didn't die and I wasn't knocked unconscious, I don't think, but it was certainly bad enough. My whole head was a church bell someone had clanged back and forth with too much enthusiasm, and my elbow and hips would have been in screaming pain if screaming out loud wasn't the equivalent of shouting, *Dinner is served!* to every mal in hearing range. Instead I curled into a ball like a child and shut my mouth tight over stifled high-pitched sobbing, both my hands wrapped around the throbbing back of my skull and my whole face screwed up with tears.

I didn't move from there for much too long. The second warning bell went off somewhere behind a distant mountain range, and only the certain knowledge that I was about to be incinerated got me into motion. I levered myself onto my hands and knees and started lurching down the corridor in a three-legged crawl, still pressing down on the back of my skull with the hand that had got banged. Of course I should have pulled myself together and taken some kind of remedy, but at the time, I was still completely sure on some visceral level that I was keeping my brain from falling out of the back of my head.

Somewhere behind and above me, I heard a door bang shut loudly and footsteps coming, along the metal walkway and down the spiral stairs and into the corridor. I kept on creeping along, too slow but moving. I knew it wasn't anybody I knew, and then I knew it was Liesel, but I still kept crawling because I couldn't do anything else yet. Then she caught up and grabbed me under the arms and heaved me standing. Her face was still angry and flushed under the pink shimmer, but what she said, harshly, was, "Where is your room?" and she helped me limping on towards it.

We got about halfway before the final warning siren went off, and as it did, the door three down from where we were slid open and Orion came out. He froze like a deer caught stealing hubcaps in the headlamps of a police car, then noticed that I was there to fall down in front of a wall of mortal flame and die rather than to yell at him. Not that I didn't do my best to combine the activities as he grabbed me under the other arm, but he ignored the violent wheeze I aimed in his direction and helped Liesel get me into his room just as the loud crackling went off behind us, accompanied by the first panicked scrabbling of mals starting to run. Orion paused in the door to throw a last longing look down the corridor, then slid it shut with an unhappy bang as Liesel heaved me onto the bed.

"What happened?" Orion asked, coming over.

"She fell coming out of the bathroom," Liesel said shortly.

I didn't fill in the additional details. Knowing she got furious enough to commit murder but also couldn't go through with it in the end gave me rather a fellow feeling for her. "Give me a glass of water," I muttered, and when Orion gave it to me, I took a few deep breaths to temporarily keep from vomiting and then sat up and cast the simplest of my mum's healing charms on the water. Then I took out the little plastic bottle I keep on hand for exciting emergencies like this one, downed it, and drank the whole glass of water as fast as I could. I managed to keep it down for a count of fifteen, and then I lurched over to the floor drain and did vomit, energetically. Afterwards I rolled away and curled on my other side with a groan, but it was a conscious protest, not whimpering; I was already better.

"What is that?" Liesel said, picking up the bottle from where I'd dropped it, and giving it a wary sniff.

"Tabasco and butterscotch," I said. That isn't actually part of Mum's charm; it's my own addition, of which I'm sure she'd disapprove quite a lot, but something about forcing the horrible mixture down makes the healing charm work lots quicker. I think there's even some kind of science behind that, worse-tasting medicine works better or whatever, but it might just be the mana from deliberately making myself swallow something that awful. It doesn't actually have to be Tabasco and butterscotch, it just has to be absolutely vile and yet still technically edible, so you don't waste the healing charm on being poisoned.

Anyway, after that I wasn't concussed or in howling pain anymore, but I still felt extremely sorry for myself. I climbed back onto Orion's bed and just lay there for a bit to recover. Liesel started talking to Orion like a normal and civilized person, getting back only mumbled and distracted answers. "If he tries to open the door, brain him with the chair," I muttered after the third time.

"I'm not going to open the door," Orion said sulkily.

"Shut up, you lunatic, you'd absolutely open the door," I said. "What if the wall down by Aadhya's had gone this time?"

"I'd just—have come back here," Orion said, as if it were that simple to deal with being caught between two walls of mortal flame sweeping towards each other, each with a lead-ing wave of frenzied mals, and no exit anywhere in between. Nobody would open the door in a cleansing, not even if they heard Orion Lake or for that matter their own mum calling on the other side. Anybody stupid enough to do that died during freshman year when they *did* open the door and got eaten by the myna grabber on the other side. "I wasn't plan-ning to go anywhere."

I opened my eyes to glare at him. "That just means you didn't have a *plan,* not that you weren't *going.*"

He scowled at me and stomped off to his desk and pre-tended he was working on something in a notebook. Liesel made a faint snort and sat down on the bed in an open spot near my midsection. I eyed her. "What?"

She looked at me pointedly, but I still didn't follow until she said, "And *your* room?" and I realized she thought Orion had actually been planning to creep down the corridor to spend the day with me. I was about to explain that Orion wasn't enough of a moron to risk going out in a cleansing to spend the day sitting in my room getting yelled at for having gone out in a cleansing, he was in fact much *more* of a moron, only then it occurred to me that she was half right: if he had got caught between two walls of flame before reaching the main stairs, he would indeed have come and banged on my door for safety. And yes, I'm stupid enough that I would have opened it when he banged, even if I'd have kept a jar of left-over etching acid handy. Which meant spending the day with me had been his *backup* plan.

I even got confirmation: he was sitting with his back to us, but he'd got his hair buzzed lately at my insistence—let's not talk about the state it had got into—and the tops of his ears were visible and bright red.

"Lake, if you've ever for a second entertained a lurid fantasy that you might possibly have it off on some occasion and that I might in any way be involved, I want you to erase even the memory of having the thought from your brain," I said deeply and earnestly.

"El!" he squalled in protest, turning to dart a mortified look at Liesel. But it was nothing more than he deserved.

Anyway, so that was loads of fun, spending the day in Orion's room with him and the girl who'd tried to kill me. Actually, Liesel was all right. She and I ended up playing card games; she had a deck of tarot cards she'd made herself that she carried around with her, and she taught me canasta using all the major arcana as jokers. She got a bit narrow-eyed when I kept getting the Tower and Death, but it wasn't my fault; she was the one carrying them around and imbuing them with divinatory power.

Orion joined us a couple of times, but he kept getting distracted and going to the door to listen to the crackling as the wall rolled back and forth through the hall. On New Year's they go several times, which in theory and not in practice makes up for the reduced number. We did hear the dying shrieks of mals a few times, and there was a scrabble at the drain at one point that made him jump up hopefully and scatter the cards all over, but it didn't come through even when the mad muppet actually pulled off the drain cover and stuck his head close to peer inside it.

Liesel flinched away from him with her expression somewhere between horrified and just disgusted. I took the chance to scoop all the cards back into a facedown pile before she noticed that the Tower *and* Death had both landed faceup in my lap that time, along with the Eight of Swords, which in Liesel's illustration was a woman sitting cross-legged and blindfolded half caught in a thicket of eight massive silver thorns in a circle pointing in at her. How encouraging.

"Why don't you try putting out milk?" I said to Orion snidely. That technique did actually work in the olden days, when there were more minor mals that don't need much mana to survive, and more mundanes who sincerely believed in them and were therefore vulnerable to them. If you deliberately put out a bowl of milk for the little people, or whatever equivalent gesture, they'd come and suck up the tiny bit of mana that came from your intent, and then they'd leave your house alone in order to preserve the regular supply. But most of those mals are gone now; they got eaten up by more powerful mals who consider a mundane person the equivalent of an already open packet left on the side of the road with suspicious stains and two stale crisps in it.

Orion didn't bother looking abashed. He just sighed and put the drain cover back on and slunk back to the game, for lack of anything better to kill than time, but he didn't even notice that I didn't deal him in for the new round. Liesel and I played several more games, until the sixth time I turned over the Tower, and she grabbed it out of my hand and shook it in my face. "You are cheating!"

"Why *would* I?" I snapped at her. "Just take it out of play if you're going to be so fussed about it."

"I *did*!" she snapped back, and grabbed her case and opened it up in front of me to display its entirely empty innards to us both, and after staring into it for a moment, she collected up all the other cards and put them into the case and stashed it away in her pocket without saying another word.

After that it was awkward silence all round. I shoved aside

enough of Orion's dirty laundry to clear a rectangle of floor and did push-ups for mana, spiced up by the faint throbbing still going in my head. I was tired and sore and hungry enough that the exercise was highly productive as long as I could do it, but I ran out of steam sooner than I ran out of time and then I just flopped myself back onto Orion's bed and lay there even more tired and sore and hungry and now sweaty, too. Liesel was sitting at Orion's desk working on something, which I only realized was *his* work when he did and said, "Hey, you don't have to . . ." in the most halfhearted way those words had been spoken ever.

"I have nothing else to do now," Liesel said. "Later you can pay me back."

"He's guarding the room, isn't he?" I said.

Liesel shrugged. "He's here, too. It doesn't count." I rather thought it did, since he didn't want to be in here and would have gone like a shot if we hadn't been here, but I was the only one arguing his case. She added to him, "I will need amphisbaena scales."

"Oh, sure, no problem," Orion said, very enthusiastically. I scowled at him across the room, but I didn't have a leg to stand on even metaphorically; that was a completely reasonable trade for someone doing your homework, and even if you thought it was in some way his duty to go hunt down amphisbaena for nothing, which I didn't, that still wouldn't mean he wasn't entitled to get something back for taking the trouble to collect the scales.

Anyway he probably *wouldn't* hunt amphisbaena for nothing; they're only slightly more dangerous to us than the agglos, which they eat. Their worst quality is every decade or so enough of their predators get wiped out in a cleansing, and then the amphisbaena lay a bumper crop of tiny rubbery eggs in nice warm damp spots like for instance around the hot-water pipes, and when they hatch shortly after New Year's, the babies pour out of the taps and the showerheads in droves, both heads hissing and biting. Which you'd justifiably say is in fact nightmarishly bad, but the poison isn't strong enough to do more than sting at that stage, and it doesn't get stronger until they're big enough that they don't fit through anymore. You just hear them stuck in there and hissing as you wash and hope very hard that the showerhead doesn't break off today.

There almost certainly *would* be an infestation this year, now I thought about it. I'd have to pass the word, and also spend some of my crochet time making mesh bags to put on the showerheads. Liesel must have seen it coming a while ago and worked up a strategy using what was about to become an abundant resource; clever of her. Even more clever to take advantage of a golden opportunity to have Orion do the harvesting, in exchange for her doing the remedial homework she would probably knock off in the next two hours.

I sulked on the bed in completely unjustified resentment while she motored through the entire stack of worksheets with about as much effort as it was taking me to lie there. The only thing that slowed her down even a little were the places where Orion had dripped food and/or maleficaria innards on some of the questions, and she had to get him to help her reconstruct what the unspattered words had been. Actually I overestimated vastly: it took her thirty-eight minutes, and that includes the time she spent sorting it neatly into deadline order and putting it into a pair of folders for him and also tidying up absolutely everywhere.

I veered from being annoyed at her to being annoyed at Orion when he received the folders and just perfunctorily put them on the side of his desk and said, "Great, thanks. How many scales do you need?" It wasn't effusive enough for *me,* much less by American standards.

"What Lake means is, he's pathetically grateful that he doesn't have to spend the last six months of term dodging vats of strong acid because he couldn't be arsed to do his own homework," I said peevishly.

Liesel just shrugged with all the weariness of a veteran of the wars—I suppose she'd worked her way through the entire time doing homework for enclavers—and said to Orion, "Can you get thirty hides? I need them at least two weeks old."

"Sure," Orion said blithely, and I didn't literally gnash my teeth because no one does, do they, but I *felt* as if I were gnashing my teeth. With no justification in the slightest. Liesel had made a good deal for her, and so had Orion, and for that matter it was good for *me,* too, because I wouldn't have to keep saving his thick plank self all the time. I didn't even need to be worried that he was neglecting something important that would come back to bite him the way neglected assignments usually did. He didn't *need* to practice his alchemy, either to graduate or for any other reason; he didn't have any special affinity for it as far as I'd ever seen. I didn't even know why he'd done alchemy track in the first place. New York surely had all its lab space packed with geniuses; he wasn't going to graduate and go be a modestly competent alchemist the rest of his life.

It annoyed me more and not less because I didn't have a good reason for being annoyed. I couldn't even come up with anything to say about it. If I'd tried to put into words what I was feeling, it would have been something unpleasant and envious and whinging like *Why should you get to make easy deals that suit you perfectly to get out of the things you don't like* with the strong implication of *when I never do,* which wasn't even true anymore since I had a New York power-sharer on my wrist.

So I didn't put it into words; I just lay curled on his bed in an unpleasant stew of cooled sweat and resentment while they discussed their happy arrangement. Orion even stopped being so distracted: even if the mals *did* get purged back, Liesel had just cleared his slate completely of anything but hunting and eating and sleep, with the last two as optional as he wanted them to be. She even offered to help him brew up some amphisbaena bait.

The one thing I wasn't, at all, was jealous. I was so far from it actually that I didn't even think about being jealous until Liesel shot *me* an exasperated look and I realized that she'd very much have liked to make me jealous, and would have had a strong go at it if the field had been the least bit open. I couldn't blame her. She wanted that guaranteed spot in New York enough to have seriously contemplated both Magnus Tebow and murder for it; I certainly ranked Orion higher than those alternatives. If he had so much as taken a first glance at her cleavage, she'd have been a plonker not to make sure he got a second.

But he hadn't, and when I realized he hadn't, I started to feel more than a bit panicky, because he hadn't any excuse not to be taking a first glance. I'm only mildly motivated in that direction myself and I absolutely *had* taken both a first and a second glance at the cleavage and the bouncy golden curls and shiny pink lips. I think anyone who wasn't really impervious would have. If you haven't eaten anything but tasteless slop in years and suddenly someone offers you a slice of chocolate cake, so what if you don't especially like chocolate cake; if you were interested in food at all, you'd at least think it over before you said *no thanks.*

Orion had no business saying *no thanks*. I was fairly confident he *did* like cake, or at least was quite ready to give it a try, and he wasn't getting a bite off my plate if I had anything to say about it, which I did. He ought to have at least licked his chops, even if he didn't want to dive in, and instead he didn't so much as drop his eyes for a peek. He wasn't a good enough actor to have been faking it, either.

Which irritated Liesel, understandably. It was like the homework; that much bloody effort deserved a smidge of appreciation. So when the all-clear bell rang, she said stiffly, "I will be going to my room now," and cleared out before I had a chance to jump on the bandwagon and leave with her.

"I'll be going too," I said in a hurry, swinging my legs over the side of the bed, and Orion came over and said, "Are you sure you're okay?" a little wistfully and then had the unmitigated nerve to have a quick peek at *my* breasts, which were currently under a second-day top marred with alchemy stains and soot, with the sawn-off ends of my hair obscuring the view.

"I'm fine," I said sharply.

"I'll walk you back to your room," he said.

I should just have let him; Precious was in my room. Instead I said, "I don't need help going nine doors down, Lake," and then my stomach growled and he said, "And you threw up your whole breakfast, you need to eat something," and jumped to grab me a sealed muesli bar only eight years past its best that he must have been gifted by some adoring fan. It wasn't cake maybe, but by Scholomance standards it still qualified as haute cuisine. I stupidly took it and stupidly sat there on the bed eating it—so stupidly that I have the bad feeling I did it on purpose—and obviously he sat down on the bed next to me. He tentatively crept his arm round my shoulders when he thought I wasn't paying attention, and I pretended I wasn't paying attention, and then he said in a faintly hopeful voice, "El," and I told myself to shove him off the bed.

I didn't. In fact, mortifyingly I kissed him first, and then it was all up, because I'm starving, and I *do* like cake, and after I'd taken the first bite I wanted another, and another after that, and I put my hands under his shirt to press them flat against his warm bare back, and it was so good to be this close to someone, only it wasn't just *someone*, it was *Orion*, and he shivered all over and put his arms around me and I could feel how strong he was, the muscles moving under his skin that he'd built over years of fighting all the very worst things that come out of the dark. His mouth was all warm and wonderful and I can't even describe how good it felt and how much better it made everything. I was one of those poor stupid freshmen longing inside the gymnasium fantasia I'd made, only this was real and I could really have it, inside and after we graduated and *forever*, and the rest of my dream along with it—a life of building and creation and good work, and every prophecy of evil and destruction could go fuck right off and I could start the rest of my life right now, and I *wanted* to, so much I couldn't stop, couldn't want to stop.

So I didn't. I just kept kissing him and running my hands all over him and breathing in time with him, our foreheads pressed together making a warm private space between us to catch our breath in, full of gasps. Orion had a hand all tangled up in my hair, moving around like he wanted to feel the strands running over his fingers, tightening his grip and relaxing in small bursts, his own breath coming out in hard panting raspy gulps, and it felt so good I laughed a little into that open space between us and reached down to grab the bottom of his shirt.

He gave a convulsive shudder and jerked back, pushing me

to arm's length, and crackled out, "No, we can't," in a rawly agonized way.

I've been mortified in all sorts of awful ways in the course of my life, but I think that might possibly have been the worst. It wasn't because he didn't want to; that would've been all right. But he wanted to just as much as I did, and he'd nevertheless managed to stop himself, and I *hadn't*, like some undisciplined yahoo grabbing at the shiny treat that I knew perfectly well would lead to complete disaster. He even heaved himself off the bed in the next moment, all but levitating to the other side of the room.

"Right you are," I said, and fired myself out the door and into the still-lightly-toasted corridor at once.

Precious was right on the other side of my door when I shot it open, so frantic she was leaping almost as high as my waist. I caught her right out of the air and said furiously, "Will you stop? Nothing *happened*, no thanks to you."

I slammed the door hard behind me and slumped onto my bed. Precious crept up my arm to my shoulder and sat there silently until I finally admitted, "No thanks to *me*, either," as bitter as rotten squash. She crept closer to my ear and rubbed the lobe with the tip of her little nose and made a few comforting squeaks as I put up my hands to rub away a few leaking tears.

Chapter 7
ALLIANCE

Orion didn't even have the bare decency to avoid me the rest of the day. In fact, he spent all of lunchtime casting pathetic looks of desperation and longing in my direction, exactly as though I'd been the one who'd fired him up only to cruelly leave him hanging. Nobody made a peep about it in my direction, but I could tell they all assumed that I had done just that. When I complained to Aadhya about it that afternoon, she told me—with a total lack of sympathy— that no one was spending that much time thinking about my love life, but what did she know?

"You should just be grateful he saved you from yourself, anyway!" she added.

I glared at her. "And *who* was just asking me for all the salacious details?"

"That doesn't mean I wouldn't have thrown a bucket of cold water on your head if I'd been in range. What were you thinking? Do you even know when your last period was?"

I really couldn't argue with her especially since no, I had no idea when my last period was or when the next one was due. Thankfully, that's one thing magic is good for; whenever the first signs show up, you brew yourself a cup of nice go-the-fuck-away tea—an easy alchemical recipe every wizard girl can brew in her sleep—and that's the end of it. Some of us do have to keep a sharp eye on the timing, because theirs starts with blood spotting, and you don't want mals to get a whiff of that. But my first symptom is a nice sharp whanging cramp in the midsection, completely unmistakable, and it arrives with a good five hours' warning.

Unfortunately, one thing magic is *not* good for is avoiding pregnancy. The problem is, if you deliberately do something that you are conscious and deeply terrified might cause pregnancy, the magical intent gets confused. Protective spells are about as reliable as the withdrawal method. Science is much more reliable, but then you have to either invest some of your very limited induction weight allowance to bring in condoms or pills and then use them properly, or get an implant or an IUD before you get inducted and cross your fingers that nothing goes wrong with it over the four years you're hopefully going to be in here before you next get to see a gynecologist. I didn't see the point. Or rather, I hadn't seen the point four years ago, when I'd been reasonably sure no one was going to talk to me, much less date me.

"It's just—" I stopped squabbling and sat down on the floor of her room in a thump and said, "It was just so *nice*," and maybe that sounds stupid but I couldn't help my voice wobbling. Nice was what we didn't have in here. You could manage desperate victories and even dazzling wonders sometimes, but not anything *nice*.

Aadhya sighed out a long deep breath. "Well, forget it. *I'm* not getting eaten by a maw-mouth because you got yourself knocked up." I sat up with my mouth open in low-blow outrage, but Aadhya just looked at me hard-faced and serious, and she was *right;* of course she was right. I'd already been screwing around excessively without making it literal, and if I kept on, I'd very likely end up with something even less helpful than a pewter medal.

We didn't know what we were going to find when we got down to the graduation hall, and in some ways that was worse than knowing it was going to be the same terrible horde of mals that seniors had faced every year for a hundred years and more. We couldn't even guess based on the early accounts of the days when the cleansings had been running, because the school had been brand-new then, and the only mals had been the first squirming pioneers to find their way through the wards. Now there were century-old infestations and colonies buried deep in dark corners, ancient maleficaria rooted into the foundations, generations who'd never lived outside the machinery. Maybe there had been enough survivors of the cleansings to start a sudden population explosion in the available space, like the oncoming wave of amphisbaena, and we'd be dumped into a ravening horde of recently hatched and starving mals, so many of them and so small that most of our strategies wouldn't apply, just like that horrible mass we'd accidentally lured with Liu's honeypot spell only ten thousand times worse.

Or maybe they'd all be dead. Maybe they'd eaten each other all the way down the food chain, and there would be no maleficaria left except Patience and Fortitude themselves, guardians on either side of the gates, and they'd have nothing left on the menu except us.

If that's what we found down there—I had no idea what I'd do. There was an obvious and sensible thing to do, which was to pass the word to our entire graduating class in advance that if it was us against the maw-mouths, they'd all make one enormous circle and feed me mana, and I'd try to take them out. But just because that was obvious and sensible didn't mean I was going to do it. I had killed a maw-mouth the only way you could, from the inside out, and if I tried to think even in a very vague distant way about doing it again, a faint incoherent screaming started up inside me that took up all the room there was in my brain, like standing next to a fire truck with siren wailing while someone tried to talk to you, their mouth moving with no sound at all coming through because the whole world was full of noise.

Maybe I'd get over it if I saw the maw-mouths coming and there wasn't any other choice. Maybe. I wasn't at all confident, for all I was about to have six months of honing my reflexes to razor sharpness. It wasn't the same. It wasn't remotely the same. Having to choose to go inside again—I don't know if it's a choice anyone could make more than once. There certainly haven't been many people who've had the chance to consider it. If I do make it out of here, I should look up the Dominus of Shanghai. He's the only other living person who's ever done it. We could compare notes. Or we could look each other in the face and just start screaming together, which feels more appropriate to me.

Of course, it was extremely likely that it wouldn't work anyway. The maw-mouth I'd killed had been a small one, maybe budded off one of the big ones or however they spawn—no one's spent much time studying the reproduction of maw-mouths as far as I know. It had managed to squeeze through the wards and make it upstairs. I don't know how many people had been inside it, how many lives; I'd been far beyond keeping count of the deaths I'd dealt out. But I did know that it hadn't been anywhere near as big as Fortitude, much less Patience, who's been lording it over the killing grounds almost since the hall first opened. I don't think even

I can do that much killing. The only way they're going is if the whole school goes.

The point being that we still needed a better strategy for graduation than *Wait and see if El can keep her big-girl pants on,* and here I was whinging on about how *nice* it would be for me to do something unbelievably stupid instead, like Orion. Aadhya had every right to cram my face in it.

"Sorry," I muttered. She just nodded, which was kinder than I deserved, really, and then said, businesslike, "So I think I've figured out a good gym schedule," and rolled out a timetable for me to look at.

After New Year's, half of the gym gets cordoned off exclusively for the seniors, and every week, it lays out a fresh new obstacle course for us, so we can get as much practice as possible running flat-out through forests of sharp things trying to kill us. It's excellently realistic, full of artificial constructs pretending to be mals, and also the many real mals who show up helpfully to populate it. It's a testament to our top-quality educational experience how few of us die. Please envision me saying this with my hand held piously over my heart. But really, we were all hitting our stride by now. There isn't anything much more dangerous in the world than a fully grown wizard. That's why the mals have to hunt us when we're young. We're the real apex predators, not the maw-mouths that after all just sit by the doors mumbling to themselves and occasionally groping around for some supper. Once through the gates, we'll be carving our dreams into the world like gleeful vandals scratching graffiti on the pyramids, and we won't look behind us. But only once we're out.

Ordinarily the reserved gym is a useful and highly valued privilege. No one was very enthusiastic about it this year, but there wasn't any other option for practice. The fundamental goal of graduation is to get from the nearest stairwell to the gates as fast as possible without getting stopped along the way. It's roughly a distance of 150 meters, about the same distance as from one end of the gym and back, and aside from throwing spells left and right, you also have to *run*.

"Mornings?" I said, in protest, because Aadhya had us meeting three times a week at eight, which meant hauling ourselves out of bed at the first quiet chiming to get breakfast and make it downstairs; we'd be first through all the corridors, not to mention—very important to mention—first into the obstacle course every week, without any warning how bad it was going to be.

"I talked to Ibrahim and Nkoyo today, during the cleansing," Aadhya said. "We made a deal. They'll go right behind us with their teams, on either side. We take the heat up front, and they keep us from getting flanked. We'll practice together each morning."

That kind of arrangement is normally a supremely terrible strategy for the lead group, to the point that you're explicitly warned against it in the pre-graduation handbook we'll all be getting in about three months—much too late to be of real use; we're all using copies we bought in our sophomore years off that year's seniors, who'd bought their own copies two years before, et cetera. The advice changes a little from year to year, but one of the most consistent points is that taking the lead is absolutely not worth whatever advantage you might get from the groups covering you. As soon as you're in any danger of being overwhelmed, they'll hop to one side and let whatever they're holding off come at you, meaning that you won't even have a chance to recover, while they take the opening created by the pile-on and go sailing onwards with a substantial improvement to their odds, taken out of yours.

It's not great to be the one taking the lead even within an alliance, but at least in an alliance, you've been practicing together and integrating your skills tightly, so it's not actually a good idea for your allies to cut and run. Unless you're close enough to the doors, at which point loads of alliances do fall apart. And that, boys and girls, is why enclavers never take the lead.

Aadhya wasn't making a mistake, though. There's one situation where having someone covering you does in fact make excellent sense: if it's *never* going to be a good idea for them to ditch you. For instance, if all they've got is knives and your team's got a flamethrowing machine gun. So she was confirming that yes, our entire strategy was going to rest on my keeping my big-girl pants on. "Right," I said, grimly, because what else was I going to say? *No, don't rely on me? No, I won't do my best to get you to the gates, the way you've done for me?* Of course she was going to build the strategy around me. And of course I had to let her.

"El," Aadhya said, "you know we'd take Orion," and you might think that was a hilariously absurd thing to say—yes, out of the generous goodness of our hearts we'd take the invincible hero along with us—but I knew what she really meant. She was saying *Orion's not on our team,* and if I was, that meant I couldn't ditch them to go help him, even if, for instance, I looked over and saw him being dragged into the guts of a maw-mouth, screaming the way that Dad's been screaming in Mum's head since the day she crawled out through the gates with me in her belly. If that was the monstrous fate Mum had been trying to warn me away from, she'd know, she'd know the way no one else in the world would know just how horrible it would be to live with someone you love screaming in your head forever.

"I'll ask him," I said without lifting my head, pretending I

186 of NAOMI NOVIK

could still see anything when actually I had my eyes shut to keep from dripping on Aadhya's carefully written timetable. She put her hand on my shoulder, warm, and then she half put her arm around me, and I leaned into her a moment and then shook my head wildly and sucked in a big gulping breath, because I didn't want to get started. What was the point? I couldn't do anything about that, either.

I did ask him that night as we walked up to dinner, because I had to, just in case. He had the nerve to say, "El, you're going to be fine," in reassuring tones. "There's plenty of mana in the pool, I'll get more in now that there are more mals around, you've got Chloe and—"

"Shut *up*, you cartwheeling donkey," I snarled at him, and he recoiled and wobbled between baffled and offended for a moment, then said, sounding confused, "Wait, are you worried about—?" and just stopped to gawk at me as though the shadow of the idea that any living being might at any point entertain a fraction of concern for *his* health and well-being had never crept across the windowsill of his molluscular brain, and I ran up the rest of the flight of stairs away from him because it was that or punch him in his beaky nose, which I'd caught myself idly thinking just that morning across the table at breakfast had a hint of young Marlon Brando, which might convey to you the depths to which I was sinking if your mum thinks, like mine does, that the height of appropriate children's entertainment is antique movie musicals.

Aadhya and Liu and Chloe had gone on ahead, but I caught up to them before they actually went into the food line. "Thanks for holding a spot," I said, grabbing a tray, without saying how it'd gone, and Chloe bit her lip and Liu looked sorry and thank goodness Aadhya just said, "What do you guys think of asking Jowani?" and got us discussing the merits.

I could list them out for you. He had a really top-notch perimeter-warning spell, the kind you cast once and then it lingers for half an hour; his was notable because it worked off intent rather than physical presence, which meant it would warn you about incorporeal mals. He'd give us a solid personal connection across our little trio of alliances, because Cora had teamed up with Ibrahim and Nadia and Yaakov. And boys are undeniably useful for heavy lifting; I was the closest thing to brawn on our team at the moment. The discrepancy hadn't seemed as significant at the start of the year, but lately it felt like all the senior boys were expanding up and out when we weren't looking, and they were suddenly doing things like toting an entire crate full of iron all the way across the shop under one arm.

You might think those all sound like minor advantages, and they were, relatively speaking. Everyone in the school could make themselves somewhat useful—that's what all of us have been doing all four years of this, finding ways to *make ourselves useful*. And now that everyone knew I was *very* useful, we could have cherrypicked ourselves one of the top kids. In fact, I suspected that at least two of the near-miss valedictorian candidates had made overtures of their own to Aadhya: I'd seen them stopping by her room.

None of us raised those objections. We all agreed that Jowani would be helpful and a good strategic addition to round out our team. But we didn't talk about why. We didn't say that we didn't want him to get left behind. Ever since Cora's arm, we'd all been eating together as a group almost every day, and each day at the start of breakfast, he would bring out a tiny book full of incredibly thin pages—one for each day of four years, I realized after the first few times—and he'd softly recite out loud a short poem or an excerpt of one that his dad had copied out by hand into the book, in one of a dozen languages, each one a piece full of love and hope: *have courage*. His voice reading them smoothed out even my most snarling mornings.

Before then, I'd never heard him emit more than a monosyllable. I'd always assumed that was dislike on his part, but actually it hadn't anything to do with me in the slightest. He had a stammer, which didn't trip him up when he recited poetry, and luckily also not when he was casting spells, but made it almost impossible for him to get out a word in conversation unless he really knew you. And that was why he'd held on to Nkoyo's social coattails past when that had stopped being a good idea, and why he was now having a lousy time of finding himself an alliance. And if he didn't get an alliance, he wasn't going to make it out.

We didn't say any of that to one another. You didn't, ever. Ibrahim and Yaakov and Nadia hadn't taken Cora because they remembered making the circle around her, mana flowing through us all like a river to heal her arm, a gift that hadn't cost anything but caring to give. They'd taken her because she and Nadia both knew how to dance spells—there's quite a lot of spells that get more powerful if you dance them along with the incantation—and were now working out a magical sword-dancing routine using blades that Yaakov was making; Ibrahim had scored a major matter-phasing spell to put on them from one of his other enclaver friends, who'd traded it to him on the cheap after putting together his own alliance, as apology for not asking him. That was a good solid fighting team, and they'd got offers from at least two or three enclavers to join up. That was why. You couldn't choose people because you liked them, or because you wanted them to live.

But we did scrape together good enough reasons to say yes to Jowani, and when we got to our table, Aadhya pulled him aside and asked him, and after that all three of our alliances were firmed up, and everyone agreed we'd go for the first run the very next morning. Even Orion. He was clearly not even bothering to think up any kind of plan for getting to the doors beyond *Kill things until there aren't any more,* but he overheard us discussing the merits or lack thereof for going first thing, and how we'd have to keep a sharp eye out for any *real* maleficaria that had crept into the gym overnight and hidden in the course. At which he perked up and said, "Oh hey, do you mind if I come down with you?" It will shock you to hear that nobody minded.

So we all trooped down after breakfast the next morning. I hadn't been back to the gym myself since Field Day. I was braced, but not enough. The place had got even worse. Some birdwitted freshmen—it could only have been freshmen— had replanted the big planters along the walls with seeds out of the alchemy supplies, and the spell machinery had worked them in, currently as hedges, so now you couldn't even tell where the walls met the floor, and it was an even more perfect illusion of being outdoors. The big trees in the distance had let their leaves fall, and there was a feathery dusting of snow on their wet dark branches, broken by the occasional red huddle of a tiny bird, and every delicate blade of the grass underfoot was crisp with frost. Our breath fogged.

"*What,*" Jowani said, and stopped there, which actually did pretty well to encapsulate all our feelings, I think.

Well, not *all* our feelings. "It's so nice, El," Orion said to me, almost dreamily, arms outstretched and his face turned up to the artful flurry that the sky allowed to fall to greet us. "I can't even tell we're not outside." I think he meant to be complimentary.

You could pick out the boundaries of the obstacle course with a good squint: there was a low wooden fence running down the halfway mark dividing the obstacle-course area off from the rest of the gym. But apart from that, the illusion artifice had integrated the obstacles fully into the environment: bristling thornbushes, trees with grabby-looking limbs, a steep hill covered with snow; a thin grey fog lying over a wide black slick of icy river ready to break into jagged shards and an ominous handful of ways to cross: a thin rickety board, a scattering of slippery rocks poking up above the ice, a healthier-looking narrow stone bridge that was undoubtedly the most dangerous option. If you looked up at the inside of the gym doors, they seemed to be two enormous iron gates set in the wall of a mysterious and alluring stone tower.

We'd already started wrong. The best way to use the obstacle course is to just throw yourself at it instantly, the first time you see it, without taking time to look it over. After you come out bruised and limping—assuming you do come out—that's when you go over all the things you did wrong, and try new things the rest of the week, and then the new course comes out on Monday and you do it all over again. And if you're lucky, every week you get better at doing it the first time, with no planning. You don't get any planning time at graduation. But in our defense: *What*.

"Let's get going before the next teams show up," I said. Then I realized that everyone else was waiting for *me*, which was both obvious and terrifying. I stared out at the perfectly lovely expanse of winter-touched wilderness. Any mals out there were in hiding, except for the faint dancing lights visible on the other side of the river, glowing in colors through the fog, exactly as if will-o'-wisps had moved in to take up residence, only those are largely decorative constructs and not much use for the purposes of practice. They might have been some variety of soul-eater, but real soul-eaters that close to one another would have merged into one very hungry soul-eater, so a pack of them wasn't much use for practice, either. But that would be useless in a more dangerous and unpleasant direction, and therefore more likely. The fake mals the course produces are very much like the ones that get put on display in Maleficaria Studies—just because they're not real doesn't mean they can't kill you, and sometimes the real ones sneak in and pretend to be fake just long enough to get hold of you. But we weren't doing ourselves any favors by waiting to find out which these were. I took a deep breath, nodded to Liu, who started playing the lute, and I sang out the mana-amplification spell in a slightly squeaky voice and ran straight in.

The snow burst open all around us before we were more than a stride away from the doors, jagged scything blades curving out with the tips lunging for our guts, and after that I couldn't tell you what order any of it came in. We had to cross the river both ways, both going and coming, but I don't remember whether I turned it to lava on the way out or the way back. We didn't actually make contact with the wall, since the gym illusion was trying very hard to convince us there wasn't one: when we got close, a sudden blizzard came howling into our faces with quavery ghost voices, telling us to turn back.

Actually the lava was definitely on the way in, because on our way back out, the obstacle course was still trying to reset around the lava spell, so instead the river fired geysers of superheated steam at us through cracks in the ice. One of them caught Yaakov's leg. He fervently yelled out what I'm absolutely sure were wild curses with every step the rest of the way back to the doors: he was usually such a nice, proper boy, carefully polite; it would've been funny under any other circumstances. But not here: it meant he was in the kind of desperate pain where all you can do is drop where you are and howl, and he couldn't do that, because he'd die. The instant he got out into the corridor, he did drop, and started trying to pull out a bandage to wrap around the blistering skin, still gasping curses under his breath with tears gathering in his eyes. His hands were shaking so hard he couldn't unroll it.

"You can't keep yelling!" Ibrahim snapped, even as he dropped to a knee next to him. He dragged his arm across his forehead—not very effective; each one smudged some streaks of blood on the other—and took the bandage out of Yaakov's hands to put it on for him.

"No," Liu said, panting; she was on her knees on the floor mostly draped around the long neck of the sirenspider lute. "No, it was all right. It went into the music. We should all yell, I think, or sing." She was better off than most of us; she'd been playing the whole way from inside the sheltered place at the center of our alliance.

Chloe was shivering with her eyes wide enough to be on the edge of shock, and she was fumbling out some bandages of her own; Jowani was helping her. Her whole right side— the exposed side—had been perforated with one too-close swipe from one of those clawing tree branches, blood and skin showing through open gaps in her clothes from her shoulder down to her thigh, the frayed edges stained dark. Aadhya had been bringing up the rear; she was standing with her arms wrapped around herself, her hands still clenched tight on the fighting-sticks she'd made for the run. I didn't see any wounds, but she looked pretty sick. I was just about to go to her when she pulled in a deep breath and then went to Liu to look at the lute and make sure it had stayed in tune.

Nkoyo's team had been hit by a spray of razor-blade-sized

THE LAST GRADUATE ✦ 193

slivers of sharpened ice and were all even bloodier than the rest of us, except for their resident enclaver, a boy named Khamis from Zanzibar, who'd been very firmly ensconced in the most protected spot in their team, at the center. He was an alchemist and armed only with a bandolier of spray bottles, one of which he was wielding right now on Nkoyo's slashed arm: the wound underneath was disappearing along with the blood as she wiped tears from her face.

All of us were freaked out and shaking, from a dozen near-death experiences crammed into the span of five minutes and also from the even worse knowledge that this was nothing, absolutely nothing. It was the first obstacle course on the first day after New Year's, it was warm-up material, and there was nowhere to go from here but a long steep road uphill all the way. Most of us were used to being jumped by mals, but there's a substantial difference between one attack and an unending stream of them. About half of us were crying, and the other half wanted to cry.

When I say *us*, what I mean is *them*. I felt fine. No; I felt like I'd woken up after a long sleep and had a good workout in the fresh air and a really nice stretch and was now contemplating with interest the idea of a hearty lunch. Sitting on edge in a classroom for hours surrounded by fluffy peeping freshmen waiting for one mal to pop out at me: nightmarish. Summoning a river of magma to instantly vaporize twenty-seven carefully designed attacks at once: nothing to it.

"Hey, that looked pretty good," Orion said encouragingly, coming to join us with a bounce in his step and the mangled corpse of something spiky dangling from his hand: he'd somehow managed to sniff out the one real mal hiding amidst the fakes. Normally every word out of his mouth automatically produces a burst of adulation, but everyone in our group had spent enough time sitting at meals with him for the shine to wear off a bit, and under the circumstances, they all glared at him with pure hatred. I'm fairly certain I saved him from bodily harm when I interrupted his attempt to dig himself a deeper grave—"I mean, you all made it okay"—and said, "Lake, what is that dead thing and why are you carrying it around?"

"Oh, it's—I don't know, actually," he said, lifting it up: it had a vaguely Doberman-sized body with dachshund legs and was covered with narrow cone-like spikes that had tiny holes at the tips. I had no idea what it was myself. Mals are always mutating, or being mutated, or new ones get made, et cetera. "The spikes put out some kind of gas. I didn't want to leave it out there; it was covered with snow and the gas blended into the fog. I thought somebody might step on it." Very thoughtful of him.

Other seniors were beginning to cautiously trickle down from breakfast by then. As we dragged ourselves off to lick our wounds both metaphorical and literal, I overheard someone asking Aadhya, "Hey, you're taking first run?" and she shrugged and said, "We're thinking about it," meaning that we were open to offers: at least one or two teams would be glad to bribe us to be the very first ones through the doors, so they could come down bright and early themselves and still know that someone else had already cleared the way. If we were going to do it anyway, we might as well get paid for it.

She negotiated the arrangement at lunchtime, with three alliances who wanted to share the time slot after us, and got us a promise of cleanup help from them, meaning we wouldn't have to waste our own healing and mending supplies. That was a good deal for us: helping us right after we slogged out meant they had to wait instead of starting their own runs before anyone else showed. They agreed because they had to wait anyway: the obstacle course took a good long while to finish resetting itself after we'd gone through.

Normally that process takes place in the time it takes for the doors to close on your heels and open up again. The runs aren't actually real. A thousand wizards all hurling their most powerful spells around three times a week would wreck the place almost instantly, and also if we were actually casting our most powerful spells, we wouldn't have enough mana for graduation, our works of artifice would get worn out, our potions would get used up, et cetera. So instead the obstacle-course magic fades everything out: when you cast spells inside, it feels the same, but you're only casting half of one percent of a spell, and the course fakes the reaction so it's as if you've cast the full thing. You think you're taking a big swallow of potion, but it's being diluted down; you think you're using a piece of artifice, but it's wrapped in a traveling-protection spell. And when you come out, swish, everything goes back to normal—except for any injuries you've picked up, those are entirely persistent, the better to encourage rapid improvement—and the next round of eager seniors gets to go in.

And all of that works because we voluntarily enter the course: consent is the only way for someone else's magic to get at your mana and your brain on that level. Well, except for violence. There's always violence.

However, apparently there was still substantial effort required to clean up even one half of one percent of a giant river full of lava. The particular spell I'd used on the river this morning had come from an overambitious maleficer from the Avanti kingdom who decided his evil fortress would be much more impressive if only it was surrounded by a moat of lava. How right he'd been. The teams behind us had been forced to twiddle their thumbs on the threshold for ten minutes until the doors opened up again on the charming wintry landscape of murder.

We spent the rest of the day the way we'd be spending all our days from now on: gathered around a table in the library, going over every move we'd made and trying to decide what we'd done wrong. As noted, I had almost no idea what moves I'd made, and no one else did, either, which made our first postmortem difficult. Everyone did very clearly remember the river boiling up into lava, points to me, so we frittered away quite a lot of time discussing whether we should make that the centerpiece of our strategy: just have me bang a molten river of magma down the middle of the graduation hall, throw a cooling spell on our feet, and all run along it to the doors. It did sound good, nice and simple, but there are plenty of mals who are just fine with even boiling-lava amounts of heat, and anyway every single kid would get on the highway to heaven right behind us, which would concentrate mal attention too much. Mals would force each other into the lava by sheer pressure of numbers, and the second wave would climb over the charred bodies to get at us. Also, not only would the maw-mouths not mind the heat, they'd just flop parts of themselves over onto the path and make it their serving tray as soon as we started running towards them. It's not like we could just *stop*. There aren't a lot of cooling spells that will last long if you keep standing on lava for any length of time.

"What if you throw it across the room the other way, right behind us?" Khamis said. "You could keep the mals off our backs."

I said levelly, "I'd also block any other *kids* behind us."

He clearly considered that their lookout and not ours, but he was a smart guy; he didn't say so to my face. I'm fairly sure he did say so to Nkoyo's face, though, in the vein of *Can't you reason with your silly friend?* I saw him pull her back to talk to her as we went downstairs for dinner, and she was all controlled resignation when she got to the queue, her usual sparkle dimmed.

There was a man who came to the commune once with his girlfriend and patronized everyone, asking overly polite questions with a sneer in the smile that he always tacked on, *and you all really believe in this sort of thing?* It was a familiar sneer: the exact one that filled my own heart every time someone tried to tell me earnestly about how I would really clear my chakras if only I would wear this set of beads or that magnetic copper bracelet. They'd always get wound up when I told them that putting on a thing churned out of a machine from ore that had been strip-mined by underpaid laborers wasn't likely to improve my mana balance any. But I still hated this wanker the instant he turned up. He'd only come, as far as I could tell, to make his girlfriend feel bad about having a nice weekend doing yoga in the woods with people kind enough to ask her how she was feeling, even if they did it with a bunch of blather about her chakras.

The tired way she had looked, that was how Nkoyo looked, and it made me just as cross to see, cross enough that back at the commune I'd actually gone up to the guy and told him that he should get out and stay away. He laughed and smiled at me and I just stood there looking at him, because that usually did the trick even though I was only eleven years old at the time, and fifteen minutes later he did indeed leave. But he made his girlfriend go with him.

So I didn't go tell Khamis to get out. I just made sure to bus my tray with Nkoyo and told her, "Feel free to tell that prick that I kicked off at you when you even tried to suggest the idea," and she glanced at me and her mouth quirked, a little of the sparkle coming back. I should have felt proud of myself; I'm sure Mum would have told me I'd grown. I'm afraid all I felt was an even more passionate desire to drop Khamis down a maintenance shaft.

When we ran the course again two days later—we each get to go every other day; anyone who tries to hog the course more than that starts to have unpleasant experiences, like for example their spells not working at all at a critical juncture— I didn't turn the whole river to lava. Instead I summoned just enough lava at the bottom of it to boil the whole thing up while simultaneously cooling the lava down. The variety of traps and simulated mals lurking in the river almost all got encased in the new stone, or at least became completely visible, and we could just walk across at any point we liked.

"El, that was the right thing to do," Liu said to me afterwards, intently. We'd made it to the far end and back without any serious bloodletting that time, which made that seem obvious, but she meant it more generally. "It was the right thing to do because it gave us choices. Having a choice is the most important thing."

I'd heard that before. It's a bullet-point line in the graduation handbook: *As a general rule, regardless of the specific situation in which you find yourself, at every step you must take care to preserve or widen the number of your options.* It hadn't quite sunk in properly, but now it did. Having a choice meant being able to choose something that worked for you and whatever you were carrying and whatever you'd prepared. Having a choice meant you got to choose getting out.

Liu looked back at the doors. "Six months left." I nodded. We went upstairs to get back to work.

Chapter 8
SLITHERJAW

I'D LIKE TO SAY Khamis improved on acquaintance, but he didn't. The second week of the obstacle course, we did it properly: I sang the mana-amplification spell before the doors even fully opened and charged in without stopping to let myself look. I went straight into a knee-high snowdrift in a glacial mountain landscape, empty except for massive tall stone boulders jutting out of the ground like pillars, intermittent blasts of snowy wind coming into our faces almost as hard as the boundary blizzard from last time. It was still beautiful, but it was the kind of beautiful that normally you only get to see in person if you spend a week hauling yourself up a mountain with a backpack longer than your torso.

I floundered a few steps in, and then my foot just went out from under me and I headed over backwards. If it hadn't been for Aadhya's shield holder—after I'd told her about my little run-in with Liesel, she'd tweaked them to handle accidental falls along with deliberate impact—I'd probably have concussed myself properly that time. As it was, I went down hard, and the snowdrifts on either side of me fell in on top of my head and started actively trying to smother me. Jowani hauled me out of it and put me back on my feet—oh I was glad to have him along—just as the boulders all unfolded themselves into troll shapes like Transformers made out of rock and started flinging chunks at our heads.

We all came out with numb bodies and a lot of bruises, and Chloe had a broken collarbone and cracked shoulder and a bad limp: she'd been hit by one of the flying rocks. Our helpers patched her up a little, while inside the gym the boulders reassembled themselves out of the mass of crushed pebbles and dust that I'd left behind me, but she was going to need more healing than we could expect from the deal. "Let's get you to your room. We can work in there instead," Liu said, and Chloe just nodded without saying anything, her eyes lowered and her mouth thin, and Khamis came up and said to her, "*You're* the one putting up the mana. Next time, *you* go in the middle."

I'd spent the week congratulating myself repeatedly on my self-restraint, but it had run out, and I was about to tell him that actually Liu was bringing at least as much mana, by carrying the mana-amplification spell on the lute the entire time we were running, and also I was going to lay out exactly what I thought of him, and offer some detailed suggestions of where he could shove it, but before I could open my mouth, Aadhya said, "Seriously? A big boy like you, afraid of some scrapes and bruises?" He rounded on her; she just waved a finger back and forth across his chest in over-the-top disdain. "You want to take your first hit when it's for real, son, you go ahead, keep hiding in the middle. Chloe's going to be out the doors before *you* are, for sure."

Chloe darted a look up at her out of shiny eyes. To be honest, I don't think she'd thought of it that way any more than I had, but Aadhya was right. Enclavers didn't get hit, not like the rest of us, not day-to-day. Once a month maybe they'd see a mal, with mana at their fingertips and lots of help and easier targets both close to hand. Enough for practice. Not enough to get *hurt*. I don't know that Chloe had ever actually been tagged before. Definitely not the way I had, but not even the way Liu or Aadhya or Jowani or any average loser kid had, at least half a dozen times. It didn't matter sometimes if you had all the mana in the world, all the equipment in the world. All it took was getting unlucky once. If you got hit hard enough, you went down, and if you didn't get back on your feet fast enough, you stayed down forever. And you couldn't learn how to get back on your feet until after you'd been knocked down.

Chloe swallowed and said to Khamis, "Thanks for looking out for me. I'm good with my team."

He didn't like it, especially since he probably couldn't help seeing that Aadhya had an alarmingly good point that he was now going to have to worry about, but he took it, although he gave a snort and looked at Aadhya as if he'd have liked to have a minion push her over in a corridor sometime before he turned around and walked away back to his team.

That said, good point or not, I'd never seen Aadhya have a go at an enclaver before. She wasn't a committed suck-up like Ibrahim, just too sensible to do anything that—well, that stupid. Unlike certain other people who will remain me. "Wow," I said to her just under my breath as we went downstairs.

"Yeah, like I had a choice," she said, with a huff, and gave me a pointed look. I would like to say I felt ashamed of myself for putting her in the position of having to snap someone back just so I wouldn't try to disembowel them, but I was too unrepentantly happy that *someone* had told Khamis off. Aadhya sighed. "Just do me a favor, keep a lid on it until the end of the month."

"Then what?" I said.

"Then he can't walk away anymore *with Nkoyo*, hello."

My turn to sigh. "Yeah, all right." Sometimes when your friends are right, you're pleased, and sometimes it's unbearably annoying.

But she was right, so I bit my tongue repeatedly over the next weeks while the last alliances got locked down and we invested enough mana and time in our collaboration that he really couldn't just flounce off and find himself another arrangement, dragging Nkoyo and her friends with him. The jerk even started taking a partially exposed position on our *second* runs, trying to arrange himself just the right amount of pain.

I was counting down the minutes until I'd get to slag him off properly when we started our fifth week. All the runs so far had been varied winter wonderlands of death: a thick forest, deep and hushed; a wide frozen lake stretching so far we couldn't see the other bank. Today it was a wide snowy meadow scattered with placid ordinary shrubs and tiny blue flowers peeking out from the snow—and absolutely nothing came at us. We ran to the wall of trees at the far end and back like we were doing an ordinary sprint, and then just as I'd made it to the doors, there was a deep rumbling noise and the snowfield split open maybe ten meters behind us and what seemed like a thousand spiked thornbush vines burst lashing up out of it.

Almost everyone had made it to the other side of the split by then; it was only Yaakov and Nkoyo still behind the line. Yaakov was close enough that he just yelled and threw himself over before the vines got high enough; he fell down on the other side with them grabbing at his legs and trying to pull him back. Cora and Nadia were close enough to slash through the vines with their swords while Ibrahim and Ja-maal grabbed his arms and hauled him away.

But Nkoyo had been one step further back, and that one step had put a solid wall of vines between her and the gates. I tried to cast a spell of putrefying rot at the vines, which ought to have wiped them out along with most of the rest of the landscape, but instead nothing happened, and I looked down and realized I hadn't just made it clear, I was *out:* I was standing in the corridor, just outside the gym doors. I couldn't help Nkoyo any more than I'd be able to help her in the grad-uation hall once I'd passed through the gates and was stand-ing back in Wales.

But if I'd gone through the gates downstairs, I also wouldn't have still been standing there to *watch* my friend get torn to shreds. Nkoyo was casting withering spells, whirling-quick touch spells, but she could only do them one vine at a time, and she was running out of both mana and breath. She couldn't make an opening big enough to jump across the chasm without being pulled down, and the vines kept com-ing and coming. One of them made a darting lunge out of the mass and got round her throat and started to strangle her so she couldn't cast anymore, blood running down her neck and her arms from the thorns as she grappled with it desper-ately.

I didn't know what I was going to do, but I *wasn't* going to stand there. Even though I would have to do something real, something permanent—as bad as what I'd done to the gym in the first place. The mana was at my hands and the spell was on my breath, my tongue curling around the words: a spell of destruction and tearing-down, a spell to rip the obstacle-course machinery apart, bring the whole gym down if I had to—

And then that absolute wankstain Khamis *went back for her.*
He poured a bottle of green liquid out over several writhing
nests of vines, and they burst into flames and burnt up in
a single roaring instant, opening up a wide gap in front of
her. He jumped through, grabbed Nkoyo under her armpits
and knees, and more or less threw her bodily through the
opening—he *was* a big boy—before he jumped after her and
shoved her along the rest of the way ahead of him through
the doors, staggering as the last vines grabbed and clawed at
his own legs, leaving a trail of fresh blood drips on the
churned snow before the doors slammed shut on his heels.

And yeah, you never wanted to lose a member of your alliance this close to graduation, and it was Nkoyo's team more
than it was his; he'd just agreed to put up the resources and a
shedload of mana, and she'd pulled everyone else together
out of her big network, the loads of people who were happy
to join up with her. But that work was done, and she wasn't
irreplaceable as an incanter by a long shot. In fact there were
enough losers left floating around without an alliance that he
could have subbed in two kids as replacements, who'd be desperate enough by now to agree to an even more exposed position further in the rear and a smaller share of team resources.

Instead he'd put himself as far out as anyone would go,
just to save her. Mum always told me that you couldn't know
what people would do in a crisis, but I'd thought she just
meant you should forgive people for behaving like weasels
under bad circumstances, not that a stale biscuit like Khamis
might suddenly come over all heroic in a tight corner.

After the first moment of *what just happened,* the rest of
our crew gathered round the two of them in the corridor, a
yammering of noise and congratulations; even the next
group of seniors just waiting their turn to go crowded in:
they were helping gladly this time, offering bandages, hand-

kerchiefs, good salves. We're all fans of near escapes, of far escapes, of any escapes at all; we want so much to believe in them, even after all these years in here. Nkoyo just sank down on her knees on the ground in front of the doors, her eyes shut with two fat streaks of tears running shiny down her face; her other allies Janice and Fareeda were holding up her limp arms to bandage them. Khamis was sitting next to her staring at the bloodstained gashes in his trousers and shoes. He seemed roughly as shocked as anyone that he'd done it.

I'd got out of the way at some point, I don't remember when; I'd backed up from the doors to make room for everyone helping, the crowd of them framed in the archway of the big metal gym doors. Only Ibrahim was off a little way down the corridor with Yaakov, their foreheads together and his hands cupping Yaakov's face, tears streaming down his own; he jerked in to snatch a fast desperate kiss that made Yaakov lose it and shut his eyes and start crying, too.

I stood there with my back against the far side of the corridor, well away from them all, the working of destruction still alive in my mouth and the mana I'd pulled still churning inside me. We'd been running the obstacle courses for a month and we were already so much better, so much faster. We *needed* the gym, we *needed* the course. If I'd smashed the whole thing to save Nkoyo, I'd have been making another bargain with the lives of people I didn't know, faces I wasn't looking at, the way I'd traded those kids from Shanghai for the ones the quattria ate.

I didn't have the right to do that. I didn't have the right to do anything except the one thing I had the right to do—to get out of the gates—because we all agreed that we had that right. We all agreed we had the right to get out any way we could, within the one narrow limit of actually killing each

206 ◆ NAOMI NOVIK

other—and even that could be handwaved off as long as you did it unobtrusively enough. It was understood that you only promised to help other people because they'd help you back, and it was understood that your promises stopped counting when you got close enough to the gates, and nobody would ever blame you for going through as soon as you could, even if everyone else on your team died. Nobody would ever expect you to turn back and nobody would promise to do it.

If you even tried, nobody would believe you, because maybe you couldn't know what people would do in a crisis, but you could know that. If you turned back, you didn't save anyone, you just died along with them. At best you died *instead* of them; you put yourself into a maw-mouth for eternity to get them out the doors *instead* of you. That's all anyone could reasonably hope to do, so it wasn't something you could ask anyone to do. You could ask people to be brave, you could ask them to be kind, you could ask them to care, you could ask them to help; you could ask them for a thousand hard and painful things. But not when it was so obviously useless. You couldn't ask someone to deliberately trade themselves away completely, everything they had and might ever be, just to give you a chance, when in the end—and the gates were the end, the very end of things—you knew you weren't any more special than they were. It wasn't even heroism; it was just a bad equation that didn't balance.

Except for me. I could turn back. With just an ordinary amount of nerve, not even as much as Khamis Mwinyi had dug up out of his own guts with no advance warning to anyone, I could turn around at the gates and wave everyone on my team through and wreak destruction on every mal that came in range, until all of my friends were safe. So I had to. Of course I had to. I couldn't go running through the gates to safety, to the green woods of Wales and Mum hugging me tight, while anyone I loved was still behind me. I had to turn back and keep the gates clear for them until they all made it through. They hadn't asked me, they wouldn't ask me, because that went against the rules we all understood, but I'd do it anyway, because I could. I could save Aadhya and Liu and Chloe and Jowani, and I'd save Nkoyo and Ibrahim and Yaakov and Nadia.

And then, once I'd done that, then I could go through the gates myself. I'd rescue the people I cared about, and then— I could turn my back on everyone else. I could go through, and leave them to find their own way out or die. I didn't owe them. I didn't love them. They'd done nothing for me. Except Khamis, who was sitting on the floor there shaky with blood trickling over his legs in rivulets and puddling beneath him, blood he'd spent to save Nkoyo when I couldn't. I'd save Khamis. I'd keep standing by the gates long enough to save Khamis, who I didn't love in the least, because how could I do anything else now?

I stepped back from the knot of people gathered round him and Nkoyo, the strangers helping someone I cared about, in the small ways they could afford. I took another step back, and another, and turned, and three breaths later I was halfway down the corridor and running, running like the gates were up ahead of me and I could make it out, I could escape. There were more seniors heading for the gym by then. Their heads turned, anxious to follow me as I passed, wondering what was I running from, only I was running from them, from any of them who might turn out to be a decent person, who might turn out to be just as special as the people I loved. Who might deserve to live just as much as they did.

I sped up even more, which I could do because for the last five weeks I'd been sprinting for my life on a near-daily basis, only that turned out to be a terrible idea because I ran straight

into Magnus. He was coming off the stairs to go practice with
his own team: a pack of five boys who took up nearly the full
width of the archway so I couldn't dodge round them and
had to pull up hard instead, and he reached out instinctively
to steady me and said, "El? What happened? Is Chloe okay?"
as if even *he* had a thought to spare for another human being,
as long as she was someone he'd grown up with. Or maybe as
long as he could risk caring about her because he knew the
odds were she wasn't going to die before her eighteenth
birthday.

"Oh, I hate you," I said, childishly stupid; I was about to
burst, into tears, into something else, I have no idea what,
when Orion got literally bowled down the stairs and knocked
all six of us off our feet like a perfect strike. A monstrous roaring slitherjaw, thrashing squid-sucker tentacles around a
prehistoric-shark mouth, came humping down the stairs after
him, gargling and grabbing, and all of the boys screamed and
tried to get away, which was hard to do when we were tangled up on the floor in a heap.

At least Magnus didn't do anything heroic; he scrabbled
wildly for escape just like the rest of them. There wasn't any,
though; it was on us, arms already grabbing Orion and all of
Magnus's teammates and dragging them towards its gnashing mouth, more coming for him and me, but after it pulled
Magnus off me, I sat up and screamed at it, "Shrivel up and
die, you putrescent sack of larva!"

Those weren't actually the right words of the rotting spell
that I had been trying to cast on the vines, but apparently that
didn't matter, because the slitherjaw obeyed me without the
slightest hesitation, its skin shrinking down until it popped
along seams that unleashed a writhing mass of tiny horrible
maggot-like grubs all over the floor, half burying the boys as
it dropped them—still screaming, possibly even louder—in

its disintegration. They all flung themselves out of it and went wildly careening into the corridor, frenziedly shaking off grubs in every direction and crushing them underfoot as they went grape-stomping around. Except for Orion, who just surfaced out of the sea of maggot-things, shook himself off without an iota of decent horror—they were *in his hair*—and looked around at the rapidly disappearing remains of the mal: the larvae were fleeing down the drains en masse, leaving behind nothing but the two enormous bony jaws full of serrated teeth, hanging still wide-open on the floor like something out of a natural history museum.

He didn't have the nerve to reproach me, but he did heave a faintly disappointed sigh. "Don't even start, Lake," I said. I felt better; maybe because I'd blown away my gathered mana forcing a new spell into existence, or maybe it was just the same kind of calm as going through a crying jag and coming out the other side, where you know nothing's changed and it's all still horrible but you can't cry forever, so there's nothing to do but go on. "Tell me something, what's the plan? *Is* there one, or were you just going to improvise the whole thing?"

"Uh, the plan?" Orion said.

"Graduation," I said, making sure to enunciate every syllable in case he missed one. "Taking out the mals. Before they *eat* everyone."

He glared at me. "I don't need a plan!"

"In other words, you can't be arsed to think of one besides 'run in and start killing mals until one of them gets you.' Well, too bad for you, that's not what we're doing."

"What *we're* doing?" he said after a moment, warily.

"Well, look at you," I said, making a condescending wave to take in the still-writhing mess of the stairs. "If I let you clear the hall on your own, you'll trip over your own feet and

get yourself eaten by a grue in five minutes; it'll just be em-
barrassing."

He wasn't sure whether he wanted to be offended more
than he wanted to be pleased, and he obviously also had a
brief thought about making a chivalric protest of the *no you
mustn't do something so dangerous* variety, but he thought better of that and shut his mouth before it escaped him. Instead
he folded his arms over his chest and said, coolly, "So what's
your plan? Turn all the mals into maggots? That would be fun
for everyone."

"They'd take it and say thanks if they knew what was good
for them," I said.

I hadn't any better plan to offer, in fact, than "run in and
start killing mals until one of them gets you." I didn't know
what I was going to do. I only knew what I wasn't going to
do. I wasn't going through. I wasn't going through until everyone was out.

Chapter 9

DRENCHER

O F COURSE, NOBODY ELSE even noticed my grand noble decision to save all their lives, as I started with the only thing I could think of, which was in fact just not going through the gym doors until everyone else had made it out. But that wasn't noticeable, because given this week's ridiculous course, that was the only sensible thing to do. The course usually doesn't change throughout the week, but we thought possibly this one time there would be additional attacks during our second and third runs, because it was so aggressively useless otherwise, but no. For that whole week, for everyone who ran it, that's all the course was: a good sprint with one not-actually-surprise attack at the end.

Even if I had been full of ironclad determination to abandon everyone behind me and run through the graduation gates at the first chance, it would still have been stupid to let my teammates get picked off in the gym during practices.

So no one batted an eye when I stopped at the doors on Wednesday and Friday and turned round to disintegrate the entire forest of vines even as they came whipping out. We

212 + NAOMI NOVIK

didn't even discuss strategy or anything; there wasn't any strategy to discuss, except to agree after the Wednesday run that Nkoyo and Khamis should just take Friday off and build mana while they healed up. That wasn't even a nice break for them; it was making the best of a bad situation. None of us wanted a break. What we wanted was more of the practice that we desperately needed to get out alive. Personally, I wanted it even more than I had before.

I tried going round the school hunting with Orion to make up for it, but that was even more useless. Nothing whatsoever attacked us, and if there was ever a faint scritching noise somewhere, he'd instantly abandon me and take off at top speed to go and get it. At best I'd catch up and there he'd be satisfied with himself standing over some dead thing. At worst, I'd have to spend half an hour wandering around the seminar-room labyrinth trying to find him again. Wait, no, sorry. At worst, I spent half an hour wandering around trying to find him, slipped in a giant puddle of goo that was the solitary remnant of whatever thing he'd killed, and then gave up and found him in the cafeteria eating lunch, still satisfied with himself. He didn't say outright that I'd asked to be covered in goo, but his expression was perfectly explicit. At that point I realized the only thing I was going to kill was him, so I gave it up.

Then the next week rolled round, the course changed again, and the school made clear it was more than ready to make up for the slow week. We couldn't cover ten meters of ground before yet another thing came at our heads. To fully convey the experience, on Friday the previous course had taken us a grand total of three minutes start-to-finish, including the time it took for me to wither all the vines into dust. Even on a more typical course, the average run only takes ten minutes. When a real graduation run takes more than fifteen minutes, it normally means you aren't getting out at all.

On Monday, I didn't come out until the twenty-seven-minute mark, into a crowd: we'd taken so long that there were about eight other alliances already downstairs and waiting outside the doors for their turn. None of them looked very enthusiastic. Usually you avoid finding out what's in the obstacle course so you can have a blind first run, but this time the waiting teams were all busily interrogating everyone in our group who'd come out, and going into huddled negotiations with other alliances to run it together.

I don't think my appearance was reassuring. I emerged trailing clouds of dark-green smoke flickering phosphorescent with crackles of lightning, the dwindling remnants of the hurricane I'd whipped up to dissolve the shambling army of frozen-mud-things. There was also the large ring of glowing orange-purple balefire spheres orbiting round my waist. The workings all fizzled out as I came through the doors, but they hung in the air just long enough to make a fashion statement of the *behold your dark goddess* variety, and anyway I'd been standing there just short of the threshold for five minutes, siccing spheres and thunderbolts on strategic targets to clear a way to the doors. Everyone else on our three teams was staggering. Nkoyo even sat down in the corridor right there and shut her eyes and leaned her head on Khamis's shoulder when he sat down next to her. The worst of the gouged marks around her throat were barely healed and some of the scabs had cracked and bled again.

"Righty-o, who wants a rundown?" I said, waving away the last trailers of smoke in as prosaic a way as I could manage. Which wasn't very, but desperation still drove people to talk to me, or at least to creep close enough to overhear what

I said to the braver ones. I stayed there in the corridor for the next ten minutes, answering questions to help everyone work out their strategy for running the course. Then the four alliances who'd been lined up to go after us gave it a go, together. They made it about ten meters from the door and then gave up and ran back out. At that point, everyone else just left. The new course was useless in the opposite way: it was too hard for anyone to get through. Except for me.

On Wednesday morning, we came out of our run after only fourteen minutes; we'd thought up loads of better ways for me to take out everything in our path. There was nobody outside waiting at all. We had to patch ourselves up, which went slowly; everyone in our group was exhausted. Except for me. I felt energized and extremely ready for lunch.

During which, it occurred to me that if no one else was trying, the course was wide open. Normally the school goes after you if you try to run the course more than three times a week, to keep people from hogging it, but you're allowed to take an extra run if there's literally nobody else queued. "I'll be up to the library in a bit," I said abruptly to everyone as we got up to clear our trays. "Come on, Lake."

Orion whinged all the way down the stairs—all the real mals had abandoned the gym, since nobody was down there trying to run the course, so as far as he was concerned there wasn't any point—but he gave in and came with me. We ran it together.

It was an even worse idea than hunting with him, in a completely different way. Blazing through endless hordes of fake mals, Orion killing them left and right in a sulky bored way and keeping me clear, with no one at my back I had to worry about, utterly free, utterly fearless. I made him do it three times in a row, and when he balked at a fourth run, I jumped him right there in front of the gym doors. We were kissing and everything was going really well in my opinion, and then he put a hand on the side of my breast mostly by accident and panicked and jerked back from me and babbled, "I've got, it's, uh, I didn't, you have, we," incoherently, and nearly walked himself backwards right onto the corpse of the very real drencher he'd killed in our first run, which was still sopping wet and perfectly capable of dissolving the flesh off his feet and legs if he touched it on his own. I had to jump after him and drag him to one side, and he didn't even notice why, he just pulled free of me and fled, leaving me standing alone in front of the doors.

But this time, not even that humiliation could bring me down. I went upstairs breathing deep and full of my own power, helplessly happy, even though it had obviously been stupid in every respect. I'd already known that I could get out if I didn't bother worrying about anyone else. I didn't need to shove my own face in how lovely and easy it would be, and especially I didn't need to contemplate how much fun I could have with Orion in the process.

If I *had* needed help recognizing the stupidity of it all, Precious was waiting eagerly to provide it, perched on a shelf just inside the library doors. We weren't taking the mice with us on the obstacle course; they weren't the kind of familiars that help in combat situations, so instead we were practicing with small stuffed balls tucked into safe places in our gear. But I didn't need to be bitten on the ear by the time I got up there; I'd had several long flights of stairs on which to contemplate the folly of my ways. "Yeah," I told her shortly as I reached up to take her down, and she just nosed at the knuckle of my thumb and scampered back into her bandolier cup.

In the reading room, I stopped by one of the teams Aadhya had made our cleanup deal with, and told them if they did come down on Friday, I'd do another run with them after ours. They all stared at me like a herd of wildebeest being offered safe passage across the Nile by a very large crocodile. "Or don't," I said crossly. "I can use the practice if you want it, that's all."

They couldn't decide that they did, but evidently they shared the offer around to get opinions, because on Friday, the other two teams were waiting when we came out. They didn't actually ask me outright to go with them, like I was a person or anything; they just looked at me sidelong. I swallowed it and told Aadhya shortly, "I'll see you upstairs," and after my team had gone off down the hall, I said, "Let's go," and marched myself back in.

The other team weren't as good as mine—or at least they weren't as good as we'd become after six weeks of running the course together—but I got them all out again still alive. I did have to turn one of them to stone at one point to save her from being bitten in half, but I turned her back afterwards, so I don't see what the problem was.

Everyone but me was waiting with enormous anticipation for that course to be swapped out, but on Monday, the next one was just as bad. All three of our cleanup-crew teams were waiting by the open doors when we came out, with their faces blankly appalled. I turned right round and did another run with them, and when we got out, there was a new team waiting—Liesel's team. After New Year's, she'd apparently crossed Magnus off and had instead settled for allying with Alfie, from London. I didn't know what she had against the Munich enclave, which had three strapping senior boys to choose from if that was really one of her primary criteria, but there was presumably *something*, since these days Munich was a better choice than London for a German girl who was apparently viciously determined to get a seat on a top-tier

THE LAST GRADUATE ✦ 217

enclave council before she was thirty. Unless there was something especially *right* with Alfie, but I hadn't seen any notable signs of that in the last three years and change.

"El, how are you?" he said, exactly as if we hadn't seen each other for ages and he was delightfully surprised to find me here.

I ignored him and said to Liesel, "Right, let's go." She nodded back coldly and we went. A woman after my own heart.

Also, she was really good. She wasn't Orion, but she was miles better than anyone else I'd run with, even though I tried not to notice out of loyalty. Her whole team was better, actually. Even Alfie wasn't remotely a weak link: he'd taken the middle, obviously, but he wasn't sitting there cowering; he was using the position to throw complicated defensive spells to all sides to cover everyone else, and he was really good at it. He had fast reflexes and what must have been an encyclopedic defensive collection that he knew backwards and forward: he kept steadily pitching exactly the right spell at exactly the right time to exactly the right place, so the rest of us could just trust him and go totally on the offensive. We made it through in eleven minutes; it had taken me twenty-two on the first run with my team.

Of course, twenty-two was better than never, which is what it would've been for Liesel and company if they hadn't had me along. They all flinched when we got to the home-stretch and the icy ground we'd been running over abruptly folded itself up round us into towering slabs toothed with jagged spikes the size of tyrannosaur femurs, and seething with ectoplasmic vapors that suggested they had psychic form and not just physical. Alfie threw up what was the very best group shield I'd ever seen, which might have held for one or two hits, but there literally wasn't anywhere to go.

Until I spoke the seventh spell of binding from *The Fruitful*

Vine, which was the very first Marathi-language spellbook ever written. It was put together by a group of poet-incanters from the Pune area who wanted more spells in their own vernacular—the better you know a language and understand its nuances, the better your spellcasting is going to be—so they gathered for a writing and spell-trading session. It went so well that they formed a long-term circle and kept going, their spells went on getting more and more powerful, and eventually the collection was so valuable they were able to trade just the one book to Jaipur for enclave-building spells.

Immediately after which, their group imploded into a massive internecine fight. Most of them died and a few went to Jaipur and a couple of others renounced magic and purged all their mana and went to live in the wilderness as ascetics, and that's why there's no enclave in Pune. But *before* that, they wrote some real corkers, including this series of increasingly complex binding spells, the hardest of which really only ever gets hunted up by the sort of maleficer who wants to bind one of the more nasty mals in the manifestation category as a personal servant. Well, or by a circle of decent wizards trying to get rid of one of those mals, but you can guess why the school gave *me* a copy. The soles had started to come off my trainers halfway through my freshman year, and I thought I was being adequately specific when I asked the void for a spell to securely bind them back up, but no. You'd be amazed at how little call I've had in the last four years for a pet benibel that would need to be fed on a steady diet of human corpses, although I suppose you could accuse me of a lack of imagination.

But it was just the spell you wanted when facing a possessed entity the size of a glacier. This was my third time through this course, and I'd got the hang of doing it, so it was fairly painless as an experience; I just banged out the spell, commanded the gnashing ice peaks to lie flat, and off to the doors we went. But that didn't make it less maddening for Liesel and her crew. The problem was, no one other than myself, no matter how brilliant or hardworking, could have done much of anything in the situation. Even if you'd got hold of the binding spell, it normally calls for a circle of twelve wizards chanting for an hour. Her face was rigid with fury when we got out the doors. I didn't even blame her for stalking off without so much as a thank-you. Alfie was better programmed, so he did say, "Thanks, El, fair play," before going after her, but even for him it was mechanical.

By lunchtime word had got round, and everyone started to panic. Aside from the very real danger of dying for basic lack of practice, the new course made no sense in a particularly alarming way. There are some mals as big as mountains out there in the world, but you might as well say there are blue whales in the world. If a blue whale happened to appear smack in the middle of the graduation hall, it would certainly present a challenge to us all, but it wouldn't have got there on its own initiative. So why was something like that suddenly showing up in the obstacle course? Either the school was just throwing it at us out of nastiness, on the justification that at least *one* student could get past it, even if that made the course totally useless to everyone who didn't have me along—which would be bad enough—or there *was* something on that scale down below.

No one else could think of any other reason why it was happening; as far as they knew, nothing had changed. I was the only one who knew what had changed. *I'd* changed. And the brutal courses were too obviously a response. You want to save everybody, you silly girl? Right, let's make that harder

220 + NAOMI NOVIK

for you: nobody gets any practice the rest of the term, so they'll all be panicking and fumbling around down in the hall. Good luck saving them then.

I wasn't sharing my grand plan, though, so everyone else kept laboring onward in ignorance and spreading alarm. That afternoon in the library, a couple other teams got up the desperation to ask me to do a run, and the next morning, Ibrahim did them one worse: he cornered me on my bleary way to the girls' and sidled round the subject for nearly five minutes before I finally understood that he was trying to work out if I had any sort of opinion about him kissing Yaakov.

He hadn't done anything wrong by Scholomance standards, not telling me. You *do* have to disclose any conflict of interest like that to your potential allies before you ask them to go with you and your significant other—it clearly wasn't an accident that in his team, he was in the lead and Yaakov was bringing up the rear, the two most dangerous positions and the most separated, where they wouldn't have a chance to ditch the others and take off together. But I *wasn't* one of his allies. My name wasn't written up on the wall with him and Yaakov, so he hadn't owed me a thing, my opinion shouldn't have made a difference. But here he was trying to find it out, as though it should have *mattered*.

It was horrible, and I couldn't even howl at him, because it *did* matter, now, by the standard operating procedure of Scholomance losers. Aadhya had made a tactical deal for us with their alliance, but it's always understood in those deals that either side has the right to jettison the other and trade up if the opportunity permits. And the opportunity did permit, now that I had become an extremely scarce and valuable resource. If we took the chance to, oh, upgrade to running with Liesel and Alfie, Ibrahim and his team would suddenly be just as stuck as everyone else who didn't have me to run with.

And it wasn't an accident that he and Yaakov hadn't let on that they weren't just friends, all those nights we were sitting together studying in Chloe's room. We're all fairly nose-to-grindstone in here, but one of the most reliable topics of conversation was nevertheless gossip about who was dating who or wanted to. It was second only to gossip about who was getting allied with who.

There wasn't actually very much of the gossip to be had, because oddly enough constantly being on the verge of malnourishment, exhaustion, and mortal terror isn't really conducive to romance, but we extracted all the entertainment we could from the couples that managed to have the energy—most of which involved at least one enclaver, unsurprisingly. We knew when Jamaal started coordinating his snack runs at the same time as a girl from Cairo—her with a group of girls, him with a group of boys, all very by the book. We knew that Jermaine from New York had spent the last year in a competitive love triangle with a boy from Atlanta over one of the top alchemists, and we all knew when in a perfect storm of gossipy delight it turned into a trio *and* an alliance, halfway through the first month of term. Everyone else also had the fun of pestering *me* about Orion while they were at it. Ibrahim and Yaakov had decided not to share the information. They'd decided it was a risk they couldn't afford to take.

Lots of enclavers, especially from the most powerful Western enclaves, like to go on about how enlightened wizard society is, relative to the masses of the mundanes. From their rarefied perspective, I suppose it's true. Spend decades recruiting the most brilliant wizards from all round the world, because they're the ones who can best save your kids' lives and make your enclave even richer and more powerful, then you can look round your diverse and tolerant international enclave and pat yourself on the back in a congratulatory way. But that doesn't mean there aren't any bigots among us. It only means that we've got this one additional dividing line of our own that stops right at the enclave doors, and it's sharp enough to cut your throat.

And Ibrahim wasn't on the safe side of that line. He's not an enclaver; he's not one of the top students, who could count on getting an alliance with one. His primary gift, the one talent that he'd marshaled to get himself all the way through school and into his alliance with Jamaal—the boy from Dubai who was going with his team—was that he was a really determined and enthusiastic suck-up. If you liked a tidy bit of flattery and someone who'd cheer you on and comfort you when you were down, pat you on the back and tell you that you were brilliant and in the right even if you were really quite blatantly in the wrong, help you talk your way through any inconvenient fits of guilt or conscience, then he was your lad, and loads of enclavers did indeed like that.

Which is hardly a unique approach. Roughly half of the indie kids are at least partly on the minion track: some of them offer up labor or muscle; the more desperate ones offer themselves up more or less explicitly as human shields. They take the worst seats at the cafeteria tables and in the classrooms; they fetch supplies and drop off homework; they walk the enclaver kids to their dorm rooms at night and keep watch for them in the showers without even asking for turnabout. Because almost all enclavers except the very richest ones will end up with a few filler positions in their alliances, open to average kids who can do four or five decent castings in ten minutes and have built a modest sum of mana on top of their schoolwork, and have been lucky enough to stay able-bodied and in solid physical condition through years in the Scholomance.

That was the kind of opening Ibrahim was aiming for, his whole time here. He didn't have other options. He was perfectly competent, but that didn't make him anything special, not by the standards of the graduation hall. And if you're on the minion track, you can't afford to prioritize anything as unimportant as your most passionately held beliefs or your deepest emotional needs. You don't even get to prioritize your own bloody life when you're going down the stairs first with your heart in your throat, just so if there *is* something waiting, it'll get you instead of the enclaver seven steps behind you, who you're both pretending really hard is being such a good friend for letting you have the chance.

That was why he'd kept it quiet. He wanted to keep the option to glom on to an enclaver who was the kind of rusty hinge who cared about other people's business, and now he was asking me if I *was* one of those—because his life depended on it.

I wanted to yell at him in a fury and stomp away, but I couldn't. He looked ready to cry, the way you would if you had to desperately beg some girl you'd been rude to on the regular for your life and the life of someone you loved. He'd have been a complete nutter not to lie to me in any way I wanted him to, if that got me to keep running with his alliance. For that matter, if he were really clever, he'd know I didn't care and have the conversation anyway, as an excuse to exhibit his commitment to servility.

But I knew Ibrahim wasn't that kind of clever. He was so good at sucking up because he was sincere about it. I think he really liked people to begin with—a foreign concept to me—

and he was *earnestly* starry-eyed. He'd kept on sucking up to Orion long after it'd become clear that Orion wasn't in the market for minions. For that matter, Ibrahim had been stupid enough to fall in love inside school; and it really had to be love, because hooking up with Yaakov for an alliance was an obviously bad idea that had put them both in those more dangerous spots.

So instead I muttered, "I'm not a wanker, Haddad. Have your own fun. See you tomorrow morning," ungraciously, and *then* stomped away.

That same day at lunchtime, Magnus had the bald-faced cheek to ask Chloe to pass along an *invitation* to join his team if I still wanted more practice, which I suppose in his mind was the equivalent of Ibrahim's desperate begging. I gritted my teeth and did a run with them that afternoon. They were just as good as Liesel's team, and they would have been just as dead without me.

When I went down with my own team again on Wednesday morning, there were roughly thirty people downstairs waiting even before we got there, and they were all angry—furiously angry. They still didn't know I meant to help them. What they did know was, if they wanted any practice, they had to go to me hat-in-hand for help that they weren't going to have on graduation day, because of course I wasn't going to help them then, and when they saw thirty other kids lined up to ask, they knew that today was the day I'd start charging for my help, and I'd want things they couldn't afford to give away.

I don't know if I could have fixed the situation by telling them I was going to save them all. I don't think they'd have believed me. But I can't say for certain, because I didn't even try. They were looking at my friends; they were looking at

Aadhya and Liu and all the people who'd taken a chance on me; and they were losers looking at enclavers, except fifteen minutes ago they'd *been* the enclavers, the ones who were going to live. Alfie with Liesel and the brilliant team she'd built, Magnus and his wolf pack; they hadn't spent four years being slowly taught over and over that another kid had the right to live and they hadn't.

And I could see in their faces that if they could have *taken* me, if I'd been a piece of artifice they could wrestle away or steal, they would have: they'd have used every unfair advantage they had and gone after my friends, and at this very moment probably most of them were trying to think of some way to do it, just like Magnus with his Field Day stunt.

"Lots of us up for first run today," Alfie said, in the bright sort of way that someone might say, *Well, looks like rain, doesn't it!* when it's sheeting down and you've taken shelter under an awning with five people who've all got knives drawn, and you're quietly reaching into your pocket for a handgun.

So I didn't say anything reassuring like, *You can stop fretting already, Orion and I are going to get all of you useless gits out.* I didn't even say anything sensible about going with everyone in turn. Chloe glanced at me and I could see her getting ready to say something sensible for me, play peacemaker with the enclave boys, and before she could, I said, "No sense waiting for any more to show," and I marched for the doors, flung them open, and sailed in. There was a confused scramble behind me, and then everyone reached the same conclusion at the same time: if they wanted to be sure of getting in a run with me, they had to go *now*. They all poured in after me together.

Doing the course with fifty people at once isn't normally a

good idea, because you make it through all right, but you don't get enough practice. That wasn't a problem when we were being deluged from all sides. I realized afterwards that actually it had been terrific practice for *me*, the closest I could get to the real thing, all of us being dumped into a sea of maleficaria at once. But right then in the moment, I didn't have time to think about anything but fighting, casting desperately in every direction to take out attacks that were about to overwhelm someone's defenses. It was like one of those horrible twitchy games where there are seventeen things to do on separate timers and you frantically dash from one to the next and you're always on the verge of missing one. It was just like that, except I had forty-seven timers running, and if I missed even one of them, somebody was going to die. It was a massive relief when we got to the final attack and I could just cast the one nice relaxing hideously powerful spell and let everyone else run for the gates while I held the eldritch glacier down.

We limped out with skins more or less intact but utterly exhausted. Even I felt drained, my whole rib cage aching; my heart was banging around inside like it'd had an argument with my lungs and now it was in the kitchen putting pots and pans away angrily while they tried to find a way out through my breastbone. Which I suppose was good really, as it meant I'd got some proper exercise in, but I wasn't for taking the long view at the moment. Some other teams had come down and were waiting, but after I staggered out, they took off without even trying to bribe me for a run, so I gather I looked the way I felt.

There wasn't any conversation afterwards. Aadhya said, "I want a shower," and I said, "Yeah," and basically all twenty-seven girls of our group trudged off to the showers together.

It was almost time for Orion to harvest the amphisbaena for Liesel; the juveniles had stopped coming through with the water a week ago or so and now were just hissing and banging impotently at us from inside the showerheads like the steam pipes had gone mad. There was one moment when the wall cracked around one of the showerheads and the amphisbaena inside started to thrash around wildly to try and finish breaking out, but it was just an amphisbaena, so the girl using the shower didn't even stop rinsing her hair, she just grabbed a long enchanted stiletto-knife out of her bathroom bag and stabbed it into the opening. The showerhead stopped moving around. It would be unpleasant if the dead amphisbaena started rotting in there, but probably the others would eat it before that happened.

None of us talked. We took our turns washing in almost complete silence broken only by the occasional "has anyone got shampoo to trade for toothpaste" and the like. We got our clothes back on and straggled up to the library for our respective postmortems, and still no one said anything to me or to each other until I sat down at our group's table. But the boys were there waiting for us—and stinking, which was a lot more noticeable since we'd got ourselves clean—and before I'd even quite got my arse in the chair, Khamis demanded peremptorily, "What was that?" like he'd been holding the words back on a tight leash until I got in range and he could let them loose.

I gawked at him. Yes, I'm perpetually complaining about everyone cringing away from me, but of all the people to think they *could* safely have a go at me without getting knocked back—and then I had a moment of even greater indignation as I realized *he'd* been biting his tongue for a month the same way I had, waiting until enough of the term was gone and we'd locked things down and I couldn't shove him off anymore without crossing the line of what passes for common decency in here.

"What's the matter, Mwinyi?" I snapped back. "Picked up a splinter today?"

"What's the *matter*?" he said. "I'll tell you what's the matter! Six times today—*six times*—Fareeda went down." He jerked a thumb at poor Fareeda, who was just sitting down herself, three chairs away from him. She was an artificer friend of Nkoyo's I didn't know very well, and she very clearly did *not* think she could safely have a go at me. She darted her eyes between us and slid the rest of the way into her chair while doing her best to convey that her entire being was on another plane of existence and it was just a mistake on our parts if we thought she was there. "On Monday, she only went down once. What do you say about that?"

There's a lovely spell I know that makes your victim's organs all desiccate while still inside them. The original was developed ages ago for perfectly respectable mummification purposes and fell out of fashion roughly along with that practice, but the version I've got is the really nasty nineteenth-century English one that everyone's favorite Victorian maleficer, Ptolomey Ponsonby, worked up in translation out of his father's collection of Egyptian artifacts. At the moment, I felt roughly as though someone were casting it on me.

"She didn't *stay* down, did she?" I squeezed out of my shriveling entrails. Khamis wasn't wrong to be concerned if Fareeda was going down a lot: she was in their team's lead position. She'd spent all the fall semester building a massive forward shield, which would have been a bad strategy on an individual level except it had bought her a place in an enclaver's alliance, even if it was an extremely dangerous place.

"Nkoyo pulled her up three times, James pulled her up

THE LAST GRADUATE ✦ 229

twice. I got her up once myself," Khamis said. "What were you doing? I'll tell you. You were taking out a razorwing coming at Magnus Tebow. I don't see Magnus at this table. Do you think we're putting ourselves out to cover you so you can help all your New York friends?"

Chloe was on Aadhya's other side, or on the astral plane along with Fareeda—almost everyone at the table was halfway to joining her, or trying to transmute themselves into unmanned ventriloquist dummies—but at that she let out a small strangled squawk, and then covered her mouth and looked away when everyone glanced at her.

"Tebow had a really good go at killing me about seven months ago, right in that corner over there," I said, stupidly grateful for Khamis to have given me ground I thought I could stand on. "I wouldn't lift a finger to put him at the gates ahead of one single person in this school."

"Ah, so he's not your friend," Khamis said, loading on the sarcasm. "You don't like him, you don't want New York to take you."

"El's already got a guaranteed spot," Chloe said, obviously deciding that she had to come in after all if this was going to be some kind of challenge to New York.

Everyone round the table twitched instinctively; it's the kind of gossip we all pay attention to because you can usually trade it for something, but no one really looked surprised. "Which I'm not taking," I said through my teeth. "I *don't* like Magnus, and he's *not* my friend, and I'm *not* going to New York."

Everyone did look surprised then, and Chloe flinched. But Khamis just stared at me incredulously, and then got angry, really angry, like he thought I was telling him a lie so stupidly obvious that it was insulting I expected him to swallow it. He leaned forward and said through his teeth, "Then I have to ask you again. What was that? Why are you helping Magnus Tebow, who you don't like, who isn't your friend, whose enclave you don't want to join, when you're supposed to be helping *us*?"

But getting mad at me isn't safe, because it gives me permission to get mad, too. I put my hands on the table and half came up, leaning forward, and I didn't do it on purpose, but I don't have to do this kind of thing on purpose: the lights in the room started to dim and stutter, except right around me, and the air got cold, and the words came out on a thin stream of fog when I hissed, "I helped Magnus because he *needed* it. The way I blocked the stone storm from crushing your skull when *you* needed it, and if Fareeda had gone down and stayed down, I'd have helped her, too. And if it's too much to ask you to help her cover your massive front so I can save someone else's life in the meantime, then you can try going it without me at all, you selfish toerag."

Khamis was leaning far back by then, with the iridescent green sheen of the light reflecting off his cheekbones and in the dark rings of his wide eyes, but he was stuck, after all. Maybe if he *had* been a coward, he'd have shut up just to get me to back away, but he wasn't, worse luck for both of us, and I had to be lying, because that couldn't be the truth in here. He took a gasp of cold air and said thinly, "That's crazy. What are you going to do? Save everyone? You can't save everyone. Not even you *and* Lake."

"*Watch* me," I said, furious and desperate, but even while I was snarling at him, I knew that the wheels were coming off and the wreck was coming. I'd just barely made it through the obstacle course with fifty kids—not quite fifty kids—and there were more than a thousand of us: the largest senior class in the history of the entire Scholomance. The senior class that Orion Lake had made by saving us and saving us. A thousand timers running out, all at the same time.

Khamis had been in the gym for the run himself, so after I said those stupid words, he wasn't angry at me in the same way anymore, because he'd worked out that I wasn't lying to him. It was the difference between someone threatening to shoot you and someone running around in circles screaming wildly while emptying a gun into the air. He shoved his chair back and stood up. "Get everybody out? You *are* crazy!" He spread his arms to the whole table. "What happens to us while you're busy saving all these people you don't like? You're going to get us all killed while you pretend to be a hero. You think you can take our mana, take our help, and do whatever you want, is that what you think?"

"Khamis," Nkoyo said, low and urgent; she'd got up too, and she was reaching out to put a hand on his arm. "It's been a hard morning." He stared at her incredulous, his whole expression twisted up with indignation, and then he looked round the table at everybody else—everybody else who wasn't saying anything to me, in exactly the same way no one had ever said anything to him, all these years—while he took their mana and their help and did whatever he wanted, because there was no point saying anything when the answer was *yes*. It was just rubbing your own face in it, and the only reason he didn't already know that was he'd never been a loser before, lucky enclave boy.

But he was now. He was a loser, and so was Magnus, so was Chloe, so was every last enclaver in the place, because they weren't getting through the obstacle course without me. It was entirely possible that they weren't getting through the graduation hall without me. So if I offered any of them a place at my side, in exchange for everything they could possibly scrape together, mana and hard work and even friendship, and if I took everything they gave me and used it to pretend to be a hero—even though of course they didn't want me to, because that was, actually, very likely to get them killed—still they'd take it and say thanks, if they knew what was good for them. Thank you, El. Thank you very much.

The silence got longer. Khamis didn't say anything else, and he didn't look at me. He wasn't stupid any more than he was a coward, and he'd got it now that he *had* rubbed his own face in it. And mine, of course, but that wasn't quite the same thing. From this side, it was only embarrassment, really. How unfortunate that someone had made such a scene, such an unnecessary fuss. If only I'd been an enclaver myself, I expect I'd have been trained up to handle moments like this with grace. By now, Alfie would have said, a little rueful, *Do you know, I think we could all do with a nice cup of tea,* and he'd have reached into his ample purse of mana and turned our jug of water into a big steaming teapot, with milk and sugar on the table—just the soothing comfort his own lightly chafed spirit needed. And everyone else would have taken it, not because it helped the gaping wound on their side, but because when you had nothing, you took what you could get.

But I wasn't an enclaver, so I didn't handle it gracefully, and they didn't even get a cup of tea for their pains. I just turned and ran away into the stacks.

Chapter 10
THE HIMALAYAS

ADHYA FOUND ME A WHILE LATER. I don't know what time it was. There isn't any daylight in here and the surroundings never change and I was alone in the little library room where you couldn't hear the bells, the room where no one else had ever had a class, where the Scholomance had tried and tried all this year—not to kill me, but to make me turn my back and let other people die, kids I didn't know. As though the school had known what it needed to worry about, long before I'd worked it out for myself. The way it had known that I could kill a maw-mouth, and had tried to bribe me into going the other way.

My freshmen were still coming up here for their session every Wednesday, but Zheng had told Liu that the attacks had stopped completely. This ought to have been the safest place in the school to begin with, and now it was. There wasn't any point shunting mals over here anymore. The school had tried, and it hadn't worked. I hadn't learned my lesson; I hadn't turned my back.

"So this is nice," Aadhya said, from the doorway, looking around the room and seeing it the way I'd seen it my first morning, a promise of safety and shelter and quiet, before I unwisely signed my name on the schedule and picked up the gauntlet the school had hurled at my feet. She came in and dragged around the desk in front of me, sitting down to face me. "The others went down to lunch. Liu and Chloe are going to get us something. Everyone's still on board, if you were wondering."

"Not really," I said, and laughed a little, jangly and helpless, and put my hands over my face so I didn't have to look at her, my friend, the first friend I'd ever had, besides Orion, who didn't count; the first normal sane person in the world who'd looked at me and decided she was going to give me a chance to not hurt her.

Then Aadhya said, "I had a sister," so I picked my head back up to stare at her. She talked about her family all the time. She'd given me a letter for them, the way she and Liu and Chloe had letters for Mum, just in case, but even without looking at the envelope, I already knew the address of the big house in the New Jersey suburbs with the swimming pool in the backyard. I'd heard endless painfully appetizing descriptions of the ongoing and deeply vicious cooking competition between her grandmothers, Nani Aryahi and Daadi Chaitali, and a whole line of bad jokes acquired in her grandfather's garage workshop, where he'd taught her how to solder and how to use a saw. I knew all about her sharp and sharp-dressed mum who wove enchanted fabric by hand, fabric that went to the enclaves of New York and Oakland and Atlanta. I knew about her quiet dad who went out six days a week to do technomancer work at whichever enclave had hired him for that month. I knew their names, their favorite colors, which Monopoly tokens they liked to play. She'd never once mentioned a sister.

"Her name was Udaya. I wasn't even three when she died, so I don't really remember her," Aadhya said. "Nobody in my family ever talked about her. For a while I thought that I made her up, until when I was ten I found a box of photos of her in the attic." She gave a snort. "I freaked *out*."

I knew what she was doing, and what I was supposed to do. I was supposed to ask what happened, and then I was supposed to let Aadhya tell me about her sister who'd died in here, maybe during graduation, and then Aadhya was going to tell me she understood I had to try and save as many people as I could, and then I was supposed to come downstairs and if I couldn't get my head out of my arse long enough to make everyone a nice cup of tea, Chloe would probably do it for me, and we'd all go back to work on our strategy this afternoon as if nothing had changed. And I knew why: because that was the only sensible, practical thing for her to do, even if what she really wanted was to yell at me twice as loud as ever Khamis had.

"I can't do this," I said, my voice as quavery as if I'd been crying, even though I hadn't been, I'd just been sitting there alone. "I'm sorry. I can't."

I fumbled for the power-sharer, and Aadhya reached out and grabbed it down around my wrist, pinning it to the desk. "Again? All I actually need is for you to put aside the drama in your own head and shut up and sit there and listen to me for like five minutes. I think you *can* do that much."

I couldn't exactly say no. Anyway, she'd have been in her rights to smack me into next week, because what good would it do her for me to pull out? Liesel had Alfie's buckets of mana, and brains and ruthlessness and a team totally dedicated to getting the hell out, and it hadn't been worth two shits when the Himalayas attacked. Everyone else was still on board for exactly the same reason everyone was ever on board with anything in here, which was exactly the same reason everyone ever put themselves into this hellpit of a school, and that's because it was better than the alternatives. That was all I could be: the lesser evil.

Aadhya gave it a few narrow-eyed moments, until she was sure I'd been cowed, before she took her hand off and sat back. "Okay, so, let's pretend after I told you about Udaya, you said, *What happened to her?* like a normal person."

"She died in here," I said, dully.

"This is not a guessing game, and no," Aadhya said. "My parents were really young when Udaya was born. They were living with my dad's parents, and his dad was incredibly old-school. He insisted that my mom homeschool, and we were never allowed to go anywhere, not even the playground down the block. We couldn't even play in the yard without a grown-up right there. I actually do remember that; he put a ward on the back door that zapped us if we tried to go through it alone. Udaya got sick of it. When she was eight, she climbed out the window and headed to the playground. A clothworm got her before she made it halfway down the block. They would come around our house sometimes to lay eggs, so their babies could sneak in through the wards and chew on my mom's weaving. It just got lucky."

"I'm sorry," I said, feeling stupid in the way *I'm sorry* always feels stupid when you mean it.

Aadhya just shrugged back. "Mom asked her parents to stay in the States after the funeral. My aunt had married into Kolkata by then, so they could. She took me to live with them in a one-bedroom and put me in a mundie preschool next door. Dad joined us after a month. A couple of years later, they took everything they'd been saving to buy into an enclave, turned it into cash, and got our house across the street from a good school, and they made sure it was always full of tons of food and toys so all my school friends would want to come over to my place, even though it meant they couldn't do magic when my friends were around. Daadi came to live with us when I was in kindergarten. Daduji was dead by then. Nobody's ever told me for sure, but I'm pretty sure it was suicide."

I was, too; there aren't that many causes of death for wizards between the ages of eighteen and a hundred. Cancer and dementia eventually get too aggressive to stave off with magic, and if you live outside an enclave, sooner or later you become the slow-moving wildebeest and a mal picks you off the end of the pack, but not until then.

"I yelled at my mom for hiding it from me," Aadhya said. "She told me she didn't want me to be afraid. Daduji loved us, he wanted so bad to protect us, that's all he was trying to do, but he couldn't. And Mom wanted to protect me, too, but she also wanted me to live as much as I could while I had the chance, because Udaya never got to live at all."

Really, it wasn't a shocker or anything. It was just maths. Have two wizard kids, odds are you're not going to see them both grow up. Possibly not either. Udaya had only got a little more unlucky than the average. Or a lot more unlucky, if you considered she'd spent every scarce minute of her entire life shut up in a nicer version of the Scholomance itself.

"Anyway, that's how long I've known that I was probably going to die before I was old enough to vote," Aadhya said. "And I don't want to die, I want to get out of here, but I'm not going to put off being a person until I make it. So I'm not going to pretend like I didn't know. I knew when I asked you to team up, I knew that I'd just gotten lucky. It wasn't anything I did. I was just a loser girl like you and a desi girl like you, and I wasn't a complete jerk to you, so you let me get close enough to figure out that you were a rocket and I could grab on."

"Aad," I said, but I didn't have anywhere to go from there, and I don't even know if she heard me. It came out as thin and crackly as broken glass, and she wasn't looking at me; she was staring down at the desk and tracing back and forth over the graffiti on the edge with her thumb, LET ME OUT LET ME OUT LET ME OUT, and her mouth was turned down.

"Somebody always gets lucky, right?" she said. "Why not me? Why shouldn't I be the one who wins the lottery? I told myself that, but I didn't believe it, because it was *too* lucky. I knew I had to do something to deserve it. Like I knew you'd had to do something to deserve that book you got. And I hadn't. So first I kept waiting for you to ditch me, and then I kept waiting to have to do something, but I didn't. And I'm telling you about Udaya because, in my head, at some point, I think I decided, okay, it was like a trade. I didn't get to have my sister, so I got you."

I had a horrible gargled noise stuffed up in my throat, because I couldn't ask her to stop. I couldn't want her to stop, even if I had my hands pressed over my mouth, and there were tears building up along the ledge of my fingers.

Aadhya just kept talking. "I knew that was bullshit, but it made me feel better about not doing anything. So all these months, I've been letting that sit in my head, and that was stupid of me, because if you're who I get instead of my sister—I can't just leave you behind and still be a person." She looked up then, and it turned out she was also crying, tears trickling down her face and just starting to drip off her chin, even though her voice didn't sound any different. "I'm not leaving you behind."

I really wanted to be blubbing like a child, but instead I had to pull myself together and stop her. "I don't want that! I'm not asking you or anyone else to stay behind with me."

"Right, obviously." Aadhya swiped her sleeve across her face and sucked in a snuffle. "You'd rather run away and wallow in angst than *ask* for *help* or anything else extremely horrible like that."

"If you want to help me, you'll get out the gates as fast as you can. That's the whole point! Whatever Khamis thinks, I'm going to get you there—"

"Not all on your own you're not," Aadhya said. "Khamis is a bag of wieners, but he's not wrong. I don't care if you get your biggest superhero cape on, you can't just carry a thousand people out the door on your back."

"So what are you going to do? If you turn round at the gates and make a stand with me, you'll just be another target for me to cover. I'm not going to stand by and let people die, but that doesn't mean I'm going to *trade* you for them. I'm *not*."

"Uh, not telling you to?" Aadhya shook her head and pushed herself up out of the chair. "Come on. I don't know what I'm going to do, but I know I can come up with something better than *Book it out the gates without giving you a second thought* or *Die tragically and pointlessly at your side,* neither of which sound genius to me. Since that's all you've got so far, pull your head out of wherever you've shoved it and consider the crazy idea that maybe us pathetic little people could help you solve this problem. I know it's against your most sacred principles to ask anyone for anything, and obviously we don't have any reason to care about figuring out how you could save everybody's lives, but maybe some of us are really bored and don't have anything better to do."

It still sucked. Maybe Aadhya didn't want to leave me behind, but Khamis would've been just fine with it, and I was pretty sure that the difference between him and everyone else was, he had either the nerve or the guts to let it show. Of course they didn't want me saving anyone else's lives if it meant I didn't have as much time to save their lives. That didn't make them grotesquely selfish; it just made them *people*. It was even fair, when they were the ones I'd actually made a deal with, the ones who were planning to have my back. That deal meant I was supposed to have their backs, too. And yeah, Aadhya had given me an out, saying she hadn't done anything to deserve me, but they'd all done more to deserve me than anyone else had, if I even did call for being *deserved*.

The only thing that helped was Aadhya had done more than any of the rest of them. If she wasn't demanding that I put her first, nobody else had the right to demand it, either. But that didn't give her or me the right to volunteer them to save everyone. I didn't have the right, but I had the power, because their only alternative was to quit our alliance, or maybe open up one of the floor drains and jump in, which looked roughly as good a survival plan. And they all knew it, and I knew it, and that meant I was *making* them do it, just as much as Khamis taking the nice safe center position in his team.

But my only alternative was to tell them never mind, I wasn't going to save everyone, I was just going to concentrate on getting our group to the gates, and after that I'd help whoever was left. Which wouldn't be very many. No long tedious graduation ceremonies for us. Historically, according to the graduation handbook, about half the deaths happen before the first person reaches the gates, and the time between when that first lucky survivor gets out and when the last lucky survivor does is close to ten minutes, year after year. I'd be tenderly shepherding my own little flock to safety past a few hundred kids screaming as they were butchered. By the time we got to the gates and I turned back, most of them would already be dead.

I couldn't stand it either way, which was too bad for me, since there wasn't a third option as far as I could tell. The way I attempted to make one appear was sitting at the library table like a plank without looking anyone in the face, staring fixedly at the bread roll that Chloe had brought me without eating it. I pretended the stabbing pains in my stomach were hunger, and left it to Aadhya to say, "Okay, let's figure this out," to everyone else sitting round the table in the depths of awkward silence.

"What is there to figure out?" Khamis said coldly; he was sitting with his arms folded over his chest, glaring at me so hard that I could tell he was doing it even without looking anywhere near his face. "Are *we* supposed to be worrying about how to save Magnus, now, too? I don't think he's returning the favor."

Everyone shifted awkwardly, and then Liu said, "Well, he should."

"What?" Khamis said, but Liu wasn't talking to him; she'd turned to Chloe. "What if we invited Magnus and his team to join up with us? Wouldn't they say yes?"

Chloe stared at her. "Well—" She looked at me and then back. "I mean, yes, of course, but—" She stopped and looked at me again, and fair enough, I'd clearly conveyed to her on more than one occasion that I could think of many uses for Magnus, in the line of testing sharp objects and toxic chemicals, so she had a reasonable cause for doubting whether I'd be on board with signing him on. But I didn't look up. I didn't

242 • NAOMI NOVIK

feel I had the right to object to any other ideas anyone had, given I'd rejected the one that involved all of them getting to live.

"That's the only way this can work. Anyone who wants to run the course with El has to join us, really become allies," Liu said. "It can't just be El and Orion covering all of us. They won't be able to do it. We all have to help cover each other so they can fight the worst mals, or save anyone about to go down."

No one else was really participating in the conversation; almost certainly all just wondering what on earth they were going to do to save themselves while I was busy saving everyone else. But Yaakov had been listening, and apparently he was sincerely giving it a think, because he said, "But if this keeps happening, soon we will have everyone trying to run the course at the same time." Ibrahim actually blinked over at him in surprise that he was taking the conversation seriously.

"Okay, so?" Aadhya said. "Most years, sure, we're all trying to get private time on the course. But that's not the problem we actually have. Did anyone here feel like the course wasn't hard enough this morning? Even with fifty kids running?" Nobody had, very clearly; Aadhya didn't even bother answering her own rhetorical question. "Let's say El and Orion run the course twice a day. Everyone who wants to run with them gets to go once every other day, like we're all supposed to. Even if literally everyone joins up, that's fine; the gym can handle a few hundred kids at once, no problem. This isn't rocket science or anything. We already know that we need allies. If we *didn't* team up for graduation, if we all ran solo, practically everybody would die. This is just—the next level. We're *all* going to be allies, because it's worth it to help some rando kid if that means five minutes later, El's going to be able to stop the volcano from falling on your head."

"All of which is true right up until we all get to the gates at the same time, and Patience and Fortitude come for everybody at once," Khamis said, the bastard, and Aadhya looked at me, asking the question I still wanted to run away from while screaming loudly. But it was only fair, after all: if I was making them jump through all these hoops, just so I could be a hero, I had to be a bloody proper one, didn't I?

"I'll take them out if I have to," I said. I was just trying to get the words out without hysterics, but it came out like I was performing deadpan. Half the table thought I was making some sort of joke and gave it a polite laugh by way of telling Khamis to shut up and stop making things unnecessarily awkward, but Liu and Chloe both understood instantly that I wasn't joking at all, and Khamis was still glaring daggers at me so hard that he presumably could tell that I was thirty seconds from projectile vomiting into his stupid face, and with all of them staring at me, the tittering died off and then everyone went through a round of looking at one another sideways to check *Do we think El's gone off her trolley for good,* and then there was a round of uncertainty over whether I was just saying it or whether I had any actual reason to imagine that I could do anything of the sort.

I don't think everyone had decided yet when Nkoyo said, "We should split up by language. You've got the big four, right?" she asked me, meaning English, Chinese, Hindi, and Spanish, and I managed a short nod. I suppose now I had to be grateful for my library seminar after all, and all Liu's coaching.

Liu said, "We'll write it up next to the gym doors," and after a very abbreviated discussion, we broke up to start spreading the word.

Aadhya took me in tow—I think she felt I wasn't to be trusted not to go skulking off again—but she didn't move quick enough. As soon as I was plausibly but not actually out of hearing range, everyone else started whispering about it and I overheard Cora say, "Orion never found it, and she was so sick that day," and I told Aadhya, very calmly in my opinion, "Sorry," and ran ahead to the stairs and down to the nearest loo, outside the cafeteria, where I threw up what felt like most of my stomach lining, and then just sat crouched there over the toilet crying with my hands over my mouth. In here, by the end of freshman year you learn to cry with your eyes open, without making noise. Except of course nothing was going to come after me anyway, because I could kill maw-mouths as long as I had the mana, and there was a New York power-sharer on my wrist at the moment, apparently not to be removed no matter how ludicrous a swerve I took, so what mal would be stupid enough to come after me anymore?

Aadhya came in after a few minutes and waited for me outside the stall. I finally got hold of myself and crept out to wash my face. She kept watch for me until I had finished and then said, "Let's get started."

Orion gave me a poke in the back at lunchtime—the kids behind me in the queue let him ahead of them without his even asking—and said, *"Hey Orion, I've got this great idea, how about you stop hunting actual mals that are eating actual people, and spend six days a week doing fake gym runs twice a day instead."*

I didn't stop; I wasn't going to miss out on the rice pud that for once was actually rice pud. There was a colony of the usual glutinous maggots growing rapidly through the big metal pan, but they'd only got halfway through so far, and I managed to get a bowlful. Ah, the privileges of being a senior. I also got three apples, despite the faint greenish shine you could see if you held them to the light at just the right angle: Chloe had a really brilliant spray that would take off the toxic coating. "Lake, I know you like your walkies, but fewer than twelve people have been eaten this year so far, and five hundred are due to be gobbled in the first ten minutes downstairs. Don't be a twat. You can run around and play with the mals after the work's done." He scowled at me, but the numbers were too pointedly on my side, so he stopped arguing and sullenly took a scoop of the spaghetti Bolognese, and sprinkled it with a thick helping of shaved antidote in lieu of Parmesan.

We gave it an hour after lunch, to let the word spread a bit, before we went down for the first Hindi run. There were perhaps twenty kids waiting: two teams mostly made of friends and trading acquaintances of Aadhya's, including one girl from Kolkata enclave who knew her cousins. My freshman Sunita had talked her older brother Rakesh into talking his team into coming, which included one wary enclaver from Jaipur.

The handful left over were stragglers, kids who hadn't got into any alliance yet. There aren't many Hindi-speaking stragglers. The enclaves in India and Pakistan only have enough spare seats for half the indie kids who would like to come, so there're brutal exams and interviews before you even get inducted, and even the worst of the kids who make it in are almost always a cut above the straggler level of Scholomance loser. But some parents will spend huge amounts of money buying seats, even if their kids can't qualify on their own merits. Sometimes those kids turn out to be great at making friends, or sometimes they get better under the pressure, and sometimes they get lucky, and these were the ones who hadn't.

They'd come down for the run because they didn't have

much hope anyway, so a grasp at any straw was worth it. It was a tiny bit useful just to come here and meet some kids who *did* have alliances, because those kids might end up with openings they'd have to fill. But they all looked deeply skeptical while Aadhya gave everybody the official lecture that they each had to help anyone they could, or they wouldn't be welcome to run again. This boy Dinesh with really awful alchemy scars that had melted half his face—an accident it would probably cost five years of mana to fix if he got out of here—stared at her while she was talking as if she were an alien from several galaxies over.

But when we crossed the river for the first time, and the rilkes came out of the half-frozen mud on the banks and lunged with shredding claws for him and the two straggler kids next to him, he went ahead and threw up a shield over them all instead of just himself, which won me the ten seconds of casting time that I needed to finish disintegrating the massive hungerhowl erupting from beneath the ice, which was about to swallow them whole along with the rilkes and several other members of our group.

They all still looked fairly shell-shocked coming out of the gym, but one of them offered Dinesh a drink from a water bottle, and he walked away down the corridor with them. And I came out panting for breath, but nobody had got killed, and I wasn't a twitchy wreck, either.

Orion wasn't panting at all, just sullen and bored as he trailed out after me. "You really want to do this twice a day, every day?" he said, with a whinge to it. I have to confess I felt meanly pleased the next day during the first Spanish run when the crazy evil glaciers reared up a few minutes earlier than before, and he *tripped*, because he hadn't been paying proper attention. I had to use a telekinesis spell to scoop him out of the giant toothy blue crevasse and toss him—possibly a little more vigorously than necessary—into a snowbank.

"Maybe you *do* need a bit more practice, Lake," I said sweetly to him out in the hall as he irritably brushed off the snow and scowled at me. I beamed back and flicked a blob of snow off his nose, and then he visibly stopped being annoyed and started wanting to kiss me, but there were *people* there, so I glared him off.

The Spanish run was almost too easy to be good practice: it was an even smaller group than the Hindi one, just a handful of Puerto Rican and Mexican kids who'd heard about the plan from friends allied with New York enclavers, and one alliance headed by a kid from the Lisbon enclave who was friends with Alfie. But that made it easier to spot who wasn't actually trying to help anyone else; three guesses who, and no prizes if you got the Lisbon enclaver on the first go. She got huffy and indignant when I told her afterwards she wouldn't be welcome if she did it again, and that if she wanted the chance, she'd be spending her mana to patch up all the assorted injuries from the run.

"Is that what you think?" she said, sharp with outrage. "I'm following your orders now? I don't think so. Who needs you anyway? Come on, we're leaving," she added to her team, except we'd just finished a course that had made abundantly clear that *they* needed me, very badly, and her top recruit, Rodrigo Beira—sixth in the class rankings, in sniffing distance of valedictorian—got up from where he'd been crouched on the floor gulping for air and quietly went over to start help tending one of the Puerto Rican girls who had a badly lacerated arm filled with spiky bits of ice that were melting only grudgingly. Enclaver girl stared after him, and then jerked a look at the rest of her team, none of whom met her eyes, and all of whom one after another went to help Rodrigo.

If I was feeling a bit smug afterwards, which I might have been, the afternoon took care of that nicely: when Orion and I went down with Liu for the first Chinese run, there wasn't a single person there. We waited for nearly twenty minutes, Liu biting her lip and looking sorry. Chinese and English circles are fairly separate in here, since you can go your entire career doing lessons in only one language or the other, but a Chinese-speaking team of kids from Singapore and Hanoi had been among the crowd at the gates two days ago, and Jung Ho from Magnus's team did lessons in a mix of Chinese and English and had promised to spread the word, which surely hadn't needed much spreading.

Which meant, I realized when we finally gave up waiting, that someone had sent round a *different* word: *Stay away.*

"I asked around a little at dinner," Liu said that evening. She was sitting cross-legged on her bed picking softly at the lute while I sat against the wall doing crochet in a sluggish desultory way, every stitch reluctant. I looked up at her. "The Shanghai enclave had a meeting of their seniors yesterday, about the runs. After I asked a few people about it, Yuyan sent someone to invite me to meet her and Zixuan in the library."

I sat up and left the crochet in my lap. "And?"

"They wanted to ask me a question about how you do magic," Liu said. "I agreed I would tell them, if they told me why they wanted to know." I nodded a bit grimly; that was a sensible information trade—if also the kind you only carefully negotiate with someone you're considering a potential enemy. "Zixuan asked me if you have trouble doing *small* spells."

I stared at her. If I'd had to guess at his question, that

wouldn't have been anywhere on the list. I'd been braced for the one about what I'd do to get the power for my spells, if for instance I ran out of mana on graduation day, or maybe how exactly I was so good at controlling gigantic maleficaria. Most wizards don't give a rat's arse whether I'm bad at boiling a cup of water for tea once they see me setting lakes on fire. "I have trouble *getting* small spells."

"You've got trouble casting them, too," Liu said. "I didn't realize it was important until Zixuan made me think about it, but I did notice—you remember back in August, when we were just starting to work on the amplification spell, and I tried to teach you that little tone-keeper spell first, so you wouldn't accidentally sing the wrong tone and change the meaning?"

"Ugh," I said, which comprehensively described that afternoon's delights, which, yes, had lodged firmly in my memory. I had ten goes at the spell and my tongue felt like it had been clamped in a shop vise before I gave up and told Liu I'd just have to learn the bloody tones properly on pain of blowing myself to bits.

Liu nodded. "It's meant for really little kids who are just learning how to talk, so you can teach them the 'yell for help' spell. I could cast it when I was three." I must have been gawping at Liu openly with my doubt on my face, because she added, "It's happening for you with Precious, too."

My hand instinctively went up to wrap around the bandolier cup on my chest, where she was curled up sleeping. "There's something wrong with her?"

Liu shook her head. "Not *wrong*. But it took so much longer for her to start manifesting, and now she's already a lot stranger than the others. I saw her try to *bite* Orion once in the library when he was about to put his arm around your shoulders. That means she's exercising judgment that's independent of yours. That's not really a thing that happens with mice."

I was about to claim that my judgment was perfectly aligned with Precious on the subject of Orion putting his arm around my shoulders or on any other part of me, but Liu gave me a pointed look and I couldn't make the words come out of my mouth.

"Anyway, I also realized, you almost never *use* normal spells," she went on. "You'll even sweep the floor with a broom before you'll use a spell."

"My spells are more likely to sweep every living person in the room into the nearest rubbish bin," I said.

Liu nodded. "Yes. And those are the spells you're good at, the ones that come easily. So you don't ever use magic when you can use something else."

"But how did *Zixuan* guess all that?" I asked, after a moment. I was having some difficulty digesting the idea. I never *do* get ordinary spells, and the ones I get are almost always unnecessarily complicated—like those Old English cleaning spells I'd got last term, which turned out to be worthless for trade even beyond being in Old English, because they took twice as much mana to use as the modern cleaning charms everyone else had, and needed more focus besides. I'd assumed that was the school—or, well, the universe—being out to get me, not because there *weren't* ordinary cheap spells, for me. I wasn't sure whether that ought to make me feel better or worse, actually.

"He said it's the same way a reviser works," Liu said. "It abstracts away detail and allows you to operate on a higher scale, control more power. But you can't use a reviser to do detail work. So—you're like a living reviser. That's why you have trouble with little spells, and not really big ones. He guessed because you could channel the power from *his* reviser so easily."

"I wouldn't have called it *easy*, myself," I muttered, but that was just grousing. I would've quite liked a chat with him myself, actually; it sounded as though he might know more about how my magic worked than I did. "But in that case, they know I'm not lying—they know I really *can* get them through the course. Why wouldn't they come?"

"They don't believe you could really have hidden your power from everyone," Liu said. "They think New York knew all along, and you've been in with them from the start, and just hiding it so none of the other enclaves would know about you before graduation."

I groaned and thumped my forehead down against my knees. The problem was, I couldn't see any way to disprove it. It made all the sense in the world from their perspective, which was limited by the language barrier that runs through the middle of the school. Over my four years in here, I've shared a class with at least half the kids in the English-language track, and almost none with Chinese-track kids. I know the ones like Yuyan who are doing enough languages that we've overlapped once or twice, and the bilingual Chinese-track kids who take their general classes in English to count for their language requirement. But that's it. Most kids don't cross over very much to begin with—most group conversations in this school happen either in English or in Chinese, so you hang out with the kids who prefer the same one you do. Liu deliberately chose to spend more time with the English-speaking crowd because she's working on spell translation, which requires as much fluency as writing complicated metered poetry with lots of long obscure words in a foreign language.

But I crossed over not at all, because I wasn't in any conversations, period. I went to my classes and spoke to almost no one, ate alone, studied alone, worked out alone, tucked away in my own cramped little cell, *exactly* as I would have if I'd been deliberately hiding a very bright light under a bushel. The actual explanation, which was that I hadn't had any alternatives because no one liked me, only invited the question of why I hadn't *made* any of them like me by giving them a good look at the aforementioned bright light, thereby getting myself courted by all instead of dangerously isolated.

That was such a good question that I'd literally spent three years aggressively telling myself I was going to join up to an enclave as soon as I got the chance, and then carefully avoiding any possibility of a chance while pretending to myself I was playing some sort of extremely long game. If I'd ever acknowledged to myself that possibly my mum had been right and I didn't want to join an enclave after all, I'd probably just have lain down and died in hopelessness at the prospect of—the rest of my *life*. I'd only been able to admit it to myself after Orion, Orion and Aadhya and Liu; after I wasn't completely friendless anymore.

"I don't suppose they let you talk them out of it?" I asked, without any real hope. It looked stupid in retrospect even to *me*, so I didn't think Yuyan and Zixuan were going to believe it. Maybe someone who'd been among the kids who'd deliberately avoided me, but the Shanghai kids hadn't any clue that loser-kid me even existed until suddenly I erupted into prominence. And then Chloe and the New York kids suddenly embracing me en masse, offering me an alliance and a guaranteed spot, just because Orion had been hanging around me for a few weeks? I'd thought they were completely mad. It would make loads more sense if actually I'd secretly been part of their crew all along, or at least for a year or more.

Liu shook her head. "They were polite, but I'm pretty sure the other reason they wanted to talk to me was to get an idea if you had tricked me, or if I was trying to establish a relationship with New York."

I blew out a breath. That was Liu trying to be polite to me, but I knew what she meant was, the Shanghai kids wanted to get an idea if she—and by extension her family—were getting ready to undercut the established Chinese enclaves and make an alliance with New York to get their own enclave. "Which did they pick?"

Liu held up her hands in a shrug. "I told them that I couldn't prove anything. But you were my friend, and you really wanted to get everyone out, and you aren't going to New York. So . . . they think you tricked me." She gave a small sigh.

It wasn't even especially paranoid of them. The Asian enclaves have been in a slow and increasingly vicious decades-long wrestling match with New York and London to force them to hand over more Scholomance seats. The Chinese-language track of general classes literally only started in here in the late eighties. Before then, it was English or nothing, even after a good quarter of the school was coming in with some dialect of Chinese as their first language, and it only finally changed when the ten major Asian enclaves, Shanghai in the lead, publicly announced an exploratory committee to build a new school under their control.

Of course, the enclaves didn't really want to follow through on that threat. The wizard population has been growing steadily since the Scholomance opened, but as of right now, adding a second school and splitting the enclaver population across them would mean they'd have to *compete* with the Scholomance for indie kids. Both schools would have to sweeten the odds for us—at the cost of their own kids. And that's apart from the massive cost of building the school itself.

What they really wanted was what they got: more Scholomance seats for their enclaves to hand out, and classes in an easier language for their kids. Not much to ask, but they'd had to *make* the threat to get it, and the allocation is still a far cry from fair. I'm in here myself thanks to a spot London really shouldn't still have had to give out, and meanwhile indie kids all over Asia are still doing those grueling exams for the chance to be among the one in two kids who get a place.

But that can't be fixed any more without starting to take places away from the very top international enclaves in the US and Europe, none of whom want to give up a single one. The next reallocation is coming soon—and there's a real fight brewing over it. New York and Shanghai and their allies on both sides have been doing increasingly nasty things to one another for the last few years, jockeying for position. It would be a bit of a shocker to find out that a New York ally had gone after Bangkok and literally taken the enclave down, but we can all imagine it. Everyone knows it's entirely possible that there's a full-on enclave war happening right now.

Everyone including me, but the truth is, I've only known it in a vague background-noise way. All these years I've been a loser struggling in the soup; the geothaumaturgipolitical dancing among the top enclaves of the world didn't matter to me anymore than pariah-loser me mattered to the top kids from Shanghai enclave. But it mattered *now*, and the more I thought about it, the more of a desperate mess it looked. Of course Yuyan and Zixuan wouldn't trust me. They thought I was planning to graduate and head straight to New York, where presumably I'd be trying to help kill them and their families. Why wouldn't I just do for them in here if I had the chance?

"But what's their alternative?" I said in frustration, having gnawed it over in my head without finding a way through. "No matter what, they still can't get through the obstacle course without me, and if they don't get any practice in, they'll die anyway. I'll grant you it's a bad chance, but it's the only chance they've got. Why not give it a go? Or—why not at least send a few minions to give it a go, and make sure?"

Liu shook her head. "The course is in the *gym*."

I groaned and lay myself out flat on the ground, staring at the ceiling. The gym, which I'd *completely overhauled* this past Field Day, in a bizarre and utterly nonsensical use of power which would suddenly make fantastic sense if what I'd been doing was, for instance, arranging some kind of mysterious sabotage of the obstacle course that would force people to put themselves in my power. Ideally in some way that would allow me to maintain power over them even after they left school and went home to their enclaves. That's the whole idea behind the obstacle course to begin with—giving your consent is necessary to make it work. If some maleficer— *some* maleficer—managed to wriggle their way into it, that would be an excellent mechanism to use to force people to become their mindless zombie servants et cetera.

"I'm sorry," Liu said softly. "I did already try asking a few indie kids to come, but . . . they don't really trust me." She put her hand up to run it back and forth over the short spiky fuzz of her head, an unconscious gesture she'd picked up ever since it had been cut. She hadn't made that many more friends than I had, in her first three years in the Scholomance. Her family hadn't needed her to network. They'd needed her to stay alive, and keep her kid cousins alive through their freshman year, and she'd been meant to do it with malia. And when you're just a low-level maleficer, people pick up on that sort of thing and get nervous. "And they do trust the Shanghai kids. Most of them wouldn't have spots in here at all if Shanghai hadn't fought for them."

I'd have debated the purity of the enclavers' motives, but I'll grant you that I didn't have very good ground to stand on, me with my for-granted spot that Mum asked *me* if I wanted to take. "Do you suppose it would help things if we told them that I've actually *got* a mind control spell that works on masses of people at once?" I said aloud.

"No," Liu said, positively. Then she said, ". . . do you?"

I grimaced, enough of an answer. She was right, of course; that's not very confidence-inspiring.

But if we couldn't find a way to change their minds—if Zixuan and Yuyan and the other kids from Shanghai didn't come, if they all stayed away from our obstacle course runs, because they were afraid that it was a massive setup meant to take control of their brains and turn them all into trojan horses—and then graduation came, and they all *died*, in droves, because they hadn't had any practice, while everyone who'd followed New York's lead came sailing out home to their families—then it would in fact turn out to *be* a massive setup, in result if not intention, and I didn't think their parents would be particularly interested in what my intentions had been.

As if to emphasize the problem, next morning there were more than a hundred kids for the English run. That many kids all in one place was so much temptation that a squad of extremely real, extremely hungry mals jumped us during the run, bursting out of snowdrifts and from behind jagged towers of ice. It wasn't very wise of them; we could all tell they were the real thing, because they hadn't been in the run earlier that week, so Orion made a beeline for each one. He took them all down without a worry, except for the massive mantaray-sized digester that peeled itself off one face of the glaciers during their attack and tried to just flop itself completely over him. That one I just disintegrated whole.

I had the attention to spare, because everyone else had already got better. Thanks to Liesel, I was grudgingly forced to admit; she had been waiting right in front of the doors while everyone gathered, and as I got there, she preemptively announced in projecting tones, "We must approach the run differently. Stop thinking how you can help the people nearest to you. Think about what help you can give best, and look for the nearest person who needs that help."

That was completely unintuitive, and very few people were willing to let go of their alliances quite that thoroughly yet. But by halfway through the run, it was so obviously the better approach that everyone was at least *trying* to do it. By the end I almost felt as if Orion and I were running it on our own—the same exhilaration except even better, though the run was still a thousand times harder—because the plan was *working*. Everyone was helping everyone else, saving everyone else, and all I had to do was jump in when anyone's luck went a bit sour.

There were a lot more kids at the Hindi run in the afternoon, too: Ravi and three other enclavers from Jaipur showed up with their teams, so evidently Liesel's cooing had paid dividends after all. Still nobody from Mumbai, though; not from anywhere in Maharashtra. That wasn't really a surprise. Back at the start of freshman year, when all of us who weren't enclavers ourselves were in the first frantic rush of trying to make friends, the other kids started going to lengths to avoid me by the second time meeting me. But the kids from Mumbai would literally pick up and move away from me without another word as soon as they heard my name.

I don't know exactly what they've heard about me. My dad's family haven't actively spread the prophecy round, I don't think. If they had, surely some of those enclaves I'm supposed to darken and destroy would have taken a much more energetic interest in my well-being, or lack thereof, some time before now. So I assume all they know is that the family were going to take me and Mum in, and we didn't last a night inside their compound walls.

Perhaps that doesn't seem like enough to merit *instantly* ostracizing me, but the Sharmas have a reputation among the wizards in Maharashtra roughly like Mum's got in the UK. They've produced several acclaimed healers of their own, but what they're really known for—and how they keep their increasingly large family—is divinatory magic, with a twist. Divinatory magic doesn't generally work out well for many reasons, but one of them is because human beings aren't very good at predicting what will make them happy. I don't mean if you wish for something and then get it twisted in some horrible way like that stupid story about the monkey's paw; I mean in the same prosaic way that you can sincerely be certain that you'd like a dress you see in a shop, and you buy it and take it home, and then it sits in your closet unused for years while you insist to yourself that one day you're going to wear it, until finally you give it away with a sense of relief.

Well, my dad's family have seers who can tell you how to get what will *actually* make you happy. The most famous living one of whom is my several-great-grandmother Deepthi, who nowadays mostly gets approached in supplication by the Dominuses of enclaves that are in a difficult strategic position, who pay her in the equivalent of millions of pounds for

a single brief chat. The legend about her goes that somewhere round her third birthday, she looked up from her toys
while her family were idly discussing marriage prospects, and
very seriously told them not to worry about it until she graduated from the Scholomance. That was quite baffling to
them, since this was 1886, before the cleansing equipment
had broken for the first time, and back then the school was
only open to actual enclavers. Even enclave kids from Mumbai had to compete among themselves for the six seats that
Manchester had begrudgingly allocated to them. Not to
mention that it was perfectly obvious to them that you'd
never spend a priceless Scholomance seat on a girl.

She was seven years old when London took over, subdi-
vided the dormitory rooms, quadrupled the seats, and threw
admission open to independent wizards. By then, her family
already knew that if they ever did get a Scholomance seat,
they were absolutely sending her, and also they were going to
have to find a husband willing to marry in. No wizard family
gives away a girl who can accurately tell you about significant
future events that are years out.

She was perfectly right about not arranging her marriage
beforehand, too. By the time she graduated, her family had
racked up enthusiastic offers from virtually every Indian boy
who'd been in school with her at any point during the past
four years, all of whom she'd quietly given various bits of
advice along the way, such as, "Don't go to your lab section
today," on a day when their usual seat got incinerated in a
pipe explosion, or "Learn Russian and make friends with that
quiet boy in your maths class" who turned out to be the valedictorian and invited you to join his alliance. There was apparently even a group of boys who offered to marry her
together, like the Pandavas or something. She picked a nice
young alchemist from an independent wizard family outside

Jaipur instead—already vegetarian and strict mana—who had two older brothers and was indeed willing to move in and join the family. They proceeded to have five healthy children, four of whom survived graduation, considerably better than the usual odds, and carried on from there. My father was apparently her cherished favorite great-great-grandchild, out of several dozen. I don't understand why she didn't warn him about getting too friendly with that blond Welsh girl in his senior year, although perhaps she did, and he listened as enthusiastically as teenagers ever do to that sort of warning. I would never ignore similar good advice myself if it were given me, of course.

Whatever advice Dad got, he didn't follow it well enough, and as a result here I am, and here he isn't. And I'm not a Sharma from Mumbai, I'm a Higgins from Wales, because thirty seconds after meeting me, Great-Grandmother pronounced my quite horrifying doom—well, horrifying for everyone else alive; for all I know, I'd find my own bliss in becoming a grotesquely evil maleficer blasting enclaves into submission. I certainly can't claim the idea doesn't have a lot of visceral appeal. So then Mum had to tote me all the way back to the commune because my father's family were ready to put baby Hitler me to death, in order to save the world that I'm slated to cover in darkness and murder et cetera.

I should note that this is the same family who are so devoted to nonviolence that they turned down a priceless offer to move en masse into Mumbai enclave, because the place wasn't strict mana and they wouldn't cheat at so much as the cost of the life of a beetle.

You can see why their rejecting me might make the people who are familiar with their reputation look at me askance. Even lacking the details, it's hardly unreasonable to imagine there has to be something extremely unpleasant in my future. And at that, no one's imagining anything quite as extreme as the actual prophecy.

So I quickly stopped trying to introduce myself to any Marathi-speaking kids. In fact I've spent most of the past three years with a low-grade worry about what they might tell people about me, which helpfully filled all the hours where I wasn't worrying about more immediate problems, such as whether I'd get enough to eat that day, or if something were going to eat me.

Of course, now I didn't need to worry about that anymore. They could have stood up in the cafeteria with an amplification spell and repeated the prophecy word for word, and the people joining me for these runs wouldn't have trusted me one jot less. They didn't trust me to begin with; they weren't here because they really believed I was going to save them. They were joining me because even if I *was* a vicious maleficer, there still wasn't any other option for getting in any practice. Surely almost all of them were quietly making secret plans with their allies and other teams for what they'd really do in the graduation hall, and especially what they'd do if I did in fact turn out to be a vicious maleficer.

That was what made Liesel's edict so important. It wasn't possible to go through a run, even just one single run, with everyone round you all working to their own strengths and your most urgent needs, and not realize how much better it was than anything we could manage in a private alliance, even the very best. It was so much better that even if it turned out that I *was* a vicious maleficer and planning to cull some substantial number of the class, they were all probably still better off sticking to the strategy and accepting the risk of me instead of the risk of everything else down there.

That became just as clear to the kids in the Hindi run as it had to the ones in the morning, and word kept spreading. On

Saturday morning there were almost eighty kids for the Spanish run, and that afternoon, the first five kids did finally turn
up for the Chinese run. They were all stragglers.

There's no single thing that marks someone out as a straggler. Sometimes it's just bad luck—you've been jumped too
often, blew all your mana fighting off mals, and now you
haven't anything to contribute to a shared pool. Sometimes
it's even worse luck—you've got an affinity for something
truly useless, like water-weaving. That's tidy on the outside,
you'd make a fortune helping enclaves with their sewer lines,
but you won't have the chance, since it doesn't do yourself or
anyone else any good in here. Sometimes you're just not very
good at magic and not very good at people—you can get by
with one or the other, but if you haven't either, you're in
trouble.

I've tried not to think about what it would be like—the
idea of having to wade into the graduation hall all alone, the
mass of the crowd breaking for the gates ahead of you, a sea
of people with plans and friends and weapons, warding spells
and healing potions, and the maleficaria all around already
beginning to rip kids out of the mass, shredding them into
bones and blood—running because your only hope was to
run, knowing that actually you hadn't any hope, and you'd
die watching other people going out the gates. I spent three
years trying not to think about it, because I thought that was
going to be me.

In this case, one of the poor bastards had developed shakes
that occasionally interrupted his spellcasting, probably aftereffects of a poisoning, or perhaps just trauma. There's no
shortage of that in here. Another one of them had Chinese
about as good as mine, which was a bad sign given that it was
presumably the language she'd been taking classes in for all
four years. It's *not* actually worth it, statistically speaking, to

send your kids in here if they aren't properly fluent in English or Chinese to begin with, which generally also is a sign they're no good at languages. It doesn't matter how brilliant a wizard they are otherwise: they'll be at too much of a disadvantage when they can't keep up with their general subjects. You're better off keeping them at home, guarded as best you can, teaching them in the vernacular they *do* know. But some families try it anyway.

And in fact none of the five were any good during the run. The wisdom of our crowd is vicious, but it's rarely wrong. The boy with the shakes, Hideo, would've been a quite good incanter, except that he'd have died twice during the single run when he interrupted his own invocations. But it didn't matter; with only five kids in the run with me and Orion, we still all sailed through.

Afterwards I made myself tell Hideo, "I'll get you a potion that will hold you for the run." My mum's got a recipe for something she calls calming-waters. She makes a monthly batch to give to wizards who've got muscle spasms brought on by overcasting—when you try to cast a spell you haven't *quite* got enough mana for, you can make up the difference out of your own body, but it often has side effects that are brutal to get rid of. I was reasonably certain it would work for his shakes, too.

The sticking point was, I couldn't actually brew it myself. I had to ask Chloe to do it for me. I gave myself the reward of a silver lining: I asked Orion to come down to the labs, too. He got all bright-eyed and enthusiastic, and then gave me a look of wounded disappointment when he discovered that Chloe was coming, which was exactly why I had asked him. The next time I asked, he'd be sure to ask if there was going to be any company, and then I'd have to say yes or admit I was asking him on a date, which I absolutely wasn't going to do.

It was the best protection against myself that I could come up with.

He was even more annoyed when it took us three hours to get the bloody thing concocted. Chloe kept asking excellent questions like, "Do you grind the scallop shells fine or just pound them to coarse bits?" and "Do you stir clockwise or counter?" none of which I could answer except by panto-miming Mum doing it, trying to remember with my body, and then guessing as best I could. I'm rubbish at alchemy in general, and I'm rubbish at healing in general, too, so the combination is almost always a disaster. The last time Mum tried to teach me, the test drop disintegrated a chunk the size of my fist out of the floor of our yurt.

"That can't be right," Chloe said, looking into the seething angry yellow boil in the pot, which indeed did not look any-thing like calming-waters.

"It's not," I said grimly. "I think I got the timing of the salt and the sulfur wrong."

She sighed. "We'll have to start over."

"Oh, come *on*," Orion moaned outright. In justice, which he wasn't going to get from me, it was take four.

"Stop complaining," I said. "Pretend you're staking us out as bait. The two of us alone in this lab are as likely as anyone in the entire school to get jumped." Judging by her sidelong look, I'm not sure Chloe really appreciated my argument.

The fifth attempt actually came out vaguely resembling the cool green-blue it was meant to be, only with a thick streak of muddy yellow-brown winding through it. I had ab-solutely no idea what we'd done wrong at that point, but Chloe very cautiously dipped in a lock of her own hair, rubbed it between her fingers, then sniffed it, and finally just barely touched it with her tongue. She made a face and spit into the sink and said, "Okay, I think I've got it," then cleared the decks with a brisk cleaning spell and dived in once more. She went much quicker this time, and I couldn't even spot what she did differently, but when she was done, at the end the yellowy mud streak got swallowed up smoothly and vanished away, and a single drop on my tongue was enough to tell me she *had* got it.

The drop wasn't enough to keep away the burst of sour jealousy: I couldn't brew calming-waters, my own mother's recipe, and Chloe could. I'd have had to drink a triple dose to clear that taste out of my mouth.

But she made a big batch and we bottled it into thirty vials. It would take care of Hideo for the rest of the term, and leave enough over for anyone who panicked on graduation day: there were usually a reasonable number of unexpected freak-outs. Orion lugged the crate downstairs to Chloe's room for us and threw me one last reproachful look before flouncing off to go hunting, since I very firmly parked myself into one of the beanbags and made clear I wasn't going anywhere alone with him.

Chloe bit her lip and didn't say anything, but she continued not to say anything even after he left, which wasn't usual for her. It was clear she could have happily used a dose of calming-waters herself to stop worrying: *Is El going to take Orion away from us.* I didn't want to think about that myself, as letting the idea into my head was likely to lead me in the direction of many terrible decisions. "Were you always planning to do alchemy?" I said instead, by way of distracting us both. "Aren't your parents both artificers?"

"Yeah," Chloe said. "But my grandma's an alchemist. She started by teaching me to cook, when I was about ten. She was really happy that I wanted to learn; my mom and my uncle never did. She got in for working on the cafeteria overhaul," she added.

For all that the food in here is mostly awful and regularly contaminated, we're lucky to have it. Originally the Scholomance cafeteria dispensed a nutritious slurry three times a day—thin and watery enough to pass through the very narrow warded pipes—and if you wanted it to be something else, you had to transmute it yourself, which no one could afford to do.

Actually making a particular food out of something else with magic is almost impossible, because you aren't just interested in how you experience it in your mouth: you want the food to work as nutrition for your body once you send it down into your stomach and forget about it. If you turn a box of nails into a sandwich, you might think you've eaten afterwards, but you'll be wrong. And for that matter, if you turn gruel into bread, you'll generally be wrong then, too, because gruel and bread aren't actually that similar as far as your digestive enzymes are concerned. It *has* been done, but only in alchemy labs funded by enclaves, by the kind of wizard who will finish their Scholomance training and then go off to spend ten years in a mundane university getting advanced degrees in chemistry and food science.

You can start with something that technically qualifies as nourishment and then just put a sensory illusion on it, but the illusion will break down as soon as you start chewing. The result is generally more unpleasant than just choking down whatever you started with. The only practical solution is to selectively transmute whatever parts come into significant contact with your senses: you lose the nutrients out of the bits that were transmuted, but that sends the rest successfully down.

However, that's loads more complicated and expensive mana-wise than just waving a hand and turning, say, a stick into a pen, where you don't care in the slightest what's happening on the molecular level as long as you can write with it. Not even enclavers could afford to do it on a regular basis. Most kids came out more or less malnourished, and everyone spent most of their weight allowance bringing in food. It was enough of a factor in deaths that after ten years or so, the decision was made to open up a hole in the wards for transporting in small amounts of actual food, enough to give everyone our thrice-weekly snack bar visit.

But shortly after World War II, New York and a consortium of the US enclaves swooped in and very cheerfully took over the school—London wasn't in any shape to put up a fight—and they hired a batch of those chemist-wizards who went into their labs and developed a food-transmutation process to run on the slurry that was an order of magnitude cheaper than the best solutions before then.

Evidently Chloe's granny had been one of the alchemists who had made it possible—good enough to get a place in New York enclave for the work. I already knew her dad had been allies with her uncle, during graduation, and he'd got in by marrying her mum. So her dad and her granny had been indie wizards who'd made it in by clawing and scratching and working themselves to the bone; her family weren't high up in the council or anything, they were relatively new. No wonder she was so anxious about not losing the Domina's son.

But I couldn't say anything to reassure her. I wasn't coming to New York. I wasn't making her grandmother's bargain, not even the better version of it that I could have struck. So if Orion wanted me more than he wanted New York, I suppose I was going to take him away, and I wasn't going to feel guilty about it, either. Not after the way they'd treated him, raised him to be their hero instead of just another kid. I'd spent most of my childhood yelling at Mum for *not* taking me into an enclave. It hadn't occurred to me what any enclave would do with someone like me, what they'd want of me, what they'd tell a kid too young to resist them, just to get what they wanted.

I wasn't going to give in to them. I wasn't going to give in to anyone: not Magnus, not Khamis, not Chloe, not even Orion, if he asked me himself. I wasn't going to give in to New York, to any of the enclaves, and most of all, I wasn't going to give in to the Scholomance.

After I left Chloe in her room, I walked alone to the gym. The doors were closed today: there were no runs on Sunday. On the other side, the low grinding and clanking noises were going steadily as the obstacle course went on rearranging it-self to try to kill us, all in the name of making us stronger. I stood in front of them listening for a long time. I could; noth-ing tried to jump me. "That's right," I said, aloud, defiantly. "Don't even try. You're not going to win. We're going to get everyone out. *I'm* going to get everyone out."

Chapter 11
ENCLAVERS

DRAMATIC PRONOUNCEMENTS are all very well and good, but on Monday, two hundred kids turned up expectantly for the next English run, and Orion and I started to hit our limits.

The new course itself was absolutely awful. The gym was full of plum trees on the cusp of blooming, with a soft gurgling brook winding among their roots, the last traces of ice clinging to the banks and a pale edge of frost limning the grass. Sunlight dappled down through the leaves and small birds darted around in the distance, chirps coming from amid the branches, lovely and inviting, at least until we got close enough for the trees to start savagely clubbing us with thorny limbs that shredded most shielding spells, and the tiny birds bunched up into a flock that came at us en masse and turned out to be shrikes.

I tried to hit the whole swarm with a killing spell, but it didn't work. Just before the spell landed, the cloud of shrikes all burst apart and started attacking us separately. Orion spent the whole run weaving back and forth through the crowd, shooting them down one at a time, but I couldn't do that: throwing one of my killing spells at a single shrike while it was flying rapidly around a person pecking at them was an excellent way for me to miss the shrike entirely, and kill the person and their three closest neighbors at the same time.

The only thing that saved it from disaster was that everyone *did* keep helping one another—throwing fresh shields over people who had been clubbed, picking the shrikes out of the sky one at a time if they came close enough, neutralizing the poison clouds that occasionally spurted out of the plum blossoms. I wasn't useless, either; halfway through, the trees got inventive. A dozen of them pulled up their roots and wove themselves together into a living wicker man. It went crashing about, grabbing enormous handfuls of people and shoving them inside the basket of its own chest, and then erupted into flames with them imprisoned and screaming just as a second batch of trees followed the first.

The shields that everyone had to keep up against the shrikes were totally useless against the tree-basket-men, and even Orion couldn't make a dent in the things. They weren't consumed by their own fire, which was presumably psychic instead of corporeal. They just kept merrily burning on, right until I tore them all apart with a handy spell I have for constructing a ritual dark tower. It uses whatever construction materials are in the area. The people inside got dumped out, and the trees got shredded apart and reassembled into a tidy hexagonal tower of solid walls bristling with upcurved sharpened stakes placed at intervals that looked exactly as though the structure was designed to have people impaled all over the surface. Even dodging shrikes, everyone gave it a very wide berth.

Nobody died, but seven people came out with exposed bone, a dozen with severe burns, and two people had lost eyes. A couple of enclaver alchemists grudgingly shared drops of restorative tinctures, which were good enough to heal the damage once they emerged from the gym, and nobody complained if they made it out of graduation alive at the cost of an eye, but it had been a sharp lesson in our limitations. There were plenty of small, quick mals. In fact they were excellent candidates to have survived the cleansing, down below.

In the library afterwards, Magnus pulled Orion aside into a corner of the reading room for a deep heartfelt chat, out of earshot of where I'd been before I got up and quietly snuck after to eavesdrop. "Look, bro, I'm sorry to have to be saying this, I know you're trying to move mountains here, but— we've got to have a plan for when you can't," by which he meant, a plan for leaving people behind. That was what every enclaver had.

"If that happens, I guess we'll have to let the best-prepared fend for themselves, Tebow," I said, sweet as a poisoned apple, from behind his back. He flinched and glared at me before he could help himself.

But the truth was *everyone* had that plan: how to recognize when one of your allies had gone down too hard, and it was time to cut them loose and keep going. I'd lived with that plan in my own head for years and years, and just declaring that I was giving it up wasn't actually a solution to the underlying problem. We needed a plan to save everyone instead, and we demonstrably still didn't have one. Magnus wasn't wrong about that.

But we still had a better option than any of the other available ones. More kids kept joining the runs all week long, except in the still-almost-empty Chinese section. One of the former Bangkok enclavers did show, warily, and later in the week, Hideo—calming-waters did beautifully to stop his tics, for half an hour at least, which was plenty of time to do the run—brought a group of three other kids with him, a loser-alliance that he'd had an agreement to follow after in the graduation hall, with no other benefits: even the worst stragglers can get that kind of lousy deal. I think he'd asked them to come and watch him perform with the tics medicated, in hopes they'd agree to let him properly join up, and the prospect of a real fourth brought them—that, or they liked him, and wanted to be convinced.

Apparently they were convinced, and it was contagious, because the following Monday—after the gym debuted yet another completely unsurvivable course—all of the Japanese enclavers turned up for the Chinese section en masse, bringing their allies with them, which made it suddenly a substantial crowd. The biggest Japanese enclaves all have each of their kids make their own team, with no more than one or two carefully picked potential enclave recruits from among the independent Japanese kids, and the rest of the kids are foreign wizards whom they'll aggressively sponsor into foreign enclaves after graduation, the idea being to create relationships all over the world. Loads of kids take Japanese and compete for the slots as a result, since it's substantial help to get into the enclave you actually most want to live in. Mostly people consider themselves lucky to take whatever enclave they can get, even if it means moving halfway round the world from your family.

Some of them had been coming to the English runs before now, since most of them knew both English and Chinese, but it obviously made more sense to come to the less crowded run. They just hadn't wanted to pick a fight with Shanghai enclave, and who could blame them. Turning up like this was the equivalent of them saying publicly they were convinced that they weren't getting out alive otherwise, a vote of no confidence in whatever the Shanghai kids were trying to organize.

What they certainly weren't organizing was runs of the obstacle course, since as far as I knew, no one in the school but me could mind-prison a castigator, which was this week's special guest star. It took *me* a full ten minutes of wrangling the thing while it bellowed and roared and thrashed hideous slimy limbs dripping with acid all over the gym, eating enormous holes in the wide spring meadow buzzing with seventeen different swarms of mana-eating insects that everyone else desperately had to keep off. Orion literally had to go across the gym and back thirty-two times in the single run with a net spell, which kept coming apart every time one tiny drop from the castigator's arms hit it.

"Maybe it doesn't matter," Liu offered wearily, that afternoon in the library, as we sat slumped round the table. Orion had put his head down in his arms and was snoring faintly from inside them. The rest of us were trying to think of ways to talk the Shanghai enclavers round. "Nobody will turn down help on graduation day, and the really desperate ones who will need the most help are coming to the run. Maybe we'll be able to just include them."

"Yeah, it's not like they're going to be useless," Aadhya said. "They're doing *something*. They're in the workshop all the time; I've seen Zixuan in there working with at least a dozen kids every time I go in for supplies."

"This is nonsense. They are not going to be *prepared*," Liesel said. If you're wondering how Liesel came into our discussions, so were the rest of us, but she was both impervious to hints that she wasn't wanted, and also hideously smart, so we hadn't actually been able to chase her from the planning; in fact she had edged her way further up the table at every session. "There are more than three hundred of them and they are not coming to a single run. We cannot yet manage a group even of two hundred properly. Are *we* useless? Have *we* not trained? But it is only lucky that no one died this week. And it is still only the beginning! If they don't start practicing before the end, there will be no hope for them. Put that out of your heads."

"I suppose you'd like me to just abandon three hundred people, then," I said sharply.

She rolled her eyes. "Oh, the great heroine is angry. If they want your help they will come. Until then you should worry less how you will save them and worry more how they will get in your way. Now is it possible we can talk about the order of entry? We cannot keep running in without any organization. This is not a good strategy when we are all collaborating."

She then hauled out four separate diagrams with multiple color-coded alternatives and spread them out on the table. "We must systematically try each of these options over the next six runs. First we will begin with the students with the strongest shielding, and attempt to create a defensive perimeter which can be monitored closely—"

I'll draw a merciful veil over the rest. Liesel was clearly right, so we couldn't stop her marching us off firmly in the proper direction, but for my part, I did feel very much like I'd just been put against the wall by the most dragonish dinner lady at primary school.

That week, without bothering to mention it to anyone, Liesel also marshaled every creative-writing-track kid out of our runs and gave them marching orders to invent minor cantrips that would do things like highlight anyone in trouble with an aura that would shade from amber to bright red as their situation worsened—not something that anyone in the graduation hall would ever previously have wanted, since it was more or less like putting out a beacon for mals—and automatically mark the ground where a person last saw a mal, to warn off the people behind them. Again, not something anyone would've spent mana on in the past. The first I knew about this clever program was when people started glowing all over the place on Friday, and Liesel lectured me and Orion sternly after the run not to even bother looking at anyone who wasn't bright red.

I'd have had several things to say about her high-handed behavior, except I was lying flat on the floor with my eyes shut trying to convince my heart and lungs that really everything was fine and they should just calm down and keep working, and Orion was sunk over his own knees gulping for air, his entire shirt soaked completely through with sweat. We'd reached three hundred kids in the English run.

All of whom had in fact come out alive, and no one had even suffered a half-dissolved limb in the process, because launching behind a perimeter of the students with the best shielding was, in fact, extremely effective, and so were the new warning systems. By the time I had managed to haul myself up to the cafeteria and fork in my lunch and recovered enough energy to contemplate squabbling with Liesel, I had grimly realized that the only possible grounds on which I could squabble with her were that she was seizing authority that nobody wanted to give her. As grounds went, that had the solidity of a bog. At least she was doing it on the basis of terrifying competence and not just the random chance of affinity.

Anyway any spare energy I might have had for squabbling was soon to disappear. That afternoon we were up to 150 kids in the Hindi run: the Maharashtra kids all finally turned up. They were still keeping as far from me as they could, but they'd come. The next morning the Spanish run had more than a hundred as well. I was pathetically grateful that the Chinese run was still thin; running with forty kids felt like a relaxing stroll by comparison. It was all the more clear that without Liesel's ruthlessly imposed improvements, we'd have been losing people left, right, and center.

Which didn't actually reconcile me to her approach. "How exactly have you managed to spend your entire career until now pretending to be a nice person?" I demanded grouchily as I stomped down to the cafeteria on Monday the next week: in our library session after the English run that morning, she'd brought out a long checklist of the many, many things I'd done wrong or inefficiently that needed correcting, all of which she'd carefully observed while somehow managing to sail through the run completely undistressed herself. She was still demanding my attention for a few more of them on the stairs even after the lunch bell rang.

She sniffed disparagingly. "It is not a complex problem to appear nice to people! You identify the most popular targets in each of your classes, learn what they value about themselves, and give them a minimum of three relevant compliments each week. So long as they think you are agreeable, others will follow their lead."

It hadn't occurred to me that there was an *answer* to my question, complete presumably with regularly tended checklists. I must have looked aghast, because she scowled at me and said sharply, "Or instead you can spend years sulking around the school letting everyone believe you are an incompetent maleficer. Do you know how much simpler everything would be now if only you had given us any reasonable time to prepare? Not to mention we would not be having all these difficulties with the Shanghai enclavers! You had better be careful. They are waiting too long." She flounced on from me to join Alfie and the London kids further ahead in the queue. They all moved back to make room for her right be-hind him, even Sarah and Brandon, although they were en-clavers and she wasn't.

"She's a monster," I said flatly to Aadhya and Liu as we queued. They were both quite shadowy under the eyes them-selves: on top of all going in the English runs together, Liu was going with us in the Chinese runs, and trying to push the mana-amplification spell out to cover as many people as she could each time, and Aad was doing the Hindi runs, not to mention they were both actually suffering Liesel far more on a regular basis than I was, since they and Chloe had been doing all the managing. I was grateful to have to spend much more of my time running desperately for my life.

"She's the *valedictorian*," Aadhya said, which was in fact a good point: terrifying ruthlessness is close to a necessary cri-terion. "Stop picking fights with her. We need everything that's coming out of her giant brain. We're all getting wiped out as it is. Even the kids doing only one of the runs."

I was tired enough myself that I hadn't really been paying attention, but when she waved an arm round the cafeteria tables where people were already sitting, I could see instantly she was right: anyone who'd been doing the runs with us was more or less slumped over their tray in a way that would've been an invitation to be pounced on by at least three different mals in an ordinary Scholomance year. You could literally pick out the lingering objectors just by seeing who *wasn't* fall-ing into their vegetable soup. Loads of the kids who'd come out of the English run this morning were literally not eating yet; they were taking turns doing catnaps on the tables.

"Why *are* we getting so wiped out?" I said. "Do you think the school's draining our mana somehow?"

But I looked back and Aadhya and Liu were both giving me the same kind of level, murderous looks I'd seen aimed at

Orion in the past. "We're all being attacked much more in every run than ever before," Liu said. "It's not just the extreme maleficaria. At this time last year, the obstacle course only had ten attack stations, all separate. The general melee runs aren't supposed to start until June."

"Oh, right," I said awkwardly, as if I'd just needed to be reminded.

We went through the line and loaded up our trays with bowls of spaghetti—we had to pick out the red mana leeches hiding among them, but we were all used to that—and big helpings of sliced peaches in hallucinogenic yellow syrup that Chloe would probably be able to neutralize for us when we got it back to the table she was arranging. Annoyingly, the last helping of sponge cake they were meant to accompany went just in front of us, to a boy from Venice who had a tidy fishing tool he used to snag it from among the surrounding spikegrubs. Even more annoyingly, once he'd got it, he paused and turned and *offered* it to me, exactly the way people sucked up to enclaver kids all the time. And Aadhya gave me a jab with an elbow before I could erupt in the boy's face like I wanted to, so instead I just had to say in as ungracious a tone as I could manage, "No. Thanks."

"We need to think about it, though," Aadhya said at the table, a while later. I was sullenly eating the peaches without even being able to enjoy them, and it wasn't just because the neutralizer gave them a faintly metallic taste. "What if the school *is* making it harder on purpose? What if it's trying to wipe you out so bad that it can hit you in a gym run, take you or Orion out?"

"Well," I said, trying to think how to word it so I wouldn't get more death glares from the entire table. I *was* tired, but to be perfectly honest, I'd mostly been whinging. You're *supposed* to be tired during graduation training. If you aren't, you aren't working hard enough. I was working-a-full-day tired, not falling-into-my-soup tired.

Orion *was,* and I'd saved his bowl twice so far this meal, but that's because he was sneaking out to go hunting real mals after curfew. I'd tried to persuade Precious to keep watch on him, but she wouldn't; the only thing she'd do is insist on coming along anytime I went over to his room to force him to actually get into bed and shut his eyes and turn out the lights before the curfew bell rang. If he did, he instantly fell asleep and stayed down until morning; otherwise he'd be in the cafeteria at dawn, eating from a giant heaped tray before anyone else got there. In case you're wondering, staying out past curfew is normally a death sentence and probably still was for any other student even in this strange year, but at this point mals were all fleeing Orion very energetically. Mostly he only ever got to kill them in the runs, when one of them got too distracted trying to eat another student and blew its cover.

"Or maybe it wants to kill some of us now in practice, in case most of us do get out," Liu put in, a perfectly reasonable concern which helpfully relieved me of having to make a bright and cheery point of explaining that it wasn't that bad really, at least for me.

"What should we do?" Ibrahim said, anxiously.

"Why don't we just take a break?" Chloe said, which I suppose was the obvious solution if you were someone who had ever had the luxury of being able to *take a break.* "We could take the rest of the day, skip tomorrow, and Wednesday morning. Nobody would miss more than one run. That's not much."

Almost everyone endorsed the idea as soon as it percolated outwards. Even Orion perked up dramatically as soon as he woke up enough to hear it. I assumed he was planning an all-day hunting extravaganza. I personally slept in to the glorious hour of eight, just early enough to still make it upstairs for breakfast dregs if I rushed, and was up and stuffing my hair into a short ponytail when someone knocked. I'd got much more cautious about that sort of thing since my delightful encounter with Jack last year, but with a vat of mana available, that now just meant I kept a nice murder spell on the tip of my tongue and opened the door at arm's length.

Orion was standing there looking a bit nervous, carrying a large mug of tea and an alchemy lab supply box heaped with three buns, a small glass full of apricot jam and butter pats that were starting to permanently intermingle, a bowl full of congee with a whole egg on it, and a half-green clementine. I stared at him and he blurted, "Would—would you—have breakfast with me?" and then realized as the words left his mouth that he hadn't made the situation horrible enough and added, "On a date?" in a squawky warble.

I slammed my hand down on the door of Precious's enclosure, where I'd tucked her in with some sunflower seeds, and latched it shut just in time. I ignored the furious chittering and squeaks from inside and blurted back, "Yes," before anything resembling good sense could assert itself.

I had to work extremely hard not to think better of what I was doing, even as I followed Orion through the corridors. I couldn't even distract myself by watching for attacks or traps; nothing with a mind, right or otherwise, was attacking Orion lately. He'd grown three inches so far this year, at least, and his shoulders and arms were straining every seam of his t-shirt, and he'd showered and his silver hair was dark and curling round his neck, and I was having to devote really enormous effort to ignoring that I was being a truly colossal wanker, when I suddenly realized where we were, and stopped, everything forgotten in appalled outrage, on the threshold of *the gym*.

Orion didn't even break stride. He sailed onwards through the doors and into the half of the gym that was left over from the obstacle course. The famed cherry trees had appeared this week and were just getting ready to make a proper scene, tiny pink and white buds dotting the dark limbs.

I almost couldn't believe he'd done it. I went after him blankly, waiting for him to explain this was some sort of joke, which would itself be in poor taste. He just stopped under one particularly laden tree and earnestly began spreading out a ragged blanket for our picnic, while I stood staring down at him, trying to decide if he was literally insane, and whether I liked him enough to pretend he wasn't. I had already liked him enough to drink the horrible tea-stained hot water he'd brought me, so the answer to that was almost certainly yes, but I wasn't sure I liked him enough to *picnic in the gym* with him.

It's just as well that I was too appalled to move, I suppose, because that's why I was still on my feet when Orion looked up and saw something coming. I had no idea in that first moment what it was he'd seen; his face didn't actually reach any kind of positive or negative expression, he only focused on something behind me. But I knew that something was coming at my back, and that I hadn't heard it or picked up on it. That was warning enough.

Even as I turned round to find out what it was, my hands were already moving in the shielding spell that Alfie had given me, two weeks ago. I'd bitterly made myself ask him for it, knowing he'd say exactly what he said, "Of course, El, delighted." Bollocks. It had to be one of the best spells even his London enclave family had, worth loads in trade. In here it would probably have brought more than my sutras, since a decently skilled senior could cast it during graduation, and the sutras wouldn't do anyone any good until they got out alive.

It wasn't a shield spell, really. It was an evocation of refusal—not to be too boringly technical, an evocation is more or less taking something intangible and bringing it into material reality. What the evocation of refusal produced—in Alfie's hands—was a neat translucent dome roughly seven feet across. As long as he could hold it up—casting alone he could manage as long as three minutes, which is an eternity in the graduation hall—he could refuse anything he didn't want inside, including mals, hostile magic, flying debris, loud farts, et cetera. And while there're plenty of spells that will let you seal out the world, the extremely special quality of this one was that it let in all the things you *did* want, such as oxygen untainted by any poison gas in the vicinity, or healing spells from your allies. I'd seen Alfie use it for the first time back during our run against the evil ice mountains. He'd brought it out several times since then to save random other kids' lives. He wasn't one of the enclavers who whinged about helping other kids; his grace went both ways, or maybe he'd secretly internalized the fantasy of noblesse oblige, because he'd dived wholeheartedly into the project of rescuing everyone in his path.

But when I cast the evocation, I got a globe nearly twelve feet across, which showed every sign of staying up for as long as I bothered to keep it going, and after I put it round something, I could *move* the globe and all its desirable contents, meaning I could scoop up a double handful of kids and deposit them in a different spot on the field, no mals included. That was a game-changing move. I could claim that was why I'd asked for the spell, for everyone's sake, but that would be bollocks, too. I hadn't known for sure what I could do with it when I asked him to give it to me. I'd just known it was a really top spell, and I could see that it had room to grow—the kind of room that I could fill up.

I had the smooth dome of it up over me and Orion before I finished turning round, which was good, because we very much didn't want any of the literally twenty-seven different killing spells and deadly artifices that came flying at our heads, five of them backed by a true circle working. I don't think I could have blocked or turned them all any other way. But none of them could make it through the impenetrable *no thanks very much* of the globe. Most of them just dissolved. The more elaborate workings slid down to where the globe intersected with the floor, and dissolved into a frustrated cloud of churning smoke in a dozen different colors that ringed us, bubbling and seething, until one after another they finally dissipated.

By then Orion was standing up next to me, staring out of the shimmering wall into the faces of the thirty-two kids who'd just had a really good go at murdering us. I recognized Yuyan at the front, and Zixuan was standing with the circle—all of the Shanghai seniors, in fact, along with their allies, and a dozen other kids I was pretty sure were from Beijing and Hong Kong and Guangzhou.

It didn't surprise me at all, except that I'd been taken by surprise. I ought to have known it was coming. But Orion just looked confused at first, as if he didn't understand how they could possibly have made such a bizarre mistake. It took the grim disappointment on their faces as they watched their spells dissolving to drive home the idea that they'd *meant* it.

I imagine they were very sorry about that a moment later, and so was I, because that made him angry, and it turned out I'd never seen Orion angry before. Not *really* angry. And I realize I haven't one metacarpal to stand on here, but I didn't like it. And I wasn't even the one he was angry at. For a horrible moment I had the vivid sensation that I wasn't holding the dome up to protect him anymore: I was keeping *him* away from *them.*

"Lake!" I said, trying to make it sharp, but it came out with an awful wobble I didn't like. I couldn't help it. His face looked all *wrong,* his lips peeled back in a snarl and a faint glimmer of eldritch light coming through his eyes, so much mana gathered for casting that you could almost see it with the naked eye, like a fist clenching. I had a clear and terrible vision of him just mowing gracefully through them, the way he did with a horde of maleficaria, conscious thought going entirely out of it until everything—*everyone*—was dead.

But thankfully, he grated out, "They wanted to *kill you,*" and despite my visceral horror, I managed a spark of indignation over that, just enough to light up my ever-helpful reservoirs of irritation and anger.

"I don't seem to have been in any danger!" I said. "What were *you* going to do, I'd like to know. Probably get your bones dissolved into goo, if you'd had it all to yourself. That's up to eleven for me, by the way."

It distracted him from the confrontation, just long enough to crack his own fury a bit. "Eleven!"

"I'll write out the tally for you later," I said, managing a decent façade of coolness. "Now let's pack this up and go and have our picnic in the library, like *normal people.* What are you going to do otherwise?"

That was a wrong question to ask, because Orion looked back at them and still clearly felt that *kill them all* was a perfectly valid response—and when I say perfectly valid, I mean that he was an inch away from going at them, and I hadn't any idea what to do, but the choice was abruptly not mine anymore, because people literally started appearing round me in bunches, starting with Liesel and her crew: Alfie with his face screwed up in strain, holding up his own casting of the evocation of refusal as they flew in through the doors.

It wasn't just them, though; other teams were all shooting into the gym around us with the bungee quality of yanker spells going off, all of which I realized after an incredulous glance were keyed off the shield holder on my belt. Ibrahim and his team appeared; even Khamis had come, with Nkoyo.

And more to the point, Magnus and his team sailed in, along with Jermaine and his; then a team from Atlanta, another from Louisiana—and in minutes, what any outside observer would've said was going on was that the New York and Shanghai enclaves had squared off, with their various allies, all of us ready to tumble down into the open waiting jaws of Thucydides's Trap together. It would be at least as effective at killing wizards off as a horde of maleficaria, especially once any survivors went home and told their parents that the war everyone was half expecting had started here on the inside.

I had no idea how to stop it. One look told me Orion wasn't going to be any help: he was going to be the spearhead. Magnus had already led the New York kids to form up behind him. And the only people who *weren't* there were Aadhya and Liu and Chloe, presumably because whoever had organized this protective scheme—three guesses, all Liesel—had known that they'd tell me about it in advance, thus denying her the satisfaction of getting to *rescue me.*

As if things weren't bad enough, at that very moment the school jumped on the bandwagon, too: we all paused as we heard the grinding of the obstacle-course machinery disengaging—the way it did at the end of each week before the place reconstituted itself, only it was twice as loud when we were all inside at the time—and then the entire floor beneath our feet lurched and went *pliable,* open to reshaping.

We're all on alert for anything like a potential advantage, so everyone started grabbing for it immediately. Like the opening rounds of some strategy game where everyone's trying to establish their positions before they start lobbing bombs. The green hills swelled and heaved like rolling waves as everyone tried to re-form them into handy things like trenches and fortifications. It felt like trying to surf a continental plate over the ocean with nothing more to steer by than a horse bridle.

And as soon as I came up with that metaphor, I realized I only had one possibly useful working: the one and only spell I've ever successfully written by myself. It's also the one and only spell I've ever tried to write, because what I produced in that shining burst of creativity was a spell for setting off a supervolcano. I burnt the parchment instantly afterwards, but the spell has remained firmly lodged in my mental catalog along with all the other most horrible spells I've ever seen.

I pulled mana in on one breath and spread my arms out on the exhale, chanting the opening incantation. Two glowing ley lines branched out over the floor to either side of me and began spiraling over the entire floor like the arms of a galaxy, and everywhere they touched was abruptly and vividly in my head, brought under the power of my incantation. Everyone else kept trying to hold on to the small chunks they'd managed to control, but the spell ruthlessly tore them away and gave them to me, until I'd got the entire gym seething and shuddering in my mental grip.

And round then, the better incanters all began to realize where my spell was very clearly *going*—namely straight for some kind of gigantic mass-extinction-level eruption that would take out everyone in the room and quite possibly all four floors directly overhead.

"What are you *doing*?" Magnus yelled at me in absolute panic—he was in fact quite a good incanter—and there was a perfectly clear tipping moment when everyone in the gym stopped worrying about the other side and started worrying about me.

As well they should have, since I'd hit the end of the opening incantation, and once I started into part two, there wouldn't be any stopping it. I halted with my whole body clenched up around the gathered power and flattened the gym out with both my hands, so abruptly that half the kids fell over as hills vanished from beneath them and trenches popped them up into the air. Everyone still on their feet was backing away from me, eyes wide with horror, and I snarled at all of them universally, "Stop it. Just *stop*. If I wanted you dead, if I wanted any of you dead, you'd be dead! *Rú guǒ wǒ xiǎng nǐ sǐ, nǐ men sǐ dìng le!*" I translated, in my flabby Chinese.

Which was so patently true under the circumstances— since I was having to work extremely hard to *not* kill them all—that it made a visible impression all round. Well, as much as it could while everyone was actively terrified that I was in fact about to kill them all. At least they had certainly stopped worrying about doing any killing of their own. Even Orion had got over being enraged and was just standing gawking at me—in an infuriatingly starry-eyed way, in his case, demonstrating his continuing total lack of judgment and sense.

When I was satisfied that everyone had stopped, I let my control over our alarmingly malleable surroundings slide slowly out of my hands, hills and valleys lurching themselves back into place, trees unfolding up from the ground in an unnatural fashion as they crept back into the illusion. Untangling from the spell took me nearly fifteen minutes, but absolutely no one did anything to interrupt or distract me; a few kids even went to the gym doors to stop anyone else coming in. I was shaking when I'd finished, nauseated. I'd have liked to go lie down in a dark room for a significant amount of time, but I gulped air and grated out, "What I want is to get you *out*. To get *all of us* out. Do you think you could pull your heads out of your collective arses and *help*?"

Chapter 12

INTERMISSION

O N THURSDAY, four hundred kids showed up for the Chinese run. Afterwards Orion and I dragged ourselves into the library and each crawled onto one of the couches and lay there letting everyone else do the postmortem over our heads. I felt like a sheet of kitchen roll that had been used more than once and wrung out thoroughly in between.

It wasn't just the larger number: most of the new kids hadn't learned any of our completely unfamiliar strategies, and apart from that, the obstacle course bloody *works*. So skipping it for seven weeks had put them substantially behind the rest of us. The only reason there hadn't been a metric shedload of deaths today was because I had cheated in pure desperation by using Alfie's evocation to toss bunches of students and mals together out of the obstacle course into the other half of the gym. The mals had then dissolved, as they were just fake constructs. The mals in the graduation hall were not going to dissolve conveniently of their own accord, so it wasn't going to be a helpful maneuver in the actual event. But I'd had to do *something* just to get everyone out of practice alive.

I wasn't paying much attention to the discussion, since everyone agreed the main point was that the new cohort all had to catch up, which was fairly obvious. Yuyan—she'd joined the planning team—suggested letting them run every day for the next two weeks and giving everyone else—except for me and Orion, obviously—more time off. Everyone agreed on this, and then Aadhya said thoughtfully, "Actually, we probably want to have everyone from the Spanish and Hindi runs join up with either English or Chinese anyway pretty soon. We want to start doing five-hundred-person runs—in a month!" she added, when she noticed I'd craned my head up from the couch in outrage.

I put my head down again, briefly mollified, but Liesel gave a loud exasperated sigh, too pointed to miss. I glared at the patched threadbare upholstery just past my nose and gritted out, "Next week for English. The week after that for Chinese." Orion groaned faintly on the couch perpendicular to mine, but he didn't argue. We were already looking April in the face. Less than three months left.

I'm not going to claim that I enjoyed the next week, but by Wednesday, the Chinese run was in spitting distance of survivable, and after Friday's run, Zixuan approached Liu and Aadhya and offered to use his reviser to improve the siren-spider lute. They spent the whole evening in the workshop together, and on Saturday, when Liu struck the first chords and I sang the spell, the mana-amplification wave rolled out over the entire mass of kids and gonged against the gym walls and came *back* for a second pass that quadrupled the power of everyone's workings. I didn't have to cheat once; I wasn't even exhausted at the end.

"He didn't make you *give* it to him?" I muttered to Liu

afterwards: everyone was clustered round Zixuan gushing congratulations. I'd just incinerated an entire anima-locust swarm so large that it had blotted out all of the hideously blue sky: they just kept spawning afresh so I had to literally keep a hurricane-sized psychic storm burning over everyone's heads the entire fifteen minutes of the run, but I was old hat at that by now. Or possibly the storm had been so disturbing that everyone was blocking it aggressively out of their memories; one or the other.

Liu and Aad had already talked over the lute and agreed that Liu's family would pay Aadhya for it, assuming Liu and it got out. The deal would establish Aadhya's going rate as an artificer and give her a big chunk of seed resources to start a workshop with, and Liu's extended clan would have a lot more use for the lute than just Aad and her family. But usually the cost for revising some piece of artifice is three-quarters the value of the *result*. Zixuan had every right to consider himself majority owner at this point, and since he was a Shanghai enclaver, he could probably buy Liu out a lot easier than she could buy him out.

I was just asking, I didn't mean anything by it, except to wonder if there were some angle involved. Of course the upgrade was clearly in everyone's interest, but someone was going to get the lute after, so it would have struck me as odd if there hadn't been *any* negotiation on the subject. But Liu turned very red and then compounded the effect by putting her hands over her cheeks as if trying to squish the red out of them, which certainly wasn't effective if her goal was to stop me gawking at her.

"He asked to come meet my family after we get out," she said, in a choked, stifled voice. I didn't gawk any less; that was quite the declaration. It's not that enclavers—or people as close to becoming enclavers as Liu's family—all officially arrange dating and marriages or anything, but there's often *some* family involvement. All of the wizards in her parents' generation and the two before had been working themselves to the bone to get the resources to buy the enclave-building spells. And not for a poky old-fashioned little Golden Enclave like the ones out of my sutras, either: they were getting ready to put up towers in the void, another modern star in the Chinese constellation. Once they put together a package with the last of the core spells, they'd take bids from the independent wizards in various Chinese cities. They'd pick the city whose wizards put together the biggest offer, and the mana and resources they provided would get the new enclave put up. The wizards who'd contributed the most would get to move in straightaway; the rest would get in over the next decade or two as the foundations settled and the place expanded.

Liu had been born into that project, and she was expected and expecting to contribute. And anyone she so much as dated was absolutely going to be evaluated as a potential part of it, too. Her family might not be planning to get actively involved with the process, but they'd certainly be *pleased* if she brought home an impressive candidate. Which an artificer from Shanghai who was already good enough to whip up a reviser in school certainly would be.

"So is that . . . good?" I prompted.

Liu stared at me with a half-bewildered expression, as if she didn't know what it was, then looked over at him and then back. "He's—he's nice? And he's very cute?" as if she were asking me. She'd never had a crush that I knew of; I suspect she'd considered it as much a long-shot as I had, all those years she was on the maleficer track. Maleficer relationships tend to go Bonnie-and-Clyde or Frankenstein-and-Igor:

not very appealing. So now she was opening a newly delivered box and peeking under the lid for the first time.

"I see," I said, solemnly, so obviously I stuck round until the very end. I felt it was my job as her friend to observe closely and also my chance to revenge a lot of giggling at *my* expense.

Liu might not have been sure about Zixuan, but she was definitely sure that I should go away and stop making her squirm and kept whispering that I could leave. I kept pretending not to understand her while the crowd very slowly ebbed away from round Zixuan, until he managed to politely detach from the last few hangers-on, at which point I casually edged back from Liu but not so far away I couldn't hear as he came over and asked her to walk to the library with him.

Liu did turn to me and ask, "El, are you coming?"

"You go ahead," I told her, and beamed at her as obnoxiously as I could. She turned red again and made a quick face at me, then smoothed herself down to calm dignity before she turned back to him. I was smiling the whole time as I watched them walk away; it was just—so normal, an ordinary fumbling towards a future outside this horrible place.

I suppose you could say the same of my own complicated dating situation, but it felt a lot more uncertain and dramatic and fraught when I was the one inside it, not to mention more impractical, seeing as me dragging Orion off to join a quixotic project of building tiny enclaves round the world was a lot less likely to be acceptable to *his* family. This was a happy ordinary human thing I could actually enjoy, and it felt like the perfect period to that magical run.

For the first time, I almost felt that I could even let myself believe in the plan—so much that when they'd gone out of sight, I gave a huff of laughter out loud and turned back to the gym doors and said exultantly, "Still think you're going to stop me? You're not. I *am* getting them out. I'm getting them all out, and nothing you do is going to make me leave any of them behind. You're not going to get a single one of them. I'm going to beat you, I'm going to *win,* do you hear me?"

"Who are you talking to?" Sudarat asked.

She gave me a bad start, which I entirely deserved since I'd been so enthusiastic about my stupid ranting that I hadn't noticed her, and when I'd calmed down my racing heart and shoved down the sixteen different killing spells that had instantly leapt to mind, I said with an attempt at being cool and collected, "Nothing, I was only thinking out loud. What are you doing down here?"

Then I looked at the little bundle she was carrying with the end of a loaf of bread poking out of it, and realized, appalled, that she was of Orion's mindset about picnics in the gym. "You've got to be joking," I said, revolted. "Didn't I yell enough? You're only going to mess your own head about, if you don't get yourself killed. You've been in here long enough by now, you must've started to understand. It's *not the real thing.*"

She just stood there and took the lecture, small with her shoulders hunched forward, gripping the handle of her little carrysack with both hands, and then she said softly, "My mother used to tell me for a graduation present she would take me to see the cherry blossom festival in Kyoto. But I will never see it now."

I stopped talking, stopped breathing more or less. She paused, but when I didn't say anything else, she said, "In my school—in the enclave—they taught us how to pick out the smart kids, the good ones, the best ones to help us. So I know what the good ones are like. And I'm not very good. And nobody wants to be my friend. The enclave kids are all afraid.

They don't know what happened in Bangkok. And I don't know, either. Everyone thinks I'm lying, but I don't. I took my grandmother's dog out for a walk and then we came back and the door—the door to the enclave didn't work anymore. It was just a door to an empty apartment. And everyone was gone." She swallowed visibly. "My auntie was working in Shanghai, she came home and took care of me. She gave me everything she could spare. But it isn't enough to save someone who isn't very good, that nobody likes. I know it's not."

She stopped. I still couldn't manage a word. After a moment I suppose she got tired of hanging about in the corridor with a mute statue, and she went politely past me and pushed the doors open. She went a decent way in: not so far that she didn't have several good escape routes, but far enough that she was clear of the area round the doors. She settled herself at the base of a tree putting on an immense display, dark boughs sagging with bloom, and took a small box of strawberries out of her bag, which she must have wasted gobs of mana enchanting out of some dingy fruit from the cafeteria. She sat there eating them and reading a book, making a picture straight out of the freshman orientation handbook, with tiny petals drifting across the scene like pink snow. Living as much as she could, because she wasn't going to get much more of a chance.

The doors swung shut over the scene, wafting a sweet fragrance into my face as they banged shut, and I said to them stupidly, "No," which obviously helped loads, and then I just laughed out loud at myself, high-pitched and jeering. "God, I'm stupid, I'm so stupid, I can't believe," and I couldn't go on. I put my hands over my face and sobbed a couple of times, and then I lifted my face and screamed at the doors, at the school, "Why did you even try to stop me? Why bother? There's no use. There's never been any use at all."

Like an answer, there was an immense crash of glass and cracking wood behind me. I whipped round instantly. I'd been training for my Olympic-class event in uselessness so hard, so earnestly, that it wasn't a voluntary reaction; I'd programmed my muscles so they could skip past my brain and just get on with it, with saving all those lives, all one thousand of those fantastically insignificant lives, so I whirled and my hands came up in casting position and the adrenaline was already flowing like a smooth-running river in my blood-stream before I even saw that the crash was just one of the heavy framed blueprints off the corridor wall that had come down behind me, a glitter of shards sprayed all round and the frame broken into kindling sticks, pale where the dusty gilt-slathered wood had splintered apart.

I dropped my hands as soon as conscious thought was in-volved in keeping them up, gulping for breath between the sobs and the instinctive alarm. "So why shouldn't I just give up after all—is that what you're trying to say?" I said, just a girl talking to myself in the hallway, a stupid girl pretending she was a hero because she was going to save a thousand kids before she *then* went skipping merrily through the gates, leaving behind—what were the numbers? Twelve hundred kids dead out of every year, and it's been 140 years, which worked out to a number I couldn't fix even if I stayed behind to guard the gates for my entire life. However many ticking minutes I had left, I'd still only ever be a girl with her finger stuck into a hole in the dike, and whenever I finally fell down, here the torrent would come.

"Is that what you wanted me to learn?" I said savagely to the pale blank square on the metal wall where the frame had been, a window through the grime of a century and more. "You should've done it quicker. At this point, I might as *well* save everyone as not," and then I looked down, and the crashed frame wasn't a blueprint. It was the front page from the May 10, 1880, issue of *The London Whisper,* dominated by a large photograph of a gaggle of men in Victorian suits, a grandly mustachioed blond one out in front with his arms cocked out from his hips and a self-congratulatory air. There were copies of that all over the building, too. For years I'd been reading it without paying attention, in droning history lectures and the cafeteria queue, the way you read the back of cereal boxes while you're eating because you haven't anything else to do with your eyes.

But now I picked it up and looked at it properly. The men were standing in a small and familiar wood-paneled room, lined with bookcases and full of small heavy cast-iron chairs with wooden desks, and at the very edge of the photograph a thick scroll covered with signatures was lying upon a massive roll-top wooden desk. It was my own special classroom, up at the very top of the school.

The article said, *The final Scholomance binding spells were successfully laid today through what must be considered the most extraordinary circle working ever conceived by the mind of man, with fully twenty-one representatives of the foremost enclaves of the world, uniting their wills and the marshaled resources of all their several domains under the visionary leadership of Sir Alfred Cooper Browning of Manchester, for the singular goal of establishing an institution beyond all quarrels and disputes, whose fundamental purpose shall be to offer sanctuary and protection to all the wise-gifted children of the world.*

I read it again and again, until I couldn't possibly avoid understanding it anymore. I knew all the words already, of course; I could probably have recited it from memory. The same photo was literally in the freshman orientation handbook they sent us before we came in, the exact same self-aggrandizing article was on the wall in a dozen of my classrooms and in the history textbooks. The words are even engraved on the stairway railings and the upper molding of the library reading room, those precise words: *to offer sanctuary and protection to all the wise-gifted children of the world,* only absolutely nobody ever took them seriously. Even Sir Alfred Cooper Browning and all his fellow smug waistcoats didn't believe their own nonsense at the time. They didn't let in any children from outside their enclaves until they had to, and when they did have to, they did everything they could think of to give their own every possible advantage, and certainly not a single student ever got through a single day in here believing them. No one thought it was true.

Except, apparently, the Scholomance itself. And fair enough: twenty-one of the most powerful wizards in the world had made a circle and forced the words into the very bones of the place—the words they'd wrangled among themselves into a warm mealymouthed lie they could all agree to tell together. They built the Scholomance and told it very firmly that its fundamental purpose was *to offer sanctuary and protection to all the wise-gifted children of the world.*

And perhaps the school hasn't been able to do that very successfully, but apparently it still *wanted* to be—something besides a lesser evil.

I can't pretend that I completely understood at first; quite the opposite. I got the first vague inkling of the idea and then dropped the article back onto the heap of broken frame and walked away down the corridor. I was moving aimlessly, a cloudy blob of static from ear to ear, and anything at all could have killed me. But nothing came at me, even though I kept wandering along. I couldn't have told you where I was, until the door I was passing slammed open, loudly, and I saw it was the corridor going to my delightful private seminar room, the one where I'd been attacked relentlessly the first two months of the year.

Which suddenly took on a very different light. I stopped and stared down the passage. The school hadn't been trying to kill me, and it hadn't been trying to make me go maleficer. It didn't want me to suck everyone dry and fly out to darken the earth. So what *did* it want from me?

I went down to the room. The door was waiting open. I paused at the threshold looking inside, and with a bang, one of the outer wall panels next to the sink literally fell in, exposing a narrow shaft with a ladder, tucked into the wall. I knew what it was: I'd been inside it at the end of last year, for another one of the delightfully unique school experiences I hoped never to relive. It was the maintenance shaft that went down to the graduation hall.

The message was extremely clear. My head wasn't, which is why I didn't think as hard as I probably ought to have before I went and got on the ladder and started climbing down, in the dark. But I didn't even hear any sounds of maleficaria, no scuttling or rasping or hisses or breath; only the gurgles and bangs of the school itself, the vast conglomeration of artifice running on, steadily pumping air and water and cafeteria slop and wastes all round, the low burring hum of mana being channeled into the wards. The climb didn't take very long: the school wanted me to get there quickly, and my brain was so empty that it didn't insist on the climb taking a rational amount of time. It felt like only a few minutes, and then I was climbing down off the ladder into the skinny maintenance chamber at the bottom, the place from which we'd sallied forth on our grand mission to repair the cleansing machinery.

I made a light. It shone onto the blank, curved metal

wall—dented a bit from the outside, as if the mals had beaten on it trying to get through after we'd made our yanked escape. The graduation hall was on the other side, along with whatever the school had been preparing us all—preparing *me*—to deal with. This whole term, all the endless outrageously horrible unsurvivable runs, pushing and pushing and pushing all of us to find completely new strategies, to learn to work as a single enormous alliance, to defeat—whatever was on the other side. That's what we had to overcome.

And apparently, it was time for me to face it. I didn't have a maintenance hatch with me, but one of the metal wall panels just popped itself open, rivets pinging out of the seam and onto the floor one after another. I just stood there and watched. The two panels of the wall fell open with an enormous clanging, one towards me and one away.

Nothing came through the opening.

It wasn't especially shocking; I'd understood by then. I knew what was on the other side waiting, and they weren't going to bother coming after one measly student. I'd known all along what it was going to be, really, no matter how hard I'd pretended I didn't. It wasn't going to be evil glaciers, or an anima-locust swarm, or a castigator demon. The school had been treating me gently, with kid gloves, bringing me along little by little, but time was running out now, and I had to face it, so I could be ready on graduation day. I'd promised, after all. I'd promised Khamis, and Aadhya, and Liu, and Chloe, and everyone in the entire school.

I couldn't make myself step through. Even if it was safe right now, in some ridiculous sense of the word, I didn't want to go look. I didn't want to have to go back upstairs and tell everyone what we were up against. I didn't want to spend the next three months thinking about them every single day, making plans, discussing *strategies* for me to relive the most horrible thing that had ever happened to me. I wanted to huddle into a ball against the back of the chamber. I wanted to sob for Mum, for Orion, for anyone at all to save me, and there wasn't anyone. There was only me. And them. Patience and Fortitude, waiting by the gates, so hungry that they'd licked the entire graduation hall clean.

I knew I had to go look at them, so I couldn't go back up the ladder—if the school would even have let me run away—but I couldn't move forward, either. I stayed down there for a very long time. I think it had been close to an hour when there was a small anxious chirp from the shaft, and Precious poked her tiny nose out, clinging to the last rung of the ladder.

I put my hands up to get her, and I cupped her in my hands and put her against my cheek, and my whole face crumpled like discarded classwork and I just sobbed a few times, getting her fur wet with leaking tears. She just poked at me with her nose and put up with it. When I managed to get myself under control, she climbed onto my shoulder, tucked behind my ear, and made soft small encouraging squeaks. I took a deep breath in through my nose and made myself go out into the hall before I could lock up again.

The hall wasn't completely empty: a family of mature agglos, their tidy shells glittering with mana-infused jewels, bits of glowing artifice, and tiny jars and vials of potions and unguents, had been sleeping peacefully against the far wall, near the cleansing machinery we'd repaired last year. They all woke up at the sound of my footsteps and started humping away into dark corners at top speed, which in the case of adult agglos is about a quarter mile per hour.

The floor was crunchy with amphisbaena scales and the dried-up moltings of juvenile digesters, none bigger than a handkerchief. None of them were actually in sight. The ceiling had faint dark lines patterned across it, the ghosts of the century-old sirenspider webs that had been incinerated in the cleansing. The only things left of the sirenspiders themselves were a few hard melted lumps stuck to the ceiling among them, the stubs of legs poking out in a few places. There was nothing left of other mals at all except a few droppings and skeletons; a few construct mals had collapsed in mechanical heaps here and there, out of mana. A few more scuttling larval things ran away from me, so small I couldn't even identify them, as I clenched both my hands tight and turned myself bodily to face the gates.

"But," I said, after a moment, out loud. I stood there stupidly until Precious gave me a nudge, and then I walked across the whole graduation hall, directly up to the massive double doors, the gates to the school. There were two enormous scorch marks on the floor to either side, blackened outlines where the maw-mouths had been, like a police tape to show the position of a removed corpse. The marks had ripples: you could see the mortal flame had burnt off a good few layers, although there had certainly been plenty left of them afterwards.

I'd been half right. The cleansing had worked. Patience and Fortitude hadn't been killed, but they'd been burnt and blinded, probably thrashing wildly, while the seniors ran out. They had missed their one annual meal. Afterwards, they'd recovered and tried to fill their hollow bellies by devouring all the rest of the surviving mals instead. But after they did that—when there was nothing at all left for them to eat, they'd—*gone*.

I had no idea where. Had they hidden away somewhere inside the school? They certainly hadn't got into the main levels—we'd all have heard the screaming. There're pockets of dead space, many of them, in the hollow area between the top of the graduation hall and the bottom of the workshop floor, and those aren't really warded, so they could have crawled in there, but they still wouldn't have had anything to eat. Maw-mouths don't generally hide, anyway. Had they left entirely? They could have; the wards stop maleficaria from coming in, not going out, and if Patience and Fortitude had gone off to roam the world and trouble enclaves for their suppers, we wouldn't hear about it until after we got out ourselves.

Which we'd apparently be able to do with no trouble at all. None of us needed a day's practice, not a single run. We could stroll right out.

I stared up at the enormous doors, cast from solid bronze. There were diagrams and paintings of them scattered all round, like the blueprints, all a bit different from one another. But I can't imagine anyone had actually spent as much as a millisecond looking at them since the day the school first opened to students. A massive seal in the middle was engraved with the school motto *In Sapienta Umbraculum*—In Wisdom, Shelter—and nested circles round the seal were engraved with a warding spell that had been layered through languages: so the same spell in English and Middle English and Old English, one after another, all going round in a ring. It wasn't just English, either; there were rings of the same spell in dozens of languages, and all the ones I knew well enough to recognize had multiple versions, too—there was modern Arabic and medieval, modern French and Old French and Latin.

Translating a spell and actually *getting* a spell on the other end is almost impossible; it had probably taken a genius poet or a team of twelve for every version of every language, and only possible at all because they weren't very complex spells: all the ones I could make out without a dictionary were just one or two lines and a variation on *Don't let anything evil through these doors.* The English inscription was *Malice, keep far, this gate wisdom's shelter guards,* tied to the motto, obviously not a coincidence; some version of the phrase was there in all the other languages I knew.

And they weren't *just* an inscription. The letters had been engraved all the way through the top layer of bronze, and some kind of illuminated alchemical substance was being piped through behind them so the light shone out through. They weren't just glowing steadily, either: the light moved through each inscription, at the speed and rhythm you'd have used to speak each spell. It was effectively casting the incantations over and over again, renewing them steadily. And the separate spells were even synchronized somehow—I couldn't follow it exactly, but I could tell that several of them started or ended at the same time, new ones began as previous ones went out. Like a massive choral piece with a few dozen separate lines of music going at once.

It mesmerized me; I could almost hear the spells going, and then I realized I really was hearing them: there were bands of tiny perforations in the metal, what I'd thought were just decorative dots, and when I leaned close and peeked I could see there was a bit of artifice behind them that opened and closed each hole individually. And when one of them opened, a puff of air came through with a sound like a single letter or syllable, breathed out, and each sound matched one of the characters being lit up at the time. I could barely hear the whisper over the faint metronome ticking of the machinery that was controlling the vents, the shushing and gurgle of the liquid being pumped through, but they were there.

I'd never seen anything like it before, even inside the school. I know from much droning in our history lessons that Sir Alfred had talked the other major enclaves into build-

ing the school in stages—the expense of the thing was as ru-
inous as you might imagine. He initially proposed just
building an ordinary enclave for kids to live in, just with these
really powerful doors. After the doors were built, that's when
he showed everyone the rest of his even more elaborate
plans, and supposedly they looked at the doors and signed on
for the rest. Standing here, I wasn't surprised. I'd spent nearly
four years living inside the school, nearly dying over and over,
and I still almost believed it, believed that these doors would
keep out all evil, keep out the monsters and keep us all safe.

And obviously they had, more or less. I couldn't even
imagine how many maleficaria would have been coming at
us without them. The Scholomance was a honeypot, the
most alluring honeypot you could imagine: all the most ten-
der, mana-plumpest wizard children in the world gathered in
a single place. Any mal that so much as gets a whiff of this
place would try to get in. And some of them would make it,
even with the doors. Every once in a while, a letter didn't
light up, a puff of air didn't make it through; there were
surely a few places in the massive composition that were a
little weaker, where the spells didn't quite sound right at the
same time, making cracks in the warding where a really determined mal could make an effort and wriggle through, like
poking a loose brick out of the fortress wall. More than
enough had made it through, even in the first few years, to
make this hall into a slaughterhouse. The doors weren't *impenetrable*.

But they were close. So after the mortal flame had actually
worked last year—and after Patience and Fortitude had eaten
their way through everything else—and after Orion had done
for every mal that had dared to poke its nose into the classroom levels—the whole room had been cleared. For one
shining moment, our one unbelievably lucky year, we'd be

able to come down here and walk straight to safety, the first class in the history of the Scholomance to make it through graduation without a single death.

And then—the mals would all come back. Every single portal that opened up to send one of us home would make an opening in the wards; two or three mals would squirm through for every one of us that left. More of them would tag along later that day with the newly inducted freshmen. Psychic mals would follow a parent's worried dream of their child; the eldritch and gaseous mals would float up through the ventilation shafts, and the amorphous ones would pour themselves through the plumbing.

And sooner or later, if Patience or Fortitude didn't come back, a new maw-mouth would ooze in through one of those openings and settle into pride of place by the gates. The cleansing would break again. The death rate would likely be back to normal by the time the current freshmen were graduating, or at best a year or two later. Sudarat and Zheng and my other freshmen wouldn't get a free ride. That boy from Manchester, Aaron, who'd brought me my tiny scrap of a note from Mum, for nothing. All the kids I barely knew or didn't know or had never met or who hadn't been born yet.

That's what the school had been working me up towards, all this time. Luring me onwards with one crumb of power after another to teach me that it wasn't useless for me to care, that I could let myself care about my friends, and about their allies, and then even about everyone in my year, and once it had got me over that hump, now it was showing me that I didn't need to worry about any of them after all, so surely now I had the spare capacity to care about—everyone *else*.

"But what do you want me to *do*?" I said, staring up at the doors. Surely the Scholomance didn't want to save one year's worth of kids, or even four years'. The school had already chewed up a hundred thousand children during its relentless triage operation. No human who cared enough to try could have stood it. But the school wasn't human, wasn't soft. It didn't love us. It just wanted to do its job properly, and here we were, dying all the time on its watch, inexorably, three-quarters of every class lost. It wanted us to take this wide-open shining window of opportunity and—"*Fix* you?" It was the only thing I could think of, but it didn't actually provide any direction. I looked round the empty killing field: even the bones had been cleared away. "How?"

No answer came. I didn't get any more helpful guidance, except from Precious, who gave a chirp and prodded me with her nose, wanting to go back. "I don't understand!" I yelled at the doors. They went on placidly ticking away: the work of an army of geniuses with all the time and mana in the world at their fingertips, trying to build the safest and most clever school in the world for their children, and that hadn't been good enough, so what did the Scholomance expect *me* to do?

Precious gave another squeak, vaguely exasperated, and poked me again. I thumped the left door resentfully with my fist, and then wished I hadn't: it moved a little. Not really, not actually enough to go ajar or anything, it just trembled, barely, under my fist, enough that I could tell that if I braced myself on something and put my back and legs into it, I could have *opened* it. It wasn't held shut from this side. The outer edges of the gates were stained with green and black mold, and the puffs of air coming in were coming in from outside. This was the one place where the school wasn't just floating in the void. The real world was there, right there on the other side. If I pushed the doors open, I could *walk out,* into whatever secret hidden place the enclaves had chosen as the anchor point, and that would be a real place, somewhere on the

Earth, with a GPS location and everything, and surely I could find someone in a day's walk with a mobile who'd let me ring the main line of the commune and talk to Mum.

It would be an absolutely stupid thing to do, because I wouldn't have *graduated*—we don't march through the doors to get in, since if you turned the physical doors into a single point of entry, all the mals in the world would eventually be massed round it, and not a single freshman would survive the gauntlet long enough to get inside. My vague understanding of the induction spell is that we're borrowed into here with the same kind of spells that enclaves use to borrow space from the real world, and when we go through the gates, what actually happens is we're being paid back with interest, through a portal that sends us right back where we were taken from in the first place. If I hopped out the doors into the real world instead of going back out through the proper portal, I'd more or less be making off without paying the debt. I have no idea what the consequences would be, but they were bound to be unpleasant.

But I *could do it*. It was the opposite of everything that was unbearably horrible about the gym. The other side of the doors was undoubtedly deep underground in some unpleasant and probably dangerously spiky place to discourage both mals and mundanes from coming near; the smell coming through had the thick mucky stink of a stagnant sewer—an entirely likely location—and absolutely none of that mattered because it would be *real*, it would be *outside*, and I wanted to go so badly that I turned round and ran back to the maintenance shaft without letting myself look round even one more time.

The climb up was *not* abbreviated. It felt more as if I were paying back the speed from the earlier climb. But Precious was along with me, a warm lump on my shoulder, or scampering up a few rungs ahead of me, her white fur bright even in the dim light I'd cast on my hands. I finally crawled out of the shaft and lay flat on the floor in the seminar room with my arms and legs starfished out round me, too tired to groan more than faintly. She sat on my chest washing her whiskers fastidiously and keeping an eye out, if that was even necessary. The *school* was obviously looking out for me really hard. It had only sent just the right level of mals to make me swallow the indigestible lump of my pride and take mana from Chloe. If it *hadn't* gone after me, Aadhya and Liu and I would've spent this year working so hard to build a decent pot of mana that I certainly wouldn't have had the time and energy—much less the mana—to imagine saving anyone *else*. And no one else would've listened to me even if I had.

I stared up at the stained ceiling overhead as that thought sank in, and with an effort lifted my still-leaden arm with the power-sharer up in front of my eyes. I'd got so used to it by now I didn't think about it anymore. But I had been pulling oceans of mana with every run, even at the discounted gym levels. Magnus and the other New York kids had probably gone round to the other enclaves at some point and demanded that they share the burden—implying that I'd kick them out of the runs if they didn't.

No one would have listened to me if I'd gone to them with a crazy plan to get us all out together. The school had *made* them listen, had *made* them all come to me, by laying out one unsurvivable run after another. It had forced everyone to give me those oceans of mana, to put their lives into my hands. None of them had wanted to do that. So the moment I told everyone that there was nothing down there at all, that we could sail right out—

"Mu-uum," I groaned faintly, as if she were there for me to argue with violently, but she was only inside my head, looking at me with all the desperate worry in the world furrow-ing her face. *Keep away from Orion Lake.* Was *this* what she'd seen? Had she caught some glimpse of what it would mean to stack me and Orion up together in a single year, and what I'd have to do in order to pay it off? Because of course I wouldn't be able to do a thing if everyone took back their mana. But if I took their mana with a lie—it wouldn't be freely given, after all.

Which wouldn't hurt me in any obvious way, not the way outright maleficers get hurt. If Prasong's little freshman-flaying scheme had worked, his anima would've been scarred so badly he'd probably never have been able to build mana of his own again even if he'd spent the rest of his life trying to atone and purify himself. That wouldn't happen to me; I wouldn't even get black nails and a faint cloud of disquiet, like Liu had, punishment for sacrificing a couple of defense-less mice to survive on. Maleficers got that kind of damage because they were yanking mana out of something that was actively fighting them, resisting them. That's what turned it into malia. But when you got someone to *hand* you their mana—it didn't hurt. You could trick someone, pressure them, lie to them, all you wanted. It wasn't going to damage you in any way that anyone else would ever see.

Which is why that's what enclavers did. And then they pre-tended it wasn't malia, but it was. There's a long distance be-tween cheating someone out of a scrap of mana they didn't urgently need, and turning into a slavering murderous vam-pire who couldn't do anything decent ever again, but it's all on the same road. Mum taught me that, spent her whole life teaching me that, and it had taken a while, but the lesson had stuck.

I knew what she'd say to the idea of doing it for someone's *own good,* much less for the sake of future generations. I was only alive because she would never make that bargain. She'd been told flat-out that I was going to be a monstrous killing scourge by people who hadn't been lying to her, and she hadn't refused to hand me over because she didn't *believe* them. She hadn't even refused because she loved me: if that had been the only reason, she'd have taken me to live in an enclave when I was nine years old and mals started to come for me, almost five years ahead of schedule. She hadn't done that either. She'd only refused because she wouldn't take the first wrong step.

So maybe this was what she'd seen. Me with a beautiful gold-paved road Orion had laid out in front of me, with all the best intentions in the world, while never doing a wrong thing himself. But if I took my first wrong step onto it, who knew how far I'd go? No one could stop me flying down it at top speed, once I got started.

I sat up slowly. Precious scrambled up onto my knees as I folded myself up and twitched her nose at me anxiously. "Well," I said to her, "let's go and see."

I put her into her cup and slogged up to the library. Half the reading room had more or less been turned into a war room. Everyone else from our half-official planning committee was up there: lunch had finished and Liu and Zixuan were telling them all about the upgraded effects of the lute, with pleased and happy—and massively relieved—faces all round. Orion was snoozing on a couch with his mouth hanging open and one arm dangling off limp.

"El!" Aadhya said, when I walked in. "You missed lunch, are you okay?"

Liesel didn't wait for me to answer, just gave a quick exasperated flick of her eyes as if to say *You were skiving off, weren't you,* and said to me sternly, "We have more work to do now, not less. We still do not know how far the lute will reach. It may be able to amplify everyone's mana, but to find out, we must make an attempt at a full run sooner rather than later."

"No," I said. "We don't need to do any more runs." Everyone stopped and stared at me—most of them with absolute terror on their faces; I suppose they thought aha, it was time for the curtain to pull back from the monster or something. One girl from Mumbai enclave who I suspected had joined the planning committee to keep an eye on me even started doing a shielding spell. "Not like that," I said crossly to her, and let the irritation help me say it. "I've just been down to the graduation hall. There's nothing there."

She paused with her hands in midair. Everyone else just gawked at me in total confusion. They'd probably have felt more sure of themselves if I had given out a maniacal cackle and told them to run for their lives.

Aadhya said tentatively, "So it's just Patience and Fortitude . . . ?"

"No," I said. "They're gone, too. There's nothing at all. The whole place is cleared out."

"What?" Orion had sat up and was staring at me. He sounded actually dismayed, which was a bit much, and got most people to look at him sidelong—and then actually take the idea into their own heads, to think about what it would mean, if there literally wasn't *anything*—

"Are you sure?" Liesel demanded peremptorily. "How did you go down? How close did you—"

"I kicked the bloody doors, Liesel; I'm sure. Anyone who doesn't care to take my word for it can go down themselves for the price of a ladder climb," I said. "The shaft's in my seminar room, other side of the north wall of the workshop. The school just popped it wide open and sent me down there to see."

That got variations on "What?" coming out of roughly

thirty mouths, and then Chloe said, "The school *sent* you? Why did it—but it's been making the runs this hard, it's been making us do all this—"

A sudden roaring of wind blew through the room, the ordinarily murmuring ventilation fans suddenly starting up loud as jet engines, and the blueprints spread out on the table—the big central table, the largest one in the reading room—all went flying off in every direction along with the sketches and plans in a gigantic blizzard of paper, to expose the silver letters inlaid into the old scarred wood: TO OFFER SANCTUARY AND PROTECTION TO ALL THE WISE-GIFTED CHILDREN OF THE WORLD, and at the same time all the lights in the reading room dropped to nothing except for four angled lamps that swiveled to hit the letters with broad beams that made them shine out as if they'd been lit up from inside.

Everyone was silent, staring down at the message the school had given me, given us all. "It wants to do a better job," I said. "It wants us to help. And before you ask, I don't know how. I don't think *it* knows how. But I'm going to try." I looked up at Aadhya, and she was staring back at me still stunned, but I said straight to her, "Please help me," and she gave a snort-gasp kind of a laugh and said, "Holy shit, El," and then she sank down in a chair like her knees had given out.

Chapter 13

MARTYRDOM

I DON'T THINK ANYONE really knew what to do with themselves. We've all spent the best part of four years training as hard as we could to be inhumanly selfish in a way we could only possibly live with because all of us were going round in fear for our lives—if not in the next five minutes then on graduation day at the latest—and you could tell yourself everyone else was doing the same and there wasn't any other choice. The Scholomance had encouraged it if anything. Everyone-for-themselves worked well enough to get 25 percent of the students out through the unending horde: I suppose up until now that had been the school's best option. And yes, it *now* very clearly meant for us to start collaborating instead, but a large building might not understand that human beings have a bit more difficulty shifting their mindset. I wouldn't have been surprised if all the enclavers had pulled out instantly. I wouldn't have been surprised if literally everyone had pulled out instantly. In fact I expected the library to empty out within two minutes of my announcement, theatrics or no.

Then Orion said, "I could come back? Whenever it needed to be cleaned out again?" He didn't even make it sound appropriately martyr-like; just threw the idea out there as if that were a perfectly reasonable option for us all to consider. I glared at him, but it did have the effect of making a lot of other people shuffle uncomfortably.

"Yeah," Aadhya said. "Look, Orion, we all know you're practically invincible, but that's not the same as totally invincible. If you keep hopping in through the gates, sooner or later some mal will get lucky."

"They haven't yet," he said, perfectly sincere.

"*Eleven times,* Lake," I said through my teeth. "*This year alone.*"

"I would've had them!" Orion said.

We were both ready to pursue that line of discussion further, but Liesel headed us off. "Don't be stupid," she said loudly. "And give us back some decent light." That was directed to the room at large, and the library lamps instantly put themselves right again, as if they were as afraid as the rest of us to refuse her marching orders. "We *must* help. Do you not understand?" She slapped the letters. "The purpose of the school is to protect wizard children. But if *we* are in no danger, we do not need protection. This obviously creates a thaumaturgic flow towards protecting the *other* children."

I felt that *obviously* was a strong and unjustifiable word in this context—as, I suspect, did three-quarters of the people in the room—but Liesel wasn't pausing to take questions. "If we do not assist the school to help the younger children, then the flow will create an incentive for the school to trade away our extreme safety to improve theirs. For instance," she added pointedly, in response to the blank expressions all round, "it may begin to lock us out of the cafeteria. Or turn off the plumbing in our bathrooms. Or if another maw-mouth should enter the school, open the wards to direct it towards *our* dormitory."

We'd all got the point by then. I'm not sure it was any better if everyone else was forced to help by the school instead of by me lying to them, but I couldn't help being grateful that everyone had a good reason to do it. It didn't feel as wrong as me lying them into it, anyway. It was fair, as much as anything in the hideous bargain of the Scholomance is fair: if you had offered any of us a deal at the beginning of the year, that we could just walk out of the graduation hall at the price of going filthy and hungry for three months, eating nothing but what we could beg or trade from the other kids, we'd have taken it like a shot. You could fatten yourself back up as soon as you were safe at home.

"Okay, so—" Aadhya said after a moment. "This is all because the cleansing machinery worked. So we just need to find a way to keep it working, for good."

That did sound promising, but Alfie said, "Oh, bugger," half under his breath, and then said, "You can't. The cleansing machinery can't be preserved. You can fix it, but you can't keep it working. Four years is the absolute most you can get. The agglos will do for it by then."

"The *agglos*?" Aadhya said. We all think of agglos as party favors rather than maleficaria. Technically, they do need mana and they can't build it themselves, but they never hurt anyone. They just creep around very slowly and collect any stray bits of mana-infused creations that have been left out and then tack them onto their outer carapaces, like oversized caddisflies. We'd all be delighted to meet a fully grown one that's been accumulating scraps of artifice and alchemical products for a decade or so. Which is why you never *do* meet agglos in the classroom levels, except the tiny larval ones. But there are colonies of grown ones in the graduation hall, like the group I'd seen. They hide until graduation is over, and after all the other mals are well fed and snoring, they creep out and collect up all the tidy bits that got dropped by the students who didn't make it out.

Alfie ran a hand over his face. "They get through the outer shell and just gnaw on the machinery until it breaks."

"That doesn't make any sense," Aadhya said. She wasn't by any means the only artificer looking baffled. "Why don't you throw a five-minute warding on it? They're just agglos!"

"That's *why* you can't ward them out," Alfie said. "Mortal flame is—well, it's arguably an *entity,* and one that consumes mana that it doesn't make itself. If you want to conjure a mortal flame and send it *out,* you can't ward the artifice you're doing it with against mana-consuming creatures. You have to ward it against malice. But the agglos aren't malicious. They never take mana against resistance. They just nibble on this thing we've left sitting out near them, and sooner or later they make a hole in it, and then they squirm inside and take bits of it until the whole thing comes apart. London enclave's got a laboratory with an agglo farm that's been looking for ways to keep them out for the last century. If we could, it would be worth doing anything, spending any amount of mana, to get another team in to do a real repair. But we can't find anything that works for longer than bloody wrapping the thing in tinfoil—the agglos like that stuff so much they'll eat all of it before they *bother* going into the artifice. And that would get you four years."

We stood around dumbly for some time after he finished. The cleansing was so stuck in all our heads as the obvious thing to fix that even after Alfie's explanation, at least half a dozen people opened their mouths to suggest some other way to do it, only none of them managed more than "What if . . ." before they realized that whatever their clever notion was, the brightest minds of London had already thought of and tried it at some point in the last hundred years.

"What if we just fix it every year from now?" one of Aadhya's acquaintances from Atlanta said finally, the first one to make it past the sticking point. "A crew could go down right after New Year's, when the hall is freshly cleaned, and," picking up enthusiasm, "we could make it the same deal as last year. Anyone who signs on for the fix gets a spot, enclave of their choice. Right? People would go for it."

He was absolutely right; some desperate kids *would* go for it, year after year, losing a few each time but keeping the machinery tidy, until finally one group went down only to discover that surprise! The machinery had finally broken again before they could fix it, and there was a hungry crowd of maleficaria waiting for them. I was about to put up a howl of protest, but Alfie was already shaking his head, in weary exasperation. "They've thought of that. Posting guards, sending in maintenance crews every month, all of it. And that would handle the agglos. But you can't pay anyone enough to do it, because a new maw-mouth *will* come into the school, very soon. There's a trace on the doors. Usually one or two manage it every year—they're oozes, those are always the hardest to keep out of anywhere. And they'll set up shop in the hall. Patience and Fortitude were protecting us, actually. They would eat the newer ones."

Everyone's faces had downturned into masks of appalled horror; I cringed inwardly and tried to tell myself that it wasn't very long until graduation, and surely there wouldn't be a new maw-mouth *that* soon.

"What if we breed some mals to eat agglos?" some bright lad blurted out, I didn't see who; I think he ducked away behind someone else as soon as he realized what he'd suggested and everyone turned to stare in his direction. Breeding maleficaria is a very popular pastime *for maleficers,* because it always ends in roughly the same way, with variation only in the amounts of screaming and blood. Trying to do it with good intentions generally makes the results worse, not better.

"We could build a construct to do it," someone else suggested, which also wasn't going to work, since the other mals coming in would happily eat the agglo-eating constructs, but at least that was less likely to create some kind of hideous monstrosity shambling around the school devouring kids forever.

But more to the point, it was *another suggestion,* and the crowd in the reading room was breaking up into small groups along preferred language lines and starting to argue and discuss, to come up with ideas. Trying to *help.* I didn't care that all the ideas were useless; we'd literally only just started thinking.

Aadhya came round to me and put her arm round my waist and said under her breath, "Hey, she can be *taught,*" with a tease in her voice that wobbled a little, and when I looked at her, her eyes were bright and wet, and I put my arm round her shoulders and hugged her.

I did begin to care that the ideas were useless after an entire week went by without any useful ones. We'd enlisted the whole school in the brainstorming project, but so many people came up to the reading room to suggest that someone go down to fix the machinery on some arbitrary day each year that by Tuesday we were all yelling, *"Maw-mouth!"* before they got halfway through their first sentence. All of these clever people were enclavers, I note.

A junior came up to propose our staying on an extra year to guard the other students. He called his idea *paying it for-*

ward, and it had the novelty of making literally every senior in the room squirm with a violently stifled *shove it up your arse* even before Liesel said in exasperation, "And where will we be *sleeping* during this year? What will we eat?" He then revised it to suggest that we come back in just in time for next year's graduation. That didn't even merit a response beyond a flat stare: no one has ever volunteered to come back into the Scholomance, and no one ever will. Barring the one incredibly stupid glaring exception, who didn't count.

For variation, one pale and bedraggled-looking freshman girl came up with the notion that all of the underclassmen should graduate with us, instead. I think she just couldn't stand school any longer and wanted to go home to her mum, and fair enough, except that her plan wouldn't have protected and sheltered her at all. She'd just be snapped up in a few months by some mal on the outside, like ninety-five percent of the wizard kids who aren't lucky enough to get into the school. We more or less gave her a bracing pat on the shoulder and sent her on her way, and that was all the time we alloted to her suggestion.

But that afternoon as I was leaving lunch I saw her slumped in the freshman queue, standing alone, and on an impulse, I stopped by Sudarat, who was alone in the queue just a little further back. "Come on," I said. "You've got someone holding a place for you."

She trailed after me uncertainly, and I took her over to the other girl: she was an American, but just an indie, and I vaguely thought she was from Kansas, or one of those other states you never hear about on the BBC news, far from any enclaves. The point being, she didn't have a smidge of a reason to care about what had or hadn't happened to Bangkok. "Right, what's your name?" I demanded, and the girl said warily, "Leigh?" as if she wasn't quite willing to commit.

"Right, this is Sudarat, she was from Bangkok before it went pear-shaped; you're Leigh, and you're so miserable in this place that you'd rather trade for the odds outside; that's introductions sorted," I said, getting the worst bits out in front, for the both of them. "See if you can bear to sit together; it's best to have company for meals."

I sailed away and left them to it as quickly as I could, so none of us including me could think too hard about what the bloody hell I was doing. I don't think I could have done it, even a week before. I wouldn't have imagined doing it, I wouldn't have imagined either one of them *letting* me do it: a senior putting two underclassmen together, why? I'd need to have an angle, and if I hadn't an obvious one, they would have made one up for me, and more likely than not actively avoided each other afterwards.

Maybe they still would: Sudarat had more reason than most to be wary, and I didn't know a thing about the Kansas girl beyond her being as miserable as I'd once been, which might mean anything. Maybe she, too, was secretly a proto-maleficer of unimaginable dark power, or maybe she was such a reflexively nasty person that everyone avoided her for good reason—I immediately thought of dear old Philippa Wax, back in the commune, who almost certainly hadn't got any nicer just because I wasn't there, although she'd often implied she *would*—or maybe Leigh from Kansas was just a loser kid who was shy and bad at making friends, and who had nothing going for her, so no one had bothered to make a friend of her. She wasn't an actual maleficer, because a maleficer wouldn't have been that desperate to get out.

Anyway, Sudarat could decide for herself if it was worth enduring her company. At least it was *someone*, someone who wasn't going to be suspicious of her, or even just hesitant to make a friend of her because *other* people were suspicious of her. And I could imagine trying to help her, and help the other girl into the bargain, because that was now a thing that could happen in the Scholomance.

Assuming that they actually did sit together for at least that one meal, it was also the most successful example of help that entire week, at least that I knew of.

There were any number of charming additional proposals for maleficaria-breeding, some of which got so far as to include detailed specs. One alchemy-track kid actually had the gall to suggest to Liu that he could do it with *our mice:* enchant them and leave them all living forever in the pipes of the Scholomance to breed and eat agglo larvae. Liu didn't get angry very easily, but she did get angry then, to the point that Precious woke me up out of a nap and sent me racing to her room just in time to collide with Mr. Animal Cruelty, who beat an even more enthusiastic retreat when he saw me outside the door with Precious poking a quivering-whiskered nose out of the bandolier cup on my chest.

People also generated some less obviously bad ideas, like plans for installing some kind of major weaponry in the dead space under the workshop floor, which would be used to blast the graduation hall mals more directly. The problem was that anything you installed outside the graduation hall would require openings in the extremely powerful wards that keep the mals *in* the graduation hall and *out* of the classroom levels.

We were a fairly glum group as we gathered in the reading room the next Saturday. The obstacle course had reversed itself full-bore: instead of being impossible to survive, it had suddenly got so easy that even freshmen could manage it, so now *they* were doing runs instead of us. The school *had* in fact started randomly locking seniors out of the cafeteria, and the only way to get in was to give something useful to one of the younger kids. Small things like individual spare socks or pencils were working this week, but you could see the writing on the wall perfectly well. And grotesquely, of course most seniors were giving the things to *enclave* kids, in exchange for nothing more than the promise of putting a good word in with the enclave council when they graduated.

"All of the proposals are still trying to repair the cleansing," Yuyan said, spreading the papers out over the tables. She'd taken over gathering them, because she could read so many languages so fluently, and because unlike Liesel she didn't traumatize people with her comments, so we'd got a lot more submitted after she put out the word that people should bring them to her. "I think we have to accept that the cleansing approach to graduation is just a failure. We need something *different*."

"Yeah, well, we're trying," Aadhya said grimly. I knew she'd been in the shop almost all week with Zixuan and a bunch of the other top artificers of our year, trying to come up with things. "We've experimented with making a corridor to the gates—like a tunnel of safety. But . . ." She shook her head. She didn't really need to say what the problems with that strategy were: you'd be offering a single irresistible target to every last one of the mals, and how did you decide who went first? "Anyway, it still feels too obvious. The grown-ups would have tried something like that before."

"Hey—here's a thought. What if we *did* all graduate?" Chloe said. "What if we bring all the younger kids out with us. When we graduate back to the New York induction point, Orion's mom will be there—she can get the board of governors to cancel induction. If we did that, the school really would stay clear, because no mals would try to come in if there weren't any of us inside. And then instead of just us trying to come up with something, we could have every wizard in the world thinking about a better solution."

Yuyan sighed. "We *have* been thinking about it, for years," she said, which made sense: if Shanghai had been able to develop a better solution, it *would* have been worth their building a new school, and *everyone* would have moved. She gestured to the nearest copy of the newspaper article, mounted against the end of one of the stacks. "London has been thinking about it for a century, and New York nearly that long. Nothing we've found gets us better odds than the Scholomance."

"Well, okay, but if we can't think of anything better, at least nobody is any worse off," Chloe said.

"The younger children would be," Liu said. "They'd be out there undefended."

"Just for a little while—it could be like summer vacation. We could all help look out for them. And if it turns out there isn't a fix, or it takes too long, they could come back in," Chloe said.

"Would *you?*" Nkoyo said, with an edge I felt in my own gut. "Come back in? After you'd got out of here?"

Chloe paused. "Well," she said, with a wobble. "They'd get to choose . . ." but it was only a faint protest, fading off.

Liu was sitting on the couch next to her; she leaned over and bumped shoulders with Chloe, comfortingly. "We should send the mals to school instead," she said.

Ten minutes before curfew that night, she came and banged furiously on my door. I didn't know it was Liu, so I jumped out of bed and threw up a major shield, got a killing spell ready, and yanked the door open ready to fight. I had to fling my arms to both sides as she lunged in and grabbed me by the shoulders, with a few pieces of scribbled-on paper crumpled in her grip. First she said something in Chinese too fast for me to follow, because she was so excited, and then she said, "We should send the mals to school instead!"

"What?" I said, and the final curfew bell rang, and she

jumped and said, "I'll tell you tomorrow!" and ran back to her room, leaving me to lie awake for an hour trying to figure out what she was thinking. The crumpled papers she'd left with me didn't help: I could tell it was maths, but it was all in Chinese numbers, in two sets of handwriting, hers and I thought Yuyan's, and even after I laboriously translated them, I could only guess what the numbers were referring to.

"The honeypot spell," she said, the next morning, meeting me halfway down the corridor between our rooms.

"Right, I got that far," I said: mals come swarming into the school through the graduation portals anyway; if we used our honeypot spell, we could lure a proper horde of them in. Theoretically tens of thousands over the half an hour of graduation, if Liu's calculations were right and I'd understood them properly. "But what's the idea? Are you thinking if we pack the whole hall completely full of mals, they'll— eat the agglos?" That was the best guess I'd come up with in a night of thinking, although if mals were going to eat enough of the agglos, they'd have eaten them already, but Liu was shaking her head vigorously.

"Not the *hall*," she said. "The *school*. The whole school. We leave, and we fill the school with mals."

I stared at her. "And *then* what? Boot it off into the void or something?"

"Yes!" Liu said.

"Er, what?" I said.

I could tell you all the details of the next two weeks, during which we came up with five or six alternative plans and discarded all of them, and also had about ten different false starts working out the rough details of this one, but it was agony enough going through it once, so I won't.

The main question was whether Liu's idea would in fact work to *protect the wise-gifted children of the world*. The Scholomance wasn't built out of some kind of passionate dedication to the concept of boarding-school education. It's just a casino, meant to tilt the odds in our favor, because surviving puberty is a numbers game. Any wizard parent can save their kid from any *one* mal. But when mals come fifteen a day, sooner or later one of them is going to slip through your wards and shields and gates and get the tasty treat you're hiding from them.

And that's why we get crammed in here instead, past the guarded gates and only reachable through the narrow pipes covered with wards, and why we spend a healthy chunk of our formative years in a prison out of nightmares. If we could cut down the maleficaria population enough to give us odds of survival *outside* the school that were as good as, oh, one in seven, most people wouldn't come to the school to get the one-in-four odds here. It's too horrible. And after Liesel pounced on poor Liu and dragged her into a room to check the calculations a few million times, the two of them came back and announced that we had a decent chance of getting the odds outside down to one in *two,* and they thought the effect would last for at least a couple of generations. That made it one of the few ideas on the list that couldn't just immediately be crossed off, unlike for instance that morning's suggestion of creating a flock of flying snake-tailed piranha vultures that would absolutely have polished off the agglos in ten minutes and then come up to start on the rest of us.

The rest of the issues with Liu's plan were logistical. After poring over the blueprints and maintenance documentation, we worked out that when you touch the gates, your portal home opens at that precise moment, stays open just long enough to return you to your induction point, and then slams shut again in seconds—a sensible design meant to keep mals *out*. If we wanted to lure in as many mals as we could, everyone would have to queue up and leave slowly: a steady stream of kids going out, a steady stream of mals coming in, so we could keep the honeypot spell working through the full half hour of graduation.

Sorry, so *I* could keep the honeypot spell working. No one even bothered discussing who exactly was going to be casting the spell intended to call up a vast tidal army of maleficaria. Well, it was a fair cop.

"How are we going to keep the mals from just killing everyone in line?" Aadhya said.

"As long as the honeypot spell is going, they're just going to follow it, I think," Liu said.

"So El has to be somewhere far from where they come in, to pull them deeper," Magnus said. "Can she cast the spell up in the library and still have it work at the gates?"

"How am I getting *out* of the library afterwards in this scenario?" I said pointedly. I was very conscious that if the school didn't mind being hacked off into the void itself—it hadn't raised any objections so far—it would certainly consider *me* expendable, too. I couldn't refuse to risk my life, but I wasn't keen on accepting martyrdom before we even began.

"For that matter, how are you just not getting smothered in five minutes?" Aadhya said. "If this even works, a billion mals are going to be coming right at you."

"Why don't I just kill them all as they come in?" Orion said, without the slightest doubt in his ability to kill a billion mals.

"Shut up, Lake," I said, having *many* doubts about his ability to kill a billion mals.

That left Liu's idea as just one of the many very-long-shot

possibilities on our list, but Yuyan talked it up to Zixuan, and three days later, he came up to the library with a solution for the problem of luring the mals throughout the school: a speaker system. The idea of it was we'd make hundreds of tiny speakers—magic ones, not the electronic sort—strung on a line, and then run this line in a gigantic loop throughout the entire school, starting and ending in the graduation hall, through all the corridors and stairways on every level, branches going off into every classroom; up to the library and winding through all the endless stacks, and then all the way back down into the hall. At one end of the loop would be me, standing near the gates: I would sing our alluring honeypot spell into a capturing mouthpiece, and it would get piped through the entire system and come back out at the very last and largest speaker, standing right in front of the gates, to broadcast the song out to any mals in listening range of the portals.

What would make the mals actually *follow* the line and go into the school was a single brilliant twist to the design: an enchantment so you only heard the sound coming out of the one speaker just *ahead* of you, and as soon as you got too close to that one, you'd start to hear it only from the next speaker along instead. The mals would come because they heard the song being blasted out, and then they'd chase it onward to the next speaker, and the next one, all the way through the school.

That certainly made Liu's plan seem tidy, until you considered that there would be more than four thousand kids going out the gates, spanning the whole globe, and with hundreds of them headed to the huge city enclaves that were surrounded by hungry maleficaria. Broadcasting a honeypot spell out of the Scholomance—already the most tempting honeypot in the world—would be gilding the lily. If any of the mals *didn't* come, it would likely be because they'd got stampeded or eaten by other mals rushing to get to the suddenly wide-open doors, or because they couldn't make it to a portal in time.

"We'd be luring in all the mals in the world," Chloe said nervously, and she wasn't wrong. It was obviously insane.

However, it still didn't get crossed off the list, because we only crossed ideas off the list when we were sure they wouldn't work, not just because they were mad. The list wasn't long even so. Most of them came off when Alfie said, "Yes, tried that," often without even taking his head off his fist where he was slumped next to Liesel at the head of the table; others got crossed off because Yuyan or Gaurav from Jaipur admitted their own enclave laboratories had tried it. Surprisingly, no one in any enclave had ever explored the brilliant idea of destroying the entire school.

More seriously, it was an idea that they *couldn't* have come up with, because it needed—me. You could have cast the honeypot spell with a circle of twelve wizards, or thirty if you wanted it to keep going for half an hour, and then you could have taken *another* thirty wizards and cast a spell to break the school off from the world, but you certainly couldn't have got them all out again in time. As it was, I'd be yelling the last syllable of what was turning out to be my surprisingly handy supervolcano spell *as* I was jumping through the portal, or else I'd go toppling off into the void with the school. Oh well; if that happened, hopefully the accumulated mals would eat me before I had an opportunity to experience the full existential horror of being totally severed from reality.

And no, I wasn't nearly that blasé about the prospect.

But we hadn't found any better ideas, other than Chloe's solution of just running out and throwing the problem into the laps of the adults. We all liked that solution quite a lot: the only problem with it was that it didn't provide us with any work to do, and meanwhile the Scholomance was impatiently tapping a metaphorical foot. Over the next week, Zixuan started actually tinkering around and building the speakers, and other senior artificers started asking to help him, because anyone who *wasn't* helping in some way started having their already dim room lamps go completely out, or having the water shut off to the bathrooms just when they got there, or being shut out of the cafeteria or the workshop.

The school only got meaner from there. There didn't seem to be any big dangerous mals left—if there were, Orion was undoubtedly nabbing them before anyone else caught a glimpse—but we were all shaking ratworms and cribbas out of our bedclothes and having to cast purifications every night or wake up with mallows infesting our tear ducts, and one morning we got to the cafeteria and the food line was nothing but vats of the original thin nutrient slurry until after the last senior went through.

I have to say, I have no idea how anyone survived eating it long enough to graduate. We all ended up eating mad things: full English breakfasts, waffles slathered in berries and whipped cream, shakshuka with gorgeous heaps of fresh tomatoes and cucumbers; Aadhya had this amazing thing her nani had invented, thin pancakes stuffed with a puree of cholar dal and topped with toasted meringue. Once you're spending the extremely expensive amount of mana it takes to transmute a meal in the first place, you might as well transmute it into something you actually like. But we'd all had to spend a week's worth of mana to do it.

After breakfast every last senior was fairly clamoring for *something to do,* and since we didn't have anything better on offer, they all started to grab bits of Liu's plan, because it was the only one that was far enough along to start doing work, and it began to lurch down the runway like a half-built plane that people were literally holding up and carrying while other people were still putting on the wheels and wings and seats, trying to get the steering and the engine in order, and other people were running after it carrying the luggage.

The artificers and the maintenance crews started spinning out the speaker cabling and running it through the school, and building the speakers themselves—Zixuan had got a prototype working just in time; they'd have stolen the sketchy designs and built dozens of wrong ones otherwise. We even got the first positive sign that the school was endorsing our demolition plan, because after a fight broke out in the workshop over the last coil of metal wire, one of the metal ceiling panels fell in painfully on the squabblers' heads, like a pointed message.

After that, maintenance-track kids started ripping down less important panels throughout the school and delivering them to artificers in the workshop, who shredded them into speaker cabling and wound them onto fresh coils and handed them right back. Alchemists started brewing actual honeypot bait—seniors unexpectedly did prove willing to donate blood to this project, since, creepily, a 10ml syringeful turned out to be good enough to get you into every meal of the day—with the idea that we'd spread it in the dormitories to lure some of the mals off from the crowded main stream of the spell. Other seniors started dragging the younger kids down to the gym at regular intervals and making them pretend to queue up for the doors, so they could work out the right pacing.

Liu and Aadhya and I didn't have to look far for work: we spent our mornings up in the library trying to find some better alternative plan, and our afternoons down in the workshop with Zixuan, tweaking the lute and the speakers and the mouthpiece—he was building that crucial bit himself—to work best with the honeypot spell. Yuyan migrated along with us. She was also a musician, and had offered to be backup for Liu on the lute, in case anything happened to stop her playing; they were practicing the song-spell together most nights. No one was going to be backup for me.

The furnaces were going full blast with all the other artificers frantically trying to do *something*, so it was hot and tedious work, and my voice was ragged and croaky by dinnertime every day. For consolation, it was quite good fun wagging eyebrows at Liu, who kept turning red with confusion—Zixuan was clearly running a determined campaign on that front alongside the engineering work; he found time during the process to make her a set of tidy little metal egg-shaped protective cages for the mice that would lock into the bandolier cups, for graduation, with a tiny little spell-extension hook on the top that would attach into our shield spells.

Chloe started spending her own afternoons brewing throat-cooler for me, and salve for Liu and Yuyan's fingers, and invited other alchemists to join her. She ended up with more hands than the work needed, so she took the best of them and started working on developing a second recipe meant specifically to enhance the honeypot song-spell, which I hadn't even known you could do with alchemy.

A few days later, she gave me the first tiny thimbleful to try. The honeypot spell *had* still been doing a wonderful job of summoning larval mals, by the way, and in case you were wondering what we did about it, the answer was that for the first week, we cast it from inside a ring of mortal flame I summoned, all the while pouring out buckets of sweat. But we gratefully stopped doing that after the first week, because the swarms stopped coming. By the time Chloe gave me the sample, we were pretty sure we'd completely cleared the workshop environs of every last living mal.

And we had, only an isk had apparently laid a batch of eggs in the workshop furnaces some time ago. They weren't due to hatch for a decade or so yet, but after I drank Chloe's potion, the enhanced song managed to persuade them to break their shells and come out anyway. Their exoskeletons hadn't hardened yet, so they were just floppy and slow-moving squiggles of molten metal, not a direct threat, except as they came out of the furnace they fell to the floor, melted through, and vanished away into the void below. By the time we managed to smother the rest of them, the floor of the shop was looking like one of those tin cans someone had punched full of holes with an awl for decoration. We spent the rest of that day repairing it, very gingerly.

By the end of May, we were far enough along with all the pieces of the project that when Liesel chivvied us all up to the library for a review of all the various planning ventures, the one major practical issue left with Liu's plan was how to get the horde of mals up from the graduation hall and into the main levels of the school.

Which was quite an issue, as the entire school was designed from the beginning to make that journey as difficult as possible for even a single mal. The maintenance shaft was going to be a tight fit for an entire horde, even if a juvenile argonet had managed to squish itself up that way last year, and what about when the first mals circled all the way around through the school and then tried to come back *down* the maintenance shaft? As soon as a bottleneck developed, a mass of them would build up in the hall and eventually they'd start eating us after all.

No one had any good ideas, but we hauled out the big official school blueprints and spread them out onto the table to try to find a solution, and discovered to our confusion that there were two enormous shafts in the blueprints, right there on opposite sides of the graduation hall, each one wide enough for seven argonets to climb up and come down again on the other side if they liked.

I assure you that there had absolutely never been two enormous shafts on the blueprints before, or for that matter in the school.

But when we grabbed another set of blueprints off one of the walls, the shafts were there, too, and after we got a third and still they were there, one of the maintenance-track kids said suddenly, "There are pieces of machinery that weren't here when the school was built, but they're too big to have come up the maintenance shaft. The school must have bigger shafts that only get opened for major installations."

Chloe sat up. "Wait, that's right, I remember this! All the new cafeteria equipment—when they were ready to install it, New York built like a hundred golems to deliver it. The golems opened the gates from outside, blasted the whole hall with mortal flame from flamethrowers, and then charged in with the new equipment. They shoved it into a shaft and closed it again before they got ripped apart. And then the kids inside installed it."

I didn't ask how many of those kids had been slaughtered by the minor horde of mals that would surely have got upstairs in the time it took for a gang of golems to load equipment into a shaft. New York's golems do have a reputation for being quicker than usual, but that means they could go thundering across the graduation hall in six minutes instead of twenty. I didn't ask if *all* the kids in the school had been warned to expect the sudden influx. I'm sure Chloe wouldn't have been told those parts of the story. You wouldn't trouble a nice, warmhearted girl with that kind of information.

I didn't ask, I just seethed about it while stomping all the way downstairs to the workshop level with a handful of volunteers—kids I didn't know very well who'd only been hanging round the library looking for work because they hadn't done very much that day and were anxious about getting into dinner—to confirm that yes, these helpful shafts were in fact there, one ending in the workshop and one in the gym, and both were wide open. They looked a lot more impressive in person than on the blueprints. It's hard to remember just how bloody *big* this place is until you're standing on the edge of a shaft, easily big enough for a jet plane, that just goes plummeting down for half a mile. An army of mals could sail up no bother.

"I don't suppose it occurred to *you* to keep them shut until the enclavers bothered to give everyone a warning?" I demanded of the nearest framed blueprints—the shafts were showing on there now as well—while my company all nervously took their own peeks down to help make sure that the shafts were there. "Not very much for fairness, are you?"

The school didn't answer me. But I already knew the answer. It didn't weigh people up one after another and even the score. It would do its best to protect an enclaver kid as much as a loser, and it wouldn't care that the enclavers had come in with a basketful of advantages. They still hadn't been *safe*, after all. That was the only line it drew, the line between *safe* and *not safe*, before it doled out its help with an implacable unjust evenhandedness. And it expected me to do the same, and it made me angry even while I couldn't see any way to do it better.

I seethed all the way back upstairs to the library—my mood wasn't improved by having to climb back up all those stairs—and announced, "The shafts are open," before I threw myself sullenly into a chair.

After that, Liu's plan was *the* plan, the only one we were working on, which was just as well, since it took every last minute of the last weeks—of what might be the last term ever—to get it into shape. Almost everything we'd done already had to be done again. Half of the first round of hastily built speakers broke and had to be replaced; we had to redo a quarter of the cabling, and then we had to make nearly a hundred new coils just to go up and down the shafts. We weren't sure where to safely get the materials until someone suggested the walls of the gigantic auditorium where we take Maleficaria Studies, which are plastered all over with a horrible educational mural of all the mals which are normally waiting below to eat us.

I hadn't been inside since last year, and I hadn't missed it, but I took a day off from singing practice to join in for the festival of destruction. I wasn't the only one. Hundreds of kids showed up; the younger kids were actually still going to lessons, but a lot of them skived off to join in and help as much as they could. We tore the place completely apart. Alchemists were there pouring precious etching fluids onto the bolts; incanters heated and cooled the panels to warp them until they fell off. Kids were flying themselves to the ceiling and prying panels off there, yelling out warnings below as they dropped. Even the freshmen—dramatically more gangly than they'd been at the start of the year—were there just whacking away at the seats with ordinary hammers in a frenzy. By the time the lunch bell rang, the room was gutted down to the girders and pipes.

Liu's plan had that one significant advantage over any

other: we all *wanted* to destroy the Scholomance. I'm not even joking; the fact that we all loved the idea on a deeply visceral level would almost certainly help carry it off. And it wasn't just resentment and spite working in us, although that would have been enough: I think everyone else felt as I did, secretly and irrationally, that if we could only succeed, if we could only destroy the whole place, we could save ourselves from ever having been in here. And every last one of us, from the most blithe freshman to the most crumpled senior, was longing more violently with every passing day to get *out, out, out.*

Well, except for our one special loony. Orion got increasingly sullen as July 2 crept closer. If he'd been resentful over the task he'd been assigned in our delightful scheme—he was going to be guarding the shaft that came *down,* facing the entire horde of mals at once—I would have considered it entirely justified. Since he didn't mind his assignment in the slightest and in fact seemed to be looking forward to it in some weird demented anticipation, I had no idea what was bothering him.

That wasn't true, of course, but I wasn't allowing myself to have an idea what might be bothering him. He hadn't asked me on another date since the disastrous attempt in the gym, which might have been out of mortification or because we hadn't had a single day to ourselves since.

Either way, it was just as well. I came in here and I've survived in here being sensible all the time, trying to always do the cleverest thing I could manage, to see all the clear and sharp-edged dangers from every angle, so I could just barely squeeze past them without losing too much blood. I could never afford to look past survival, especially not for anything as insanely expensive and useless as *happiness,* and I don't believe in it anyway. I'm too good at being hard, I've got so good at it, and I wasn't going to go soft all of a sudden now. I wasn't going to make Mum's choice, wasn't going to do something stupid because of a boy who'd come and sat shoulder-to-shoulder with me in the library, the two of us alone in a pool of light in the reaching dark all around—a boy who improbably thought I was just grand and who made my stomach fold itself over into squares when he was near me.

Everyone *else* was doing stupid things all round me—that whole last week, I was constantly stumbling over people making out in the library stacks, and making mealtime trades for condoms or alchemical brews of dubious efficacy, and even otherwise sensible people were giggling to each other in the girls' about their plans for dramatic last-night hurrahs, which was stupider than anything else; you weren't going to catch me losing sleep the night before we tried to carry out this insane scheme, even if Orion Lake turned up at my door with tea and cake.

While I spent my days with Liu and Aadhya and Zixuan in the workshop, tuning the lute and singing my lungs out, Orion was still doing runs in the gym. He'd be spending most of graduation protecting the queue, unless the horde of mals managed to circulate through the entire school and come back down before we were all out, in which case—well, in which case he'd presumably make a hopeless but nevertheless determined stand at the barricades, trying to hold the mals off long enough for everyone else to make their escape. And I'd have to go on standing there next to the gates, singing the mals onwards, keeping them off everyone else, as he was inevitably overrun and torn apart before my eyes by the monsters I'd lured in to kill him.

I couldn't stop myself going by the gym to watch him, just to poke the sore place. It didn't make me feel any better to watch him thrashing scores of fake mals and gym constructs.

I knew he was good at killing mals, I knew he was brilliant at it, but if this plan even worked, there wouldn't be scores, there would be hundreds, maybe thousands, all piling on him at once. But I watched from the doors anyway, every day after I finished practicing, and when he finished his last run we went up to dinner together without talking, my teeth clenched round the words I wanted to say: *You don't have to do this alone; you can ask for people to help you, at least to shield you; we'll hold a lottery, we'll draw straws.* I'd said them already and he'd just waved them away with a shrug and "They'll just get in the way," and he might very well be right, because no one would stick beside him with that horde coming. No one except me, and I was meant to be saving everyone else, everyone else but him.

But the last day before graduation, we decided it was best to rest my voice instead of more practice, and after lunch, I didn't go back to the workshop; I marched down to the gym and told Orion I was going to do the last run with him. He was just outside the doors getting ready, whistling cheerily as he dusted his hands with casting powder—like gymnastics chalk, only with more glitter—and he had the gall to object. "I thought you were supposed to get some rest," he said. "You don't need to worry, I'm not going to let the mals get to you . . ." at which point he caught my expression and hastily said, "Uh, sure, let's go."

"Let's," I said.

The exercise did make me feel better, even if it shouldn't have. As patently stupid as that was, five minutes into the onrushing horde that the Scholomance threw at us, I was as viscerally sure of invincibility as Orion: we could do it, we could, nothing would stop us—and of course nothing would until something *did,* at which point we'd be dead and past the bother of learning our lesson. But I let myself have the lux-

ury of insane confidence while we mowed through maleficaria together, passing the work between us with the easy
grace of partners dancing, my vast killing spells clearing
great swaths around us and his shocking-quick attacks knocking down anything that dared to survive or poke its nose in
any closer.

He lunged to one side of me to take out a swinging rack of
crystalline blades and then instantly whirled to the other to
vaporize the billowing violet-pink cloud of a glinder, finishing the sweep in close to me, and when he grinned down at
me, breathing hard and sweaty and sparkling, I laughed back,
helplessly, and threw a wall of flame spiraling out round us
both, a swarm of treeks exploding like tiny fireworks as it
caught them, half a dozen scuttling constructs melting into
glistening puddles of liquid metal, and the course was done:
we were alone in the hazy sunlit warmth beneath a stand of
delicate purple-red maples. A moment later, an unnaturally
perfect rumble of thunder sounded and a sudden torrent of
warm summer rain came down to wash away the detritus—
which wouldn't have been unpleasant, except the pipes for
the gym had evidently been infested, too, and quite a lot of
amphisbaena came with the downpour, thrashing and hissing as they tumbled. Orion grabbed my hand and ran for the
small pavilion, and he pulled me inside and kept pulling me
into his arms and kissed me.

I kissed him back, I couldn't help it. The soft pattering rain
wasn't real, except for the amphisbaena thumping down at
intervals; the beautiful trees and the garden weren't real, the
pavilion wasn't real, they were all just awful hollow lies, but
he was real: his mouth and his arms round me and his body
overheated against me, trickles of rain and sweat trapped
against my cheek and his breath gasping out of the sides of
his mouth even as he tried to keep kissing me, wanting me,

his heart pounding so hard I could feel it through my chest, unless that was my own heart.

He'd buried his hands in my hair to kiss me more and I was clutching at his back, and then his t-shirt came apart under my grip, all at once the way clothes do when you've mended them with not enough raw material. He flinched back as the scraps fell off him, my hands slipping off him, and we were staring at each other across the opened space, both of us panting.

He jerked his head away first, his face wrenched and miserable, and he was about to say he was sorry; I could tell. I should have been sorry, too, because it was stupid and I knew better, even without Mum telling me *keep far away from Orion Lake,* except standing there with only hours left ticking down, it suddenly *wasn't* stupid anymore. It was in fact the only sensible thing to do, because he might be dead tomorrow or I might, and I'd never know what it would be like to be with him; clumsy and awkward and terrible as it was likely to be, I'd never know, and I said, "Don't *even*, Lake," before he could open his mouth, and I stepped in close and grabbed him by the waist and said fiercely, "I want to. I *want* to," and kissed him.

He groaned and put his arms round me again and kissed me back, and then he jerked away from me again, turning aside, and said cracking, "El, I do too, I want to, so much, I just—"

"I know you're a mad optimist who thinks he can kill all the mals in the world, but I'm *not*," I said. "And even if I were, if I knew for certain we'd make it, I still don't want to wait until we're out of here, on opposite sides of the ocean. I don't want to wait!" I wanted his body back against me, the wave of heat back and rising higher, and it was so amazingly clear and obvious to me now that I couldn't understand why *he* wouldn't want to, which wasn't particularly fair of me, but I still couldn't help taking a step towards him, reaching out.

He wouldn't look at me. "I'm just—I'm so low."

"What?" I said, confused, because it didn't make any sense.

"I'm really low. There's almost no mals, and they're all coming at seniors, so everyone's just taking them out for themselves. Magnus gave me some this morning, but . . ."

He trailed off: I think my eyebrows had packed bags and migrated three counties north. "If *that's* dependent on mana, it's news to me," I said, with a pointed look in the appropriate direction, and immediately cursed Aadhya's mum again in my head, because obviously I couldn't help going straight to *secret pet mal* and I wanted to start howling with laughter in Orion's face, which didn't seem likely to advance my cause when he was squinched with mortification already.

But in a moment I stopped caring, because he blurted out, "You said—Luisa, you said Jack got at Luisa because—because she let—"

I gawked at him in outrage. "You think I'm going to *drain* you? Here's news for you, Lake, if I wanted to—"

"No!" he yelled. "I think *I'm* going to—"

I didn't let him finish, rising to a proper howl. "What, like one of the bloody *mals*?"

"No!" he said hurriedly, raising his hands as he backed away from me.

"That's right, *no*," I said—I don't think I literally had steam coming off me, but I certainly felt as though I did—"so get back over here and kiss me again, and if you *do* try to drain my mana, I'll tear off one of the doors and beat you senseless." Orion heaved an enormous gasp like I'd hit him in the belly, and came across the pavilion in a rush towards me.

I'd grown two inches this year, but he'd grown six, and when he gripped my arms and pulled me in, with all his strength and power, I had a dizzy top-of-the-roller-coaster moment of *wait I'm not ready*—of course I'd managed to completely avoid that while I'd been busy talking *him* into it—but then he was kissing me, and the roller coaster went and I was gone along with it, flying between terror and delight. We got my t-shirt awkwardly pulled over my head, each of us with one hand involved in the project, and he squeezed his eyes shut and pulled me in closer to kiss me, I think so he didn't embarrass himself by gaping at my breasts. But the shock of being up against him like that, all of our naked skin pressed so close, ran through me, and I stopped kissing him and started fighting with my old knotted string belt, because I wanted more, more, more of that, yes, so desperately.

He backed up a step to undo his own belt and wrestle himself out of his trousers—along with his secret pet mal, and I did start laughing helplessly, possibly in hysterics, but thankfully he thought I was just laughing about how my stupid belt wouldn't come undone, and he grabbed it on either side of the knot and said, "Now untie, open by," which had no business working, but did. My combats fell straight down and puddled round my ankles, since I'd bought them two years ago off the biggest senior boy who hadn't anyone else willing to buy them, and I tripped over them while I was heeling my Velcro sandals off.

We tumbled together down onto our heap of clothing. Orion was panting as he carefully lay down on me full-length, bracing himself up on his forearms. I was deeply preoccupied with having him between my legs, the feeling inside my own body, a drumbeat pulsing sensation already going, and then the bastard looked down at me with his entire heart crammed into his eyes and his face and said, barely a whisper, "Galadriel."

I hate my name, I've hated my name my whole life; everyone who ever said it and looked at me and smiled, it's packed full of their smiles. Mum was the only one who didn't think it was a good joke. Even she wouldn't have saddled me with it if she hadn't been a shattered child herself at the time, clinging to a scrap of dreaming that had helped her make it out of the dark, without thinking about what it would mean to make me carry that name around. But Orion said it like he'd been holding it in his mouth for a year, an unreal vision he hardly believed he'd found, and I wanted to cry and also thump him at the same time, because I didn't want to like it.

"Don't get soppy on me, Lake," I said, trying not to let it wobble.

He paused and then gave me a wide, obnoxious smirk, settling himself down on his forearms as if he meant to make himself comfortable. "We might not make it tomorrow, right? So if this is *my* only chance—"

"Your chances are rapidly diminishing," I said, and then I locked my leg over his and twisted him over with me on top, and he let out something between a laugh and a desperate gasp for air, and caught my hips, and after that we were just gone, an endless lush wonderful grappling as we arranged ourselves—the slide of his thigh against the inner skin of my own, the urgent sensation of his hardened muscled body working so perfectly with mine. We hadn't very much idea of what we were doing—I'd got all sorts of detailed and educational materials from Mum obviously, but the pictures and diagrams and descriptions didn't really convey anything of what it was actually like trying to fit two bodies together. I don't think Orion had even as much of an idea as I did; I'm sure there was a sensible amount of sex ed in his past, and equally sure he'd ignored it entirely.

But we didn't need any real idea—there wasn't any goal in

mind, I was so preoccupied with the dizzy glee of having
dived in that I didn't care about getting anywhere. Which was
just as well, because he came less than five minutes into the
festivities, and then went into a spiral of writhing and apologies until I punched him in the shoulder and said, "Come *on*,
Lake, if that's the best you've got, I'm leaving you and going
to lunch," and he laughed again and kissed me some more
and then followed my pointed hints until I'd had an equally
good time, and then he moved back up on top of me and we
moved together and it was—too many things to name all of
them, with the sticky physical pleasure the least of them, far
behind the sheer relief of walls tumbling down, giving in to
my own hunger, the joy of feeding his, and if that hadn't
been enough, the unbelievable bliss of not *thinking,* of not
worrying, for at least one glorious stretch of mindlessness.

Which worked really effectively until afterwards, when we
were lying together sweaty and, at least in my case, incredibly
pleased with myself: I felt I'd accomplished something unique
and magical, that, unlike all the other actually unique and
magical things I can do, wasn't horrifying or monstrous in
the least. I was draped over his chest and he had his arms
round me, which would become intolerably uncomfortable
at some point that wasn't now, and then he sucked in a deep
gasping breath and said, "El, I know you don't want to talk
about—if we make it out of here, but I can't—" and his voice
was cracking on the edge of tears, not just leaky sentiment
but like he was barely holding on to keep from bursting into
sobs, so I couldn't stop him, and because I didn't, he said,
"You're the only right thing I've ever wanted."

I had my cheek pillowed on him, and you couldn't have
paid me to look him in the face at that moment. I stared hard
at the drain instead, from which any number of helpful ma-

leficaria could have burst and didn't. "If no one's mentioned this to you before, you've got really odd taste," I said, and wished I didn't mean it quite as much as I did.

"They have," he said, so flatly I did have to look at him. He was staring up into the dark recesses of the pavilion ceiling with a muscle jumping along the side of his jaw, a blind look in his face. "Everyone has. Even my mom and dad . . . They always thought something was wrong with me. Everyone was always nice to me, they were *grateful,* but—they still thought I was weird. My mom was always trying to get me to be friends with the other kids, telling me I had to *control myself.* And then when they gave me the power-sharer and I drained the whole enclave . . ."

Every word out of his mouth was stoking my already substantial desire to show up on his enclave's doorstep and set the entire place on fire. "They made it feel as though it were all your fault, and that as a result you owed it to all the rest of them to dump the mana you get, all on your own, into their bank, and accept whatever bits they like to dribble back out to you in exchange," I said through my teeth. "Which, by the way, is the only reason you're low on mana in the first place. You'd still be *aglow*—"

"I don't care about the mana!" He shifted and I got myself out of the way to let him get up; he went and sat on the steps, looking out into the still-falling amphisbaena rain. I grabbed my t-shirt—the New York one he'd given me, which came down to mid-thigh on me—and put it on and went and sat next to him. He had his elbows on his knees and was hunched over as if he couldn't bear watching my face, whatever he'd see on it when he told me about his horrible evil self who'd swallowed this swill from everyone round him so long that he couldn't even tell the taste was rotten. "I like the *hunting.* I like going after the mals, and—" He swallowed. "—and taking them apart and pulling the mana out of them. And I know that's creepy—"

"Shut your bloody mouth," I said. "I've seen creepy, Lake; I've been *inside* creepy, and you're nothing like."

He said softly, "That's not true. You know it's not. In the gym, when those kids tried to kill you—"

"*Us*," I said pointedly.

"—you wouldn't have hurt them," he went on, without a pause. "And I—I wanted to kill them. I *wanted* to. And it did freak you out. I'm sorry," he added, low.

I said in measured tones, "Lake, I'm useless at this nonsense, but as my mum's not here at the moment, I'm just going to feed you her lines. *Did* you kill them?"

He gave me an annoyed look that no one ever gives Mum when she's gently leading them along, so I don't think I'd got the tone quite right, but that was his own fault picking me for an agony aunt. "That's not the point."

"I think they'd agree with me that it *is*. I've *wanted* to kill loads of people. But wanting can't do harm without a pair of hands behind it."

He gave a shrugging heave of shoulders and arms. "The point is, I never wanted normal things. And that's not my parents' fault, okay? You can be mad at them if you want to be, but—"

"Thanks, I will."

He snorted. "Yeah. I know you think they're jerks for letting me hunt when I was little. They aren't. That's why they're *not* jerks. Because that's all I ever wanted to do. They tried to stop me. I'm not just saying that. You think Magnus is spoiled? They gave me anything I looked at for more than three seconds. Toys or books or games . . . I didn't want any of it. When I was ten, I started sneaking out of school to hunt. So my dad—my dad, who's one of the top five artificers in New York—literally quit working and hung out with me all day, trying to teach me himself, doing stupid kid projects with me in his home workshop. And I was *mad* at him for it. After a couple of months, I threw a gigantic freakish tantrum because he wasn't letting me hunt. I wrecked the whole shop, part of our apartment, chunks of major artifice projects . . . and then I ran away and hid down in the enclave sewage pipes. When my mom found me, she made me a deal: if I stayed in school all day and did all my homework and did a playdate every Saturday, on Sundays they'd let me take a gate shift and fight *real* mals. I *cried* I was so happy."

I scowled over this confessional torrent. I was really disinclined to be sympathetic to his parents, for what I had to acknowledge were many grotesquely selfish reasons, which was making it hard for me to winkle out the other reasons I still didn't like it. I did have to admit they had a right to struggle with a ten-year-old whose only idea of a good time was taking the guard duty shifts that otherwise would go to the best fighters that New York's mana could hire. Their gates would attract at least as many mals as the school on a daily basis, if not more. The Scholomance isn't in a major metropolitan area with five or six entrances, wizards coming and going the entire day. Ten years on a guard shift is enough to earn you an enclave spot; the only problem is very few people survive to claim it.

But Orion was saying, with perfect sincerity, "It made everything so much better. Then at least people *liked* me for wanting it, even if they still thought I was weird. And then here—"

"And why did they even send you?" I interrupted, still looking for something to be angry about. "Just to look out for the other kids? *You* didn't need protecting."

"They weren't going to," Orion said. "I wanted to come. I

know everyone else hates school. But I don't. The Scholomance—the Scholomance is the best place I've ever been."

I emitted an involuntary gargled noise of outrage.

He huffed a little. "Yeah, see, even you think I'm weird. But it *is*. I could do the one thing I wanted and also be doing something right, all the time. I wasn't just weird and creepy. I got to be—a hero." I grimaced; that wasn't on the nose or anything. "Except whenever people tried to say thanks, or anything, I always felt like it was a giant lie. Because they thought I was being brave, and if they knew I *liked* it, they'd be weirded out, just like everyone from home. And yeah, I thought something was probably going to get me at graduation, because I wasn't going to go until after everyone else was out—"

He delivered this statement with all the agonized soul-searching and drama of someone announcing he'd go for a nice walk; I suffered a burst of private irritation that died very abruptly when he said, "—but I didn't really care."

I stared at him stricken.

"I didn't *want* to die," he hastened to tell me, as if that was an enormous improvement. "I just wasn't scared of it, either. I didn't have a plan except to kill mals until one of them got me, so why *not* in here? I'd get to help so many kids, not just my own enclave. I didn't really know about that stuff, you know," he added abruptly. "Not until I met you. I sort of assumed everyone lived someplace like New York. Even after I met Luisa, I thought she had it really bad, not that we had it so much better. But it made sense to me anyway. Why should I run out on everyone just to go home and hang out on New York's gate until something got me there? I didn't want anything else. Not like normal people—"

I grabbed his near hand, gripping tight. "Stop it!" I said, on the verge of shrieking incoherently. I knew that wouldn't be helpful, but *helpful* felt so far beyond my reach, it might as well have been on the moon, so I was tempted to go the other way instead.

My whole childhood, everyone always wanted me to be more like Mum, told me I ought to be; the only person who didn't was Mum herself. But that insidious message didn't manage to get too deeply into my head, because I was always wanting her to be more like *me*. Less generous, less patient, less kind—and I don't even mean I wanted her to be those things to *other* people; I'd have been wildly glad if she'd ever have stooped to have a screaming match with *me*. But right now, with every fiber of my being, I wanted to have all her answers inside me: her clear understanding, what she would have said, the light she'd have shone for Orion onto the despair twisted like dark vines through his head, so he could see it and cut it out of himself and open up the room to grow. The only answer I had to give him was setting New York on fire, and much as I wished otherwise, I could tell that really *wasn't* an answer to his problem.

"There's no such thing as *normal people*," I said, a desperate flailing. "There's just people, and some of them are miserable, and some of them are happy, and you've the same right to be happy as any of them—no more and no less."

"El, come on," Orion said, with a weary air of being much put upon. I could have frothed in his face. "You know it's not true. There *are* normal people, and we're not. I'm not."

"Yes, we are!" I said. "And you do want things other than hunting. You're sorry enough if you miss a meal, and you minded when I was mean to you, and you certainly seemed reasonably interested in the events of the past hour—"

He huffed a short laugh. "That's what I'm trying to tell you!"

"The only thing you've tried to tell me so far is that you're a hollowed-out suit of armor marching steadily onward through the ranks of mals whilst insensible to all human emotion, so I'm not keen on listening to anything else you've got to say!" I said.

"I'm trying to tell you that I *was*," he said. "I didn't want anything else. I didn't know how to want anything else. Until—"

"Lake, don't you even *dare*," I said, appalled as the full horror dawned on me, but it was too late.

He still had my hand entwined with his; he brought it to his mouth and kissed the side of it softly, without looking at me. "I'm sorry," he said. "I know it's not fair, El. But I just need to know. I never had a plan except to go home and kill mals. I never wanted anything else. But now I do. I want you. I want to be with you. I don't care if it's in New York or Wales or anywhere else. And I just need to know if that's okay. If I can—if I can have that. If you want that, too.

"And you don't need to lie to me," he added. "I'm not going to do anything different tomorrow, no matter what you tell me. I don't think I could. Once I'm fighting, I just go flat-out and keep going; you know that's how it works. I'm not going to play it safe if you say yes, and I'm not going to do anything dumb if you say no."

"What you mean is, you'll do an enormous number of truly stupid things no matter what!" I said, mostly on reflex; the rest of my brain was running around in circles making noises like Precious in a rage.

"Sure, whatever," Orion said. "This isn't about graduation. It's about after. After I'm home, and I know—Chloe told me you won't come to New York. So I need to know if I can get on a plane and come to you. Because that's what I want to do. I can deal with graduation, I can deal with the mals. I just can't deal with being out, trying to reach you when you don't even have a freaking cellphone, and not knowing if it's okay for me to—"

"Yes!" I said, in a despairing howl. "Yes, fine, you utter wanker, you can come to Wales and meet my mum," and then, I didn't add, he could also be shut up in the yurt for a year until she had cleared the rubbish out of his skull, and if *this* was what Mum had been warning me about, if she didn't want me bringing her a shedload of work to do, it was just too bad.

I told myself that mostly because I had a dreadful feeling that this *was* what Mum had been warning me about. I couldn't help knowing she would have told me off for giving him the least encouragement, in the strongest terms possible for her, and also that she'd be absolutely right: I hadn't any business agreeing to be with someone who told me in all sincerity that I was his only hope of happiness in the world, at least not until he'd sorted his own head out and diversified.

But I'd told him the truth. I did want that, too: I wanted him to get on a plane and come to me, and I wanted to live happily ever after with him in a clean and shining world we'd purge of maleficaria and misery, and apparently I wasn't a sensible realist after all, since I was leaping after that outrageous fantasy with both hands, straight into the chasm I could see perfectly well open before me.

"I *do* have plans, though," I added, to distract myself from my own stupidity. "You might be perfectly satisfied to roam the wilds hunting and then come home to the little woman at night, Lake; it won't do for me," and I told him half defiantly about my enclave-building project, except it only made matters worse. He kept that horrible shining look on me the entire time; not even smiling, just holding my hand in his and listening to me go on and on getting progressively more fanciful, littering the whole world with tiny enclaves, sheltering every wizard child born, until finally I burst out, "Well? Haven't you anything to say about it? Go on and tell me I'm mad; I don't want humoring."

"Are you kidding me?" he said, his voice cracking. "El, this school was the best thing I could imagine. But now when I hunt, I'll be helping you do *this*," as if I'd laid a gift in his hands.

I let out a strangled sob and said, "Lake, I hate you so much," and put my head down against his shoulder with my eyes shut. I'd been ready to go down to the graduation hall and fight for my life; I'd been ready to fight for the lives of everyone I knew, for the chance of a future. I didn't need this much more to lose.

Chapter 14

PATIENCE

WE COULDN'T AFFORD to miss dinner, which thankfully gave me an excuse to put a stop to the sentimentality and horrific confessions. I gave Orion a slap on the shoulder and told him to get his clothes mended and back on. It had stopped pissing down snake-things, and the ones that had fallen were mostly dead—amphisbaena aren't very sturdy, and the gym ceiling is a *long* way—although we did have to pick our way gingerly past the ones that were still writhing a bit.

Orion clearly wasn't satisfied to put his emotions away where they belonged: he tried to hold my hand on the way up the stairs, and I had to scowl him off and put my hands firmly in my pockets. At least we caught up with Aadhya and Liu on the stairs, and they let me fall in between them to provide an additional bulwark, although they charged me in eyebrow-wagging and insinuating looks—Liu was clearly pleased to get some of her own back. It wasn't any great act of telepathy on their part: there were sparkly-dust handprints all over my clothes and even my skin. Orion all but bounced along behind us, despite having offered to carry the lute for Liu, and even hummed on the stairs, as if he'd been wafted ethereally far above minor mortal concerns such as our impending doom. Liu covered her mouth with both hands to stifle giggles and Aad smirked at me. I couldn't complain at them for enjoying the distraction—I'd have liked one myself—but I put on my dignity and refused to acknowledge it.

He did manage to get hold of my hand under the table at dinnertime, rubbing his thumb over my knuckles, and I'd already finished eating, so I didn't immediately yank it away and shove his chair over or anything. Although I should have, because after dinner, he trailed me down the stairs, and when we reached our res hall, he tried hopefully, "Want to . . . come to my room?"

"The night before?" I said repressively. "Go and get some *sleep*, Lake. You've had yours; if you want more, you'll just have to graduate."

And he sighed but went, and I went to Aadhya's room with her and Liu instead. The lute was there waiting, but we didn't have any work to do on it, we just sat crammed in there together, piled on the bed. They both teased me for a bit more, but I didn't actually mind, and then obviously we moved on to the serious business of my giving them a detailed report, and I confess that by the time I finished going over it, I was privately thinking to myself maybe I might after all stop by Orion's room before bed for just a little bit, and Aadhya sighed and said, "I'm almost sorry I turned down that junior."

Liu and I both demanded more information—turned out this junior artificer named Milosz had been helping her make some precision-enchanted strips of gold to go on the lute

tuning pegs, and he'd suggested one of those last-night hurrahs to her, which idea she, being the sensible girl I knew and
loved, had firmly quashed.

"What about *you?*" she said to Liu, nudging. "I saw Zixuan
going downstairs just before us. He should be in his room
around now . . ."

Only Liu didn't go red. Instead, she took a deep breath and
said, "I kissed Yuyan last night instead."

We obviously immediately set up a howl for more details,
and she was giggling and she did turn red again, admitting
that there had been somewhat less deadly serious practicing
of music going on in the evenings in her room than perhaps
we might have thought. "Also excuse you," Aadhya said.
"What was up with letting us hassle you about Zixuan all this
time! Or were you trying to *decide?*"

She only meant it in fun, but Liu swallowed, visibly, and
then she said, a bit wavering, "It would . . . it would have been
smart of me."

We both understood right away, and it stopped the teasing
cold: she meant, she *had* been trying to decide, but not because she'd wanted to do something stupid; she hadn't
wanted to sneak over to Zixuan's room for one last night,
hadn't wanted to rip his shirt into shreds in the middle of the
gym pavilion with a mass of amphisbaena romantically hissing and thrashing down at the base of the steps. She'd had
that insidious whispering in her ear, the calculations that
never stopped running inside our heads: *it would be smart*—to
hook a cute, talented, enclaver boy from Shanghai, when he
let it be known he was there to be hooked.

Just like it had been smart to bring in a dozen mice, small
helpless lives you could hold in the cup of your hand, and kill
them instead, one at a time, so you could suck enough mana
out of them to keep yourself alive.

There were a few tears welling up over her lashes and dripping off. She put the heels of her hands to her eyes and pressed to stop them. She said rawly, "I *wanted* to want . . . the right things. The things I was supposed to want. But I don't. Even the ones that are good." She gave a small choked sniffle. "And Zixuan *is*. He's nice, and cute, and I like him, and it would make it okay that I didn't do what they wanted. I didn't have mana to give to Zheng and Min, but I did this instead, this other right thing. And Ma would be so happy. I'd be her smart girl. I'd be her smart girl again. Like when I said I would do it to the mice, for me and Zheng and Min."

I hadn't realized before, but it made perfect sense: that was why the cleansing had worked so well on her. Because she'd said yes, not so much for her own sake, but for the boys, and so she'd taken almost no malia from the mice, our first three years. Just barely enough to survive on.

"And that's what Zixuan would like, too," she said. "A smart girl who wants the right things. He wants the right things himself. He wanted to meet my parents and help build the enclave. He's excited about it. Dominus Li is his great-uncle. He thinks he can persuade him to help us. And I want to help my family, I want to take care of them, but . . . I can't be that girl. I can't be the smart girl. I can only be me."

Aadhya reached out to her, and I did, too; we put our hands on her, and Liu reached out her own slightly damp hands and gripped ours, one in each, tight. "We're going home tomorrow," she said, and kept hold of us determinedly: we'd both flinched. We hadn't broken *that* rule. You didn't say out loud, *I'm going to graduate*. But Liu held on and said it again. "We're going home tomorrow. I'm going home. And my mother is going to be so happy, and for a long time, she won't care about anything, except that I'm back. But then she's going to want me to want the right things again. The things that the family think are the right things." She stopped, and took a deep breath and let it out. "But I'm not going to. I'm going to want the things I want, and help them the way *I* can help them. And those are going to be the right things, too."

I reached out to Aadhya, and the three of us made a circle together: not anything formal, but still a circle, still the three of us together, holding each other up. Liu squeezed our hands again, smiling at us, her eyes bright but not dripping tears anymore, and we smiled back.

We couldn't keep sitting there smiling like muppets the whole night, so eventually . . . I went back to my room—without any side trips; I did manage to resist temptation—only to find Precious sitting in a pile of stuffing in the middle of my bed, sulking ferociously, with a substantial hole dug straight through my already thin pillow. I glared at her and said, "Oh, don't be a sore loser." She gave me a narrow look out of her beady eyes and then turned her back and burrowed herself into the comfortable little nest of fluff.

We still weren't talking the next morning, although with frigid courtesy she allowed me to put her in the bandolier cup to go upstairs to breakfast. She emitted a continuous stream of what I'm fairly certain were rude remarks from the moment Orion joined me, but they didn't dampen his spirits; he beamed at me with delight and tried to take my hand again. I might have relented and let him have it for a dim stretch of the stairs going up, before we ran into other kids, all streaming up to the cafeteria.

Breakfast wasn't stuffed crêpes or anything, but there was unburnt French toast and griddled sardines and pickled vegetables and enough of it for everyone: the school giving us all one nice final meal. The freshmen were still wolfing down theirs when Liesel got up and climbed onto her table with the large mindphone she'd talked some artificer into making for her—the school had apparently counted that as helping, too, although I questioned its value. "It is time now to review the final order of departure," she announced—the message reached my head mostly in English, with a few scattered words of German sneaking in and a whispery echo underneath in Marathi flavored with bits of Sanskrit and Hindi— and began to read off numbers and names as if everyone in the room wasn't already carrying the information inscribed on their brains in letters of flame.

I wasn't paying attention, as I really didn't need to: I knew when my turn was. After everyone else had gone, and I'd pitched Orion through, and I'd ripped up the school's foundations and it was teetering away into the void like a sequoia getting ready to come down. Then I'd—hopefully—have just enough time to jump before the tidal wave of mals reached me. On paper I would, assuming Orion hadn't been overwhelmed some time before then—not a remotely safe assumption—and also assuming that Liesel hadn't fudged the numbers or, less likely, made a mistake.

So I didn't notice Myrthe Christopher getting up on her own table until she cast her own more straightforward amplification spell and said, "Excuse me!" so loudly she managed to drown out the mindphone even inside my head. "I'm so sorry, excuse me!" I knew her only by osmosis: she'd always ranked as one of the more important enclavers, since her parents were something high up in one of the American enclaves, but it was Santa Barbara, one of the California enclaves that aren't quite satisfied having New York rule the roost. My uncomfortably acquired circle of enclavers didn't overlap much with hers, and she'd never stopped by the planning sessions, either.

She waited smilingly until Liesel had lowered her clipboard, then said, "I'm so sorry, I don't want to be rude," in a syrupy way that suggested she'd been studying to be rude for weeks. "But, like—we're not actually doing this?"

"*Excuse* me?" Liesel said, with a razor-sharp edge that translated into a prickling sensation along the bottom of my skull. It landed into total silence; even the freshmen with any breakfast left on their trays had stopped eating. My own had turned into a strange cold lump in my stomach.

Myrthe cast a wincing smile around, showing how pained she was to have this awkward yet necessary conversation. "I know it's been really weird this whole year, and we've all been freaking out, but, reality check—this plan is literally insane?" She pointed down at the floor. "The graduation hall is empty right now. *Empty.* And you want us to go wait in line behind all the other kids, the freshmen, everybody," hilarious, nonsense, "and hand over all our mana, so Queen Galadriel here can summon a billion mals to fill it back up and eat us?" She gave a gurgle of laughter out loud at the absurdity. "No? Just—no? I get it, we had to work on something and make it look good, or else the school was going to screw us, but it's half an hour to graduation, so I think we're good at this point. Please don't get me wrong, I wish we could keep it this good for everybody. We should totally give the other kids all the stuff we can spare, extra mana," the depths of her generosity, really, "but come on."

She wasn't using a mindphone, but she didn't really need to. If there was anyone who hadn't followed, they were getting a translation right now, and after all, surely most of them had thought of it. Surely most of them hadn't been stupid enough to take the idea seriously, had at some point thought to themselves, *We're just killing time until we can leave, aren't we?* I was surprised Liesel hadn't announced it herself, really;

she wasn't stupid. Seduced by her own spreadsheets, probably.

And I couldn't even blame them, because the first thing that came into my head was, I *couldn't* do it alone. Without all the seniors helping, actively channeling me their mana, I wouldn't be able to keep the summoning spell running the whole time and break the school away at the end. That was why the seniors had to wait until last to go. So if they quit, if only all the seniors quit, if they refused to help and headed downstairs and out—there wouldn't be anything for me to do, after all. I'd just have to walk out of the empty hall, and Orion would, too. In half an hour, I'd be hugging Mum, and this time tomorrow he'd be on a plane coming to Wales, and I'd have the whole rest of my life ahead of me, full of good work, and I wouldn't even have to feel guilty.

I couldn't help that greedy selfish desperate thought, and it stoppered up all the furious words I wanted to stand up and yell at her. I could feel Orion gone rigid next to me, but I didn't look at him. I didn't want to see him outraged, and I didn't want to see him looking hopefully at me, and I didn't want to see my own choked feelings in his face. The silence was stretching out into eternities as if Chloe had just sprayed me with the quickening spell again, except some of the younger kids had started to cry, muffled into their hands or buried facedown onto the tables. Everyone was starting to turn their heads, to look at me and Orion, at Aadhya and Liu and Chloe; others were looking at Liesel still up on her own table, all of us bloody fools who had taken the insane absurd plan seriously, much too seriously. The kids in the mezzanine were crowding the railings, peering down anxiously. They were waiting for one of us to say something, and I had to say something, I had to try, but I didn't have any words, and I knew anyway that it wasn't going to do any good. Myrthe would just keep smiling, and what was I going to do, threaten to kill her if she wouldn't risk her life to help me save people from being killed? Was I going to kill everyone who said no? I certainly wouldn't have enough mana then.

Then the next table over, Cora put her chair back, legs scraping over the floor, and stood up and just said flatly, "*I'm still in.*"

It was loud in the room, hanging there. For a moment, nobody else said anything, and then abruptly a boy also from Santa Barbara at the other end of Myrthe's table stood up and said, "Yeah. Fuck off, Myrthe. I'm in, too. Come on, guys," and as soon as he'd prodded them, the other kids at the table were all moving, shoving back their chairs and getting up, too, until Myrthe was standing red-faced with a growing ring around her, and people all round the room were yelling that they were in, they were still in, and I could have cried—for either reason or both.

People kept piling on until Liesel put the mindphone back up and yelled painfully, "Quiet!" and everyone winced and shut up. "Enough interruptions. There is no more time to review. Everyone find your partners and go down to the senior dormitories right away."

The whole incident had probably taken less time than Liesel had been about to spend on reading her announcements, but she'd clearly decided to get us into motion before anyone else could throw out a clever idea. It was just as well, because the Scholomance evidently agreed with her. The grinding of the gears that rotate the dormitories down—and send the senior level to the graduation hall—was picking up even as we left the cafeteria, and kids were still pouring down the stairwells when the warning bell for the cleansing started to go, at least half an hour early. The last few came flying in panicked from the landing on the hissing crackle of the mortal flames going, with their shadows huge in front of them in the brilliant blue-white light.

I ran to my room and reached it with the floor beneath me thrumming. Sudarat and three of the Bangkok sophomores were already waiting inside for me, piled onto the bed clinging to one another: we'd divvied the younger kids up among all the seniors for the trip downstairs. I slammed the door shut just in time as a xylophone chorus of pinging started up outside, metal shards and bits scraped off the walls flying through the corridor as we started our violent rattling progress downwards.

We hit some kind of blockage maybe halfway down that made the whole level lock up and start shaking wildly, and the younger kids all shrieked when the gears finally forced us through the obstruction and we lurched several meters onwards in a single violent jerk. My entire desk fell off into the void; thankfully I already had the sutras in their case strapped safely onto my back, and Precious tucked inside her cage inside her cup, also strapped down.

Another roaring started to go, of monstrous fans somewhere, and a hurricane-violent air current began to tear away the outer edges of the room into jagged puzzle pieces, sending them flying upwards where they'd be reassembled into a new, hopefully never-to-be-used freshman dormitory. The floor was crumbling away at an alarming clip, actually, and we still hadn't reached the bottom. "Get off the bed!" I yelled, but Sudarat and the others hadn't waited for me to tell them the obvious and were already scrambling off; fortunately, since a moment later my bed tipped off, too. I had to yank the door open again and we all spilled out into the corridor even as it came to a thumping, jaw-rattling halt.

Kids were pouring out of rooms all over, running towards

the landing as the rooms kept breaking up around us. The bathrooms were already gaping holes of void, and the tops of the corridor walls were starting to go as well. "Keep together!" I yelled at Sudarat and the other Bangkok kids, and then they were swept away by the current, and a moment later so was I. The corridor floors got in on it and began sliding us all along towards the landing like moving walkways gone mad, dumping us all efficiently into the still-steaming and freshly cleansed graduation hall, all of us in our thousands still dwarfed inside the cavernous space.

Actually this was a sedate graduation by Scholomance standards: normally we'd all have been fighting our way through the first wave of maleficaria to get to our allies by now. And I'd known, I'd literally seen it for myself, but I hadn't quite believed my own memory until I got my feet under me and was standing there in the empty hall, not a single mal in sight.

The doors weren't even open yet, so we really were early. It was just as well, since several hundred people would probably have instinctively made a run for it even if they hadn't *intended* to. We were all milling round in confusion; people were vomiting—efficiently, we were practiced at that—and sobbing and yelling out names all over, trying to find their friends, and then Liesel was bellowing through the mindphone, "Back! Everyone back! Clear space in front of the doors!"

A gaggle of artificers emerged from the general mass, lugging several big square contraptions I hadn't even seen before, which fired out a volley of thin colorful streamers that fell to the ground and then attached themselves there and lit up like runways. The artificers kept firing them off over and over, crisscrossing one another to create small sections covering the floor, all color-coded and marked with the numbers

Liesel had assigned the teams; everyone started running to their places and lining up.

Alchemists were painting wider stripes on the outside of the queue area, imbued with spells of protection and warding that threw up hazy shimmery walls. Zixuan already had a team helping him check over the speaker cables that had been rigged from the ceiling, doing tests from the mouthpiece and making sure the sound was coming out again from the massive first speaker dangling down in front of the doors. Another large group were going over the massive barricades that they'd built around the second shaft, the one coming *down,* and Orion was there near them just tossing his whip-sword in his hand lightly.

He looked over and caught me watching him and smiled so blithely that I immediately wanted to run over just to punch him in the mouth, or just possibly kiss him one last time, but before I could put either plan into action, Precious knocked open the top of her protective egg and gave an urgent squeak. I jumped and looked round to see Aadhya and Liu beckoning to me wildly from the raised platform set up to one side of the doors, where the wide mouthpiece of the speaker system had been mounted onto a stand. Liu was saying something to her own familiar Xiao Xing in his cup on her chest, presumably *Tell Precious to get her stupid mistress over here.*

I ran over, dodging the other kids racing to their places in all directions, and as soon as I reached them, training took over, and we were just working, the same routine we'd practiced for weeks. Aadhya quickly tuned up the lute, and Liu and I ran through a few scales together. Chloe joined us with three prepared dropper vials nestled in a small velvet-lined case: I sang warm-ups while she mixed them carefully together into a small silver cup, stirring with a narrow stick of diamond glowing with mana, and gave the shimmering pink liquid to me. I gargled with it twice and then swallowed it, and all the raspy adrenaline tightness in my throat smoothed away, my lungs swelling with air as if someone had put a bellows into my mouth. I sang out a few more practice notes and they echoed around the room in an ominous ringing way, like the tolling of a bell, and everyone in their places shuffled back from the platform a bit. Probably just as well, in case anyone had thought of having a dash at the gates in the last minute.

"Ready?" I said to Liu. She nodded, and we stepped up to the mouthpiece together. Aadhya and Chloe had already run to their own places in the queue; everyone else was there, too. I took a deep breath, and Liu picked out the opening line, and then I started singing.

I was immediately glad for every last second we'd spent practicing, because I hadn't quite realized until that very moment that we wouldn't be able to *hear* ourselves. The speaker system grabbed the sound and sucked it completely in, and then carried it off through the miles and miles of speaker cable wound through the school.

Which obviously was what we wanted, of course—if the song was audibly coming from me, the mals would just stay right here and come at me; we needed the sound to come out of that last speaker right in front of the gates, and from there lead the mals to chase it down that long, long line, so they'd fill the school up before they ended up back down at the gates Orion was guarding. But it was just as well that I had every word and phrase deeply embedded in my brain and my throat and lungs, as otherwise I would have bungled the incantation completely a minute later when the first notes I'd made finally boomed out of the speaker in front of the actual doors.

The younger kids all set up a chorus of yelps and small

shrieks as larval mals started to drop from the ceiling and pop out of cracks in the floor and from under bits of rubble to chase the alluring call. Real screams started a moment later as a panel of the floor popped off and a really decrepit-looking voracitor crawled out. The thing was so antique it must have been at least two centuries old, all creaking wood and antique bloodstained cast-iron machinery held together with bundles of intestine-like flesh, with long spindly arms and fingers; it had probably been hiding down there snatching students and other mals almost since the school had opened.

It was near the front of the queue, amid a crowd of freshmen. The panicking and running didn't have a chance to get under way properly, however, because it ignored them all, fixed its dozen eyes on the line of speakers hanging from the ceiling, and set off crawling along their direction at a good healthy clip. It would presumably have kept going on into the shaft and into the school, only it didn't have the chance, as Orion dashed over from his station and pounced on it before it got halfway.

There was some more yelling after that, too, but just a few kids who'd been splattered with the gore, and then they were drowned out by loads of people yelling and pointing and gasping: behind me, the doors had cracked. The first coruscating glimmer of the gateway spell spilled out over the steps like the light on the bottom of a swimming pool, a faint staticky crackle going and thin tendrils of the maelstrom wisping out over the floor like a hungry eldritch mal. I couldn't be angry at Myrthe, I couldn't; I wanted to turn and jump through more than anything in the world. I pressed my hands hard over my ears and kept singing my silent song, concentrating on the familiar feeling in my throat.

Liesel was booming out, "Group one!" before the doors had even opened fully, and the first three kids ran up the stairs holding hands, a cluster of freshmen from Paris, and vanished out of my peripheral vision. Everyone sighed a little and leaned in, and then recoiled again as a kerberoi bounded in through the gates—what one of those was doing in Paris, I'd like to know—with its heads snapping wildly. The ones on either side had a go at biting, but their teeth skidded off the protective spells the alchemists had put up, and the middle head and the body weren't paying any mind to anything except bolting along the cable after the speakers. It was running so fast that Orion didn't manage to get it in time; it galloped into the shaft and was gone.

But it didn't matter, because more mals were coming, bucketloads of them, mostly dripping wet and trailing stinking sewer water. You can't have an induction point anywhere that mundanes might see it; if you get spotted, you don't get inducted, because the amount of mana the school would have to spend to force a portal open for you in the face of a disbelieving mundane would be absolutely insane. Which leads to having induction points in awkward out-of-the-way places, which in turn as you might imagine get ringed round by hungry mals that don't dare attack a prepared group of grown wizards, but very much want to get into the school.

That had all been part of the plan, of course, only I hadn't realized how sure I'd been that the plan somehow wasn't going to work, until apparently it *was* working. What looked like a hundred mals had already come through even by the time Liesel yelled, "Group two!" and the second group—actually just a single freshman from the far outback of Australia—went for the gate. He had to literally leap into the gate over a river of animated bones that hadn't stopped long enough to assemble themselves back into skeletons and were just clattering along.

The second he'd gone through, a huge eldritch-infested

dingo came through, so fast that it had to have been literally standing *at* his induction point—presumably guarding it, since it had a binding collar round its throat. A rather dangerous strategy for protection against mals: so much of its fur had fallen off to expose the glowing vapors inside that his family couldn't possibly have kept it under control for more than another three years at most. But they clearly had needed the help: a horde of red speckled grelspiders came pouring through almost right behind it, their talons clattering over the marble floor as they skittered alongside the line of speakers. They overtook one of the Parisian preycats along the way, and managed to devour it without actually stopping, leaving a hollowed-out furry bag of bones behind them to be crushed flat a few moments later when the radriga came stomping through after the two kids going home to Panama City had jumped.

A team of the best maths students had laid out the order of departure to maximize the flow of mals into the school. A pile of incomprehensible graphs and charts had appeared thirty seconds after the one and only time I'd asked to have the details explained to me, but I did know the general idea was to keep the open portals as far apart from one another as possible, so the turns were deliberately hopscotching round the world. Whatever the artificers had done to keep the portals open was working, too; the distinctly Australian ones kept coming for nearly two minutes.

Everything was *working*. The whole plan. I felt I could keep singing without a pause for weeks. I couldn't hear even the delayed music anymore over the roaring tide of maleficaria streaming in, but the mana was flowing into me and out again into the spell. The song was meant to be a beckoning, *Come, please come, a banquet waits for you,* an alluring invitation, but I didn't want to just hold open a hospitable door. I wanted to suck in every last mal of the world, and I didn't deliberately start singing something else, but as I got properly stuck in, the spell I couldn't hear seemed to become something harder in my mouth, a ruthless demand: *Come now, come all of you.* I don't know if I'd changed the words, or if I'd just gone wordless entirely, but the maleficaria were answering: more and more of them were coming, a solid wave of bodies streaming in. Orion wasn't even fighting any of them anymore, he was just randomly sticking his sword or firing attacks off into the mass, and some of them were falling down dead. The rest kept running along the line of speakers and going headlong up into the school.

I did start to worry that with so many mals coming in, they'd get in the way of the kids trying to get *out*. I couldn't do anything about it, the only thing I could do was the calling spell, but I didn't need to: someone else was doing something about it. Alfie had got all the London seniors to come out of their place in queue with him. They joined hands and made a circle for him, and with them at his back helping, pouring mana into him, he raised up his evocation of refusal and shaped it into a narrow corridor between the front of the queue and the gates, so it let kids go running through and shunted the mals off to the side instead.

Other kids started jumping out of the queue to freshen up the protection spells, or to help the kids on the edges when one of the mals tried to snatch themselves a bite for the road. We hadn't planned on that, hadn't practiced it. We hadn't realized it would be a problem. But there were so many mals that some of them were being pushed to the edges of the widening current and bumping up against the queue area, close enough that the tasty young freshman in the hand was able to overcome the tantalizing lie of the infinite banquet in the bush. But seniors were jumping out of the queue to help, fighting the mals off and pushing them back into the torrent; the younger kids were healing scratches for one another, giving sips of potions to anyone injured.

Liesel started picking up the pace, too: I think she realized that getting *enough* mals wasn't going to be a problem. She began firing off the freshmen at a much more rapid clip, waving them through almost without a pause, just yelling, "Go! Go!" The tide of incoming mals didn't slow any, but the queue began to melt away. Zheng and Min waved to Liu and me before they jumped; maybe two minutes later, Sudarat called, "El, El, thank you!" and ran through with the Bangkok sophomores.

I really hoped they had got clear of their induction point in a hurry, because not a minute later, a truly gigantic naga squeezed its widemouthed hissing head in—or rather its first head, which was followed by two others, before the rest of it muscled in. The heads nearly stretched the entire length from floor to ceiling, endangering the speaker cable. There were lots of yells: it might well have been what had taken out Bangkok. Naga that size are definitely potential enclave-killers, because if you don't stop them before they get inside your wards, then once they're in they'll start thrashing wildly to rip the place apart.

Which it would certainly have done here if given half a chance. I was about to frantically wave Liu in for an instrumental section, which had been our plan if I needed to stop long enough to kill anything especially gruesome, but before I could, Orion took a flying leap from the floor and straight into the middle head's *mouth*. It paused and then a moment later he shredded his way out of the base of the neck in a whirlwind, hailing unpleasantly fishy bits and bones and ichor in all directions. All three heads toppled into the still-flowing tide of other maleficaria, and sank beneath it, devoured in less than a minute.

Orion landed in the full churning current still whirling off the detritus, and the mals actually split to go around him as he just *stood* there, bright-eyed and not breathing particularly hard, and cracked his neck to one side like he'd just got warmed up properly. He even gave me a quick infuriating grin before he plunged back into the fray.

Five minutes later, the very last of the freshmen were gone, and we were well into the sophomores. The mals had squeezed Alfie's tunnel of access until it was barely big enough to go one across, and we only had fifteen minutes left, so the pacing had been thrown to the winds and everyone was just running at the gates as soon as they came to the head of the queue. I didn't know any of the kids going now: they were a river of faces that I'd never talked to, never shared a classroom with. Even if I'd sat with them at table in the years before this one, taking a desperation seat with younger kids, I would have kept my head down; I didn't remember them.

Some of them looked at me as they came up close to the head of the queue, and I saw my reflection in their faces: the ocean-green light flickering round me, the mana shining out from beneath my skin, tinted golden-bronze except where it escaped around my eyes and fingernails and mouth, turning me into a glowing lamp upon my pedestal. They ducked their heads and hurried by, and I thought of Orion saying *There are normal people and we're not,* and maybe he was right, but I didn't mind. I didn't know those normal kids and maybe I'd never know them, but each one of them was a story whose unhappy ending hadn't been written yet, and in its place I'd inscribed one line with my own hand: *And then they graduated from the Scholomance.*

They were out, so many kids were safely out, and so many mals were still pouring in—mals that wouldn't be out there to kill anyone else. I wanted them ferociously, wanted them beneath my command, and my desire fueled the spell even more. The mana should have been running low by then: the juniors were more than half gone, and taking their mana with them. But even as I felt the flow waver a little, the first sense of the tide beginning to ebb away, a fresh wave over-flowed the banks. I didn't know what it was at first, and then through my muffled ears I heard people yelling in dismay, and I looked up: the tide of mals had made it through the school, and the first ones had come crashing into the barri-cade.

I had to keep singing, but I watched them hit, clenched with fear: it was too soon, ten minutes too soon. First there were two or three, and then there were ten, and then almost instantly there was a solid thrashing wall of malice backed up, roaring and hissing and clawing each other in their hun-ger to get to Orion, and through him to us. Everyone still in the room tensed, and if they hadn't been packed into the queue by then, with a torrent of mals going by on the other side, people would have broken; I'm sure of it. We'd hoped, we'd planned, for Orion to hold the barricade for just a min-ute or two, no longer, but we still had more than a quarter of the queue waiting, and it wasn't possible for anyone to hold off that mass. It wasn't the graduation horde, it was orders of magnitude built upon it, unstoppable, and he'd simply be smothered and overrun.

Except he wasn't.

The first wave of mals came at him and died so fast that I didn't even see how he killed them, and I was watching with unblinking desperation, already tensing in agony, getting ready to do—something, anything, as wild as I'd been watching Nkoyo from the other side of the gymnasium doors. The next wave swept over him, and a handful of them made it past, but only a few steps past; he broke out of the mass of already collapsing corpses, still alight with stupid grinning satisfaction, and caught the last running sherve by its skinny rat tail and dragged it still flailing wildly along behind him as he plunged without a pause back into the fight.

Mana was surging into me; more than a wave, an ocean. "Oh my God," I heard Chloe say, sounding choked, and when I darted a glance over, I saw she and Magnus and the other New York seniors were all staggering, all their allies too. The power-sharer on my wrist was glowing vividly, like all of theirs, and they were all clutching at any kids round them who would take a handout, literally flinging mana at them— the mana that Orion was suddenly pouring into the shared power supply. The mals were still dying so fast it didn't seem real, as if they were coming apart even as they got to him.

I hadn't quite believed, even after Chloe had told me, that literally all the kids from New York had just coasted along for three solid years on the mana Orion had supplied them; I hadn't understood his whinging about how low he was. But now he was finally being filled up again, enough to share, and it was coming in what felt like a limitless flood. He hadn't let on how bad it really was, I realized belatedly; he'd only taken the bare minimum. Everything he'd done this year, he'd done starved as low as ever I'd been, in the days before I'd put Chloe's sharer on my wrist. He'd spent his senior year, the year when our powers really bloom, without enough mana to do what he could do.

And now that he finally had it, I thought I might understand better what he'd told me, because it was so *effortless* for him. He wasn't locked in a grim, desperate struggle for his life, counting every drop of mana like a tumbling grain of sand in an hourglass. His every movement, each graceful killing sweep of his sword-whip, every spell he cast, every effort he put forth, they all fed him back, and you couldn't help but feel, watching it, that he was doing what he was meant for—something so perfectly aligned with his nature that it was as easy as breathing. It made sense suddenly that you'd like it, that it would be everything you wanted to do, if there were something you were this *good* at, and it rewarded you with endless buckets of mana on top. Your own body would teach you to want it more than anything—want it so much you'd have to learn to want anything else.

Orion didn't look over at me again, even when he surfaced in between the killing waves; he was too busy. It was just as well, because if he'd looked over at me, I'd have smiled stupidly back at him. I was glad, so glad, even pinned down in this room with all the monsters in the world trying to come at me, at Orion, because it wasn't despair in his way after all; it was just the clumsiness of learning. He *could* want other things. I wasn't the only thing he'd *ever* want; I was just the *first* other thing he'd wanted.

The mals were still pouring in, a sea of horrors, and as the seniors started to go, even bigger ones started to come as well: these were the mals who'd been further away from the portals, who'd caught the song calling them in when freshmen or sophomores had first gone through, and now had reached the same induction point and were making it through. Some of them were so monstrous you could barely stand to look at them: zjevarras and eidolons, pharmeths and kaidens, deep nightmare creatures that lurked beneath enclaves waiting for a chance to devour. But even when the worst twisted unreal things came in, there wasn't any screaming or panic anymore. It was only seniors left now, and we were the survivors of a nightmare ourselves, the ones who'd endured the Scholomance—the last ones who would ever endure it. That wasn't just a dream anymore; I could see that hope being made real in the sheer number of mals coming through, and Orion was making room for more almost as fast as I could bring them in.

I was starting to believe that it was going to work. I didn't want to; I was fighting hope away as fiercely as Orion was fighting mals. But I couldn't help it. The golden seconds were counting away—Liesel had inscribed the timing midair in letters of fire so we could all watch them going. When they reached the two minute mark, that was when I'd stop singing and strike the final blow instead. Only seven and a half minutes left, only seven minutes left, and then Aadhya was calling, "El!" and I looked over and found her: she was almost at the front of the swiftly moving queue. She was smiling at me, her face wet with tears, and in their shine I wasn't a glowing marvel after all, I was just me, just El, and I wanted to climb down and run to hug her, but all I could do was smile back from up on the platform, and as she took the last few steps forward, she pointed at me and then held her palm against her face: *Call me!* Her phone number, and Liu's and Chloe's and Orion's, were all inscribed on the thin bookmark that held my place inside the sutras. I didn't have a phone, and neither did Mum, but I'd promised I'd find a way to call her, if we made it—

And then, the promise was different. It was only if *I* made it: Aadhya took the last few steps up the dais, and she went through the doors, and she was—out. She was out, she was safe, she had made it.

I knew all the faces going out now. Some of them didn't

like me; Myrthe stalked past without looking towards me, chin up and mouth tight, except as the last kid in front of her went, and she saw the gateway seething right in front of her, her whole face crumpled into sobs and she was fighting to keep her eyes open even while she ran headlong out, and I was glad, I was glad for her, glad that she'd made it, too; I wanted them all to make it. I'd missed Khamis going, and Jowani and Cora; they were already gone. Nkoyo blew me a kiss with both hands before she ran up the steps and out. I didn't spot Ibrahim, I'd missed him going out, but I saw Yaakov go past with his head bowed and rocking slightly, wearing a beautiful worn prayer shawl whose fringe was shining with light, his lips still moving even as he walked, and when he passed me, he looked up and I felt a warmth like the feeling of Mum's hand stroking over my hair, calming and steadying.

The New York seniors were coming up: Chloe waved wildly to catch my eye and put up heart-hands in the air before she went through, and right behind her, Magnus gave me a thumbs-up, condescending to the last, and I didn't even mind. I'd got them out. I was going to get everyone out. There were only maybe a hundred kids left in the queue— ninety—eighty—no one left I knew, except Liesel going hoarse and Liu beside me playing steadily on, the guiding notes I couldn't hear but felt in my feet, and Alfie and Sarah and the rest of the London seniors—who should have gone by now; I knew they'd got a higher number than New York in the lottery. But they'd all stayed back, to help Alfie hold the aisle for everyone else.

I wouldn't have expected it of them, of enclave kids; they'd been raised to do the opposite, to get themselves the hell out. But they'd also been raised on the party line, hadn't they:

they'd been told, just like the school itself, that Manchester and London and their heroic allies had built the Scholomance out of generosity and care, trying to save the wizard children of the world; and maybe just like the school, it had sunk in more than their parents might have wanted. Or maybe if you only gave someone a reasonable chance of doing some good, even an enclave kid might take it.

I didn't know anyone else, but we were coming to the very end of the line, and the last group of enclavers, going to Argentina; they'd drawn one of the lowest numbers of the lottery, but they hadn't kicked up a fuss and demanded to be jumped ahead, or else; and because they hadn't, none of the other unlucky enclavers had been able to complain. There were four of them, and they went through single-file and fast, one after another, except the last one recoiled screaming—the first screaming I'd heard for a while—as a maw-mouth came rolling in through the gates.

There wasn't any question about where it had come from, horribly. The boy from Argentina who'd just gone out of the portal was *caught*, struggling and screaming, begging for help, for mercy, to be let out, in absolute and familiar terror, as the maw-mouth went on gulping up his body, even as it came through.

I must have stopped singing. I don't think I could've kept singing. It wasn't a very big maw-mouth. It might even have been smaller than the last one, the first one, the only one I'd ever seen or touched before—the one that would keep living in me for every last minute of the rest of my life. It only had a cluster of eyes, almost all of them brown and black, fringed with dark lashes, horribly like the eyes of the boy being swallowed, and some of them were still conscious enough to be full of horror. Some of its mouths were still whimpering faintly, and others sobbing or gagging.

THE LAST GRADUATE ✦ 379

But it was going to get bigger. It caught three other mals even before it was all the way inside, and reeled them in and swallowed them—even before it had finished engulfing the boy, despite their own thrashing; they didn't have enclaver-quality shields to hold it off. And the boy would go too, soon enough; as soon as the last of his mana ran out.

"Tomas, Tomas!" the Argentine girl was sobbing, but she wasn't trying to reach out to him. No one tried to touch a maw-mouth. Not even other mals, not even the mindless most-hungry ones, as if even they could sense what would happen to them if they did.

There was bile climbing up my throat. Liu was still play-ing; she'd thrown a quick horrified look up at me, but she'd kept going. Alfie was still holding the aisle, with all the Lon-don kids behind him, even though surely all they wanted was to flee out the gates, to run for more than their lives, because the worst thing a maw-mouth did was never kill you.

I'd asked them all to help me, and they had; I'd asked them to be brave, to do the good thing that they had a chance of doing, and I hadn't the right to ask them to do it if I wasn't going to do it myself. So I had to go down to the maw-mouth. I had to, but I couldn't, except past it, far down the hall, at the barricade, I could see Orion's head turn round. If I didn't go down, he'd come. He'd leave the barricade, let the tidal wave of mals come in behind him, and come for the maw-mouth, because Tomas was screaming, screaming in rising despera-tion, as the maw-mouth's tendrils began to creep inquisitively up his chest, towards his mouth and eyes.

I stepped down from the platform and crossed the dais. The last kids in the queue parted to let me through, staring at me as I went, and the shimmer of the alchemical wards ran like water over my skin as I went through it. The mals were still coming through the portal, but they were parting in a

wide circle around the maw-mouth, which had paused perhaps for a little digesting, and to feel around inside the
scorched outline that Patience had left behind, as if it was
considering where to make itself at home. It was like a tiny
little inkblot inside that monstrous outline. It couldn't have
had that many lives inside it yet. And I had my own shield up,
Mum's simple brilliant shielding spell that she'd given away
to everyone in the world who wanted it, and all it took was
mana that you'd built yourself, or that a loving friend had
freely given, and Orion was still pouring power into me like
a waterfall.

I had to shut my eyes so I wasn't looking at it, and then I
pretended that the gates were in front of me, the gates with
Mum on the other side, Mum and my whole future, and that
was true, because I couldn't get there until I'd gone through
this, because the bloody horrible universe wanted me to suf-
fer, and I jumped forward into the maw-mouth. Even as the
horrible surface of it closed over me, I cast La Main de la
Mort with all my rage and the mana of a thousand mals behind it, and I cast it again, and again, and again, my whole
face and body clenched tight, and I don't know how long it
was, it was forever, it was three seconds, it was my entire life
stretched out to infinity, and then it was over and Liu was yelling at me, "El! El, look out!"

I opened my eyes, kneeling in wet, and turned just in time
to cast my killing spell one more time, automatically, right at
the slavering horka that had just erupted in through the portal. It tumbled instantly dead, and its corpse went sliding past
me down the steps, riding the horrible putrescent gush still
draining out of the translucent skin of the maw-mouth, and
three other kids were—they were yanking Tomas up, out of
the puddle of its remains. His legs where the maw-mouth

had enveloped him and started trying to unspool him were raw and bloody in patches, and the power-sharer still on his wrist was crackling; he'd probably overloaded it, pulling enough mana to shield himself. Sarah pulled it off his wrist and flung it away from him; it vanished into the streaming mals and the minor explosion was muffled by their bodies.

I knelt there staring at them, shaking. I didn't quite believe I'd done it, and I didn't quite believe it was over, the whole world gone unreal and blurry for me: the streaming mals still going by, Liu's music still carrying our song.

"Get up!" Liesel was yelling at me. "Get up, you stupid girl! It is time! There are only two minutes left!"

It worked, and I managed to get my feet back under me roughly at the same time poor Tomas did. One of the others had given him a drink of potion, and he was looking very calm and glazed; the last girl from Argentina had got his arm over her shoulders and was helping him balance. Then I realized why Liesel had been yelling so vigorously: Alfie had moved the evocation to cover us, to save us from simply being overrun, but that meant no one else could go. He was trying to force it back into place, against the pressure of the mals still pouring in, and the clock was almost down to the final minute.

But there were only twenty kids left. I didn't go back into the honeypot calling spell with Liu. Instead I went to Alfie and put my hand on his shoulder, then put my hands beneath his, to take the evocation over from him; he slowly and carefully eased his hands out, and gasped and nearly fell over with release as it came off him. I got a secure grip on it, and then I pushed mana into it, the mana that was roaring endlessly into me, and widened the evocation, shoving mals aside, to make an archway to the gates.

"Go!" I said, and the London kids were gone, and the rest of the line behind them; Liesel jumped down from the platform herself, shoved the mindphone into my hand—I resisted it for a moment, what was the point with everyone gone, but she so determinedly wrapped my hand around it that I gave up and took it, and then she was gone.

The queue was empty. Liu picked the last few notes, letting them fade away so the song-spell would end gracefully, and then she jumped down from the platform with the lute and ran past me through the gateway without wasting a moment on goodbye: the gift of leaving me every last second of the one precious minute we had left, with the music still winding its way through the speakers, before the mals all broke loose from the honeypot enchantment; she only reached out a hand and brushed her fingertips against my arm as she flew by.

And then it was the end. It was just me and Orion—Orion who was still fighting in the mouth of the barricade. The mals were trying and trying to get inside, to get past him, but he'd held them back. The endless tide of them would overwhelm and smother him eventually, even him. There were hours of them—days and weeks of them—already built up; sooner or later he'd fall down for sheer exhaustion, for thirst and hunger and lack of sleep, and they'd have him. But he didn't need to hold them off for hours, for days, for weeks. He only needed one minute and twenty-six seconds.

"Orion!" I called to him—of course he didn't do anything as sensible as look over, much less come running—and then, with a half-annoyed, half-grateful thought to Liesel, I yanked up the mindphone and yelled into it. "Orion!" Even though he was fighting, he jerked and looked back at me, and then he killed six more mals and threw a sprinting spell on his feet and put on a flaming burst of speed and skidded to a stop beside me.

"Go through!" I said, but he didn't even bother to say no, just swung round and put himself between me and the mals now pouring into the hall through the barricade. They weren't even coming for us right away. I doubt any of them wanted to come at Orion after the last fifteen minutes of slaughter, and the music had already stopped for them, the promised banquet vanished before they'd even reached it. They were only spilling in now because they hadn't anywhere else to go, with all the pressure pent up behind them.

I planted my feet on the dais and started in on the super-volcano incantation. The first ley lines spiked out from under my feet, running to all the walls like the coronal lines of a sunburst, and then long curving lines went swinging back and forth over the floor after them. When the whole floor was covered, all of them shot together up the walls and through the ceiling, and for a moment I could feel the whole building in my hands, yielding to me—

Yielding the same way the gym floor had yielded to me, that day with all the enclavers ready to fight each other. Yielding—to give me a chance to stop the killing. To *save more children.*

I hadn't expected to feel sorry. I hadn't allowed myself to expect that I'd even make it to this moment, so I hadn't imagined what it would be like if I did, but even if I had, I don't think I could have imagined that. But for a moment, I *was* sorry: the Scholomance had done everything it could for us, given us ungrateful sods everything it had, like that awful story about the giving tree, and here I was about to chop it down. I paused, in that moment between the two parts of the incantation, and though I had to clench every hardened mus-

cle in my gut to keep from flying apart with the potential of
the spell gathered in me, I managed to say, softly, "Thank
you." Then I plunged over the line.

I'd never completely cast the spell before, for obvious reasons. I don't think I'll ever cast it again. As soon as I was inside
it, I knew it wasn't really a spell for a supervolcano: that was
just an example. It was for *devastation,* for the shattering of a
world. I'd felt instinctively that it would work to take the
school down; now I knew that it would.

And the mals knew, too. They did come at us, then—not
to kill us but to *escape.* The honeypot spell had died out, and
the last portals had closed; no more of them were coming
through the gates. But the whole school was crammed full of
them, every last nook and cranny jam-packed, and all of
them could feel the end coming: the warning pillar of ash
and fire going up into their sky, the spreading grey cloud.

But Orion had flipped his sword-wand-thing open into a
long, whiplike length, and he was keeping the whole dais
clear; any mal that tried to set so much as a toe on the steps,
he killed, and none of them wanted to come up. Little ones
tried to dart out through the sides; he killed them with rapid
flicks that my eyes couldn't even follow. I was chanting the
final verses of the incantation, and the floor was beginning to
heave beneath us. I could feel walls parting, pipes bursting, all
through the school, and the low groaning of the floor as it
began to separate from the dais. The seam all round was
opening up, and a thin black line of empty void was beginning to show through.

The mals were going into a frenzy: they stopped being reluctant, and Orion was fighting furiously, killing them in
every direction: nightflyers and shrikes diving at us, ghauls
howling in the air, eldritch horrors whispering frantically.

There was a squealing of metal behind me, too: the doors were starting to swing shut again. The fiery letters in the air were counting down: forty-one seconds left, and time to go. If a few mals did escape now, after we were gone, it didn't matter. The job was done; we'd done it. I deliberately stopped on the last syllable but one, and let the spell go. The air around me rippled with the shudder of the spell traveling out—not quite finished, but so close that it would tip over to completion on its own in another moment. I laughed in sheer triumph and cast the evocation of refusal round us and shoved it outward, tumbling the mals away from me and Orion down the steps.

Orion wobbled himself, on the lowest step, and looked round wildly at the mals that had just been pushed out of his reach. "Let's go!" I shouted to him, and he turned and stared up at me, blankly.

And then the whole floor shook beneath us, and it wasn't because of my spell. The ocean of mals surrounding us parted like the Red Sea, frantically frothing away to either side as a titanic shape bigger than the doors themselves erupted out of the shaft and came surging towards us, so enormous I couldn't even recognize it as a maw-mouth at first: the endless eyes and mouths so tiny they were only speckles scattered like stars over its bulk. Any mal that couldn't get out of its way was consumed without a pause; it just rolled over them and they were gone.

It wasn't Patience; it wasn't *just* Patience. It was Patience *and* Fortitude. Scorched and starved, their graduation hall picked completely clean, they'd finally turned on each other. They'd chased each other through the dark underbelly of the school—the school had surely *opened* spaces up for them deliberately, luring them away from the gates to clear the hall for our escape—until one of them had devoured the other and settled in to quietly digest its enormous meal in peace, a century of feeding in a single go, only to be stirred up into a panic when it had felt the school beginning to topple.

All my triumph fell away from me like a long tail of ashes crumbling off the end of a stick of incense. I'd been getting ready to be proud of myself, self-satisfied: I'd *done* it, I'd saved everyone, I'd purged the world of maleficaria, I'd faced my greatest fear and I'd come through it. I'd been ready to go through the door and boast to Mum of what I'd done, to wait with queenly grace for my knight in shining armor to come and receive my hand, his reward and mine, and set out on our crusade to save any tarnished bits of the world that still needed to be polished up.

I actually laughed out loud, I think, I'm not sure; I couldn't hear myself, but it felt like a mad frightened giggle in my throat. It was just so utterly hilarious that I'd ever imagined I could face *this*. I couldn't form any words, any coherent plan. Patience slammed into the evocation of refusal like a tidal wave hitting a seawall, sloshing fully over it like a dome encasing us; eyes smushed up against the surface and staring down at us blankly. It slid back down and came at us again: mana *roared* through me with the impact, blinding. I couldn't have cast a killing spell even if I could have done anything whatsoever: it was taking everything I had to keep the evocation up, against a monstrosity that wouldn't ever take no for an answer.

Then Precious put her head out and gave a shrill squeak, and I realized—*I didn't have to.* "Orion!" I screamed. "Orion, come on!" He was standing there staring up at Patience through the shimmery dome evocation. I didn't actually wait for him to respond; even while I was screaming I had already grabbed him by the arm. I pulled him back with me up the stairs, towards the doors. They were grinding a bit; they had just started to swing slowly shut. The crack around the base of the dais was widening.

Patience slammed into the evocation again, and I nearly fell over, prickling starbursts filling my eyes. I was hanging on Orion's arm when my vision cleared; he hadn't moved. I didn't speak again, just yanked on him, dragging him one more step back.

But he wasn't taking his eyes off Patience. There was a fierce terrible light in his face, that hunger I'd seen in him before, wanting a thing dead. And I couldn't blame him: if anything in the universe wanted killing, it was that thing, that horrible monstrous thing; it needed to die. And the crack around the base of the dais was still widening, but it was going just a little bit more slowly than the doors were closing.

It wouldn't have mattered in the grand scheme of things if ten or twenty other mals made it out, but it *would* matter if Patience made it out, if that sack of endless death escaped, to keep gnawing eternally on its victims' bones and gobble up who knew how many countless others, unstoppable and forever.

But our time was running out: the hanging numbers of flame were counting down the last seconds. "We *can't!*" I yelled at him, and turning braced my whole body and flung one hand out, at the end of a stiff arm, to hold Patience off again through one more thundering blow. I gulped air and turned back to haul Orion up one more step, to the very edge of the gateway, and then I let go of his arm and caught his face in both hands and pulled him round to look at me. "Orion! We're *going!*"

He stared down at me. The seething colors of the gateway were shining in his eyes, mottling his skin, and he leaned in towards me, like he wanted to kiss me. "Do you want to get kneed again? Because I *will!*" I snarled at him, in outrage.

He jerked back from me, more ordinary color flushing into his cheeks. His eyes cleared for a moment; he looked back at Patience, and then he laughed once—he laughed, a short laugh, and it was awful. He turned to me and said, "El, I love you so much."

And then he shoved me through the gate.

PHOTO: BETH GWINN

NAOMI NOVIK is the acclaimed author of the Temeraire series and the award-winning novels *Uprooted* and *Spinning Silver*. She is a founder of the Organization for Transformative Works and the Archive of Our Own. She lives in New York City with her family and six computers.

naominovik.com
TheScholomance.com
Facebook.com/naominovik
Twitter: @naominovik
Instagram: @naominovik

About the Type

This book was set in Dante, a typeface designed by Giovanni Mardersteig (1892–1977). Conceived as a private type for the Officina Bodoni in Verona, Italy, Dante was originally cut only for hand composition by Charles Malin, the famous Parisian punch cutter, between 1946 and 1952. Its first use was in an edition of Boccaccio's *Trattatello in laude di Dante* that appeared in 1954. The Monotype Corporation's version of Dante followed in 1957. Though modeled on the Aldine type used for Pietro Cardinal Bembo's treatise *De Aetna* in 1495, Dante is a thoroughly modern interpretation of that venerable face.

Don't miss the riveting conclusion
to the Scholomance series

THE GOLDEN ENCLAVES

BY NAOMI NOVIK

Explore more wondrous worlds with
NAOMI NOVIK!

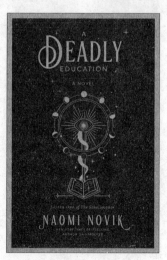

@NaomiNovik
naominovik.com

DelReyBooks.com

EXPLORE THE WORLDS OF DEL REY BOOKS

READ EXCERPTS
from hot new titles.

STAY UP-TO-DATE
on your favorite authors.

FIND OUT about exclusive
giveaways and sweepstakes.

CONNECT WITH US ONLINE!
⊙ f 𝕐 @DelReyBooks

DelReyBooks.com